WHY MUMMY DRINKS AT CHRISTMAS

BY THE SAME AUTHOR

Why Mummy Drinks
Why Mummy Swears
Why Mummy Doesn't Give a ****
Why Mummy's Sloshed
The Saturday Night Sauvignon Sisterhood

Gill Sims

WHY MUMMY DRINKS AT CHRISTMAS

HarperCollins*Publishers*

HarperCollins*Publishers*
1 London Bridge Street
London SE1 9GF

www.harpercollins.co.uk

HarperCollins*Publishers*
Macken House, 39/40 Mayor Street Upper
Dublin 1, D01 C9W8, Ireland

First published by HarperCollins*Publishers* 2023

1 3 5 7 9 10 8 6 4 2

Gill Sims asserts the moral right to be
identified as the author of this work

A catalogue record of this book is
available from the British Library

HB ISBN 978-0-00-859202-8
PB ISBN 978-0-00-861190-3

Printed and bound in the U.S.A.
by Lake Book Manufacturing, LLC

To my dearest Alison.

Meeting you made Baby Music worth it.

Friday 1 December

I've always loved Christmas. Ever since I can remember, I've been convinced every year that this year – this year it would be perfect. This would be the year when everyone's dreams would come true: the children would frolic, my carefully chosen gifts would be received with rapturous expressions on rosy-cheeked faces, I'd bear the bronzed and gleaming turkey to the table on some sort of (yet to be sourced) Golden Platter to stunned Oohs! and Ahhs!, and everyone would say, 'Oh Ellen, this is marvellous. Verily, you *are* the Queen of Christmas' before Simon kissed me under the mistletoe.

This would be the year when the carol singers would carol, the pudding would be figgy (or perhaps not … imagine the potentially disastrous effect of figs on digestions already overloaded with Christmas excess), my halls would be (tastefully) decked, the bells on high would ding dong and the merry gentleman would rest dismayless (unconnected with any quantities of port they may have imbibed).

Never had I been more convinced of it than this year, when I was going to have the cosiest, most delightful tiny family Christmas with just Jane and Peter and Simon and me! In all my many quests for the perfect Christmas we'd almost never achieved this – a Christmas with just the four of us – and I was quite sure it would be utterly magical. I hadn't seen either of the children in ages, and what could be better than a Christmas reunion? Hallmark had literally built a brand around exactly that: families reunited for the holidays, front doors flung open and prodigal offspring tumbling over the threshold on a tide of laughter and candy canes and gently falling snow!

I couldn't wait. The children had always loved Christmas too, and I was determined that I'd be making it extra special for them when they came home for this fabulous family Christmas. Perhaps on Christmas Eve we could all sit by the fire and I'd read aloud from *A Christmas Carol.* I'd steal a glance at the children, spell-bound by the old story, the firelight flickering on their dear faces that I'd so missed and realise that we were making the happiest of memories together to sustain us through darker days in the years ahead. I was sure that Peter and Jane must be as excited at the prospect of this wonderful Christmas as I was, even though they hadn't answered any of my emails about it.

Yes, this was going to be *the* Christmas to end all Christmases! Not only would the super-touching, heart-rending reunion with Peter and Jane bring joy again to my lonely, shrivelled heart and remind me of what love really meant; it would also be a special chance for festive bonding with my precious moppets, for Simon and me to walk hand in hand through festively frosty fields, watch-ing our marvellous children as they frolicked (a tick on the Perfect Christmas list), merrily (tick) with our wonderful dogs (who'd suddenly have learned about things like 'coming when called' for the purpose of the Vision), before we returned home for the afore-mentioned rapturous gifts, bronzed turkey, mistletoe snogging,

Christmas Queening, etc, etc (tick, tick, TICKETY BLOODY TICK). Nothing, literally nothing, was going to dent my Christmas plans this year.

I couldn't wait for the Best Christmas Ever.

And then, this morning, I got a phone call from Jane – at university in Edinburgh. This never boded well, because Jane is of the generation that regards actually talking on the electric telephone as a deeply unnatural and suspicious practice, and she can therefore only be induced to venture into such uncharted waters under great duress or in emergency situations. I'm not sure which category this fell into. For Jane, duress I suspect, knowing that a text would have merely provoked a wrathful phone call, with me shouting, 'You're doing WHAT?' and that an actual phone call might spike my guns slightly. For my eldest child – my first-born – my baby girl – was calling to tell me that her boyfriend Rafferty's parents had invited her to go skiing with them over MY PERFECT CHRISTMAS, and 'like, you don't mind, do you, Mum?'

Rafferty. I should have expected no better from a boy called Rafferty. The very name sounds too like 'raffish' and therefore is untrustworthy.

'But you can't ski,' I objected.

'Raff's gonna, like, teach me?'

'But you haven't got any stuff! Salopettes! Ski jacket! Goggles! SKIIIIIIS!' I wailed.

'Stuff' is eternally the way to Jane's heart.

'Chill, Mum. TK Maxx do loads of great ski stuff really cheap. I picked up everything I need in there.'

'TK Maxx sells skis?' I asked doubtfully, momentarily distracted from Jane's unexpected abandonment of me by wondering how, in my many detailed perusings of all TK Maxx's excellent bargain goods, I could have missed the skis.

'No, Mum. I can hire the boots and skis. I got the salopettes and everything in TK Maxx.'

'But how will you afford it? This will cost a fortune.'

'Not really. I only need to pay for my flight and ski hire. Raff's folks have a chalet out there, and they're giving me my ski pass for Christmas. And I've got a part-time job, you know that, so I've enough saved for my flight and everything.'

I wanted very much to collapse into a toddler-like heap on the floor, clutching my phone and shrieking, 'BUT WHAT ABOUT MEEEEEEEE?!', because Jane frolicking on fucking ski slopes instead of in my frosty fields was very much not part of my Festive Vision, but I knew of course that one cannot behave like that when one is a parent. I reminded myself that I must be glad for Jane that even if her boyfriend's parents had ridiculous taste when it came to naming their children, that at least they went some way to making up for that by being obscenely rich. I mean, I didn't really want Jane to *marry* Rafferty – apart from anything else, my grandchildren would probably end up with even more ridiculous names than my niece and nephew, Persephone and Gulliver – but if she did, at least I could rest easy that she'd do well out of the divorce settlement, even if it *wasn't fair* that stupid rich Rafferty's stupid rich parents were spoiling my perfect Christmas with their STUPID RICHNESS, the bastards, because how could it possibly be Christmas without *Jane*, my baby girl? It just wouldn't be right without her.

I did my best. I really did. I took several deep breaths and channelled my inner Polly-fucking-Anna, but to no avail because instead of saying what I meant to say, which was, 'You go and have a lovely time, darling. I'm thrilled for you!' what came out was actually, 'Jane, I don't think this is a good idea. It's one thing in Edinburgh, but quite another going abroad with him! Who is this boy? We've never met him – he could be anyone. What if he's a people trafficker, what if there is no ski chalet and he's just luring you onto a plane and he'll take your passport and sell you into white slavery?'

'MUM!'

'WHAT! I watch *Panorama*. It happens.'

'No, you don't. You watch clips of *Panorama* that people put on Twitter. You watch *Come Dine with Me* and re-runs of *My Big Fat Gypsy Wedding*. Raff is not a people trafficker. I've been seeing him for months, it's fine!'

'Yes, but not in *Abroad*.'

'Oh my God, Mother, it's only bloody Verbier, will you stop saying "Abroad" like a xenophobic Nancy Mitford character?'

'Uncle Matthew made some excellent points,' I muttered sulkily.

'Stop reading the *Daily Mail*. I'll be fine with Raff.'

'How do you know? Have you met his parents?'

'Not yet. I'm meeting them next week.'

'And even if he isn't a people trafficker, what if you haven't got the right stuff for skiing? Just because you've got some tat out of TK Maxx doesn't mean you're equipped. You need thermals. Have you got thermals? Shall I send you some?'

I was trying very hard to hide my disappointment that Jane wasn't coming home for Christmas, and so I resorted to my default setting in times of emotional distress of online panic shopping.

'I bet you haven't got the right sort of thermals,' I insisted, as I scrolled wildly. 'I'm looking at the John Lewis website now. Here, they've some nice merino wool things. And … and what about ski socks? Have you got ski socks? Oh, John Lewis don't do ski socks, what about … oh, here we are, Nevisport. Have you even *looked* at their website for proper ski socks? You could get frostbite. Or hypothermia. You could lose a foot. You could die, or get caught in an avalanche. I've read all the *Chalet School* books, I know about avalanches. Have you thought about any of these things?'

'Just stop it. You always do this.'

'Do what?

'Catastrophise. And then you try to take over and take control.'

'I do not. I do not do either of those things. Just because I take the time to consider the worst-case scenario …'

'CATASTROPHISE.'

'… and then try to *help*.'

'Take over like a MASSIVE FUCKING CONTROL FREAK, MUM!'

'That's so unfair. I've ordered you some thermals and ski socks, by the way.'

'I don't WANT them. I TOLD you. I've sorted out everything I need, I *don't* need you interfering!'

'I'm not interfering. I just don't think you've thought this through properly, so don't get annoyed with me because I'm *helping*.'

And even though you are *leaving me all alone* at the Most Wonderful Time of the Year, because you'd rather piss off with your rich boyfriend and his *stupid* parents, I'm *still helping*, I thought sulkily to myself.

'Mum, don't do this!'

'Don't do what? You're the one who's just announced they're not coming home. It's not like you've ruined Christmas or anything!' I snapped sarcastically.

'I haven't ruined Christmas!'

'Hmmph. And what about New Year?'

'What *about* New Year?'

'Well, what are you doing? Are you coming home?'

'I DON'T KNOW! I don't know what I'm doing. Maybe I'll drop out of university and go from Verbier straight to Ibiza and join Persephone as a bloody shot girl.'

'No! No, you are not going to Ibiza to be a shot girl with your cousin!'

'I WILL IF I BLOODY WANT TO! WHY AREN'T YOU LISTENING, THIS IS MY LIFE!'

'Jane, I –'

'JUST LEAVE ME ALONE, MUM! And I *haven't* ruined Christmas, that's such a horrible thing to say to me!'

'Jane, please –'

But it was too late. She'd hung up.

I sat on the floor and cried for a bit. Was I really asking for so much? All I wanted was my family around me at Christmas, to hug my children and see them open their stockings on Christmas morning, and spend some time with them singing fucking carols and eating sodding mince pies and having the best and most fabulous and festivest Christmas EVER. And now Jane would rather go off to some bastarding Winter Wonderland IN ABROAD (where even was Verbier, I wondered dimly through my tears. Was it in France or Switzerland? I should probably find out so I at least knew where I was being abandoned for, lest it be like the time I thought Jane was going on a school trip to France and it turned out to be Belgium. She claimed that was not my finest parenting hour, but I pointed out that really, it was a very easy mistake to make, they were right next to each other, but Jane insisted that knowing what country your teenager is visiting is really the very minimum you should expect from a parent. Oh how times have changed, now she just swans off skiing with any Tom, Dick or Harry! Or Rafferty).

I sobbed a bit more, and the dogs regarded me with consternation. Judgy, my beloved original rescue Border terrier – no longer in the first flush of youth but still as obstreperous and bloody-minded as ever – sneezed at me to encourage me to pull myself together and not forget about his dinner. He did not hold with emotions. Tears made his fur wet and he didn't like that. Flora, my other Border terrier, who I'd adopted a couple of years before at the age of fifteen so she didn't spend her final years in a shelter, and who was still going strong apart from some issues with a little leakage (but who doesn't have that as they get older?), offered me an extremely manky Kong she had hidden from the others to cheer me up. And Barry, my giant horse dog, who had been quite large enough already when I originally brought him home – I'd been assured by the nice rescue lady that he was fully grown, only for him to proceed to grow and grow – cavorted through all his best tricks to try to make me laugh, until he stood on Judgy, who objected vociferously, and Flora, not entirely sure what was going on, flung herself into the fray as well. My self-pity party came to an end as I attempted to separate the snarling cloud of fur into three dogs. I doled out chew sticks, wiped my eyes and assured myself Jane would calm down and realise I *was* just trying to help, as I considered the practicalities of her festive abandonment.

Should I change the turkey order to a smaller one? I decided not to. After all, Peter was definitely coming home, though he hadn't confirmed his flight yet, despite eleventy fucking billion emails reminding him I needed to know what day he was coming so I could book the pantomime and arrange various other Festive Treats to make up for three months without him. Peter's mouth has constantly gaped open like a baby bird's, desperately searching for food from the day he was born. And since he was currently on a gap year travelling somewhere in Asia, whatever rations he was living on (mostly beer and tequila shots was what I could surmise from stalking his Instagram videos, though I comforted myself with the thought that at least the lime wedges with his tequila shots would keep scurvy at bay, and hopefully he was using the three jumbo boxes of johnnies I'd put in his bag, despite his objections, to keep Other Things at bay) were likely to mean he'd come home hungrier than ever and shovel the contents of my fridge into his ravening maw. In fact, I pondered, maybe I should order an extra turkey, just for Peter? Feed him up before he went off on his travels again?

I tried to see the bright side of wonderful opportunities for Jane, of my unique chance to spend Christmas just with Peter, hearing about his travels and adventures, of log fires and board games without anyone shouting at their sibling to 'die in a hole'. I could make this work. The magic could still happen. And then Peter's email pinged into my inbox.

> Yo Ma,
>
> Gonna stay in Thaland for xmas is a beach party to go to hope your not mad theyres just loads going on I dont want to miss will save u money on flight to see u easter x

Once I had managed to decipher this garbled missive ('Dearest Mamma, I have decided not to nestle in the bosom of my loving *famille* for the festive period, as I shall instead be getting utterly off my tits on a Thai beach and possibly contracting a hopefully-not-penicillin-resistant STD. I do hope this in no way interferes with your doubtless careful and intricate plans and that it does not inconvenience or irk you. You see, Mother dearest, there is far more of interest here – mainly in the form of girls in bikinis and other things it is best I do not burden your delicate maternal sensibilities with – and I wish to make the most of my youth before I end up a desiccated husk like yourself. However, on the bright side, in the interests of economy and the environment, it is fewer flights to be undertaken, thereby improving your bank balance, my carbon footprint and the plight of the polar bears. I may, at some point in the not-too-distant future, see fit to grace you with my presence. All my love, always and forever, Your only son, Peter') I wasn't sure which was worse, Peter's entire lack of punctuation, grammar or ability to spell, or the news he had just delivered.

First no Jane, and now no Peter. I should really be glad for them both, I chided myself. For Jane, that she had found a super-loaded boyfriend, I mean, a lovely person to possibly spend the rest of her life with, although I had not yet been deemed fit to meet Rich Rafferty. And for Peter, that after years of lurking in his bedroom consuming superhuman quantities of Doritos and playing *Dungeons & Dragons* with his equally unsociable best friends Lucas and Toby, all three boys had managed to reinvent themselves at sixth-form college and had gone from pallid shuffling troll creatures into the party boys of their year. Obviously I was *delighted* for Peter that this had given him the confidence to travel the world before going to university, but at the same time I did occasionally miss the days when I knew exactly where he was (farting under his duvet and playing *Minecraft*), instead of having to send a barrage of texts enquiring if he was still alive and threatening to contact the British embassy in wherever he was if he did not respond to his loving and concerned mother IMMEDIATELY.

An attempt to consult my beloved husband and Peter's doting papa resulted in a response akin to the father in *Swallows and Amazons* when he said they would be better drowned than duffers and if they weren't duffers they wouldn't drown anyway. Simon thought Peter's trip would be 'character building' and 'good for him'. I suspect he was thinking both of the money that would be saved on his son's flights and the much-reduced Christmas food bill. He was equally unconcerned about Jane's defection with Rich Rafferty, and said something that sounded suspiciously like 'overwrought and overreacting', though when I coldly asked him to repeat that, he mumbled he hadn't said anything. *As if* I'd overreact overwroughtly.

'You've spent the last twenty years trying to get some peace and quiet from the kids and wishing they'd bugger off,' Simon pointed out. 'And now they have, you've come over all earth mother and decided you want nothing more than them back at home!'

'Yes, well,' I wailed. 'That was when there didn't seem to be any hope that they ever would grow up and bugger off! I only wanted a piss and maybe a bath without someone hammering on the door demanding things from me. I didn't actually want them to go off to the other side of the world *forever*.'

'Verbier is only in Switzerland,' Simon argued. Ah, Switzerland. Not France. Must remember that. 'Even Thailand isn't that far in this day and age. And it's hardly forever; it's only for Christmas!'

ONLY CHRISTMAS! Simon knows nothing.

* * *

I poured a glass of wine and sat sullenly by the fire – alone. Poor me, all by myself, on my own beside the fire when I should have been picking the perfect festive extracts from *A Christmas Carol*.

'How sharper than a serpent's tooth it is to have a thankless child,' I muttered to myself.

I should be glad, really. Oh Pollyanna, where art thou? I should embrace the simplicity that would come with a Christmas for just Simon and me. I should revel in the lack of mounds of potatoes to be peeled and the bickering over bread sauce and the panic about whether the famous jar of pickled beetroot my grandmother bestowed upon Christmas sometime around 1989, and that is reverently brought out and not eaten each year, has finally gone mouldy.

I couldn't deny that it was a nice prospect not to have to work through the complex negotiations with my immediate family – and Simon's – about who, what and where was happening. Bugger all the UN diplomats trying to bring about peace in the Middle East – send in a woman with experience of keeping both sides of the family happy at the same time. In fairness, as my precious moppets grew older and more feral, the grandparents' discussions about what was happening at Christmas turned more in favour of the festivities happening somewhere, anywhere else, rather than coming to them. Which meant more often than not that they came to us, for the Christmas Vision and the unopened pickled beetroot. Quite often, *everyone* came to us, as Simon's parents had cunningly moved to France and so 'Christmas is such a good opportunity to pop back home and see all our chums, you don't mind us staying, do you?' and no one really wanted to go and stay with Simon's sister Louisa, who had six un-housetrained children and a tendency to recite poetry naked and try to perform 'holistic' healing rituals on you when you least expected it (one good thing about reiki, I always thought, looking at the filth under Louisa's nails, was that at least it didn't require her to *touch* you). And my own sister Jessica inevitably was quicker off the mark than me in coming up with an excuse as to why they couldn't possibly host Christmas, generally due to her being far too Busy and Important.

My parents' divorce in my teens meant in theory that there were extra family groups who could potentially host Christmas, but when my late father was alive we were never quite sure who he'd be married to by Christmas, and more than once he'd found himself married to the sort of annoying woman who insisted on going on winter cruises, so hosting Christmas as well was seldom convenient.

My mother, I suspect, would have liked nothing more than a nice winter cruise, but as she had snared her second husband Geoffrey on a cruise, somewhat against his will (I suspected), he'd subsequently refused to go on another one. Lacking the cruise excuse to wriggle out of Christmas, she instead insisted that she would be *delighted* to have everyone, but it would rather get in the way of the church flower rota, and of course Geoffrey and the cats had very sensitive dispositions and coped badly with change. So that left me. Well, Simon and me. But mostly me. And so every December I'd once again be belting out 'Hark the Herald Angels' and sobbing over 'Silent Night' while trying to cope with everyone else's agendas, ideas, expectations, traditions, issues, anxieties, allergies or intolerances (unfortunately both food- and race-related in the case of my ghastly stepfather Geoffrey), and flinging mistletoe and holly around with wild abandon.

But this year, to my astonishment, instead of the barrage of emails and phone calls either dropping heavy hints or blatantly inviting themselves, everyone had other plans! Simon's parents Sylvia and Michael rang to say that they'd been invited to spend Christmas with some dear chums who had the most *charming* little bijou château in the Dordogne. Jessica and Neil and their own delightful offspring Persephone and Gulliver had decided that now the children were older, big Christmases were silly, and they'd be staying in London and spending Christmas by themselves, with caterers for Christmas dinner, obviously (Jessica was careful to drop that in). My widowed stepmother Natalia, whom Dad had married just before he died, was going home to her own relations in Russia (a pity, as Natalia was by far the sanest member of my family). Mum and Geoffrey would be going to Geoffrey's daughter Sarah and her husband Piers, who had finally decided now their gifted and talented daughter Orla was nearly ten that *possibly* they could cope with Christmas, though Mum had tried to foist their four Siamese cats on me to cat-sit for the Festive Period. I pointed out that my three dogs would doubtless consider four Siamese cats nothing more than a delightful Christmas buffet, at which Mum huffed and sighed and said of course, if anything happened to the cats in the cattery then I *really wasn't* to blame myself. And Louisa, in a twist no one saw coming, announced she'd reconciled with her appalling husband Bardo (we always referred to him as her 'husband', although no one was entirely sure about the legalities of the 'hand-fasting ceremony' they'd held to bless their union). She'd walked out on him over ten years ago when he tried to introduce a 'sister wife' to their relationship in the form of a mad rich American who'd been foolish enough to come to the 'alternative retreat' that they ran in Scotland, and therefore Louisa, Bardo and the six troll-pig children would also be spending a delightful Christmas *en famille*, in their yurt. Oh, and could

Simon lend her £200 for petrol to get there, in the spirit of Christmas and all that?

So, what bliss, I'd thought. Christmas – just Simon and me and Jane and Peter! No making bread sauce just for Geoffrey while Jessica had hysterics about gluten and carbs, no Louisa telling anyone who'd listen that she and all the children were vegan while the children went insane on Haribo and Louisa drank everything she could get her hands on before scarfing down twelve pigs in blankets while shitfaced. No Sarah asking if I was *sure* I had sterilised everything for Orla, because *germs*, while Orla toddled off to share a handful of purloined Bonios with my dogs. No hideous row between Mum and Natalia about Dad after Mum had hit the Gin & Its and insisted that everyone knew she'd been the only true love of Ralph's life and she'd have been *perfectly* within her rights to contest that will, despite his divorcing her thirty years earlier.

No. The most other people would be involved in our Christmas *might* be a very civilised *tiny* Christmas Eve drinks party with just my best friends: Hannah and her husband Charlie, and Sam and his husband Colin and their children, who most serendipitously are best friends with my children and it would all be MAGICAL and DELIGHTFUL AT LONG BLOODY LAST! And then Christmas Day with just the four of us. A turkey crown from Marks and Spencer's. Hell, I thought, why not go wild and crazy and get the whole bloody lot pre-prepared from Marksies, to save me spending Christmas Eve peeling pounds of spuds while cursing Sir Walter Bloody Raleigh for having the bright idea to introduce the bastarding things to England, and thinking jolly well done to Good Queen Bess for having the fucker's head chopped off, before flinging my potato peeler in the sink and declaring I could not do this anymore, and bolting outside to collapse on the bench at the back door and suck down the sweet sweet kiss of a Marlboro Gold while blessing the name of Sir Walter Raleigh for also bringing me fags, and perhaps he was in fact just very misunderstood. Instead I could just have a pile of little foil trays of overpriced love to be popped in the oven and served up with a flourish! So with wild abandon I'd ordered it all! In fact, I'd ordered it all so long ago I'd even secured a civilised Click & Collect slot on 23 December. Yay me, I'd thought – everything is sorted!

But now, it seems, nothing is sorted. Never in all the years I'd sat outside clutching a cigarette and a large glass of wine, looking up at the stars and fervently muttering, 'Starlight, star bright, first star I see tonight, I wish I may, I wish I might, have the wish I wish tonight, oh I WISH THEY WOULD ALL FUCK OFF,' did it occur to me that I might be wishing away Jane and Peter too, and that they would also fuck off and leave me one day. What was I going to do? Obviously, since Simon was so unsympathetic, I decided the best thing to do would be to have another little glass of wine and see what everyone else's children were doing and whether I could find either solace (or more likely schadenfreude) in their similar abandonment, or some kind of leverage for emotional blackmail to lure my babies home if everyone else's cherubs were returning for Christmas.

A quick WhatsApp to my friends' group chat revealed that Peter's travelling companions Lucas and Toby, the errant offspring of, respectively, my oldest friend Hannah and one of my dearest friends Sam, had also attempted this ploy. Toby had been given a hard no, as it was his grandparents' golden wedding anniversary on 27 December, and he'd been told in no uncertain terms to get

Poor Hannah, I thought, envisaging her frantically googling 'excessive salt dough consumption in possibly demonically possessed four-year-olds'. Still, at least Edward, her little Late in Life Surprise, meant she had someone to make salt dough Rudolphs with! I was not a crafty person, but *Christmas* crafts were fun, I mused, looking sadly into the dusty abandoned craft box in the cupboard under the stairs, filled with dried-up glitter glues and lolly sticks and tissue paper and the crumpled remnants of *my hopes and dreams*. Simon passed through the hall and I asked him if *he* wanted to help me make mini salt-dough decorations to adorn our gift tags, like I'd seen someone do on Instagram.

'You said you were never ever touching bastarding salt dough again after the year you were up till 3 a.m. baking two hundred salt-dough decorations for the craft stall at the PTA Christmas Fayre,' said Simon in confusion. 'Why the fuck do you want to make salt-dough gift tags?'

'I thought it might be nice. And you might enjoy a spot of festive crafting with me,' I retorted, trying to suppress the memories of that dreadful salt-dough night, because obviously I couldn't back down now. 'And then on the back, when they're dry, we can write in my calligraphy pen I got from Poundland "Made by Simon" or "Made by Ellen" or "Made by Mummy or Daddy", and the children and everyone else will know our gifts have been wrapped with *love*.'

'But why?' said Simon. 'Do you know how much bloody salt-dough tags will add to the postage? *And* they'll probably break in the post. Come on, why are you taking this so badly? You weren't that fussed when they didn't want to come away with us in the summer, in fact you were quite excited about it. And now you're getting your knickers in a twist about Jane going to Verbier and Peter staying in Thailand when you were perfectly chilled out about Peter going off to Xante with the rest of his sixth form and Jane going to Ibiza with Persephone. Well, until Persephone announced she was staying and being a shot girl.'

'That was different,' I sighed.

Oh, how could I make Simon understand? Summers were one thing. Despite my best Famous Five efforts at japes and frolics (why would my children never frolic satisfactorily in a seasonally appropriate way? Why? Did they refuse to do it just to spite me?), summers with your children when they were small weren't fun, they were eight-week deserts of juggling child care and annual leave and extortionate holiday prices and endless whining for snacks and demands for what were we going to do today, and stupid sodding memes about only getting eighteen summers with your children so enjoy each and every one of them despite the fact that you'd spent a whole day refereeing World War III over a fucking ice lolly, but CHRISTMAS! Christmas is different. Your children are *meant* to come home for Christmas, arriving in a snowstorm just heavy enough to be festive without actually impacting anyone's travel plans, tumbling through the door laughing, with rosy cheeks and arms full of presents, adorably clad in bobble hats and cosy scarves and tasteful woollen duffle coats, while I beam with maternal pride and welcome my chickadees back to the nest.

I rather tearfully regaled Simon with this Lost Vision over dinner and he said he was cancelling the Hallmark movies channel.

'This is our chance for *us*, Ellen,' he said. 'Come on. What's that bloody book you're always on about, some orphan who's irritatingly jolly no matter what happens and finds something to be glad about?'

'*Pollyanna*?'

'Yes. Where's your inner Pollyanna?'

'Pollyanna got run over by a motor car and was crippled at the end,' I said dolefully.

'Really? That was the ending? A crippled child? Why do you always tell me this book is uplifting?'

'Well, she miraculously learnt to walk again, and her *joie de vivre* and positive outlook caused that to happen, but she still got run over! Surely in a just world, the little girl who brought joy to the sorrowing hearts of an entire town wouldn't get run over in the first place!'

'Pull yourself together, Ellen,' Simon ordered. 'Enough of this self-pity. Like I said, this is our time now! We've spent twenty years sacrificing our cash, our sanity and our sleep to bring up our children. You always said the aim of raising children properly was to turn them into resilient and independent adults, and now you're upset that they're doing exactly that, when surely it's a sign that we've done something right and we should give ourselves a pat on the back.'

'Jane doesn't think I've done anything right,' I said sadly. 'She called me a catastrophising control freak who always interferes. And anyway, I don't want them to be resilient and independent at *Christmas*! Can't they just do it for the rest of the year, and then at Christmas be overcome with their need for their darling mama and return to the bosom of their loving family, so we can roast chestnuts over an open fire and sing carols round the piano, and laugh and laugh and be merry?'

'I mean it, I'm cancelling the Hallmark channel tomorrow,' said Simon. 'And we don't have a piano. And the year you tried to make us roast chestnuts over an open fire, Peter had to go to A&E with second-degree burns. And every year, *every single year*, darling, you start December wittering on about Festive Visions and joy and goodwill and obsessively creating Pinterest boards full of weird flower arrangements with bits of holly and you cover the house in ivy and mistletoe shouting that you are DECKING THE FUCKING HALLS, and then the dogs try to eat it and invariably there's an expensive vet bill, and you get more and more annoyed with everyone for not being in line with your Festive Vision because you *are* a bit of a control freak –'

'I'm NOT.'

'Until you culminate in your now traditional Christmas Eve meltdown where you take a bottle of Baileys and the dogs and sit in the garage crying hysterically about how much you hate everyone and watching *It's a Wonderful Life* on your phone until I lure you in with promises of helping you peel the potatoes while we listen to *Carols from King's*, and then you talk through the whole thing without listening to it while complaining bitterly about how much you hate both our families and how ungrateful everyone is and how much you wish it was just you and me, well, usually actually you say you wish it was just you and then add me as an afterthought to be polite, either spending Christmas on a tropical beach somewhere or in a decadently luxurious country house hotel, where the roaring log fires and potato peelings are someone else's problem and you can just waft about elegantly, drinking martinis.'

'I cried in the garage with the Baileys *once*.'

'You do it every year.'

'I do *not*. And I most certainly do not talk through *Carols from King's*.'

'You talk through everything. Every film, TV and radio programme. That's not the point, though. The point, my darling, is

– this is our chance to do this. To do the beach Christmas, or the country house hotel Christmas. There was always some reason before. Too expensive, the kids had things on, family was insisting on descending. But now, it's just us. We can do whatever we want!'

'We can't,' I objected. What a stupid idea. What if the children unexpectedly came home and I wasn't there? They would be left out in the snow, starving and freezing to death like the Little Matchgirl. Hallmark never made *that* into a Christmas film!

'We CAN.'

'We can't. I've ordered the food from Marks and Spencer's. I ordered it in October.'

'Well, cancel it.'

'I can't cancel it, I've paid a £40 non-refundable deposit. Anyway, it's not Christmas without M&S Mini Beef Wellingtons.'

'Oh, for fuck's sake, freeze it then!'

'But I'm not collecting it till late on the 23rd. So we'd have to travel on Christmas Eve. Flights would be extortionate. Things would go wrong, we'd end up being those people on the news spending Christmas in Heathrow. Some bastard would make us have a singalong and talk about the Blitz Spirit to the news people.'

'That would probably be you. Stuck in an airport on Christmas Eve, you wouldn't be able to help yourself organising the other passengers into some sort of Festive Vision, to cheer everyone up and make the best of things. But then you'd probably end up nicking a bottle of Baileys out of the closed Duty Free and going to cry in the corner because people were *still* thwarting your Festive Vision.'

'Also, there are no fires in airports to read *A Christmas Carol* beside, are there? Not like at home,' I pointed out.

'What? Why would you need a fire? And you hate Dickens.'

'No, I don't.'

'Yes, you do.'

'Not *A Christmas Carol*.'

'You've never read it. You've only seen the Muppets movie version.'

'I just don't think Christmas away is *right*,' I wailed. 'It wouldn't be the same, all hot and sandy and foreign and no turkey or crackers or really expensive dates with bits of almonds in to break your teeth on. It wouldn't be like at home!'

'Well, what about my suggestion for a really swish hotel then? One with velvet curtains and actual antiques? The sort we could never go to when the kids were little because they'd break things or steal things? You could collect your wretched M&S order and shove it in the freezer, and we could go on Christmas Eve. That would be pretty bloody in keeping with the fucking Festive Vision. It would be like home, only *better*.'

I considered this suggestion, trying to find the flaws. I was very discombobulated by this whole notion of going away by ourselves somewhere nice for Christmas. Going away at Christmas meant discomfort and other people's houses and rules, and possibly sleeping on a deflating blow-up bed and trying to find a loo for a discreet poo after too much rich food without anyone knowing it was you who had pooed. To go away in luxury with lavatories aplenty in which to poo at will was *decadence* and not at all in the Spirit of Christmas.

'There will be people,' I pointed out.

'I know.'

'But you hate people.'

'I'll put up with people to give you your perfect Christmas.'

'It'll be expensive.'

'I know.'

'But you hate spending money.'

'For you, my darling, I'll do anything to make you happy.'

'What do you want?' I demanded, immediately suspicious of such compliance in the face of Simon's well-known miserliness and loathing of the human race.

'I told you, I just want you to be happy.'

'And ...?'

'And ... I might have accidentally tumble-dried your favourite cashmere jumper! What!' he protested, as I opened my mouth to roar with fury. 'At least I'm admitting it. It did cross my mind to just put it in your drawer and let you think you'd put on weight. And I'm being a good and kind and loving husband by trying to make Christmas magical, so you can't be angry with me.'

'I can,' I said sulkily. 'Anyway, we can't go away for Christmas. We can't leave the dogs.'

'Get a dog-sitter. Put them in kennels.'

'Not at Christmas! Judgy loves Christmas. He'd be furious. Opening presents is his favourite thing. And Flora is too old for kennels, and what if she dies? And Barry? Well, poor little Barry, how you can abandon Barry at Christmas?'

'Last year the local primary school borrowed him to star as the donkey because he's so enormous. You can hardly call him "poor little Barry".'

'Yes, but he has issues. He'll be sad enough that Jane isn't coming home, let alone if we desert him at Christmas too. They'll know, all of them. We'll just have to stay here.' I sighed, then I brightened. 'Though if it's just us, we could do all the things the magazines suggest at Christmas. I saw this article once, years ago, that suggested about four different changes of clothes. I remember it so clearly! You got up in satin pyjamas, and then wore black palazzo pants and a simple white silk T-shirt for Christmas morning –'

'A T-shirt! On a morning in December!' said Simon in outrage. 'Imagine the heating bill. And as for sitting in your pants …'

'Palazzo pants!' I attempted to explain, as Simon huffed. 'Well, why don't they just SAY nice trousers then?'

'Oh, for God's sake. You own seventeen fleeces, every single one in black or unidentifiable sludge colour – why would anyone listen to your opinions on fashion? Shut up! So after your palazzo pants and white silk T-shirt, you laugh merrily and change into a cashmere jumper, well, you do if your husband isn't a useless arsehole who tumble-dried yours, and some nice boots and jeans, and you trip off joyously to the pub for a mulled wine with Local Characters –'

'The Local Characters in our Local Pub are all the Local Drug Dealers,' Simon objected.

'Well, they won't be on Christmas Day,' I snapped. 'They'll be bucolically adorable. And then you come home, cheeks a-glowing –'

Simon sniggered at this.

'SIMON! Don't be vulgar about the FESTIVE VISION! You come home and the Christmas lunch is all magically ready and you change again into something velvety and impossibly chic and simple and have your Christmas dinner and then probably some carol singers come round and you give them mince pies and the whole thing is completely FUCKING FESTIVE! But I don't know if it would work with just the two of us. Is that enough people to be festive? Because I have dreamed for years of changing out of my palazzo pants into a cashmere jumper and going to the pub on Christmas Day!'

'You've never mentioned it,' said Simon.

'Well, how could I? There was never any time to keep changing clothes. There were hundreds of people to be fed and diplomatic negotiations to tiptoe through, and Louisa's glass to be kept topped up, because she is marginally more bearable drunk than sober, and Jessica's OCD to be managed and Geoffrey to be kept away from Natalia lest he either made a pass at her or racist comments or both. But this year it was going to be just us, and they're both old enough to drink and so I hoped I could put on my cashmere jumper and we could all go to the pub and drink mulled wine and BE FUCKING FESTIVE. TOGETHER.'

'Is that really your greatest Christmas wish?' asked Simon doubtfully. 'To wear a cashmere jumper to the pub on Christmas Day?'

'Yes. Well, not *just* the cashmere. All of us, crunching across the frosty fields, the mulled wine, the lot. And now I don't even have the cashmere jumper!'

Saturday 2 December

The more I thought about it, the more Simon's suggestion of a lovely Christmas getaway – just the two of us – appealed far more than multiple outfit changes (think of the laundry on Boxing Day) and a visit to the local to raise a glass of Christmas Cheer to the Local Characters. These included Big Ron, who sat in the corner and was inclined to give you his disturbing views on Brexit while offering to sell you 'Charlie, cheap, special price for you love, 'cos I likes you'. Flattered though I was to have somehow earned Big Ron's approbation, I was always forced to decline, but that didn't deter him in his generosity.

On one occasion he overheard Hannah and me complaining about her useless ex Dan, and informed us he could have Dan 'offed' for forty quid. I'd be lying if I said we weren't quite tempted, especially when Big Ron went on to add, 'Course, for that sort of price, you can't expect anything too quick and clean. One of the apprentices. The lads gotta learn somehow, don't they?' We nodded politely and said, 'Quite', before making a hasty exit. I did very much want to ask more about the 'apprentice murderers', but I didn't want Big Ron to think I was a timewaster by pretending to be interested in his 'services'. I wasn't convinced Big Ron in a Santa hat, offering his special Christmas snow, was really in keeping with the Vision I'd nurtured so carefully all these years. Also, the Vision definitely involved tripping across picturesque frosty fields in one's good boots, and like most fields in reality as opposed to in glossy magazines, the ones between us and the pub are distinctly muddy, and the farmer has a habit of muck spreading on Christmas Day, for reasons we've never quite been able to grasp. It takes a lot of White Company candles to cover the eau de pigshit wafting in gently every time one of the dogs wants out for a pee.

The Christmas hotel idea, though, was by far the easiest to adapt to the Vision, especially if it did have rustic beams (to hang mistletoe from for Simon to kiss me under, much more romantic than hanging it off the hall light fitting while he muttered of fire risks) and velvet curtains. There was something very festive about velvet curtains. Also, I reasoned with myself, what could be more Christmassy than two weary travellers arriving at an inn for Christmas? It was the Christmas story! Not that I wanted to be consigned to a stable; I wanted the roll-top bath and four-poster bed experience, thank you very much, not a straw bale and a manger.

I therefore took myself off to google for 'perfect Christmas hotels'. After a brief tussle with the search engine, which kept trying to fob me off with 'best Christmas hotels' when I did not want 'best', I wanted BLOODY PERFECT, I found it. It was beyond perfect. A delicious little manor house nestling in glorious countryside, offering YOUR OWN CHRISTMAS TREE and decorations and a 'complimentary gift' under your tree (it would almost certainly just be extra shower gel like they had in the bathroom, but that was not the point) and carol singers and even the option of board games and a TREASURE HUNT on Boxing Day, and oh frabjous day, it was simply meant to be! There was a pub, owned by the hotel, open only to residents on Christmas Day, just a nice brisk walk through the gardens and down the driveway, just *crying out* to be strolled to in a cashmere jumper after changing out of your palazzo pants and before putting on your chicly elegant yet festive velvet frock! This was probably exactly the place that the magazine writer had in mind when she wrote that bloody article all those years ago that has haunted me ever since! It was really too good to be true. Somewhere *this* perfect was surely booked up months, if not years ago. But look! ONE room left. Well, suite. Quite a large suite. But actually, the price wasn't that bad really, when you took into account everything that was included. Rather reasonable, in fact! I peered closer. Ah. I hadn't spotted that pesky last zero on there. That was quite … eye-watering. But then again, could you put a price on perfection for a mother abandoned and deserted by the very children she gave life to?

When I went to explain to Simon in his shed that you couldn't put a price on perfection, abandoned mother, etc, he said that you could, and it was considerably lower than they were asking for at the Perfect Christmas Hotel. In fact, he insisted, it was considerably lower than the price *without* that pesky extra zero.

'But you said my happiness was worth anything!' I insisted.

'Yes, but when I said "anything" I didn't mean "more than the price of a mid-range family car for two sodding nights", Ellen!'

'So you *can* put a price on my happiness! I am very sad, and this will cheer me up.'

'It's not about putting a price on your happiness, Ellen. It's about not spending the next two years paying off two nights in a hotel. Which will make *me* very sad. And you, when we can't afford any wine. Anyway, what happened to "we can't leave the dogs"?'

'They take dogs. For a small supplement.'

Simon peered suspiciously at the screen. 'For £500 each! And you have three. Also, darling, look. It says, "well-behaved dogs". With the best will in the world, no one can describe your dogs as well behaved. Remember when John Lewis announced they were allowing "well-behaved dogs" in their shops and you took yours? Hmm?'

'Yes,' I muttered sulkily.

'And what happened?'

'The police and the RSPCA were called, and I've got a lifetime ban from all John Lewis stores and have to shop online with them under an assumed name after Barry galumphed with such excitement he banged into a fire alarm and set it off, and the noise so alarmed Flora she peed on a lamp fitting in home furnishings and short circuited it, so it DID catch fire. And then Judgy bit a fireman in indignation because he didn't want to be evacuated.'

'And what about the chickens?' he went on.

'You didn't care about the chickens the other night when you came up with this plan,' I pointed out.

'You also seemed to forget about them.'

'Only because they hate me so they wouldn't be as traumatised as the dogs if they were left over Christmas. I didn't *forget* about them, I just didn't need to factor in their emotional needs as well as their physical ones.'

Simon rolled his eyes. 'You know, it's funny, isn't it? You meet a girl, you are dazzled and bowled over by her, you fall in love, you build a life together. No one mentions, do they, in the great romances, that one day, that burning passion will translate to sitting in a shed discussing chickens' emotional needs during the festive season.'

'You no longer burn with passion for me?'

'The cream from the chemist helped enormously with that,' Simon sniggered.

'Simon, be serious. I need this Christmas to be perfect. For us.'

'But you say that every Christmas.'

'But I mean it this Christmas. I need something to look forward to because I was so looking forward to Jane and Peter coming home, and now they're not coming and what am I going to do? What if they never come home again?'

'Darling, they'll always come home. What are you talking about?'

'No.' I shook my head sadly. 'One day this won't be home, will it? They'll have their own homes. Their own families. This will be somewhere they visit, *then* they go home. Don't you see? For twenty years they've needed me. Needed me to the point of I've always, *always* had to put their needs first. And I've resented that sometimes, but now that's ending. When Jane went, I still had Peter, and when Peter went, I thought, well, it's only three months until I see them both again, maybe I can pretend they're just on a school trip. A very long school trip. And I had Christmas to look forward to and they would bring all their festering laundry, and I'd complain and rant and rave and they'd leave all the crockery in their rooms to go mouldy, and it would just be back to normal. But it won't be. It will never be back to normal. So what is normal supposed to be anymore, and what am I, if I'm not a mother?'

'You're still you. And you'll always be their mother,' Simon said in confusion.

'Yes, but not like I was! I don't even know who I *am* anymore,' I wailed. 'This is it. The beginning of the end. Why did it have to start with *Christmas*, though? Why couldn't it have been something no one bothers with, like … like Michaelmas? And so I just want something to take my mind off it.'

'Sweetheart, I hear what you're saying. But I just don't think bankrupting ourselves for two days in a hotel is the answer. Apart from anything else, I think you'd actually hate it.'

'What do you mean?'

'You know what you're like. Jane did have a point – you're a control freak about things like Christmas. You'd hate someone else running it all. You barely cope on the rare occasions we go to someone else for Christmas; you sneak off and start peeling potatoes and polishing already-clean glasses and cutlery to give yourself something to do. You moan and moan about it, but you like being busy and in charge.'

'I am not a control freak!' I retorted indignantly. 'It's just no one else bothers to take bloody responsibility for anything. Except Jessica.'

'Yes, Jessica is even more of a control freak,' Simon agreed.

'So I have to be in charge. If things are going to be done right. And also, FYI, I have only tried to polish other people's glasses and cutlery at Louisa's, and that's because they looked like they'd been washed in a swamp. But I'd cope just *fine* in a 6-star hotel with a little man bringing me festive cockingtails to take my mind off the fact that my children are grown and I've been abandoned and my life is essentially empty and meaningless!'

'Right,' sighed Simon. 'It's still an obscene amount of money, though. So maybe you could find somewhere cheaper in which to have your existential crisis?'

* * *

I stomped off inside in a huff. It seemed that Simon was not to be swayed, and he possibly *did* make some valid points about the dogs. Imagine the horror if Judgy bit some vile rich American billionaire or something? And, on reflection, it *was* ludicrously expensive, and what if we did spend all that money and everyone else staying there was ghastly? I could spend Christmas with my mother and Geoffrey for a fraction of the price if I wanted appalling people expressing politically incorrect opinions to me.

In the absence of my Perfect Christmas, thwarted by parsimonious husbands and obstreperous dogs, I decided to wallow in my so-called existential crisis by sorting through the Christmas decorations and having a good cry over all the hideous glitter-smeared-probably-stuck-together-with-snot monstrosities my precious moppets had presented me with while growing up and insisted on being displayed each year. If they weren't bothering to come home, why, at least I could transform my home into a tasteful bower of Christmas sparkle, with nary a sodding bog-roll angel wearing an expression suggesting that a shepherd had just made a deeply inappropriate comment to her, or a balding pipe cleaner not-quite-sure-what-it-was-ever-meant-to-be-but-I had-expressed-deep-admiration-and-love-for-it-for-fifteen-years to be seen. And then, after a good cry over the sticky Christmas tat – still managing to shed glitter dandruff everywhere after all these years, because glitter is truly the gift that keeps on giving – I could pop over to the John Lewis website and spend the money from Jane's returned thermals on some delightful new decorations that had never had a toddler stick a sequin onto them with their own bogeys.

I hauled down the box and started going through everything. Proper decorations in one box, the children's creations in another

23 December, nineteen years ago

I'd been braced for some kind of tug of love between the two sets of grandparents over who would get to experience the Festive Period with the First Grandchild when Jane was ten months old, but in the end there was no battle at all. My mother was quite surprised when I asked her how she'd feel if we went to Simon's parents instead of coming to her and Geoffrey in Yorkshire.

'Why would you think I'd mind?' she said in surprise. 'I can't possibly have you here anyway. Jessica is coming with Little Persephone and Neil, I couldn't cope with two babies in the house. I only have one travel cot! All that noise, it would upset the cats dreadfully. Not to mention Geoffrey,' she added as an afterthought.

Oh nice. My own mother had invited my sister and not me, Little Persephone, being six months old at the time, already being earmarked to be the Golden Child. I wasn't really surprised by my mother's decision to put her Siamese cats' welfare above spending Christmas with both her daughters and new granddaughters, and in truth it made it rather easier. Simon's mother Sylvia had been phoning daily since mid-October, demanding to be informed of our Christmas plans because she had to let the butcher know what size of turkey to order, and it was *terribly* important for family to be together at Christmas, especially now she had a grandchild, and she really wanted her whole family all together under one roof. She was also very keen we should be there to make an appearance at her Annual Christmas Eve Drinks for the neighbours, though I strongly suspected that was more about showing off her Only Son than about familial tenderness.

So it was that we duly journeyed to deepest, darkest Surrey, arriving at Sylvia and Michael's house, The Laurels, on Christmas Eve, feeling slightly trepidatious. Jane, precocious at just ten months, had decided to start walking the day before, and although very wobbly on her feet, was determined that nothing was going to stop her. I feared for Sylvia's antique china collection, as Jane's progress and directional skills were currently more down to luck than design.

I was dying for a pee when we arrived, Simon having that male mentality that it's better to piss yourself en route than to stop somewhere and thus fail to 'beat' your previous journey time. I got out of the car and heaved Jane from her car seat as Sylvia came rushing out to meet us.

Sylvia was a wafting, scarf-hung creature who took watercolour classes to demonstrate her creativity to everyone. A brief secretarial stint at the BBC before marrying Michael had convinced her that she was practically Mariella Frostrup, and she doted on her Only Son such that every time she mentioned him I could see her mentally capitalising the words. I'm not sure who *would* have been suitable to be married to the Only Son – perhaps some sort of royalty? – but it certainly wasn't me.

'My darling boy,' she cried. 'And my wonderful granddaughter. Who is Mamie's most precious girl?' she cooed as she snatched Jane off me and clutched her to her scarf-swathed bosom, before her nose wrinkled in disgust.

'Oh dear,' she gagged. 'This child needs changing!' Jane was unceremoniously thrust back at me.

I hopped from foot to foot as I passed her over to Simon. 'Sylvia, it's lovely to see you, but I really do need to go to the loo,' I gasped, as I dashed into the house. When I returned from the bathroom,

Sylvia was standing in the hall, holding Jane at arm's length, muttering darkly to Simon with a face like a bulldog licking piss off a nettle. Jane, quite clearly, had not been changed.

'What are you doing, Simon?' I asked. 'Why haven't you changed Jane?'

'Don't be silly, Ellen,' Sylvia sniffed. 'Of course Simon can't change Jane. I don't know what you were thinking.'

'It's the twenty-first century,' I pointed out. 'He most certainly can change his own child.'

Sylvia gave her special tinkly laugh, the one she only uses when she's really cross. I remember hearing that laugh a LOT at both our engagement party and our wedding.

'Simon is *exhausted*,' she tinkled. 'He should go and have a drink with his father, he's far too tired to change a baby,' and she plonked Jane firmly in my arms and marched away, calling, 'Come along, Simon darling!'

'Really?' I said to Simon, as he turned to trail after his mother.

He shrugged apologetically. 'Sometimes it's easier to just do what she wants.'

'Right,' I said slowly, and started up the stairs with Jane, to the Best Spare Room. We had been grudgingly granted the Best Spare Room for the Only Son (and now the Fruit of His Loins) when Simon had put his foot down, after we were married, at Sylvia's ongoing attempts to banish me to the box room and tuck up her Darling Boy in his childhood bedroom. I had always thought this most unreasonable of Sylvia, until Jane had suggested the boyfriend before Stupid Rich Rafferty could stay in her room and I desperately attempted not to clutch my pearls and shriek, 'My baby is not Doing The Sex Under My Roof,' and I realised how difficult it is, after years of trying to protect your children from such Nastinesses, to have to condone them shagging in your child's lovingly Annie Sloaned shabby-chic bedroom.

Back downstairs, I put Jane on the floor outside the drawing room to try to gain some brownie points with Sylvia by showing off her new clever trick of walking.

After some coaxing, as Jane was more interested in climbing into the hairy and malodorous bed belonging to Monty, Michael's ancient Labrador, in search of potential snackage, I proudly led her into the drawing room on her feet.

'Look!' I said proudly to Michael and Sylvia.

'Oh!' said Sylvia in delight, jumping to her feet. 'CLEVER girl, Jane. You have learned to walk at Mamie's house! Did you do this just for Mamie? Oh, just *wait* till all the neighbours see this at the Christmas Eve Drinks!'

Jane, who had now plonked herself on the floor and was investigating the Aubusson for any crumbs Monty might have missed, ignored her grandmother's fulsome praise.

'Actually, she started walking yesterday,' I told Sylvia.

'Don't be ridiculous,' said Sylvia coldly. 'Of course she's only just started since she got here, she was saving it for me!'

'No, Mum. She did it yesterday. Really,' Simon insisted.

Sylvia looked mutinous for a moment, as she tried to work out how exactly to make Jane walking *yesterday* be about her, Sylvia. Finally, she beamed.

'Yes,' she smirked. 'I expect she was *practising* because she knew she was going to see me today! I expect she'll start talking while she's here too. Can you say Mamie, Jane, darling? Mamie?'

I opened my mouth to object to the many levels of nonsense here, due to Jane being TEN MONTHS OLD and therefore having no concept of time, very little idea of who fucking Sylvia even was ('Mamie, darling. Say Mamie.' Why couldn't she just be Granny or Grandma? Where had she come up with the incredibly pretentious 'Mamie'? When asked, she vaguely said something about it being French, and much more chic than being a Granny. No doubt she'd soon rewrite history to tell everyone that Jane had come up with the *chic et française* 'Mamie' all by herself, because her Only Son's Child was Just So Bright). Before I could argue, though, Simon's father Michael thrust a cocktail into my hand. Michael is the polar opposite of Sylvia, in that he exudes charm and *joie de vivre* and gives no fucks about anything, whereas Sylvia gives so many fucks she could give Hugh Hefner a run for his money.

'I made Manhattans,' he said brightly. 'I thought we all might need them. Get that down you, my dear, and you'll soon be feeling no pain.'

I took a slug of what is basically a sociable acceptable way to consume neat booze, and nearly choked. Bloody hellfire, they were strong. Michael was right, though; almost immediately everything was clouded in a lovely pink haze. I slumped happily on the sofa and handed Jane an organic rice cake. From somewhere far away I heard a whimpering sound from Sylvia at this, and a cry of something about *the cushions*, but Michael shushed her. 'It's only a bloody biscuit. We've got a Hoover, haven't we?'

I did suppress a thought that the trouble with Jane and rice cakes wasn't so much that she dropped crumbs as she tended to suck them into some sort of paste and then *smear* them over a far larger area than you'd think one rice cake soaked in baby drool could possibly go, but fuck it, this cocktail was lovely, and maybe, just maybe, someone else could take responsibility for Jane for one minute. Like … ooh, her FATHER, perhaps?

I roused myself from my pleasant whiskey stupor to hear Sylvia saying, 'And dinner will be at eight o'clock sharp, everyone. Beef bourguignon.'

'Perfect,' I said. 'We usually put Jane down at about seven, so that gives us plenty of time to get her settled.'

'Put Jane down?' Sylvia blinked at me. 'As in, put her to bed? But what about her dinner? She'll miss dinner.'

'She has her dinner about five o'clock, though?' I said in confusion. 'She's ten months old, Sylvia, she can't wait till eight o'clock for her dinner. She's asleep by then.'

'But I had assumed Jane would just be sitting up and eating with us. Dinner won't be ready at five o'clock, there'll be nothing for her to eat.'

'I'm not sure she'd eat beef bourguignon anyway,' I said doubtfully. 'I can do her some scrambled egg or something, and some yoghurt and fruit?'

Sylvia did her best mouth-like-a-cat's-bum face. 'MY children always simply ate what we ate, when we ate it. You are making a rod for your own back, Ellen, pandering to that child like that. How do you think it will affect Simon? You need to consider his needs too; it's going to make life difficult for him as well as you. The key to raising children,' she went on airily, 'is that they must fit into *your* life, not the other way round.'

Simon started laughing. 'Come off it, Mum. What are you on about? All this "my children ate what we ate, when we ate it" guff? Yeah, we did, when we were about *fourteen* and you considered us fit to be seen in public. Before that we got baked beans in the kitchen with the au pairs.'

'I don't know what you're talking about,' huffed Sylvia. 'Baked beans indeed.'

'Anyway, Ma, Ellen's a great mum and we're all doing fine. And actually, Ellen, you look knackered, babe, so why don't *I* do Jane's dinner? At five o'clock?'

'Simon,' wailed Sylvia, 'you can't possibly do that, darling, you work so hard! Mummy will do it for you!'

Through a haze of whiskey I watched all the hard-won notions of feminism and equality and co-parenting I had battled to instil in Simon over the last few years, especially in the months since Jane was born, dissolve at the idea of simply letting Mummy do it for him. I really should say something, I thought vaguely. But I was finding it rather hard to move, other than to allow Michael to remove my empty glass and hand me a full one in its stead.

'I'd let Sylvia and Simon get on with it,' he murmured.

Despite Michael's advice, I was summonsed to the kitchen to oversee Jane's dinner. I slumped at the table, working my way through a box of mint Matchmakers that Sylvia had offered me. She'd said that her cleaning lady had given them to her, thus implying that they were good enough for me. Sylvia was cooking scrambled eggs with a martyred expression while Simon hovered around looking as manly as a man can look when he's thirty bloody two years old and his mother is showering him with praise for managing to find a spoon for his daughter's dinner like he'd just done his first poo in his potty.

'Oh well *done*, darling. Clever boy! It's very *good* of you to be so hands on with the baby, isn't it?'

'Sylvia, stop!' I yelped as she reached for the salt. 'What are you doing?'

'Seasoning it, silly,' she laughed.

'You can't give her *salt*!'

'What? But it won't taste of anything.'

'I know, but it's bad for babies.'

'Since when?'

'Since always.'

'I don't remember that.'

'That's because you spent our childhood in a haze of Valium and gin,' Simon muttered, as I earnestly explained to Sylvia about salt poisoning and how terrible it was for children and dogs (I wasn't sure how I'd got onto the subject of dogs in my explanation, but I think it might have been to do with the Manhattans. It was a mistake anyway, as Sylvia immediately pointed out that it didn't do Monty the Labrador any harm, therefore this was just one of those foolish new-fangled scaremongering notions introduced by This New Internet Thingy. Sylvia had a deep-rooted fear of The Internet, also always to be pronounced With Capital Letters, to make clear its Threat).

'Anyway ...' said Sylvia blithely, waving her Joseph Joseph spatula at me as she merrily tipped half a packet of Maldon sea salt into her Le Creuset pan and I reflected that at least it would be a very *middle-class* case of salt poisoning for Jane (surely when I explained to the social worker in A&E that it was the finest sea salt flakes afflicting my cherub and not a grain of Saxo had ever passed her rosy little lips they'd understand that I was a good mother and I just had a completely batshit mother-in-law), '... the trouble with you, Ellen, is you have an overactive imagination! I expect it's that broken home again, as you always imagine the worst-case scenario. A tiny bit of salt won't hurt. Nor will a smidge of pepper,' she added, grinding away like an overexcited Italian waiter on speed.

'I DO NOT have an overactive imagination, I just DON'T WANT MY BABY TO DIE!' I exploded.

Sylvia looked at me. 'Oh Ellen. You're not the first person to have a baby, you know! I do know what I'm doing. Now, you said fruit for afterwards. I've got some grapes, what about that?'

'Simon,' I implored, as Sylvia sat the bowl of salty death in front of Jane, cooing 'Now isn't dis yummy? Yes? Much yummier than Mummy's?' and shoved a spoonful in Jane's mouth before I could stop her. Jane, fortunately, spat it out, right into Sylvia's artfully swathed mass of scarves. Sylvia shrieked, Simon swooped in to remove the bowl and I grabbed an emergency Rachel's Organic Greek Yoghurt for Jane. Back in those distant, innocent days, as an overanxious first-time mother, all food with taste, texture and potential for enjoyment was forbidden for Jane. Sudden death lurked in every bowl. I tutted to myself and judged the mothers in cafes spooning such poisons as Petits Filous down their precious babes, and almost fainted in the supermarket one day when I saw a tot the same age as Jane happily chugging down a packet of Cheesy Wotsits. Deep down, although judgemental, I was quite jealous of Wotsit Baby's mummy, for it was sitting happily and quietly with its delicious bag of lurid toxins, while Jane was screaming in disgust at yet more Organix rice cakes.

All my conscientious work was undone shortly after that Christmas when I took Jane to her first Mother and Toddlers session, and she was handed a sippy cup of orange squash and a Rich Tea at snack time before I could intervene. She rammed in the Rich Tea in one mouthful and washed it down by chugging the orange squash in a single, long, thirsty happy gulp. She then spent the rest of the morning licking the Snack Rug for any stray crumbs, which wasn't embarrassing *at all*. And to my astonishment, despite the tartrazine, the E numbers, the *sugar*, oh dear Lord, the *sugar*, she showed no ill effects at all, and I thought perhaps I could relax

'Time is a bourgeois construct. We are not bound by it. And it's Amaris, Ma,' the yeti huffed. 'Try to remember, yeah? I don't want to be known by your capitalist names chaining me to your imperialist values. I need to be true to myself, and that is Amaris, the Child of the Moon!'

It did indeed appear that Simon's sister Louisa had made her entrance. Louisa, until her mid-twenties a perfectly normal, if somewhat spoiled, person with a job and a flat and a nice little car and a pension plan and some Premium Bonds, had suddenly chucked it all in to go and live in the woods with a creature she'd met when he was protesting outside the steak restaurant where Louisa was meeting her fiancé Brian – a reliable, if rather dreary accountant. Bardo had, apparently, grasped Louisa's hand while pressing a 'Meat Is Murder' leaflet into it, stared into her eyes and gasped that they were twin souls, destined through time and space to always be together and that he'd been searching for her all his life. Louisa, instead of telling him to bugger right off or snapping, 'I bet you say that to all the girls' or even suggesting that if they were twin souls, then his half of the souls could definitely do with a lengthy encounter with a hot bath and a LOT of soap, or better yet, a scrubbing brush and an entire bottle of Dettol, breathed, 'YES, oh yes!' and left poor Brian on his tod debating whether the fillet steak really gives value for money, or if they'd be better going for the ribeye, while Louisa joined the protest outside, took Bardo back to her flat that evening and the following week put it on the market, to invest in Bardo's Holistic Retreat in Scotland.

Louisa's father, Michael, was appalled by this turn of events and hired a private detective to find out who this charlatan ruining his daughter's credit rating was. To our surprise he turned out to be an investment banker called Kevin (not a romantic name) who'd had a bad trip in Goa and decided to reinvent himself as Bardo. He now read chakras, rather than the *Financial Times* and earnestly advised us to invest in personal growth not a broad-based stock market portfolio. This would probably have been more admirable had he not also urged us at every opportunity to invest in his Holistic Retreat. Louisa, not to be outdone by Bardo's batshittery, had announced her name was now Amaris, the aforementioned Child of the Moon, and that she was the reincarnation of the ancient High Priestess of the Mood Goddess Cerridwen.

Amaris/Louisa plonked herself down at the table and stared at Jane in confusion.

'Why is there a baby here?' she demanded.

'She's mine. Mine and Ellen's,' Simon reminded her. 'I did tell you, Lou.'

'AMARIS, if you don't mind. Did you? Well, it's very inconsiderate, Simon. I wanted *my* baby to be the first grandchild and now you've *spoilt* it!'

'What baby?' asked Sylvia.

Louisa began to divest herself of her many grubby, fringed layers, ending up in some trousers she'd apparently knitted and dyed herself and a filthy crop top that in no way contained her now terrifyingly vast tits and an enormous pregnant stomach.

'I am with child!' she announced proudly. 'The Goddess has blessed my union with Bardo and made us fruitful.'

'Your union?' said Sylvia faintly. 'You got married and didn't tell us?'

'We aren't married,' said Louisa scornfully. 'Marriage is a bourgeois concept that we reject utterly. We don't need to be married, our souls are joined. We went to the woods and prayed to the Goddess to fill my womb, then we made love, passionately, under the stars, until I could feel Bardo's seed filling every essence of my being and we knew the Goddess had answered our prayers and sent us one of her children of the moon.'

Sylvia made a small whimpering noise and clutched the Aga to stay upright. She appeared to be speechless. Simon went over and put his arm around her, and she leant against him gratefully. For once I could not fault him for supporting his mother instead of his wife. Gruesome though Louisa's conception story was for me to hear, I could not imagine what it felt like for Sylvia to be told in technicolour detail about her only daughter's impregnation by Bardo, as Sylvia regarded Bardo with almost as much horror and suspicion as she regarded me, though if he was some sort of swamp dweller who had sullied her darling daughter, I was possibly slightly worse, for I was the Scarlet Woman who had corrupted her Only Son.

Michael burst into the kitchen at that point, looking agitated.

'SYLVIA,' he bellowed. 'IT'S HAPPENING! Just like they said it would in the Neighbourhood Watch meeting after that *Panorama* programme. There's some ghastly bearded hippy sort putting up a stinking goatskin tent thing by the shrubbery. Call the police! Oh God, they're in the house!'

'Hi Pa,' beamed Louisa, pushing her dreadlocks out of her face with one hand and lovingly caressing her stomach with the other. 'That's just Bardo, putting up the yurt. We've got another smaller one for the birthing ceremony too. I thought that could go by the pond, because I think I want a water birth.'

Michael gazed at her in horror and Sylvia buried her face in Simon's shoulder with a small sob.

'Louisa?' he gasped, in the same horrified tones as Sylvia. 'What … what has happened to you?'

'I was just telling Ma and Si and Ellen, the Goddess has blessed us and filled my womb,' said Louisa proudly, heaving herself to her feet and thrusting her bump at Michael. 'Do you want to touch it? The belly of a woman who conceives beneath the eyes of the Moon Goddess is very powerful. It could restore all your lost potency, Pa.'

Michael gulped, and mopped some sweat from his brow. 'I need another fucking drink,' he muttered.

'Louisa, darling,' quavered Sylvia. 'What do you mean by the "birthing yurt"?'

'What do you think I mean?' said Louisa. 'The yurt where I'll give birth, obviously.'

'Yes, but you said something about putting it up *here*? Or did I mishear?' Sylvia asked hopefully.

'No, no, that's right,' Louisa said airily. 'We're putting it up here. I want to give birth under the stars of my ancestors.'

'We've only lived here since 1985!' Michael protested.

Louisa gave him a withering look 'You know what I mean. I want you and Mother there, to witness the love between Bardo and me, and see our love come to fruition in the world. You can cut the cord,' she added generously.

Michael bolted out of the room.

'But darling,' Sylvia said, 'you can't just give birth here. What about your midwife? Your consultant? What do they say about this? Have you even brought your notes?'

'Ha,' said Louisa disdainfully. 'Midwives! Doctors! What do they know? I don't need them. Birth is over-medicalised, Mother. I just need to trust my instincts, that's all!'

'I mean, they do know quite a lot,' I ventured, plucking up the courage to butt in to this Russell family drama for the first time.

Sylvia shot me a grateful look. 'Yes, Ellen, they *do*, don't they? What do your midwives say about you coming all the way down here, so far away from the team that's been looking after you?'

'I haven't seen any midwives,' she informed us haughtily. 'They're not necessary.'

'But what about scans? When are you *due*?' Sylvia demanded.

'Scans? SCANS?' exploded Louisa. 'Do you really think I'd let my baby's precious body be fried with those cancer rays while still in the womb? Look at that baby?' She pointed dramatically to Jane, now liberally smeared in yoghurt as I'd foolishly given her the spoon, lest I miss any of Louisa's pronouncements. 'Just look at it! I bet it had "scans", didn't it? And see how stunted and pale it is!'

'I mean, Jane's in the top percentile for her size and weight,' I objected.

'See! Over-medicalised,' Louisa said with satisfaction. 'Who decides these arbitrary measurements? They mean nothing. Anyway, I couldn't take the risk with this child of the Goddess.'

'Right,' I said furiously. 'I see. Oh well, I suppose my poor little stunted thing will have to manage as best she can then, being only a mortal child.'

Louisa just nodded at me smugly.

'But poppet, I really do think you should see someone,' Sylvia insisted, 'a proper midwife or something. You can't just leave it up to some airy-fairy notions about goddesses. There's a reason for midwives and doctors in pregnancy, you know.'

'It's just a money-making scheme,' Louisa said firmly. 'There's no need for them if a woman is truly in touch with her inner self, like I am.'

'Well, what about all the marvellous things they can do for pain relief and everything now?' Sylvia asked.

'Epidurals,' I put in helpfully. 'Gas and air. Gas and air is *lovely*, Louisa. I mean Amaris.'

'Pain relief,' said Louisa contemptuously. 'PAIN RELIEF! There's no pain in childbirth! This is a myth! The Goddess will guide me through the surges in my body, as Bardo provides stimulation to my clitoris and my nipples to aid in the orgasmic process of birth.'

Sylvia fainted into Simon's arms.

Christmas Eve dawned, bright and crisp and even. Louisa and Bardo eventually wandered in from the yurt, and Sylvia gently suggested perhaps they might like to take a shower. In return she was treated to a lengthy lecture on how showering was an internalisation of capitalist ideology that they rejected utterly in order to live their true pagan lives.

'Who knew a quick hose-down with a bar of Imperial Leather was a Capitalist Evil?' muttered Michael to himself.

Sylvia tried to change the subject – before Louisa started another lecture – by announcing her Big Surprise. She had booked for Jane to go and see the Very Posh Father Christmas at the local Stately Home. Apparently, this was a Very Big Deal, as to get a slot on Christmas Eve you had to book months in advance, and so Sylvia had secured our spot pretty much while Jane's head was still crowning.

'Um, Sylvia, that's terribly kind,' I said. 'But she's still a baby. She really doesn't have any concept of who Father Christmas is.'

'Nonsense,' said Sylvia briskly. 'You don't give her enough credit. Jane is clearly very bright, like her father. Of course she'll understand what is going on. And it cost £25, so we're going. I got us a nice early slot so I'm back in plenty of time to get the canapés in the oven for the Annual Christmas Eve Drinks with the neighbours. Simon can have a relaxing afternoon to himself, as I'm sure he needs it.'

Sylvia refused to listen to my protests about Jane not being old enough to appreciate Father Christmas and swept us into the Range Rover for the Grand Visitation. It was one of those very stately Stately Homes that go all out for Christmas with mad themes in the giant rooms, and Jane was overwhelmed pretty much from the start. By the time we got to Father Christmas she was sobbing with mild hysteria, and the sight of a potential paedophile looming over her in a big red coat and scary beard was too much and she had a full-on meltdown.

'*Do* something, Ellen, people are looking,' Sylvia hissed, and eventually, after six rounds of 'The Wheels on the Bus', and a couple of choruses of 'Wind the Bobbin Up', I managed to calm Jane down enough to perch her on Father Christmas's knee with Sylvia in position with her camera to snap her £25 money shot, so she could casually show the neighbours how they'd just popped out to the most exclusive Father Christmas event in Surrey on the most festive day of the year.

Jane, however, was having none of it. No sooner was she perched than she blew a gasket again. Her back arched, she shrieked, she thrashed. Father Christmas, God love him, valiantly attempted to clutch on to the roaring hell beast so she didn't fling herself off and concuss herself, and in return for his efforts, Jane's wild flailings led to one small, stout foot connecting with his testicles with some force, just as I reached out to rescue her. Father Christmas's eyes bulged and he went a very funny colour, before falling off his chair and curling into the foetal position while clutching his special Santa sack. He began to retch.

The queue behind, which had been growing increasingly mutinous at Jane's tantrum, began to sound menacing. An elf was approaching with a clipboard and the St John's Ambulance man was bearing down on Father Christmas, who was now making the sort of noises that I last heard from myself when I was giving birth to Jane.

'Go,' Sylvia hissed, as I stared round in a panic. 'Quick, just GO, people are LOOKING! Hurry!'

The elf was now brandishing her clipboard at me and talking about risk assessments and health and safety ('Elf and safety', I thought hysterically) as Sylvia tugged me by the arm, brightly trilling, 'SO sorry. I expect she's overtired, SUCH a fun age, it's been marvellous, we must go,' and we turned tail and fled the scene, as the St John's Ambulance man tenderly applied an ice pack to Santa's distressed package.

Sylvia did not speak during the drive home, probably because her mouth was too cat's bummed to actually spit any words out. All she said to Michael when he came into the hall offering drinks when we arrived back was, 'I need to lie down. And you might as well cancel our National Trust membership, Michael. We won't be able to use it again.'

Sylvia is a trooper, though. By that evening she had rallied, fortified I suspect by a couple of Michael's cocktails and a handful of Valium, and was busy in the kitchen flinging the Waitrose canapés into the Aga, ready for her Annual Christmas Eve Drinks Party for The Neighbours.

The Drinks Party (again, you could hear Sylvia Capitalising It) got off to a roaring start. Jane was adorable in reindeer pyjamas, and Sylvia, clad elegantly in *all* her scarves, made much of reading her 'The Night Before Christmas' in between handing round Mini Beef Wellingtons and cheese straws. In fact, so adorable and docile was Jane that I wondered if Sylvia had slipped her a Valium too. Either way, Simon and I hung up her stocking, tucked her in and looked in amazement at the wonderful little person we'd made, as she lay there, innocently sleeping, rosy-cheeked and perfect. We didn't gaze too long, obviously, as a sleeping Jane was much more lovable than an awake and roaring Jane, and we didn't want to risk that. We tiptoed downstairs, hand in hand, beaming smugly at each other about our angel, to find Sylvia's drawing room abuzz with the latest gossip about how the Posh Father Christmas had been assaulted at the Stately Home.

'I heard the child had to be tasered!' gasped Margery Dawkins, eyes shuddering at the thought of the chav children invading the sanctity of the Stately Home.

'Already had an ASBO, and a tag, apparently,' put in Nigel Kingsley.

'Father Christmas might never walk again,' sighed Evelyn Baxter.

'*I* heard there was a whole clan of them, running *amok*,' breathed Lucinda Parsons. 'Generations, grannies and great-grannies, the lot, every single one of them in *shell suits*!'

Sylvia was puce by now, and appeared to be quietly hyperventilating.

'Of course, I blame the parents,' said Jeremy Goodwell. 'Something needs to be done about feral families like this!'

Poor Sylvia could bear it no more and scuttled off, bleating something about checking on the tempura prawns in the oven. By the time she returned, bearing a platter of mushroom vol-au-vents, the conversation had returned to the safe and familiar topic of house prices, and Sylvia breathed a sigh of relief that her Elegant Soirée remained untainted by ASBO Babies and her Festive Vision was left intact in front of the neighbours, even if she'd have to spend the next year coming up with excuses about why she couldn't go to anything at the Very Stately Stately Home.

Her relief was short-lived, though, as Jeremy choked on his cocktail sausage with a honey-mustard glaze when Louisa and Bardo made their entrance. Sylvia had believed her soirée would not be blighted by their presence, as Louisa had announced at lunchtime that they would be spending the evening carrying out a pagan ritual to her wretched Goddess in the nearby woods (we all assumed she meant shagging again, but such was the general relief that they weren't getting down and dirty in the garden that no one said anything).

As Bardo and Louisa burst in, grubby as ever, we were treated to a spectacular view of just how questionable their personal hygiene was, as they were now stark bollock naked, apart from complicated garlands of ivy they'd entwined round themselves (Bardo had got particularly 'creative' about the entwining). They both carried smouldering branches that they were waving round as they pranced about the room.

'We bring the pagan spirit of Mōdraniht,' they chanted. 'We bless you all with the fertility of the Moon Child in our womb. Come, come, let us dance and celebrate the Mother!'

Sylvia dropped a tray of mini quiches and put her hand to her forehead with a whimper.

Louisa's prancing intensified as she began to sway and moan in the middle of the room, clutching her vast stomach, her swollen boobs setting up some sort of simple harmonic motion of their own with her 'dancing'. I couldn't help but notice a suspicious bulge in the front of Jeremy's red trousers as he stared transfixed.

'Come,' Louisa cried, 'come and join me, brothers, sisters. Tonight is the Night of the Mothers. We dance and feast to bring health and fertility and potency and virility in the coming year. Come!'

I was dreadfully afraid Jeremy might. Bardo's ivy garlands were also perking up in a rather disconcerting way.

'ARRRGGGHHHHH,' shrieked Louisa. 'ARRRRRGHHHHHH!'

'Louisa, stop it!' wailed Sylvia. 'Simon, *do* something!'

'Oh God, she's in labour!' I gasped to Simon. 'Call an ambulance!'

Simon looked at me and his mouth twitched.

'Don't!' I hissed.

His mouth twitched again, and he had to bite his lip.

'Stop it!' I hissed again. 'Don't you start.'

'I can't … I can't help it. Sorry!' and Simon dissolved into hysterical laughter as Louisa continued to prance and Bardo waved his ivy garlands. It was no good. As much as I tried to keep a straight face, Simon's laughter had set me off. We stood in the corner, holding each other up as tears ran down our faces and we tried not to shriek out loud with laughter in case Louisa thought we were joining in.

Louisa clutched at her belly and screeched some more.

'ARRRRGHHHH! I FEEL HER! The Goddess is here in me, I FEEL HER!' she howled, shimmying up to Jeremy and thrusting herself at him. Jeremy was looking thoroughly overexcited by the whole thing, when Michael, who had popped out to the loo, returned to this scene and flung Sylvia's tasteful Laura Ashley throw over Louisa.

'Enough!' he bellowed, handing Bardo a couple of cushions. 'Go and put some clothes on. Both of you. This is quite unnecessary.'

'Not the honeysuckle silk,' moaned Sylvia faintly, gesturing at the cushions now preserving Bardo's modesty.

The party ended quite quickly after that. Later on, the solemn magic of Simon and me filling Jane's first stocking was slightly spoiled as we both kept collapsing with laughter at the memory of the neighbours' faces.

'Well,' said Simon, 'Jane might not remember it, but at least we know her first Christmas was memorable!'

'Even if the memories are for all the wrong reasons,' I agreed.

Present day

I realised I'd been sitting on the floor, staring alternately at Jane's first decoration and my phone, willing her to reply to my text for over forty minutes, and my leg had gone to sleep. I sighed, then slowly struggled to my feet to go and feed the dogs.

As I scooped dog food into bowls, with three eager little faces (well, two little faces and one enormous face in the case of Barry) gazing up at me, I wondered if I hadn't been rather hard on Sylvia over the years. All Sylvia really wanted was for things to be done Right – for people to adhere to her bloody Vision, if you will. And I'd been as guilty as anyone of thwarting her Visions, dismissing her fussing and pernicketiness as the pretentious showing off of a bored housewife. But was I so very different to Sylvia? Simon and Jane had both accused me of being a control freak and wanting everything my own way, and while I might counter that by insisting I didn't want things my own way, I just wanted them *right*, who really was to say what was right? Sylvia had just wanted things *right* as well, we just didn't think she *was* right.

At least, though, Sylvia had had the excuse of being a bored housewife with very little to occupy her time or her mind other than obsessing over the colour of the napkins because they were half a shade different to the colour of the flowers, and what *would* people think? What excuse did I have? I had a job – a demanding job – to keep me busy, and that in theory should have stopped me from turning into Sylvia. My blood ran cold as I opened the door to let the dogs out for their wee. *Was* I turning into Sylvia? Surely not. Not *Sylvia*, of all people. Simon and I had always laughed at the old saying about men marrying their mothers, but maybe he had? Look at me, trying to cling to Jane, painting Stupid Rich Rafferty as the enemy coming between me and my baby. It was true! I was Sylvia Mark Two, minus the scarves. And the mild racism. Except … was I even minus that after Jane's comments on my judgements about Abroad? And then an even worse thought struck me. If I was turning into Sylvia, would Jane's attempts to rebel against me turn her into Louisa?

I poured myself a stiff gin, as I contemplated the horror of my new life as Sylvia 2, then quickly tipped it down the drain and made myself a vodka and tonic instead; gin was Sylvia's poison, and I didn't need any more reminders of our similarities.

For the first time, I felt a pang of sympathy for Sylvia and how desperately she'd clung to her Only Son. At the time, I'd thought she was just an overbearing mother-in-law, but now I realised that perhaps she too was just trying to stop herself becoming redundant in his life – and her own. It must have been even harder for Sylvia when Simon and Louisa grew up and left, and Sylvia found herself with nothing but Michael, who was generally too busy playing golf, and her ladies-who-lunch circuit, none of whom were really the sort of people you could lean on or confide in. Poor Sylvia, I realised, must have been very unhappy and lonely for many years until she moved to France and managed to set up a little business of her own, selling charming *brocante* pieces (or 'tat', as Michael called them in bafflement) at preposterously marked-up prices to bored women trying to inject a little of the Shabby Chic aesthetic into their identikit executive villas. She'd done even better since I'd introduced her to the wonders of Instagram; business was booming, despite Louisa's continuing lengthy lectures to her mother on the evils of capitalism, before trying to borrow 50 euros off her. But if Sylvia could change, learn to relax and become a better person, so, surely, could I. I started by ringing Jane again, leaving a heartfelt and impassioned message on her voicemail, although with hindsight I should probably have done that before I had a large vodka on an empty stomach, as I suspect I rambled on a bit, and perhaps declaring 'I will think of Rafferty as my own son from now on' was … a bit much?

Sunday 3 December

Despite my noble resolution to be more relaxed, to allow festive fun to just happen, to be a chilled-out and jolly Christmas Elf, old habits die hard. Some things are just too important to be left to chance, and some facets of the Vision cannot be relinquished, not ever! So I bullied and cajoled Simon into coming to get a Christmas tree with me, and insisted we went to the charming and adorable 'cut your own' Christmas tree farm, where there were promises of mince pies and mulled wine and reindeer.

'Why can't we just go to B&Q?' grumbled Simon. 'Why do you want to see fucking reindeer anyway?'

'Because it will be *festive*!' I snarled. 'B&Q is not festive. Christmas tree farms and reindeers are festive, so shut the fuck up.'

Simon sighed and wisely said no more until we were parking at the Christmas tree farm, when he said, 'Dear God, Ellen, we're the only people here without children. People will think we're weirdos. Or paedos!'

'Nonsense,' I said firmly. 'They'll simply think we're wonderful people, fully embracing the spirit of Christmas!'

'If the "spirit of Christmas" means mud,' said Simon gloomily, squelching across the car park.

I had to concede he had a point about the mud. It *was* exceptionally muddy, especially in the vicinity of the reindeer, who were not the gaily prancing, snorting, majestic sort of beasts I'd envisaged, but instead appeared to be a pair of depressed-looking moose, surrounded by screaming children. The homemade mince pies were clearly Mr Kipling's – they hadn't even removed them from the plastic trays – and the catering lady brightly informed us that the mulled wine was non-alcoholic.

'Come on,' I said firmly to Simon. 'At least cutting the tree will be magical!'

'It won't,' he insisted. 'You do this every year, Ellen. You make us come and cut down a tree and say it will be magical, and you seem to think we'll enter some kind of enchanted forest out of Narnia, where we'll crunch over ice and snow under dark and mysterious branches, until we find our own perfect tree, alone in a clearing, with Mr Tumnus and a lamp post, and then we'll chop it down with a single blow and carry it back to the car, as everyone laughs merrily and we skip along with rosy cheeks and there are Dickensian carol singers gathered round a lantern and happy memories abound – and you wear an adorable hat!'

'Yes,' I said in delight. 'Finally, you've grasped my Vision. That's exactly how it will be, at last you see it. And my hat is *adorable*, isn't it?'

Simon shook his head. 'No, Ellen, I haven't seen your Vision. You've been describing the same Vision for the Christmas tree cutting every year to me for almost twenty years. Ever since you first came up with the idea when Peter was three months old and you had to bring him in a baby carrier because the pram couldn't get through the mud, then you fell over and you were both caked in mud and everybody cried, including me, and Jane got hold of an axe and nearly chopped her own foot off. Remember?'

'Well,' I said airily. 'That was then. Things are different now. That's why we've tried lots of other Christmas tree farms.'

'Because every year we never dare go back to the one we went to the previous year,' Simon pointed out.

'These are mere DETAILS,' I snapped. 'THIS year will be different. We don't have the children bickering and squabbling and falling in the mud. And *this* Christmas tree farm has *reindeer*, hasn't it? So that's a good omen!'

'But you just described the reindeer as depressed moose, and refused to go over to them because in your words, there were "too many fucking children".'

'DETAILS,' I shouted again, then checked my inner Sylvia, took a deep breath and said calmly, 'Look, darling, why don't you just do your very manly thing and go and see the chap who gives out the chainsaws and the unInstagrammable goggles and the special trousers and let the magic commence, OK?'

'What if I cut my leg off with the chainsaw?'

'That's what the special trousers are for. And if you still manage to cut off your leg, well, I have Steri-Strips and a first aid kit and wound dressings.'

'Why do you still go everywhere with a first aid kit?'

I sighed. 'Years of your children forcing me to prepare for every eventuality, because you could be sure that whatever medical emergency I did not bring supplies to tackle, they would manage to create. Do you want a nip of Calpol?'

'Pink?'

'No, SixPlus.'

'No thanks. Come on, darling, let's get this over with. You can have your annual fall on your arse in the mud, we can have a massive row and then go home. If nothing else, I admire your continued optimism that one day you'll manage to find the magic.'

Ten minutes later we stood at the entrance to the magic, surveying a muddy tree plantation with endless straight rows of dejected-looking Nordmann firs.

'It's not an enchanted forest, after all,' I said sadly. It never was an enchanted forest, but one had to continue to hope, didn't one? What was life without hope? Simon always told me I needed to have more realistic expectations about things, but surely that was the point of expectations – to expect wonderful things. Surely to set off in the expectation of mud and depressed moose and Mr Kipling mince pies was a life devoid of any snatches of joy, even if that joy was almost immediately crushed by the filthy quagmire of reality. As Robert Louis Stevenson said, 'To travel hopefully is a better thing than to arrive.' He was right, because even if it was all rubbish when you got there, at least you'd had that brief spell of hope and anticipation that it might not be this time. Even so, just once, would it kill the fucking universe to come through for me and make my anticipation worthwhile?

Two hours later we were standing in the sitting room, I was covered in mud as Simon had predicted, and he was shouting, 'I TOLD YOU IT WOULDN'T FUCKING FIT. I said it was too big, you have no bloody spatial awareness at all, that's why you can't bastarding park!'

'I can so bastarding park,' I screamed. 'Just not when other people park like DICKHEADS. And it's not too fucking big. Just chop a bit off the bottom.'

'We won't be able to move. The whole room will be filled with this bloody tree.'

'That's why you need to TRIM IT. Oh my fucking God, it's not hard. I'LL trim it!'

I brandished the hacksaw menacingly, as Simon continued to witter about 'spatial awareness' until I sobbed, 'You're ruining the festive joy with your fucking spatial awareness' and grabbed the dogs and the bottle of Baileys and stormed off to sit in the garage and sob that no one – no one – got my Vision, and it WASN'T FAIR.

Half an hour later the dogs had already returned to the house in disgust, and I was getting very cold and wondering how to go back in without losing face, when the garage door opened and Simon walked through.

'I made it fit,' he said.

'Good,' I gulped. I knew I hadn't covered myself in glory with my behaviour, but I consoled myself that at least I'd refrained from expressing my displeasure in icy looks and tight-lipped sniffing, as was Sylvia's wont. Perhaps I wasn't turning into her after all, as Sylvia considered crying to be the height of vulgarity. This thought cheered me somewhat. Maybe I should have *more* tantrums – then I could hold onto my Festive Vision, while definitely *not* turning into Sylvia!

'Come on, let's go inside. And at least you've got your Big Christmas Meltdown over and done with early!' said Simon, prising the Baileys bottle out of my cold hands.

'There,' said Simon proudly, gesturing to the now slightly truncated tree once we were inside. 'It doesn't look too bad, does it? And you know how it'll look once you've decorated it?'

'Shit?'

'Magical, Ellen. It'll look fucking magical.'

'Will it?'

'It always does. You just … you overthink Christmas. I thought maybe this year, with it being just us, you might be able to relax a bit, chill out, forget about the "magic".'

I spluttered apoplectically at this notion.

'OK, not *forget* about it, but you know, not try so hard. Why is it so important to you?'

'I dunno,' I shrugged. But I did know, really. As long as I could remember, by the time the nights shortened and November came, there was an onslaught of adverts, of shiny happy women in velvet dresses clinking champagne glasses, of rosy-cheeked families laughing as they tramped through the dark streets with armfuls of gifts, of merry children building snowmen and parties full of beautiful people beaming with festive cheer, all of them just needing that little pinch of extra magic – the *right* velvet frock, the *most* tasteful wrapping paper for those middle-class gifts, an *adorable* lambswool scarf and mittens for the snowman building, the *perfect* canapés for that elegant soirée.

As a child, I longed for these visions to be true. To be that happy perfect family, instead of listening to my parents fighting, my mother sniping over Christmas dinner, and my father, the last year they were married, simply standing up halfway through the meal after one jibe too many from my mother and walking out to go to the pub, before coming home very drunk much later that night to the worst row Jessica and I had ever heard our parents have. Jessica, never demonstrative or affectionate, crept into my room that night as Mum and Dad screamed at each other, and got into bed with me, whispering, 'It's OK, it'll be OK, we'll be OK, Ellen, don't worry,' as we clung to each other. And on Boxing Day, Dad packed his bags and left. Mum tersely informed us that 'Your father has some tart, so I've told him she's welcome to him.'

And then we entered the era of the Broken Home Christmases, of Dad's new partners glowering at us resentfully, of trying to play happy families with stepsiblings we hardly knew, of feeling guilt about whichever parent we were not with on Christmas Day. The first Christmas after Mum and Dad split up was spent with Dad and Rachel, the woman Mum refused to refer to as anything but 'the tart'. On Christmas Eve, Mum put us on a train at her end and Jessica panicked the whole way about losing our tickets, and being arrested by British Transport Police. I spent the first half of the journey pretending to be a Second World War evacuee being sent off to the country, where I'd be taken in by a stern old couple, who, although initially strict and unbending, would soon have joy brought to their barren hearts by my simple, childish ways, and the second half by just staring out of the window at the dark night punctuated by flashes of the back of other people's houses and lives. I was convinced that every kitchen window we passed contained a perfect, happy, jolly family, where there were no rows, the mother was a happy soul, cheerfully dishing up some sort of wholesome Christmas Eve stew, while the father was an amiable character, playing bears with the children, who wore striped flannel pyjamas and Wellington boots (*The Snowman* was a pivotal part of my childhood Christmas viewing). Everyone in these houses would be laughing and merry, there would be no snapping and making snarky comments at each other, no one was hiding upstairs hoping that their parents would stop screaming at each other or trying to distract them from the row and diffusing the situation by pointing out the very funny thing the dog had just

chains out of the magazines, stopping wide-eyed to read the problem pages and boggle at the sex tips and wonder if such things were really possible.

Dad roared with laughter when they finally came home from the party to see how enterprising we'd been. 'See, Rachel,' he said. 'I told you we needed to get a tree. The girls clearly thought the same and have taken matters into their own hands!'

'Should we hang up our stockings?' I asked.

'You're far too old,' snapped a furious Rachel, who was not best pleased with the desecration of her *Cosmos* (perhaps she'd been hoping to brush up on some festive fun for Dad) as she packed us off to bed, muttering about the mess and our lack of respect.

We spent a miserable Christmas dinner with Rachel glaring at us in the Michelin-starred restaurant she'd demanded to be taken to, as she refused to cook and Dad claimed not to even know how to switch the stove on. We were slightly cheered by the cheques for £500 each that Dad had given us in an attempt to make up for Rachel's hostility and the general lack of Christmas joy, but we'd never been so glad to get home on Boxing Day, even if it was to find a note from Mum informing us that she too had gone out to a drinks party. 'After all,' said Jessica, 'baked beans just taste better when they're made in your own microwave.'

Dad's casual attitude to parenting did result in one Christmas that was memorable for all the right reasons, though. The next time it was his turn to have us for Christmas, it didn't dawn on him that we were coming until he'd already booked a Christmas cruise – as had Mum. Since neither of them would back down and cancel (Mum citing her need for a break as she had us the majority of the time, Dad, having got shot of Rachel, needing to keep a new popsy sweet), he hit on the idea of sending us to stay with his mother in her Welsh farmhouse. We'd never spent much time with this grandmother, as Mum did not get on with her, and we hadn't ever been to stay with her before as Mum considered the farmhouse to be unhygienic and a death trap. However, faced with cancelling her cruise (a singles cruise, no less, as we discovered when she triumphantly returned with Geoffrey's precursor, a sweaty stock-broker called Roger, in tow), she was prepared to overlook these failings and risk the certain death for her daughters that she insisted lurked in every cranny of Ty'r Ywen.

Dad collected us for the drop-off on the 23rd, before going back to his place for the night and then sailing from Southampton on Christmas Eve. He spent the drive across to Wales telling us how amazing it was going to be.

'You're going to have such a wonderful time,' he kept saying. 'I'm quite jealous, really.' Dad had made such a fuss about how much fun we were going to have, dumped on a grandmother we hardly knew, in the middle of nowhere, over Christmas, like parcels left in the sorting office on Christmas Eve because no one had bothered to post them in time, that Jessica and I had both made up our minds that we most certainly would *not* have fun, not if we died trying. Jessica in particular made a show of plugging herself in to her Sony Walkman for the whole drive and tuning Dad out, whereas I, lacking Jessica's organisation and having run out of batteries for my Walkman, contented myself with monosyllabic grunts in answer to his desperate pleas about wasn't I looking forward to it? I did point out that if he was really that jealous of us spending Christmas at Ty'r Ywen, then there was absolutely nothing to stop him staying and spending it with us – he'd be going there anyway, and he could just ring up the new popsy and tell her to go on the cruise without him. He said he couldn't because he didn't have any spare pants. Perhaps this is where my obsession with always having extra pairs of clean pants wherever I go comes from, just in case I ever get the chance to go somewhere like Ty'r Ywen again and I can't because of a lack of clean knickers?

Ty'r Ywen lay up a rutted track on a Welsh hillside. Dad swore and cursed as his snazzy BMW made alarming noises as it bumped in and out of the potholes. Although there were no other houses for me to look in the windows and imagine the inhabitants' lives, there were plenty of sheep. I suspected the rich inner lives of sheep did not provide much scope for one's imagination. Finally, the car ground to a halt and we were there. It was only half past four, but it was already dark.

We had been to Ty'r Ywen before for the day, but that was in the summer and my memories of it were hazy. There was a rope swing, I knew, as well as a stream in which I'd fallen and Mum had shouted at me for getting so wet and muddy. In the winter and in the dark it was all utterly unfamiliar. Below us everything was black, with the odd pinprick of light far down in the valley, and before us was the dim lurking hulk of a house. I'd been reading *Cold Comfort Farm* and feared the worst, though I consoled myself if I had to go full Flora Poste and set Ty'r Ywen in order, at least it would be something to do for the next ten days until Dad returned and rescued us, because something told me Granny didn't have Sky TV.

Dad slammed the car door and there was a furious baying from inside the house before the outside lights switched on, revealing a large cobbled courtyard with the house on one side and an old barn on the other, the third side bordered by an ancient wall, higher than my head. A second later the door opened and Granny Green sallied forth amidst a barking, leaping swirl of dogs.

No apple-cheeked, be-aproned grandmama was Granny Green. Indeed, it would have been a brave wolf that tried his chances with her. She was almost as tall as Dad, and her black hair was cut into the chicest bob I had ever seen. She had a martini in one hand, and a cigarette in a, oh holy fuck, an actual cigarette holder in the other hand. She wore a cream silk shirt, and a pair of wide-legged, beautifully cut tweed trousers.

'Get down, down, down, you brutes,' Granny yelled at the wolf pack surrounding her, before turning to us.

'Darling,' she cried, clanking cheekbones with Dad, 'I thought you'd got lost! And the girls! Oh, look at you, so grown up! Ralph, here, take my drink and things while I give them a hug.'

We were enveloped in a real, huge hug, and a cloud of Mitsouko perfume, before she retrieved her martini and her cigarette from Dad, but nothing daunted by having her hands full, put her arms round our shoulders and led us in, calling back, 'Dogs, COME! Ralph, do be a love and bring my darling granddaughters' things in and put them in their rooms – Jessica's in the Tapestry Room and Ellen's in the Priest's Room, then come and have a drink.'

I'd never seen anyone steal the limelight from my father before. Wherever he went, he had a sort of glamour and presence that always made him the centre of attention, but compared with his mother, his own glamour was a firefly beside a lighthouse. The last time we'd seen Granny Green was to have lunch with her in London about four years earlier, when I'd simply found her terrifying. Pre-divorce, Mum had always made excuses to get out of seeing her, while post-divorce, Dad was too busy placating his latest shags about our presence to have arranged for us to see Granny, so her sheer force of personality, not to mention her glorious style, now I was old enough to appreciate it, came as something of a shock to me.

We were led into the drawing room. 'I'll show you where you're sleeping in a bit,' she said, 'but do come and get warm by the fire for now, and meet the dogs of course!' She pointed at a pair of exuberant Border terriers and two beautiful greyhounds, who thumped their tails happily at us. 'These are Viper and Vixen, and Nancy and Nora. And this is Mr T. We tell people he's a Staffie, but he's a pit bull. He's the sweetest thing, but he'd be put down if anyone knew, so do keep it to yourselves. And of course Rupert, after Rupert Campbell-Black, because he's so very handsome.' A scruffy one-eared yellow mongrel of uncertain parentage licked her hand happily.

'You do *like* dogs, don't you?' Granny suddenly asked anxiously. 'I don't know what we'll we do if you don't.'

'Oh yes,' we assured her. 'Very much.'

'But who is Rupert Campbell-Black?' asked Jessica, as his namesake nudged her hand for a head scratch.

'Oh my dear, you haven't read Jilly Cooper?' cried Granny in horror. 'Well, we shall have to remedy that immediately. Rupert Campbell-Black is the handsomest man in England, so I had to call our Rupert that when I adopted him to cheer him up and improve his self-esteem. He was so horribly treated as a puppy.' Granny lowered her voice conspiratorially. 'And he's the handsomest dog in the *world*, in my opinion, but don't let the others hear.'

Dad came in at this point and looked round at the dogs all lolling happily on various beautiful velvet sofas, and in the case of Nancy the greyhound, reclining most elegantly on a chaise longue.

'How many dogs now, Mother?' he asked disbelievingly.

'Oh don't,' implored Granny. 'What am I to do, when there are so many poor souls out there needing a home and people are so awful to animals? Girls, *promise* me now that you'll never buy a puppy from a puppy farm, and you'll always get a rescue dog if you can. Do you promise? You *do*? Oh *good*! Now! Drinks!'

'I need to drive home, Mother,' Dad protested.

'You're not staying?' said Granny. 'Not even for supper?'

'I can't,' Dad insisted. 'We have a dinner party we're supposed to be at at 8 p.m., and Claire will be furious if I'm not back in time. I'll have more time when I come to get the girls, I promise.'

'Well,' said Granny, after Dad had departed. 'What about a drink for you two?'

'We're not old enough,' said Jessica primly.

'Nonsense,' said Granny. 'You're what, sixteen? And Ellen is fourteen. That's more than old enough. I had my first martini when I was Ellen's age. Here, try this,' and she handed us each a brimming cocktail glass.

I took a gulp and choked. When I could breathe again and my eyes had stopped streaming and Granny had given me a glass of water and thumped me on the back several times, she explained that you're meant to *sip* martinis.

'Maybe we had better start with a nice vod and ton for you,' she murmured. 'Ease you in gently. Now, is that better? Come on, I'll show you the house.'

Ty'r Ywen was heaven. Ancient and rambling, it might have been *built* for Christmas. Holly and ivy nestled behind murky oil paintings in flaking gilt frames, mistletoe hung from the old black beams holding the house up, the only downside being the giant tree in the hall, which was bare and unlit. I didn't like to ask about it, in case it was some strange tradition of Granny's, but at least, I comforted myself, there *was* a tree, and everything else was most festive.

I was overcome with envy at Jessica's room, with tapestries hanging from the walls and an old oak four-poster bed. It was SO unfair, Jessica always got the best of everything, just because she was the oldest. There was no way my room would be as good as hers. No room would. And indeed, when Granny flung open the door to my room, a small, plain room with no distinguishing features at all apart from some wood panelling, I hid my disappointment as best as I could, but it must have showed on my face, because Granny laughed, and said, 'I know it doesn't look as grand as Jessica's room, Ellen, but I put you in here because your father said you had a very active imagination.' I sniffed indignantly. I was not bloody Sara Crewe, starving in a garret and forced to furnish it with only the power of my mind! 'And I thought the history of this room would appeal to you. Do you know what it was used for, four hundred years ago?'

'Four hundred years?' I said in disbelief.

'Oh yes. This is the very oldest part of the house. And this room was used as a secret Catholic chapel after the Reformation. If you press this panel here …' Granny pushed on the wall, something clicked and the panel slid back, 'there's a priest hole behind it. Hence why it's now called the Priest's Room.'

'Oh my fucking God!' I burst out. 'Sorry, sorry, sorry, Granny!'

'It's all right,' she laughed again. 'Just try not to swear at Christmas dinner, I'd regard it as a personal favour. I'll show you how the panel works, then I'll leave you to settle in. Then come down for supper. I've made a stew.'

A stew! A wholesome festive stew! And it was not even Christmas Eve yet!

Granny's stew, in truth, was not the best stew I'd ever had. So Jessica and I were starving and ready for breakfast when we woke up on Christmas Eve morning. I flung back the curtains of the Priest's Room and gasped in delight, as the valley fell away below the house, sparkling with frost in the dim winter morning sunlight. Accustomed to central heating and fitted carpets, though, the floor was freezing and my ancient Care Bears nightie was distinctly draughty. A pair of stripey flannelette pyjamas and some wellies would have been just the ticket, but lacking such items, or even slippers, I hastily dressed and followed the enticing smell of bacon and sausages downstairs. Alarmingly, the closer I got to the kitchen, the more the smell became burning rather than bacon, and in the kitchen I found Granny pulling a charred tray of bacon out of the Aga and regarding it with a perplexed face.

'I don't know what I did wrong,' she said. 'Everyone says just put things in the Aga and leave them. Oh dear, I *am* sorry, girls, I don't really cook much.'

'Never mind,' said Jessica. 'There's lots of eggs, Granny. I can scramble some, if you want.'

'What a good idea!' said Granny. 'And there's plenty of baked beans if you want any?' She unearthed a battered enamel saucepan from a cupboard and emptied a tin of beans into it, while Jessica scrambled eggs and I laid the table and made a pot of tea.

'Isn't this *fun*?' said Granny as we sat down to breakfast. 'I am sorry about the bacon and sausages, darlings. I popped them in before bed last night, thinking we'd get up to a breakfast of kings, but obviously not. Like I said, I don't really cook. There's a lovely girl in the village who makes all sorts of wonderful things to fill up the deep freeze, then I just fling them in the Aga to heat up or in the microwave, but I thought I should *try*, you know? Be a proper granny. I should have known, really. I tried to make scones yesterday afternoon for you coming, and it was dreadful! Flour everywhere, dough in my hair and the result was a tray of horrible hard rock cake affairs that I put out for the birds and even they refused to eat them. The kitchen was such a mess that if you hadn't been coming I think I should just have burnt the whole place down and started again in a nice house by the seaside somewhere. And then I had to clean it all up and make the wretched stew. Good lord, that was disgusting, wasn't it? But, as dear Robert Louis Stevenson said, "the true success is to labour" – and I certainly did that!'

'I thought he said it is better to travel hopefully than arrive?' I asked.

'The quote is *actually* "to travel hopefully is a better thing than to arrive" and the second part is "and the true success is to labour". Both, I think, mean that the end results don't matter so much as the effort put in. No one ever remembers the second part, though, which personally I think is the much more meaningful bit. Anyway, talking of labouring, sweeties, I'm afraid I must put you to work. There's an enormous tree that needs decorating and I saved it because I thought you two might like to do it. I have twelve people coming for Christmas lunch tomorrow, so we need to look out all the good glass and china and get the dining room ready, and I must try to decipher the terribly complicated instructions Susan the lovely freezer-filling girl has left me about cooking this dreadful turkey and heating up all the potatoes and things she's done for me. Come on! Put the rest of the scrambled egg in the doggies' bowls. They adore it!'

We worked like Trojans that Christmas Eve. It was the most perfect day ever. We decorated the tree together, Jessica and me standing on stepladders and leaning over the stairs to put the higher baubles on, as Granny sat at the bottom with a martini and her ever-present Gauloises, handing up ancient glass decorations, all with a story: 'I bought this in Venice, on my honeymoon. Oh, and these ones, I got in a flea market in Paris. Your mother gave me these – you made them at nursery, apparently. Maybe put them near the back, darling.'

We walked the dogs through frosty fields and came home to mince pies – luckily made by Susan, not Granny – by the fire, and then we tackled the dining room as Granny put *Carols from King's* on the radio and we attempted to sing along (badly). The dogs took umbrage at the soloist in 'Once in Royal David's City' and started howling along.

Then we had more vodka and tonics, and Susan's shepherd's pie, unearthed from the deep freeze, and Granny had got *It's a Wonderful Life* from the video shop in the village. Jessica and I had never seen it so we watched that after supper, and then Granny gave both of us one of our late grandfather's woolly socks to hang up by the fire, along with one for each of the dogs, and we were more than ready for bed. Tired as I was, I still played with the panelling in my room for a while and poked around in the priest's hole, hoping to discover a hitherto unsuspected secret passage somewhere, but to no avail. I fell asleep at last, filled with a surfeit of Christmas spirit and vodka and tonic, and I left my curtains open so I could see the stars.

Christmas morning began with a rather shamefaced Rupert Campbell-Black being found on the drawing-room rug, looking extremely green around the gills, having managed to open the door, sneak in and eat six dog-stockings' worth of treats, along with all the chocolates out of our stockings, and he'd given a good gnawing to the make-up and toiletries Granny had put in too.

'Oh dear,' said Granny. 'Poor Rupert, he can never resist; he spent so long not knowing where his next meal was coming from. I *am* sorry, darlings.'

It was impossible to be cross with Rupert, though, who was both so sorry for his actions, and so sorry for himself.

'Won't the chocolate be bad for him?' I asked anxiously.

'Rupert has a cast-iron constitution,' said Granny. 'He ate a whole bag of chocolate coins, complete with foil and a bag of chocolate Brazil nuts last year, and he was fine. All the same, he does look a bit bilious. Pop him in the garden, Ellen, would you, let him get it out of his system?'

Half an hour later Rupert bounced back in, very pleased with himself and ready for breakfast. He laid his head on my knee and informed me that although he was most regretful about consuming the contents of my stocking, nonetheless, his terrible guilt and shame could probably be eased by giving him some of the smoked salmon Granny had provided for breakfast. And Buck's Fizz? He'd certainly give it a go.

'Do get down, Rupert,' said Granny crossly. '*No*, you're not having salmon. Or Buck's Fizz. If I give you salmon, I'll have to give them all salmon. Do you dogs think I'm made of money? You'll land me in the poorhouse, you wretched beasts.'

Despite Granny's protestations, she did divide the last scraps of salmon between the dogs. 'Well,' she said defensively. 'It *is* Christmas, after all. Now. Presents. Proper presents, that luckily Rupert has not been in! Though it occurs to me that I do hope Mr T hasn't widdled on the tree presents. He does have form sometimes.'

Mr T had fortunately contained himself, and Granny handed us both large squishy parcels.

'I had no idea what teenage girls like these days apart from pop music and mascara,' she said anxiously. 'But these were rather lovely, and I thought might be useful?'

We each had a beautiful, heavily embroidered, silk kimono-style dressing gown.

'Oh,' I breathed. 'Oh Granny, it's beautiful.'

'Do you like it then?'

'It's marvellous,' said Jessica in wonder. 'I adore it. Thank you. Um. We got you something, but it's not quite the same. Well, Mum got it. We didn't really know what to get you.'

There could surely have been no gift less appropriate for the glamorous, exotic Granny Green than the Yardley Lavender Gift Set hastily excavated from Mum's present drawer and wrapped up when Dad announced the amended plans, but Granny nobly declared it to be just what she was needing.

'Let's get dressed,' she said, discreetly laying the Yardley to one side. 'Then it's all hands to the deck again, people will start arriving soon. What are you wearing, girls? No, Ellen, you can't wear your dressing gown, however nice it is, for Christmas dinner.'

'Oh dear,' said Granny, surveying our clothes half an hour later. She looked wonderful again in black velvet palazzo pants and a red silk shirt. Jessica and I looked considerably less wonderful. Mum had insisted Christmas Day required donning the Laura Ashley abominations that she deemed suitable for Sunday lunch with her own mother and for which we were far too old.

'Do you *want* to wear these?' Granny asked.

No, we assured her vehemently, we most certainly did not.

'Well, you'd better borrow something of mine,' she sighed, flinging open her dressing room to reveal a treasure trove within.

'What can we borrow?' asked Jessica anxiously.

'Oh, whatever you like,' said Granny airily. 'I hardly ever wear any of this stuff anyway!'

Jessica took down a black silk number and held it against herself.

'That's lovely, darling, try it on,' enthused Granny.

Jessica squinted at the label and gasped. 'I can't possibly, Granny. It's Dior!'

'It's only a dress,' insisted Granny. 'Ellen, what about you? Oh, yes, that's nice. That green suits you.'

Downstairs again, hardly daring to breathe or let the dogs near us, doused in Granny's Mitsouko and with a 'very weak, darling, practically water, actually, not like the martini, I promise' cocktail in hand, we awaited the guests, and as they arrived, each more flamboyant and elegant and glamorous than the last, we were relieved to be standing there in Granny's Dior and Givenchy, instead of the sodding Laura Ashley *Little House on the Prairie* frocks. The drawing room was thrumming with conversation, drinks were being handed round with abandon by a charming man called Emile, who had not seemed to realise my age and had given me a cigarette that I was trying to smoke without being sick, when Granny burst back into the room and paused dramatically in the doorway.

'QUELLE HORREUR!' she yelled. 'C'EST UNE CATASTROPHE!'

'What on Earth is wrong, Francesca?' demanded Emile.

'Have you burnt yourself?' asked a lady called Victoria, who seemed to have come as Margot from *The Good Life*.

'The bloody Aga has gone out,' wailed Granny. 'Out! Dead! Dead as a bloody buggering dodo. That horrible turkey is completely raw, and the potatoes are colder than a witch's tit.'

'Oh, is that all?' said Emile.

'Can't you relight it?' said a man called Roland, sporting a very jaunty cravat.

'YOU relight it!' snapped Granny. 'I have no idea how the wretched thing works.'

Twenty minutes later everyone had peered at the Aga and agreed they also had no idea what to do. Oh, the dark days before YouTube tutorials. Roland went so far as to approach it with his lighter but retreated, muttering that he could be blinded.

Emile consoled Granny. 'Never mind, darling. We've plenty of drink, and you always have jars and jars of olives and things.'

Granny took a deep, shuddering breath and looked very brave. 'This is true,' she said. 'We shall have to picnic. Jessica, Ellen, darlings, come with me to the larder and see what we can find to eat.'

Christmas dinner was a riotous affair in the end, partly I think because the jars of olives and the breadsticks and the mixed nuts, and cheese and biscuits, and several jars of pickled beetroot ('It's the only thing that I can make, darlings') that took the place of the turkey and trimmings were not really adequate as blotting paper for the amount of drink that was circulating, but we lit the candles in the dining room and ate the salty snacks off the best china anyway, and Granny opened all the wine that was supposed to have gone with the turkey, and there was a terribly confusing game of charades because everyone was too pissed to remember if they were guessing a book or a film, and I'm pretty sure Granny kissed Emile, because they came back in after a long absence and he appeared to be wearing her lipstick, but oh, it was heaven. No one had a row. No one was tight-jawed with stress and hissing under their breath at anyone, not a single mince pie was thrown, and if I did wake up on Boxing Day face down on my little bed in the Priest's Room still in Granny's Givenchy with my first ever hangover, it was totally worth it, as I said to Granny as she administered Alka-Seltzer and water to me.

Granny waved us off a week later, with four jars of pickled beetroot (we lacked the heart to tell her it really wasn't that nice) and the Christmas Day dresses to keep for our very own, and we couldn't wait to go back to hers. However, it was our first and last Christmas at Ty'r Ywen. We managed a glorious summer holiday there the following year, but Mum insisted on having us spend the next Christmas with her at the Mill House with Roger and his loathsome children in order for them both to pretend a show of family unity to each other (Geoffrey's Queen Anne rectory was definitely an upgrade from Roger's Mill House of indeterminate period), and the following summer Granny died suddenly of a stroke. Ty'r Ywen was sold, and the poor dogs were rehomed among the Emiles and Rolands and Victorias. We were heartbroken, but Dad assured us that if Granny had to die, she'd much rather have gone quickly and suddenly. 'She'd have so hated to have been ill and dependent, and even just getting properly old and not being able to do things for herself.'

Ever since, I think this is what Jessica and I have been striving for – the sheer magic of that Christmas at Ty'r Ywen. But we've never managed to pull it off, however much we worked at it, even though the adverts and the Christmas specials continued to promise that if you just tried hard enough, if you did it right, if you put enough effort into the Festive Vision and bought your Christmas presents in John Lewis, then you too could waft effortlessly round your soirée in your velvet dress, laughing merrily as your beautiful family sang carols round the piano and everyone lived happily ever after. Because, lacking Granny's magic, I convinced myself that the next best thing was to *try*, that as she'd told me, the 'true success is to labour' and if I couldn't sprinkle fairy dust, then dammit I *would* labour.

I tried to explain this to Simon, that it was *magic* I was looking for, really.

'I know you just want everything to be perfect,' said Simon. 'But nothing is ever really perfect in real life, is it?'

'Yes, but I always just think if I just try a *bit* harder, I can *make* it all perfect. And if it's perfect,' I insisted, 'if just *once* I can make it perfect, then the magic will come. Like today. I really thought that finding a Christmas tree farm with reindeers and mulled wine would be the extra mile that would make getting the tree perfect. But the reindeer were shit and the mulled wine was non-alcoholic! What is even the *point* of non-alcoholic mulled wine?'

'I suppose because everyone has to drive to get there, and get their tree home?' Simon pointed out reasonably. 'Still, at least it's not as bad as the year we went to Jessica's, and she was pregnant with Gulliver and announced when we got there that she'd decided it would be a Dry Christmas.'

'Oh God!' I clutched my head in horror. 'Don't remind me!'

Eighteen years ago

Peter's first Christmas could not have been more different from Michael's booze-filled bacchanalia for Jane's first Christmas (well, Michael provided the booze; the bacchanalian aspect was mostly provided by Louisa's naked cavortings. No one was really surprised when Jeremy the sleazy neighbour had a heart attack on the third of January, as it had been on the cards since Christmas Eve, though it took Michael and Sylvia somewhat longer to get rid of Louisa, who didn't produce little Cedric until the start of February and who then lingered another month, before finally burying her placenta under the Japanese maple during a full moon and departing for the Holistic Retreat, no cleaner or saner than when she arrived). Jessica, eager to show off her perfect child, her perfect catering and her perfect life, in the dark days before Instagram came along and you could do all of that without actually having to let people into your house to show off to them, had decreed that she'd host Christmas for Simon and me, Mum and Geoffrey, and Dad and his latest wife, Jackie.

Since I had an infant Peter, not to mention a now extremely rambunctious and active two-year-old Jane, who was now talking as well as walking, having appalled Sylvia when her first word was 'fuck', however much I tried to laugh it off as 'duck' or 'fork', I was dubious about this plan, as Jessica was heavily pregnant, as well as coping with Persephone, also in the throes of the Terrible Twos.

'Are you *sure*?' I asked her over and over again, and Jessica airily insisted that of *course* she was sure, it was just a matter of being organised and she didn't see what everyone made such a *fuss* about. In fairness to Jessica, I don't think that Christmas was as much about showing off as it was her own attempt to recreate that Ty'r Ywen Magic we'd both been chasing our whole lives. She should really have known better, though. Magic was the last thing that was likely to happen with Mum and Dad under the same roof. From my wedding, where Mum heckled Dad's speech, to Jessica's wedding, where she attempted to boo him as he walked Jessica down the aisle, to Persephone's christening, when Mum loudly and repeatedly reminded Dad he was a grandfather now and he'd better not think he could go knocking up some young trollop to have a baby younger than his own grandchild, family accord was never on the cards. I was relieved that being a godless heathen I'd not had either of mine christened, something Mum was slightly bitter about, as I'd denied her two God-given opportunities to have a go at her ex-husband in public.

'Yes, but Mum *and* Dad? Together? Is that a good idea? Not to mention Geoffrey and Jackie? Another potential minefield. You know how racist Geoffrey can be; he'll make comments about Jackie being Indian, even though her grandparents moved here years ago, or worse, call her some hideous racial slur because he insists it was a perfectly acceptable word when he was young and then everyone will fall out and Jackie will be, quite rightly, upset, which will just make Geoffrey more boorish and fucking racist, and then someone will cry, probably you, definitely me, quite likely Jackie, and it will all go horribly horribly wrong!'

'Yes, well, I can't exactly invite Mum and Dad and *not* Geoffrey and Jackie. Or Mum, Dad and Jackie and not Geoffrey, can I? Christmas is about *people*, Ellen, lots of people. And family. And like it or not, these people *are* our family. Anyway, everyone has promised to be on their best behaviour, including Geoffrey, and

I've primed Mum about Jackie and warned her to make sure Geoffrey learns a list of words and phrases that are very definitely unacceptable, including anything involving the 'p' word or any references to sending people back to where they came from.'

'God, what does Mum *see* in the racist old bore?' I wondered. 'He makes Prince Philip look like a UN peace envoy.'

'A Queen Anne rectory and a large-enough pension pot to lord it over the other women at the tennis club and on the church flower rota,' said Jessica, with unusual honesty.

'Fair enough,' I said. 'But couldn't she just make sure he had some sort of accident? Or, you know, keep putting extra butter and cream in his dinners to try to finish him off? *Something* to get rid of him?'

'She can't. Well, she could, but that final salary pension dies with him. Honestly, it's just as well you married Simon for love. You'd make a terrible gold digger – you have to think of every eventuality, you know.'

'Simon hasn't got any gold to dig,' I said sadly. 'Nor will he have, the way Sylvia spends money, and Louisa and her "retreat" need bailing out. Apparently she's preggers again and she's tapped Michael up for ten grand to put in solar panels and electricity for the retreat. Anyway, never mind that. Are you *really* sure about Christmas?'

'Yes,' said Jessica firmly. 'I have a plan.'

'What plan?'

'You'll find out!'

When Jessica revealed her plan, it became immediately apparent why she'd refused to tell anyone what it was until we were all gathered around and ready to make merry.

'Of course,' Jessica announced, stroking the bump that would become Gulliver, in a tasteful yet sexy Isabella Oliver maternity body con number, in which she managed at eight months pregnant to look considerably less pregnant than I did three months after giving birth, 'as I'm expecting little Gulliver soon' (Jessica's need for control meant she'd had every scan and test going, including finding out the sex of the baby; only a small part of me hoped a story I'd once heard, about how sometimes the scans just don't pick up a second heartbeat or the twin 'hiding' behind the first baby until number two pops out unexpectedly, was true, just to mess with Jessica's perfect planning), 'Neil and I obviously aren't drinking, as we're pregnant. So what I thought would make a lovely change, and also be very supportive of me, is if none of us drink. Isn't that a nice idea?'

We all stared at Jessica in horror. Mum and Dad exchanged the first mutual look that suggested they agreed on something since that Boxing Day she booted him out twenty odd years before.

'No ... drink?' stammered Dad.

'Do you just mean no spirits? Like no vodka or gin or cocktails, but wine's OK?' put in Jackie hopefully.

'Yes,' said Mum in relief. 'Of course there'll be wine, won't there, Jessica? Wine's not really *drink* drinking, is it?'

'Neither's beer!' said Geoffrey heartily. 'Well, not when it's a real ale, anyway. I grant you those pissy foreign lagers in bottles that the Gays drink should be banned, but not a good British ale!'

Despite the horror, Simon and I exchanged a look, and I smirked. We'd had a bet on whether Geoffrey would go more for racist or homophobic slurs over the Christmas period, and I was pretty sure the presence of Jackie meant he'd go racist. But I'd backed the wild card and picked homophobia, because Geoffrey could be unpredictable, though not unpredictable enough to turn into a good person.

'Gin too,' Geoffrey carried on. 'That's medicinal. It can hardly be counted as drink! We'd never have built the Empire without G&Ts, especially the Raj. World would be a better place if we still ran the Raj and kept all those bloody P –'

Mum kicked him sharply in the ankle and he quickly piped down.

'Still counts,' Simon murmured. 'A point to me. One all!'

'Nothing,' said Jessica firmly. 'No booze at all. Think how lovely it will be, waking up with a clear head on Christmas morning instead of feeling all muzzy! Think how much less bloated you'll feel after Christmas dinner when you're not full of wine as well! You'll enjoy it, I promise you.'

The dismayed faces suggested we didn't share Jessica's faith in sobriety. It wasn't that we were all in desperate *need* of a drink, it just made the rest of the family more bearable. I pleaded this to Jessica as I was helping her get some bottles of 'lovely sparkling organic non-alcoholic elderflower' instead of champagne, which Jessica assured us was not only alcohol free but also packed with many health-giving properties, so that we'd all leave on Boxing Day without hangovers and glowing with well-being.

'Think how much drink there was at Ty'r Ywen,' I said hopefully.

'We've tried plying them with drink before and it didn't make them any better. In fact, it makes some of them even worse,' Jessica pointed out. 'I mean, I'm not sure I've ever spent any time with Geoffrey sober. He's having a "snifter" of something from pretty much twelve o'clock onwards.'

'I'd probably do the same if I lived with Mum.'

'Well, she's no better, on the sherry while she makes lunch, if she's not found sufficient reason to start on the Buck's Fizz at breakfast.'

'Again, can you blame her, when she has to live with Geoffrey?'

'And then everyone has too much to drink, and some people get overemotional and oversensitive, and other people become very insensitive and say things they really shouldn't, and you in particular reach the point where you can no longer tell the difference between what's only funny in your head and what's funny said out loud.'

'I do not! At least, I don't need a drink to do that, I can do that perfectly well sober,' I retorted crossly.

'Anyway, my point is, I think this will be really good for all of us. A sort of reset, if you will. Maybe without the booze-fuelled acrimony, Mum and Dad will be able to get on like normal people. And Geoffrey might even be less offensive.'

'Again, I really don't think that's the booze. He's already made one racist and one homophobic crack, and he's not had a drop. I think it's just that the years of conditioning by the patriarchy and toxic masculinity have convinced him that as rich, white Western man he's automatically superior to anyone else in the room who isn't a rich, white Western man.'

'Well, whatever, but let's give it a chance! Anyway, you've got an infant – and a toddler. It's hardly like you'd be mainlining the vodka from dawn to dusk, is it?'

'No, but it's the principle,' I wailed. 'It's like when you've got loads of crisps in the cupboard and you know they're there, and you can have crisps at any time, so you don't really fancy crisps. But as soon as you run out of crisps, you just really want crisps.'

'No wonder you've not got your figure back, with cupboards full of crisps,' said Jessica disapprovingly. 'And you'd have lost the weight much faster if you'd breastfed too.'

'Don't start, Jessica. You're making us all have a dry Christmas so we get on and play Happy Families, so don't start going on about breastfeeding and weight. Just because you have perfect babies who feed like a dream and a fast metabolism so you never have to worry about your weight!'

'OK, OK. You're right, whatever. Your baby, your choice. Your arse, your choice. Anyway, I've got to do this sober, so why shouldn't all of you?'

'Yes, but Jessica, that's not *fair*. You *knew* you had to be sober when you insisted, you did, you *insisted* we all came to you for Christmas. I asked you eleventy billion fucking times if you were sure you wanted to do this and you said you were, but *you* knew what you were letting yourself in for. We didn't! You *lured* us here under false pretences.'

'I didn't *lure* you,' said Jessica indignantly. 'I'm trying to do a nice thing. My therapist agrees. This might be the Christmas that finally heals our family, Ellen. This might be the year that the *magic* finally happens.'

'Hurrumph,' I said, both unconvinced by her plan and also seething at the thought that it might be *Jessica* who made the magic happen and not *me. I* wanted to be the Festive Fucking Queen, and if the magic happened on anyone's watch, it should be mine.

We handed round the glasses of sparkling elderflower and everyone sipped despondently. Persephone and Jane caused a mild distraction when they tried to murder each other over a tasteful wooden train. Peter was duly admired by his grandparents, though they both stopped short of holding him. Geoffrey asked if he was meant to look like that, but a warning glare from Mum to Geoffrey and from Jessica to me defused the situation. Jackie nobly picked him up, but handed him back rapidly after he was sick on her cashmere jumper. The weather was discussed at some length.

Jessica's plan seemed to working in a way, though, as although the room was split into two distinct factions, with Jessica and Neil and Mum and Geoffrey at one end, and Dad, Jackie, Simon and me at the other, with Persephone and Jane forming a sort of No Man's Land in the middle, outright hostilities did seem to have been suspended. I overheard Geoffrey a few times droning on about National Service and how they should bring it back, and I'm pretty sure I heard him mention flogging, and I think they were eavesdropping on our end as well, because Geoffrey's neck went more puce than usual when Jackie mentioned an article she had written for the *Guardian*. But Mum didn't throw any mince pies at Dad, Dad didn't threaten a restraining order and no one made Jackie (so far my favourite stepmother, and Dad had provided a good selection of them to pick from) cry, and Jessica and I didn't cry, and Neil and Simon didn't go to the pub to hide, so we counted it as a win. A very boring win, but a win nonetheless, being the first time in over twenty years that our parents had been able to be in the same room without trying to kill each other.

I had gone upstairs to check on Jane and Peter, who were sleeping peacefully (at least until the insatiable ravening maw of Peter awoke and demanded another fifteen gallons of milk. Jessica could tut over my lack of breastfeeding till she was blue in the face, but

I'd been quite unable to satisfy Peter's appetite myself, and I suspected that even an entire of herd of Friesians might have struggled), when my mother waylaid me on the landing.

'Ellen,' she hissed. 'I can't stand it. Have you got any tonic?'

'Tonic?' I repeated in confusion. 'What sort of tonic? I packed some Infacol, if you've got indigestion?'

'No! Tonic water. I've brought a bottle of gin. It was supposed to be a contribution to the Christmas drink, but there's no point now, is there? So I need some tonic so Geoffrey and I can have a little drinky pinky poo.'

'A drinky pinky poo?'

'Yes. Oh, don't worry, you can have one too, though I'm not sharing with your father and his mail-order bride.'

'Jackie's an award-winning journalist, Mum. Her family have been here for generations.'

'Yes, well, whatever. Anyway, do you have any tonic?'

'Why would I have tonic water? And Jessica has been quite clear, there's no drink allowed.'

'Jessica is clearly deranged with hormones and doesn't know what she is doing. I cannot spend forty-eight hours stone cold sober with your father. Or with Geoffrey, for that matter. Can't you send Simon to the shop?'

'Why does Simon have to go the shop? Why can't you?'

'It's raining. My *hair*.'

'Why can't Geoffrey go then?'

Mum gave her special laugh, the one she reserves for when she thinks you've said something especially stupid. 'Geoffrey doesn't go to shops. Well, apart from to buy a newspaper, and nipping into the wine shop. He says shopping is a Pink Job.'

'*What*?'

'Also, there was that incident in Waitrose when he was asked not to go back.'

'What incident? What did he do?'

'Nothing. It was all a big misunderstanding. He didn't *mean* to show that woman his winky at all. She just got completely the wrong end of the stick!'

'Not literally, I hope. Oh my God, Mother, are you telling me Geoffrey is a *flasher* on top of everything else?'

'Of course not. Like I said, misunderstanding.'

'Oh Mum, *why* do you stay with him? Is the Old Rectory and his pension and lording it over Cynthia and Margery really worth it? You could leave him, get a job and some self-respect?'

'Ellen, you're just being difficult. Now are you going to send Simon to the shop or not?'

'No. Jessica's trying really hard, we all are, so you're not spoiling it for her.'

I stomped off downstairs, feeling extremely virtuous that I had taken a stand against Mum to preserve Jessica's Vision, despite the thought of the delicious gin and tonic that would have been my reward. Virtue, I reminded myself, is its own reward, and enough people thwarted *my* Visions that helping Jessica realise hers seemed like the least I could do.

My virtue wavered somewhat, though, on the way to bed, when Dad opened his bedroom door and hissed, 'Pssst. Ellen, in here. Yes, Simon too, quick, before anyone sees.'

Dad had four Emma Bridgewater mugs sitting on the dressing table and was busily unwrapping a package. Jackie was sitting on the bed, with a look of huge relief on her face.

'I know Jessica is trying really hard, darling,' he said, 'but frankly that was a godawful evening. You've had a tough old year, what with Jane and having another baby, and I'm sure after all that you were looking forward to a little Christmas drinky.'

'I *was*,' I said sadly. 'I know it sounds dreadful, but after nine months of pregnancy, and then Peter being so constantly starving that I'm a sleep-deprived zombie most of the time, I've only managed about two glasses of wine since he was born. It's terrible, but I was hoping I might be able to relax and have a couple of drinks here, with Simon off work for a few days to help out more.'

'Well,' said Dad, 'taaaadah!' And he brandished a rather lovely bottle of 25-year-old Glenfarclas at me.

'It was meant to be Neil's Christmas present,' he said. 'But not much point since Jessica's banned drink, and apparently even after Christmas Neil isn't allowed to touch a drop until Gulliver is born, so it's wasted on him, really. And I didn't have any glasses, but the mugs were for Jessica, and then I saw she already has a set of twenty-four of them in her kitchen, so coals to Newcastle and all that. Clever Jackie here pretended she'd forgotten to print our boarding passes for when we escape on Boxing Day, so she borrowed Neil's office to print out a gift voucher for some ghastly sounding couples' pregnancy massage that Jessica was talking about, which means, my darling, we can regift their presents to ourselves and enjoy a dram or two! Isn't that marvellous?'

'It's dreadfully disloyal to Jessica,' I said.

'Yes, I know,' said Dad unrepentantly.

'The way I look at it, Ellen,' said Jackie, 'is that as long as Jessica doesn't know, it won't hurt her, will it? And her plan has worked so far in that it's kept your mum and Geoffrey sober so Yvonne doesn't start hurling insults and baked goods round the place, and Geoffrey has only referred to "The Gays" and "The Blacks" once each, which apparently is quite good going for him, so as long as the peace is kept, everyone will be happy, won't they? And since Ralph and I have no intention of knocking back a dozen whisky shots and going and picking a fight with Yvonne and Geoffrey, there really will be no harm done.'

Simon was already clutching a mug and sniffing at it appreciatively.

'The thing is, Ellen,' he said earnestly, 'this is really good stuff. We're drinking it to savour the taste, not just drinking for the sake of drinking, aren't we? Also, we have two very small children and a large mortgage, so God knows when we'll get to try something like this again. It would be *rude* not to. And it might help you relax. You know how stressed you get about everything, worrying if Peter's had enough milk and if Jane's getting scurvy and should their nappies be that colour.'

Jackie blanched at this, and Dad quickly changed the subject away from my children's nappies.

'Actually, I've got you a bottle too, Simon,' said Dad, 'so you'll get to try it again soon, if you don't want to lead Ellen astray?'

'Oh, fuck it,' I said, and took the mug Dad was brandishing at me, and sniffed. It smelled heavenly.

'No,' I said regretfully, handing it back. 'It's not fair. This means a lot to Jessica. Come on Dad, this isn't fair.'

'Your mother's got a bottle of gin, I saw it sticking out of Geoffrey's hold-all.'

'So? She's not got any tonic, though. And I think her standards do not permit her to glug neat gin from her toothmug. So if Mum can do it, you can do it. Come on, Simon, we better try to get some sleep before one of the kids wakes up.'

I staggered downstairs at 6.30 a.m. the next morning with Peter, rather regretting my noble gesture and thinking I might as well have had a drink, as Peter had woken up so often in the night, discombobulated to be in a strange place, that I felt as groggy and bleary-eyed as I'd have done with a hangover.

Jessica was already up and peered at me in horror as I started making Peter's bottle.

'Are you all right?' she asked in concern.

'Knackered. He didn't sleep much. So neither did we.'

'Didn't Simon get up with him at all?'

'A bit, but by the time I've woken him up and made him get up, and then he faffs about being fucking useless, half the time it's easier to just get up myself.'

'Haven't you tried sleep training?'

'Oh yes. But he declines to be trained. He clearly hasn't read *The Contented Little Bastarding Baby Book*, has he?'

'Well, think how much worse you'd feel if you'd been drinking,' said Jessica smugly.

'I don't think I could feel much worse,' I groaned. 'Are you *sure* we can't just have a little glass of wine with Christmas dinner?'

'Yes! Look how well last night went!'

I didn't dare tell Jessica about our parents' attempts to flout her rules, and luckily Simon caused a distraction by coming in with Jane, shortly followed by Neil with Persephone. The girls happily spread porridge everywhere for some time, successfully rubbing it in their eyes, hair, ears and any other orifice they could find except their mouths, as we dutifully waited for their doting grandparents to appear to watch the magical spectacle of their grandchildren opening their Christmas stockings. When no grandparents appeared and the children were thoroughly caked in porridge and had been borne upstairs at arms' length by their reluctant fathers to be bathed again, Jessica had had enough.

'Where *are* they?' she complained. 'Right, I know how to sort this,' and she slotted the *Carols from King's* CD into Neil's swanky sound system that had speakers wired up through the house. Next minute, the Herald Angels were Harking at full volume in every room.

'That should do it,' she said smugly, as Peter started wailing.

Within five minutes there were sounds of life and showers running from upstairs. The freshly washed and glowing toddlers, adorable in velvet party frocks that were sure to be ruined immediately by them smearing some sort of bodily fluid or matter over them, were installed by the Christmas tree, ready for Operation Stockings yet for the time being entranced by CBeebies, which I'd convinced Jessica would not stunt Persephone's development. Peter was dressed in his Christmas Babygro and the children's fathers were left in charge with strict instructions that no parcels were to be touched until the proceedings were lovingly observed by their grandparents. I was helping Jessica in the kitchen when Mum and Geoffrey and Dad and Jackie stumbled downstairs in search of coffee. Neither Mum's Elizabeth Arden, Jackie's Jo Malone, or Dad and Geoffrey's Aramis and English Fern respectively were any match for Jessica's super-sensitive pregnancy nose, which twitched suspiciously as they came in.

'Why,' she demanded, 'can I smell alcohol off you all?'

Furious denials were issued, and protestations of innocence. I wondered if I should sneak, but Dad cracked first under Jessica's steely glare.

'They started it,' he cried, pointing at Mum and Geoffrey. 'They had a bottle of gin, but Ellen said they didn't have any tonic, but then I met Geoffrey coming upstairs with a bottle of that blasted elderflower stuff and I thought why would he be drinking that in

'Lots of grandmothers are only too happy to do that,' I pointed out, though even if Mum had lived closer, I wouldn't have asked her. She had made it only too clear that bringing up her own children had been burden enough on her, and her grandchildren were to be viewed merely as lifestyle accessories when it suited her.

'We're not *here* to talk about FUCKING GRANSNET,' screamed Jessica. 'We're talking about the fact that despite all my best efforts, you've all ruined Christmas again! HERE! Jessica yanked open a drawer and fished out a key, which she flung on the floor. 'There's the key to the cupboard where all the booze is, I hope you're all happy, MERRY CHRISTMAS!' and she stormed out and slammed the back door behind her. I was about to follow her when I was summonsed to the sitting room by blood-curdling screams and panicked shouts of 'Ellen! Jessica!' from Neil and Simon.

I dashed into the sitting room to see what was going on and found carnage resulting from Neil and Simon being too transfixed by Sarah Jane's tits in the *Higgledy House Christmas Special* to notice that Persephone and Jane had started opening all the presents. They'd found a box of liqueur chocolates that Neil's Great-Aunt Julia had sent him, and had managed to open it and eat them all, while Sarah Jane bounced, and then they had some sort of drunken brawl that involved them battering each other with an Early Learning Centre wooden shape sorter, which at least brought Simon and Neil out of their trance. Fortunately Jessica had the sort of swanky American fridge freezer that had an ice dispenser, and Mum and Dad had not emptied it for their secret tipples, so I hastily applied ice packs and Steri-Strips and chocolate buttons (oh how I laughed at last Christmas's no-sugar rule), and explained once again to Neil and Simon how it was not possible to 'babysit' one's own children, and turned a blind eye to the team work from Mum and Dad in raiding the sideboard to get their hands on the drink, and finally went in search of my sister.

I found Jessica in the garage sitting at her garden table, which had been carefully put away for storage, unlike mine which was still rotting in the garden at home under a pile of leaves that I insisted we mustn't disturb because there might be hedgehogs, but really, I just could not be arsed with moving it into the garage only to have to move it out again come spring. It was wood, wasn't it? I reasoned. And trees managed perfectly well outside all winter, so a table made of trees should do the same. Simon insisted it didn't quite work like that, but also seemed to be lacking in much inclination to do anything about it, other than blame me for it still being out. Jessica was hunched over a bottle of Baileys, which she was sniffing deeply.

'Where did that come from?' I asked. 'What about the Dry Christmas?'

'I put it in the outside fridge and forgot about it when I hid the rest of the booze. Here,' she passed the bottle over to me, 'you might as well have some. Do you have any fags?'

'Maybe,' I said warily.

'Light one, will you, and blow some of that smoke over here. Just a little bit, just enough for me to get a sniff of that too,' she said wearily.

'Jessica,' I choked in astonishment. 'What the actual fuck? You're *pregnant*!'

'I know,' sighed Jessica. 'Believe me, I know. And I've eaten nothing but steamed organic vegetables and sustainably sourced organic fish and *fucking tofu* for months, in order to have the perfect bloody pregnancy, so frankly the baby can put up with a half lung of passive smoking and some Baileys fumes, and everyone knows Baileys is not *proper* booze. I mean, for God's sake, our own mother never tires of telling us how she puffed away on thirty a day and was on the gin and how we were totally fine, so I'm sure it won't hurt. Though no doubt Mumsnet would disagree and ask me if I'd put Baileys in a newborn's bottle, since what I'm doing is just as bad.'

'I mean, if you were to put anything in their bottle, Baileys is probably the best thing,' I reasoned, 'it's got cream in it, so it's high in calcium. Probably be quite good for them. But you don't smoke though, Jessica?'

'There's a lot of things you don't know I do,' said Jessica darkly. 'Because I'm the Perfect One, aren't I? And what good does it do me? The more I try to make everything perfect, the more everybody else fucks it up! The more *I* try to be perfect, the more *you're* Dad's favourite, however much you mess up. It's fucking *hard* being the oldest, you know!'

'I know,' I said. 'I used to be so jealous, felt you always got the better of everything: bigger bedroom, never had hand-me-downs. But then, since I've had my own children, I realised how much you had to grow up to look after me. And bigger bedrooms and new coats weren't much compensation for that. But still, you're Mum's favourite! That's something. Me and Jane and Peter are very much second-class citizens in her eyes, and she doesn't even bother to hide it.' I was trying to cheer Jessica up but without much success.

'Yes, but it looks so much more *fun* being Dad's favourite,' said Jessica slightly tearfully. 'And they *both* told you about their secret drink stash. I bet they asked you to join them too.'

I made a non-committal noise.

'See?' Jessica sniffed.

'Well, you did ban booze,' I pointed out. 'And you're pregnant.'

'And what was the point of all that effort? I've tried and I've tried to create the perfect family Christmas and nobody cares except me –'

'I care!' I put in. 'I do, Jess. I know how much it means to you, and why. And I know why you do it. Maybe no one else understands, but I do. All of it. The pickled beetroot and everything. "The true success is to labour."'

Our eyes met over the Baileys bottle.

'Ty'r Ywen,' we said together.

Eventually, we braced ourselves to go back indoors. To our astonishment, the fragile truce between Mum and Dad as they fell upon the Sideboard of Joy had held, and everyone was really quite jovial. Mum and Geoffrey were halfway down a bottle of Bombay Sapphire and Dad had embraced his favourite role of the Angel of Booze, dispensing strong drink all around with him, with his stock phrase inherited from his mother when anyone tried to demur, of looking sorrowfully at the bottle and shaking his head and saying, 'But darling, it's practically water! Just have a little one! Practically water!'

Mum was so thrilled to have a large G&T again that even she was allowing Dad to top her up and agreeing that indeed, it *was* practically water. Jessica and I looked at each other again as Dad tipped the remains of a bottle of red into Jackie's glass, insisting once more that it was 'practically water', and Jessica managed to laugh.

'When I have had this baby,' she whispered. 'We are putting on those dresses and going out for fucking martinis. Deal?'

'Deal,' I agreed. 'Though I'll have to lose about three stone to fit in the Givenchy again.'

Geoffrey meanwhile, was helpfully explaining to Jackie that really, *anyone* could learn to play golf, even –

'Geoffrey!' said Jessica just in time. 'Where are Simon and Neil and the children?'

Simon and Neil and the children, it turned out, were in the kitchen, on their second bottle of red, attempting to placate three screaming children with *The Tweenies* (Jane), dummies (Peter), LeapPads (Persephone), bouncy chairs (Peter) and offers of pink Calpol (all of them, including Neil and Simon).

'What on earth is going on?' we demanded.

'They won't stop crying,' wailed Neil, looking close to tears himself.

'We've tried *everything*,' Simon whimpered, gulping down another spoonful of Calpol with a Rioja chaser. 'We haven't even been able to get ourselves so much as a snack?'

'Did they eat any lunch?' I asked.

'Lunch?' Both men looked at me blankly. '*Lunch*? You didn't say they needed lunch?'

'Well, of course they need lunch!' Jessica said in exasperation, rifling through the fridge and flinging out snack plates of fruit, carrot sticks, houmous and rice cakes, which Persephone and Jane fell upon like ravening beasts, while I plugged Peter's gaping and sobbing mouth with a bottle, and blissful silence fell.

'Oh,' said Simon. 'That's better.'

'Yes,' agreed Neil happily. 'I'm starving. When's Christmas dinner?'

'When you make it,' said Jessica tartly, marching out of the kitchen with a bottle of champagne in her hand. 'Ellen and I are going upstairs to watch *It's a Wonderful Life*.'

Much later, after most of the bottle of champagne (for me) and a little nap (for both of us), we descended to find Mum had finally deigned to take over Christmas dinner, if for no other reason than to show off to Jackie. All three children were also napping (as was Geoffrey), and Dad, who'd had quite a lot of *practically water, darling*, had taken charge of the complicated music system and swept Jessica off to dance, to her delight.

Present day

'Actually,' I said to Simon, 'it wasn't that bad, Jessica's dry Christmas that wasn't.'

'You abandoned me with the children all day. Your mother gave everyone food poisoning.'

'Well, yes, that was unfortunate. But I had a nice time with Jessica. And we didn't have that many Christmases with Dad after we grew up, and he was on good form that year.'

'Practically water,' laughed Simon. 'My God, the hangovers your father caused me with that line. But he was always so persuasive about it that I never learned!'

'None of us ever did,' I said.

'I expect that's where you get it from.'

'Get what from?'

'Your insane desire to always break out the shots, when any normal sensible person would be winding down the party and going to bed. You always use a similar rationale – "They're only tiny," you say, "they couldn't possibly do any harm." And again, I usually fall for it. You're very much like him.'

'Am I?' I said in surprise. 'But he was always the life and soul of the party. And so chilled out about everything.'

'You're usually the life and soul of the party too. And I suppose he got to be chilled out because he never had to worry about things like you do. He just assumed someone else would deal with them. If you hadn't had children to stress about, you'd have been even more like him.'

'Do you mean that in a good way?' I asked.

'Yes,' said Simon, 'I do. When you're not stressing about details, you're tremendous fun.'

'Oh,' I said. 'Well, thank you.'

It was nice to hear I was fun. I didn't feel very much fun at the moment, I felt more like the stressing-about-details part of me was taking over. Maybe I needed to focus more on the fun part.

'I think maybe I get the stressing-about-details part from Mum,' I sighed. 'In her case the details she stressed about were mainly because of "What will people think?" But still, I should probably give her more credit. She was the one who made sure we had clean pants and new school shoes and all the boring stuff that never occurred to Dad that we needed. He would just swoop in and be the fun one and get all the kudos. And maybe even if Mum's reasons for making sure we were clean and fed and clothed weren't the most maternal, at least she *did* it. But, oh God, Simon, I think I've been so busy trying to be a better parent than mine were, to give the kids a totally different family, that I've fucked it up anyway with them.'

'Of course you haven't fucked it up with the kids,' he reassured me. But I wasn't convinced.

I'd been so desperate that my children would not grow up like Jessica and me, that Jane would never have to feel responsible for Peter and be the one to look after him, that they would always feel loved and secure and wanted and cared for, that somehow I'd gone to the opposite extreme. Instead of the casual, generous affection of Granny Green, the day-to-day minutiae of looking after two children meant that the more mobile they got, the more stuff I seemed to need for them: sunscreen, water bottles, spare clothes, snacks, so many fucking snacks. And then once they started school, the only way to survive and try and keep track of assemblies, sports days, PE days, crazy hair days, Bring-a-Fucking-Inconvenient-Object-We-Don't-Have-Any-of-to-School-Days, gymnastics and dancing and football and music lessons, because I was determined To Be There for Them, and Give Them Opportunities, was to become slightly militant about it, and even then I only ever really achieved the most basic level of Mothering 101. I was far from being one of the Uber Mummies who devoted their every waking moment to their children, had special drawers containing greetings cards for every possible occasion and never ever gave their children beige freezer food for dinner.

There was the guilt to contend with as well. It is constantly drummed into you when you have small children that you are #SoLucky, that you must #BeGrateful, that you are #SoBlessed and you must #TreasureEveryMoment because #TheyAreNotLittleLong. And I did not enjoy those days. Not even slightly. I found them exhausting and overwhelming and disorientating and yes, *boring*. Some people find small children, their innocent chatter, their wide-eyed curious view of world to be a source of endless fascination. I did not. For me, small children were dull and inane, and I knew they learned by asking the same thing over and over, but dear lord, sometimes I did just want to scream, 'Just google it, just FUCKING GOOGLE IT' when I was asked the eleventy fucking billionth pointless question of the day.

I never did, of course. I gritted my teeth and smiled and said Proper Mummy things like, 'Why don't we find out together, darling, about what would happen if you held your farts in forever and whether you could die of it, how interesting, oh yes, it says the farts will eventually be excreted through your lungs, well, that means you'll breathe them out, I suppose that does mean that some people have fart breath, *no*, you are *not* to ask your teacher if her breath smells like that because she has fart breath, and no, it doesn't mean you never ever have to hold farts in because it's bad for you, there is a time and a place for farting and you will survive if you do not fart on your sister's head, FFS!' I still attempted to answer even the most stupid questions, like 'Why is the sky?' Why is the sky *what*, darling? I tried to ask, only to be met with a stubborn and repeated 'Why is the sky?' I still consider that never telling my children to actually fuck off to their faces (I may have muttered it under my breath once or twice) is my greatest parenting achievement.

But I did feel guilty. About finding them so tedious. About not Treasuring Every Moment. And so I overcompensated for the guilt by keeping busy and trying to stay organised and keeping up the appearance of a mummy who just *loved* #MakingMemories. The Most Annoying Meme in the World popped up every year to remind me that I had eighteen bloody summers to enjoy with my children, so next summer, *next* summer I'd enjoy it. And then all of a sudden, there were no more summers and it turned out that one of those sayings was right after all: the days might be long, but the years *are* short, and now the guilt is worse than ever that I didn't enjoy it enough when I should have.

Somehow, though, amid the guilt and the overcompensating for not #TreasuringEveryMoment, and trying not to turn into Mum and Dad, I'd forgotten that eventually I'd need to take a step back and let the children find out who they were. All I'd really wanted was that the children didn't turn into me, and that the chain of hurt between the generations was broken, but now I found that I couldn't let go and let them be themselves. And by trying to make my kids into better, happier, more well-adjusted adults, all I'd done was to push them away. Jane in particular, as an elder child like Jessica, had probably borne the brunt of this. How could I explain to her that I had meant it so well? That it all came from a place of love. Because I *had* always loved them fiercely, even at their most incredibly annoying; I'd never not loved them, I'd just wanted them to shut up a bit. After so many years of being so responsible for so many people other than myself, and organising and bossing everyone, how could I learn to lose the habit? And after trying so hard not to be Sylvia, and not to be Mum – or Dad – I seemed to have entirely lost sight of who *I* actually was.

better than blissful darkness surely is water. Cold, icy water, which my dry and sandpaper-rough tongue absorbed like a sponge as I lay here whimpering to myself. What fucking sadistic bastard came up with the idea of having the office Christmas party on a Thursday night while still expecting any degree of productivity from anybody the following day? I begged Simon to ring in sick for me, but he refused, saying it would be blatantly obvious that I was only hungover, and the rest of my teams would be expected to make it in, so as their boss it was only right and proper that I should set a good example by going to work.

Free bars are always my downfall at the best of times, and I think somewhere around 9.30 p.m. I decided to chuck it all in the fuck-it bucket. My children weren't coming home for Christmas so I didn't even *need* to be a responsible adult anymore ('drowning your sorrows,' said Simon disapprovingly). Oh God, the flashbacks are very bad. So very bad. Why was I sitting in a sink? I think I remember. Debbie, the extremely Busy and Important Head of HR, was very upset because she thought she had found The One on Tinder and he'd ghosted her. I was attempting to give her wise counsel and life advice, because obviously I still cannot resist the urge to know better and organise everyone else's lives, even if I cannot sort out my own. For some reason, I dispensed said advice while sitting in a sink, wearing a paper crown and sternly waving half a cracker at her, as I reminded her that almost all men on Tinder are awful and take topless photos in toilets standing in front of urinals, and so really, it was not Debbie, it was them. And also, given that she seems to get ghosted by some fucking arsehole on Tinder weekly, she should either toughen up or give up on it. Then I think we scrolled through Tinder for a while and cackled and shouted mean things about the men and judged their bios and declared them all to have small willies. Shit. I think I might have insisted she message some of them to *tell* them they had small willies. Oh fuck, it's no good, I'm going to be sick.

I did not feel better for being sick, but I did have a brilliant idea while I was puking, and Lydia, one of my team leaders, was also vomming in the next cubicle. I met her by the sinks (how long before sinks stop making me burn with shame) and asked her if she knew if the utterly wanky 'Blue Sky Thinking Zone' had been booked for this morning, and if not, to go and book it for the rest of the day *right now*. We were in luck and it was free, and once Lydia had it booked, I crawled back out from under my desk and went into the main office, where I looked round at the ashen-faced remnants of humanity huddled at their desks, softly moaning because they were not as busy and important as me, so had to work in a brightly lit, open-plan 'zone', where hiding quietly with the blinds closed while you wait for death is not an option. But I'm a kind and benevolent boss to them, and could not allow them to suffer so. I clapped my hands briskly, and winced at the noise.

'Right guys!' I said brightly. 'Come on. Let's pull ourselves together. What we need is a brainstorming session, and Lydia has booked the Blue Sky Zone for us to do it in! Get your stuff and let's go. We'll come up with some great ideas for the new projects.'

Fifteen blank and horrified faces looked at me.

'Today?' mumbled Rob, the new graduate, whom I think I tried to teach the Macarena to last night. 'We're doing this *today*?'

'Oh yes! No time like the present. Chop chop,' I chivvied him. Today may not be our most productive day, but goddammit, I'd make it into the best team-building exercise ever.

'Seriously, Ellen?' Vicky, normally one of our brightest stars in the team peeled her face off her desk and glared at me through bloodshot eyes encrusted with last night's mascara. 'This is sadistic. You're not normally like this.'

'Yeah, Ellen,' groaned Rob. 'You're not supposed to be like the other bosses. You're the *cool* boss.'

'Shut up, Rob, and pull yourself together. You'll feel *much* better once you stop feeling sorry for yourself and turn your mind to something else. And actually, Lydia, can you ask Debbie to pop down from HR and join us, I think there's some personnel issues with the new projects she could be of help with?'

Lydia shrugged, clearly concentrating too hard on not vomiting on her shoes to argue, and I gathered my sorry army of jaded, shuffling high flyers and herded them out the door towards the Blue Sky Thinking Zone. Outside the door we met Tom, the big scary American boss who had ostensibly joined us from San Francisco for the Christmas party to 'boost morale', but whom I suspected was there to judge us for how much we drank and report back to HQ about how it would be far better if the last bastion of fun in the company was ripped away from us and instead of a proper old-fashioned British booze-fuelled Christmas party, resulting in at least one unplanned pregnancy, fight and divorce, we should instead have some hideous team-building day where we celebrated the festive season by all doing goat yoga together or something awful.

'Ellen!' he said in surprise. 'Where are you all going? Not all sneaking off to the canteen for a whatdayoucallit – a "bacon butt" for your hangovers, are you? Bacon is so bad for you. You should try green juices instead.'

Lydia retched quietly at the back.

'Not at all, Tom,' I replied. 'And it's a bacon butty, actually. We're all off to the Blue Sky Thinking Zone for a brainstorming session about the new projects. We're taking it offline today to circle back and really move that needle to break the paradigm to take us through the next gen pain point and blockchain into integrating our core competencies and optimising our scalable optics and strategic analytics, you know?' I had no idea what any of that meant, but I had heard Tom say all those things at one point or another when he was giving one of his impenetrable energising pep talks.

Tom beamed in delight, as I heard what sounded distinctly like a sob from Rob. 'Awesome, guys!' he roared. I winced. 'You are rock stars. I'd love to do some onboarding with this and hear how you drill down to ideate the disruptive values we're looking for in our digital transformation going forward!'

'Absolutely,' I said warmly. 'The thing is, though, Tom, right now, we really just work in a circle of trust, you know? My "rock stars" need a safe space to properly explore a deep dive and lean into their mental bandwidth alignment, so at this stage we keep it strictly to the teams. The rock stars have to feel totally comfortable with each other to give it 110 per cent, and you're such a great guy, Tom, but not everyone knows you that well yet, and that's something we should definitely explore unpacking, maybe with some teambuilding, you know, but right now, they might not be cool with someone there with a 30,000-foot view and so I'd *love* you to onboard next time, but for today, it's important it's just me and these guys. Rock stars, I mean.'

'Of course, of course,' Tom nodded importantly. 'I hear you. I feel real strongly about that mental bandwidth alignment, and I totally get they can't open the kimono when I'm there, but I'm totally gonna set up some teambuilding for us so I can get on the same page. Have you done goat yoga here yet?'

'No. But that sounds great.' My face hurt now with the over-bright smile I'd plastered on for Tom's benefit, while I was also very glad of the Extra Strong Mint I'd popped in my mouth before leaving the office to cover any last traces of stale booze. 'Also, Tom, you know how it is when you're in the zone? It's super-important we stay focused, so I'll need to be putting a Do Not Disturb on the door. We'll order out for lunch.'

'Sure, sure! Communal eating is a super-great way to strengthen bonds between our rock stars and increase efficiency. Cool idea.'

'And we're going to be pretty burnt out by the end of today, so I might let everyone go early, especially if we're working through lunch.'

'Yeah, sure. Work smarter, not harder!'

'Exactly. Well, great chatting, Tom, but we'd better go. Those paradigms won't shift themselves. Come on, fellow rock stars,' and I herded my sorry little gang along the corridor, as Tom yelled 'GO TEAM!', and I summonsed the last of my strength to give a half-hearted fist pump and a feeble 'Woo!' as we tottered off.

Once in the Blue Sky Thinking Zone, by far the wankiest room in the entire building, with its wipe-clean walls where we were supposed to scrawl our groundbreaking thoughts and ideas, and its artificial grass instead of carpet because … actually fuck knows why, and its lovely lovely blackout blinds for when someone was giving a PowerPoint and most importantly, its *blissfully comfy beanbags* instead of tables and chairs to give an informal atmosphere that was meant to enhance our creativity, I rallied and snapped into action.

'Rob, close the blinds. Vicky, get that Do Not Disturb sign and put it up. Hang on, who's this? Come in, Debbie,' as poor Debbie crawled through the door, with a sob of, 'Ellen, today? Really? I can't. Also, it seems I'm banned from Tinder for messaging loads of guys with "Ellen says you're a narcissistic gaslighting prick and all men need to fuck off and get in the sea!"'

'Shhhh,' I soothed her. 'Come in. Safe space. OK, Vicky, that's everyone, lock the door. Everybody grab a beanbag and *sleep*.'

'What?' everyone stared back at me in shock.

'Come on, guys. Nap time. Those paradigms won't shift themselves, will they?'

'Um, I hate to have to ask, but what *is* a paradigm?' asked Rob.

'No fucking clue,' I told him. 'But it makes Tom happy if you say it enough. Hurry *up* everyone, we're wasting valuable sleep time. We'll grab a couple of hours, get a Domino's delivered for lunch when we're able to face food and are in need of healing fat and carbs and full-strength Coke, then another little snoozle and Tom will think we've been working so hard that we can be out of here by 3pm.'

Poor Lydia actually started crying. 'Oh sweet Jesus,' she wept. 'I thought I was going to have to go and sleep in the toilets for half an hour, just so I didn't die, like I used to have to when the twins were babies. Tell me it's real, and not just a wonderful dream and I'm going to wake up on the bog with my head propped against the cubicle wall.'

'It's real,' I assured her. 'Go to sleep. We're safe now,' and with that I collapsed onto my own bean bag and went nighty bed. We woke up around midday and blearily consumed the pizza and Cokes and rubbery mozzarella sticks I'd had the foresight to schedule delivery for before I nodded off. Rob, with the hubris of youth, announced after lunch that he reckoned he could go back to the pub now. We were not impressed by this, as the very thought of a pub or filthy booze was enough to threaten to topple the fragile equilibrium that naps and lard had achieved for us.

By mutual agreement we all returned to our beanbags for an Afternoon Nap, except Rob, who devoted himself to watching TikTok videos with his headphones on, occasionally chortling out loud or saying things like, 'GUYS! You need to see this!' until Debbie told him that if he didn't shut the everlasting fuck up, he could consider this a verbal warning from HR for antisocial behaviour. Rob silenced, sweet sleep descended on us all again.

It was surprising how well you could sleep on a beanbag when you were a perimenopausal woman who still treated nights out like she was eighteen and started shouting for SHOTS! far too early. I drifted into a lovely dream, where I was lying on a rug by a river, under a willow tree, in a white linen dress. There was a wicker hamper, and a man in a punt waving to me. I couldn't make out his face, and in my dream I got up and walked down to the river to see who he was. He held out his hand and said, 'There you are. I've been waiting for you, darling. Come on,' and I climbed into the punt and collapsed in his arms and he held me tight and said, 'It's OK. I'm here. Everything's going to be OK,' and he kissed me and then I woke up with a gasp to another guffaw from FUCKING ROB.

I felt actually winded by the dream. The man in the punt had not been Simon, as I'd initially thought, but James. My guilty secret, James. I felt an awful longing to just curl back up and go to sleep again, and see if I could recapture those glorious moments of feeling desired again. They were dream moments of course. I'd never worn a white linen dress for James, or been in a punt with him, or even near a river. I wasn't sure of the practical logistics of kissing in a real punt rather than a dream punt either. But lovely as the dream had been, I felt overwhelmed with guilt and shame, because James was my secret. James was the one thing in the world I'd never told Hannah about. Most of the time I tried to pretend even to myself that James had never happened, but sometimes, something would catch me off guard and I'd remember.

Fifteen years ago

I was stuck in a dead-end job in a dead-end office, bored out of my skull, doing a job I was vastly overqualified for, but which fitted in around childcare and 'kept me on the career ladder', and also enabled us to pay the mortgage every month. There were no Blue Sky Thinking Zones in this office, or floor-to-ceiling windows, or minimalist glass reception areas, fancy Fairtrade orangutan-friendly latte machines or punchy upbeat Americans insisting we refer to ourselves as rock stars. There *were* a lot of slightly sticky beige carpets, a Sovietly lit canteen where a depressed woman called Big Lil served tepid chips and rolls filled with worryingly unidentifiable meat matter, a faint aroma of despair – and a smoking shack. And one day, in that smoking shack, there was James.

The smoking shack had been introduced when the smoking room was banned along with smoking in the workplace. As we were all far too depressed and downtrodden to give up the one small spot of brightness in the endless grey trudge towards the grave that working at the Cunningham United Nautical Trust (someone didn't think that through) felt like, we'd complained vociferously about the lack of a smoking facility until the Powers That Be provided us with a small wooden canopy beside the bins. We were not supposed to refer to it as the smoking shack, as they were not supposed to condone the foul habit, but it was a small nicotine-filled haven where we could escape the outdated computer systems and peeling 1970s décor.

There was a little hardcore crew of us that used to gather in the hut at the same time every day: Tony from Finance, Mike from Sales, Lisa from HR and me. A few others would drift in and out, and no one really looked up the day James wandered in with Carl from Marketing. Carl introduced him as a new contractor, brought in to try to jazz things up a bit. He had a nice smile, but I didn't really register much else about him. But over the next few weeks he was always there with the rest of us, and he became part of the Smokers Inc. gang. Somehow, he always ended up standing next to me. He smelled nice, despite the fag smoke. And he had lovely eyes. And he was funny. Married, of course, with three kids in secondary school. He was just a nice man who made me laugh and with whom, it turned out, I had a lot in common. I didn't really think any more of it until the day I realised that at some point he'd become more than that to me.

The weather got worse as the autumn went on, and only the hardcore smokers now braved the hut. I wasn't really a hardcore smoker, but anything was better than my dingy basement cubicle that was deemed sufficient for the lowly IT staff, so I continued to traipse out to the shelter and puff away. One day in October James was there as usual, and while everyone else had drifted back into the building, I couldn't face it just yet and lit another cigarette. James stayed for another one too. We started talking about books, and he told me about this strange but brilliant Ukrainian novel he was reading about penguins and gangsters.

'Andrey Kurkov? *Death and the Penguin*?' I said in surprise. 'I've just read that. I loved it!'

'I've not finished it yet, but it's so good, I'm really enjoying it.'

I was thrilled to find someone else who liked this book, as I'd adored it and tried to persuade Simon to read it. He had managed one chapter before declaring it the worst book he'd ever read and that there must be something wrong with someone who enjoyed it.

Guiltily we had another two cigarettes as we talked about the book. When I finally slunk back to my desk, luckily unobserved, I found I felt happier than I had in months. For a few minutes with James I'd felt like *me* again. Not someone's wife, mother, employee, or a cog in a relentlessly turning machine that I was trapped in till death, but like a *person*. Someone with interests, and opinions, and thoughts and things to say. And it was a very long time since I'd felt like that.

Jane was five and had just started school, and three-year-old Peter was at nursery. I think this is when I truly started to lose sight of myself, and Fun Ellen became replaced by Control-Freak-and-Catastrophe Ellen. Once my children were out there, abandoned alone in the educational system, I was suddenly aware of all the dangers facing them. And on top of that, life felt like an endless juggling act of balls I was constantly dropping. I was pulled in all directions at once, trying to be a good mother to my children and feeling like I was failing them by going to work; trying to be a good employee (apart from the smoking breaks) but having half my mind on what the children needed or were doing; worrying that I was wasting my life at Cunningham United Nautical Trust and this career ladder I was trying so desperately to stay on would turn out to be nothing more than a step stool, and trying to be a good wife to Simon, who was far too busy being so Very Busy and Important to notice I was drowning, existing not living, or indeed to really notice me at all – which was not conducive to being a good wife, frankly, and meant that a lot of the time I wanted to smash the last few plates remaining from our wedding china over his head, just so he'd look up from *Wheeler Fucking Dealers* and see that I was *there*.

This was when my world seemed to shrink to a regimented calendar, colour-coded spreadsheets and endless, tedious organisation. I could never seem to make Simon grasp the need for this, though. If he got the time of Jane's swimming lesson wrong, he'd just laugh and say, 'Oh well, there's always next week.' I could not make him see the bigger picture. To him it was only a missed swimming lesson, but what it might mean in reality was that Jane could end up missing vital aquatic skills, and so when she was swept away in a raging torrent or fell into a frozen lake, she wouldn't have the necessary know-how to save herself and she'd be drowned. And then what if Peter was there, and he tried to save her and he drowned as well – and all because she missed that swimming lesson? Simon would just look at me and say, 'It's just one lesson, babe. Chill out.'

But to me, it wasn't 'just one lesson'. It was all part of the big scary world I needed to keep my children safe from. His 'one swimming lesson' was actually one of the precarious threads forming the fragile safety net that I was trying to create around my children, and my sanity, and that *one thread* of that *one swimming lesson* might be the thing that unravelled everything. The whole mental load of this seemed to fall on me, because Simon did not seem to have taken any of those Public Safety Adverts in the 1980s and 90s seriously. I knew this because I had quizzed him one night on the proper way to put out a chip-pan fire and he had no idea and just kept saying, 'But we don't have a chip pan?' And the more I obsessed about chip pans and drownings and stranger-danger and pylons, the more Simon gave up trying, because I'd just insist he'd done it *wrong*, because the only right way was my way.

Truly, until I became a parent, I'd had no idea how death is never more than one slightly abstracted second away, but Simon somehow simply couldn't appreciate that. Perhaps it was because he'd always had Sylvia looking out for him, hovering anxiously, ready to plunge into icy lakes like a well-coiffed Newfoundland to save him from himself, whereas Mum and Dad would doubtless have remarked how nice it was that I was waving to them and wandered off to make a G&T. And so, like Sylvia, but with somewhat less Elnett, I prepared for every eventuality, while Simon sighed and asked did we *really* need to take wound dressings, Steri-Strips and three different kinds of antiseptic with us every time we left the house.

Talking to James, though, that short conversation about books, had made me briefly feel like I could stop worrying, like the Lurking Death had receded somewhat (only the day before I'd been slightly concerned Peter had bubonic plague till it turned out that the purple swelling in his armpit was actually Play-Doh). For a few minutes I was more than a provider of food/clean clothes/nose and bum-wiping services (for the children, not Simon! He wasn't into *that* sort of thing, thank God). I liked that feeling, so I went home after work and tried harder with Simon to attempt to make him see me more like James had seemed to. I resolved not to snap at him, and to try not to stress over the children and accuse him of not caring because he didn't know the symptoms of bubonic plague. I smiled, and asked him about his day, as he slumped in front of *The Car's the Star*, but he just grunted and said, 'Shit, as usual'.

'Don't you want to ask about mine?' I ventured.

'You're going to say shit as well,' he said. 'And then you'll try to Top Trump me with how yours was even shitter than mine because the kids did this or that, and then I'll point out that at least you get home early enough to spend time with the kids, unlike me, and then we'll just have another row. So really, what's the point?'

'Maybe I won't,' I said. 'Maybe I'll tell you I met a dashingly attractive and handsome man and discussed art and literature with him, and it improved my day immeasurably!'

Simon laughed and laughed. 'Where?' he hooted. 'Where did you meet this man? At Cunningham United Nautical Trust? In Sainbury's buying the fucking yoghurts you are so obsessed by, while Peter shoplifted cumin again? At the school gate? Did you run the gauntlet of all the yummy mummies, pushing them aside to hurl yourself on this sensitive literary soul? Come on, Ellen, if you're going to make crap up to make your day seem more interesting, then at least make it plausible!'

I was hurt by his derision and his dismissal of the fact that I might be capable of attracting another man's attention. 'Doesn't it even bother you that I might have met another man, whose company stimulates me and brightens my day?'

Simon stopped laughing. 'I mean, yeah, obviously, it would. If you had. But seriously, where are *you* going to meet someone else?'

'You think I'm just a saggy, old, has-been, past-it mum that no one's ever going to look twice at again?' I demanded, on the verge of tears. It was certainly what the mirror had said to me at 3 a.m. when I went for a wee, after reassuring Peter for the fourth time that a Venezuelan Vampire Squirrel wasn't living under his bed, no matter what Jane might have said.

'Of course not. You've still got it. But you don't go anywhere to use it. I mean, where *would* you meet a man? Not at work – they're all sweaty boring arseholes according to you. And not at the school – it's all wall-to-wall yoga mummies circling like sharks around the one lone father who occasionally ventures in. I saw them that time I picked Jane up, and you wouldn't stand a chance, babe. You don't have the killer instinct to take on those bitches. No, Sainsbury's is your best bet, but even then, apparently to pick up men you have to go there on a Tuesday evening and put a pineapple in your basket –'

'A *pineapple*?'

'Yes, apparently it's a sign. Tuesday evening, pineapple, means I'm up for a bit of how's your father. Whereas 4.30 p.m. on a Wednesday with a trolley full of Petits Filous and Peter repeatedly shouting how itchy his bum is, like you complained he did today, doesn't give off quite the same vibes, does it?'

'How do you know this? About the pineapple and the Tuesdays?'

'I dunno. Probably an urban myth. Or some stupid internet article or something. I thought it was one of those things that everybody just knows.'

'*I* didn't know. Is that where you are, when you're late home on Tuesdays, sauntering round Sainsbury's with a basket full of pineapples?'

'No, of course not. Don't be silly.'

'What if it's a Tuesday and you just really want pineapple, and you innocently go in to buy a pineapple and all of a sudden you've got all these men hitting on you?'

'Why don't you test the theory? Prove to yourself that you've still got it. I'll come home early next Tuesday and you can whack a bit of lipgloss on, get yourself down Sainsbury's and see if the man from Del Monte says yes.'

'Don't be stupid,' I said. 'Of course I'm not going to Sainsbury's to try to pick up a man with a pineapple!'

'Why not? It might be fun. You're always complaining we never do anything fun.'

'Yes, but I want us to do the fun things *together*? I don't want to pick up some dodgy bloke who hangs around the fruit and veg section waiting to lure in lonely spinsters with his *produce*. Also, what if he expected you to, you know, *use* the pineapple in some way?'

'You mean other than in a sweet and sour chicken?'

'Yes!'

'Darling, I wasn't suggesting that you went home with some man you met with a pineapple, just so you could test the theory. But see if anyone chats you up, make your excuses and leave, come home with your confidence boosted a bit.'

'Well, knowing my luck, I'd get chatted up by a serial killer and wouldn't be able to make my excuses and leave because he'd bundle me into his rusty Transit van and *murder* me. Or worse, *no one* would chat me up!'

'How is that *worse* than being murdered by a serial killer?'

'You know what I mean. And I don't want a stranger to boost my confidence. I want you to do it!'

'Me?' said Simon in surprise. 'What do you mean?'

'I want you to notice me! I want you to tell me I look nice! I want you to want to spend time with me, and do things with me.'

'Oh, I want to do things to you!' Simon growled.

'NOT LIKE THAT!' I howled. 'Like … make me feel like I *exist*! Like you notice me.'

'What do you mean? Of course I notice you exist.'

'It doesn't feel like it,' I said sulkily. 'I feel like a housekeeper slash cook slash nanny. You never notice what I'm doing, or wearing or reading or interested in. I'm just a piece of the furniture. This is the first proper conversation we've had in weeks, and it's about trying to pick up someone else with a fucking *pineapple*.'

'You don't fuck the pineapple, Ellen, that's not how it works. Sorry, sorry.' Simon saw my face. 'I'm sorry, babe. God, I'm sorry. It's just hard right now, isn't it? Work's so full on, you're so busy with the kids, we're both knackered all the time, there never seems to be any time for *us*, does there?'

'Well, help me more with the kids and we might have more time for each other?'

'You're right. But you need to *let* me help and stop being convinced they have obscure diseases and criticising so much.'

'The Black Death killed 200 million people. It's hardly an obscure disease,' I protested, and then, as Simon looked at me, I conceded a little: 'OK. OK. But it is spread by rats, well, fleas, and Peter does find some filthy places to roll in. It wasn't that much of a stretch.'

'Look, why don't I see if Mum can take the kids for a weekend and we could get a couple of nights away?' Simon suggested. Sylvia, I reflected, despite her many faults, would at least be vigilant against medieval poxes.

'I thought we were broke?'

'Fuck it, we'll stick it on the credit card and worry about it next month.'

* * *

After this conversation, I went into work the following day determined that James wouldn't turn my head again with his witty literary banter. I was even determined that I wouldn't smoke, so as to save money to put towards our mini break, but my resolve crumbled after half an hour of trying to show Cara the Sales Director that her laptop *wasn't* broken, she just didn't know how to use Excel, and attempting to give her a brief masterclass in it, only to have her look utterly blank and ask me why I kept talking about cells. Oh dear God, I thought, was this my life for the next thirty years? Get up, come to work, deal with fuckwits, go home, make fish fingers, answer endless questions about who would win in a fight, that sodding vampire squirrel (where *did* Jane come up with these things to terrorise her brother with?) or a zombie badger, retire and buy a nice pair of elasticated slacks and some gardening shoes out the back of the *Sunday Times Magazine*, and DIE. I decided I could bang my head repeatedly off Cara's desk while sobbing pitifully, or I could just go out for a nice soothing fag.

I passed James's desk on my way out, and he waved. I waved back – because obviously it would be rude not to – and he got up and came over, asked if I was going for a cigarette and said he'd come with me. So it really wasn't my fault that I ended up alone in the smoking hut with James again. I was simply being polite.

'Here,' he said, reaching into his coat pocket. 'I have something for you.'

He handed me a small, battered book with a blue cloth cover called *Modern English Short Stories*.

'After yesterday's chat, I thought we might have similar tastes and maybe you'd enjoy borrowing this. It's one of my favourites.'

I didn't have to take it. I could have shut everything down there and then by being honest and saying, 'Um, thanks, but I don't think that's really my sort of book. I did like the penguin book, but I'm more of a Jilly Cooper sort of a girl, actually.' But I didn't. I put on my best highbrowed and cultured face, and said, 'Thank you. Um, yeah, that's great, I look forward to reading it.'

'Cool. Well, you can have a shufti and let me know what you think. It was nice having someone to talk about books with.'

'Yes,' I said. 'Yes, it was. We should definitely do it again.' And so, instead of being honest, I was even worse, because I actively encouraged him. I was so flattered to be thought literary, and it was so nice, after Cara's spreadsheet, to think that there was more to look forward to in life than 'stylish' (never has a word done so much heavy lifting) polycotton unisex trousers, that I simply couldn't help myself. Obviously, I could have helped myself, but in truth, I just didn't want to.

And that was the beginning of it. Over the next few weeks we gradually changed our break times so it was just the two of us. We talked about everything, he made me laugh until my sides hurt, he noticed if I wore a new top or changed my hair, but not in a sleazy way, just in a nice way. Time spent with James felt like moments stolen out of time, moments when I didn't have to think about convincing Jane that strawberry Petits Filous were just as nice as raspberry, or wondering if her loose tooth was a sign of scurvy or tooth decay due to so many Petits Filous or just a baby tooth coming out, or checking anyone for nits or worms, or staring at the third packet of mince I'd defrosted that week because I'd discovered a big yellow-stickered pile in Tesco for 30p a pack and had bought the lot in the interests of economy and now had to use the bastarding stuff up. They were just little pockets of freedom.

As time went on, my feelings for James seemed to develop. It wasn't like the thunderbolt I'd had with Simon, where we'd both known from the first night that something important had happened that was going to change our lives forever. With James it crept up on me so quietly and gently that I didn't notice it was happening until he looked up at me across a meeting one day and smiled at me like I was the only person in the room, and I thought, 'I might love him.' They weren't exciting, these feelings for James – there were no secret thrills or frissons or jolts when our hands touched, none of the electricity I'd felt with Simon at first, and could still feel with him, surprisingly, despite everything.

James didn't stop me loving Simon, but when I was with him it felt like he'd given me back all the parts of myself that I'd lost to marriage and children and daily drudgery; he'd returned the confidence that had been stripped from me by the years of baggy leggings and baby sick in my hair and black circles under my eyes from permanent sleep deprivation. It made me look more kindly on Simon and notice how hard he worked, and for what long hours, and when he finally booked our mini break away, this better version of myself – this Ellen that was far more like the girl that Simon had fallen in love with than the shrieking, yoghurt-obsessed harridan I'd somehow turned into – meant that we had a more intimate weekend than any we'd had since Jane was born, with not a single pineapple in sight.

And yet neither James nor I said anything. He was the bright spot in my life, the thing that made the bad days bearable, and I saw from the way his face lit up when he saw me that he felt the same way. Our happiness existed in such a fragile bubble, I think I knew even then that it wouldn't have survived facing up to the ugly reality of our situation, discussing our partners, our families, the lives we had away from each other. I think that's why I didn't even tell Hannah about him – I was afraid to risk what we'd found in each other. But as anyone who has ever tried to placate a sobbing toddler clutching a bottle of bubble mixture knows, every bubble bursts in the end.

It was the office Christmas party. This was usually a fairly dreary event, held in a mid-range hotel with twenty-five other office parties containing over-excited middle-aged women in shiny Next 'occasion wear' dresses shrieking loudly over crackers after getting stuck into as many glasses of the lukewarm 'complimentary welcome prosecco' as they could, and the sleazy office managers who'd been eying them up all year hoping for a furtive snog under the mistletoe.

For once, however, Cunningham United had pushed the boat out and splurged on a glorious country house hotel for our Christmas party. There was even accommodation thrown in, although we were informed that this largesse was in fact in lieu of any sort of Christmas bonus, which would have been a damned sight more useful than a night in Farmforth Manor. On the other hand, I thought, *mentally* a night away from the bedtime and bathtime routine, and Peter jumping on my head at 5.30 a.m. to tell me about his really interesting dream about Moshi fucking Monsters, would probably be invaluable for me. Along with the chance to have a leisurely bath, and get ready without anyone needing their arse wiped, or a snack, or Simon jangling his *fucking* keys at me and asking why I wasn't ready yet, *he* was ready, *he'd* been ready for ages and we were going to be late if I didn't hurry up, as I snarled that maybe if *he* was capable of finding the bastarding Mini Cheddars in the cupboard instead of either telling the children to ask Mummy or standing in the kitchen plaintively shouting he didn't know where they were until I cracked and went to find them, then maybe, just maybe, I'd be ready. A night in a hotel by myself would mean I could apply different colours of eyeshadow and blend them. I could choose an outfit without the main criterion being 'Doesn't show sticky finger marks'. I could sleep for hours and then enjoy a delicious hotel breakfast, without anyone spilling their orange juice or somehow managing to squirt tomato sauce over the next table or needing their sausages cut up or suddenly shrieking like a half-murdered banshee because they were the WRONG KIND OF SAUSAGES THAT I KNEW THEY DIDN'T LIKE! Yes. The money from a Christmas bonus would have been very handy, but I couldn't deny that I was looking forward to this night in a hotel like John Mills looking forward to his first pint of Carlsberg in Alexandria. And of course, though I tried not to think about it, James would be there.

I told myself repeatedly that James was nothing to do with why I hadn't told Simon that partners were invited. I just needed a bit of time and space to myself, that was all. A weekend not having to worry about anything. I knew he'd have jumped at the chance of a free night in a nice hotel, but he wasn't the one who'd have to do all the work to make it happen. I could do without having to arrange for Sylvia and Michael to come and stay again, cleaning the house from top to bottom first and leaving meals ready for everyone, and changing all the beds and all the other things that had to be done before your mother-in-law babysat for you. I just needed twenty-four hours off without having to pay for it in blood, sweat and tears over the preceding week. Nothing more. Anyway, Simon got *plenty* of swanky work trips and nights in posh hotels at other people's expense while I was stuck at home with his children, so I refused to feel bad that he'd miss out. And if my heart skipped a beat when James said he was coming alone too, well, it didn't *mean* anything, did it? It just meant I was glad I wouldn't be the only one there on my own.

Despite my insistence to myself that I wasn't going to do any more than Simon did before departing on a work trip (i.e., pack my bag and say, 'Bye, darling, see you soon'), obviously I panicked, and in an attempt to stop myself spending all weekend worrying about what was happening at home I left a detailed list of instructions and a fridge full of healthy and nutritious meals for him and his children that I'd lovingly prepared so they could feast in my absence, complete with another detailed list of how, what and when to heat it all up, with 'DO NOT GIVE THE CHILDREN BOTULISM' written in big letters at the bottom and underlined in red pen. This was partly to ease my guilt over the very slinky new black dress and beautiful make-up I'd treated myself to, telling myself that this was a nice place we were going to and the now slightly faded and bobbled dress I'd worn to the last three Christmas parties because it didn't really seem worth making an effort, and the Rimmel eyeshadow palette I'd bought in 1997, just wouldn't cut it.

That was just the start of the lies I told myself that weekend. I told myself I was leaving ludicrously early, so I arrived long before I'd be able to check in, because I wanted to 'enjoy the grounds' of the hotel or sit by the fire in the bar and read, and not because I hoped James would be there early too and we might manage a few precious minutes alone together. I told myself I'd barely eaten in a week so the dress looked better on, not off. I told myself that the incredibly tedious and confusing Booker Prize-winning novel I'd skim read had been enjoyable and I'd wanted to read it, and I definitely hadn't just read it in order to look clever and offer Importantly Intellectual Literary Opinions to James. I told myself the spare time once I was in my room was for napping and maybe a facemask, and not tarting myself up to the nines for James. None of it, I said most firmly to myself, had anything to do with James. Not a sausage.

I'd almost convinced myself of all these things as I parked on the pleasingly crunchy gravel drive and heaved my (perhaps slightly overlarge for one night) bag out of the car and attempted to nonchalantly sashay inside as if I rocked up alone for stays at swish hotels *all the time*, while simultaneously hoping they wouldn't think me a prostitute arriving in search of business. It was quite hard to sashay confidently when your enormous bloody overnight bag and unaccustomed Good Boots, which only had a kitten heel but it was still a kitten more than I was accustomed to, were causing you to list quite alarmingly to starboard, so I was more relieved than anything when a familiar voice behind me said, 'Can I help you with that?' and James appeared and took the wretched bloody thing out of my hand.

'Christ,' he gasped, as he went for a manly 'casual heft' of my bag and nearly gave himself a hernia.

'Are you all right?' I asked anxiously. 'It's quite heavy. I've … er … brought some books to read while I have some free time.' (Not entirely a lie. I did have the new Jilly Cooper to actually read in the bath and a tedious biography of someone clever to leave on my bedside table to look intelligent should anyone happen to see it, which obviously they wouldn't, but just in case, and the rest of the bag was stuffed with all the make-up I'd ever owned, including the bits that dated back to 1997, and six different pairs of shoes because I couldn't decide where exactly on the slutty/classy scale I wanted to land.)

'No, no,' James whimpered. 'It's fine. Is it heavy? I hadn't noticed,' and he gallantly staggered into reception.

'You're early,' he remarked. 'Have you come to see Virginia Woolf's house too?'

'Oh er, I thought I might try to fit it in,' I bluffed, having had no thoughts really beyond cocktails, roaring fires, hot baths and the illicit ravishments of a man who wasn't my husband. Vaguely I'd thought that a delightful walk through some frosted gardens while I said clever things and laughed charmingly and my cheeks became adorably pink with the cold might feature before the cocktails, etc, etc, but culture and museums hadn't really appeared on my radar.

'But we've got loads of time,' said James. 'It's only about twenty minutes away, if you fancy it. Have you read much Virginia Woolf?'

'Um, oh, you know! A bit,' I said vaguely. 'Who hasn't! She was the one who wanted a room with a view, wasn't she? I liked that. Florence and all that,' I added, nodding wisely.

'No, that was E. M. Forster. Virginia Woolf wanted a room of her own.'

'Ha ha ha, well who doesn't! Hopefully they'll be able to provide that for us! No sharing!' I said, in the worst attempt at sexy banter ever.

James laughed and deposited our bags with the nice reception lady, as I babbled on that we were checking in *separately*, of course, not together, no no, just *colleagues*, obviously, here for the Christmas party, two cars in the car park. I managed to stop just short of saying 'no funny business here', but it was a close-run thing. I was sweating by the time James ushered me out to his car to go and see Virginia sodding Woolf's bloody house.

* * *

Virginia Woolf's house was very green. Not as in Louisa's we-must-compost-our-own-pube-clippings-to-save-the-polar-bears green (not that I thought Louisa trimmed her bush in a million years, mind you. On the more times than I cared to remember I'd had the misfortune of seeing Louisa's lady garden, all I could think of was the line from the children's song about Sleeping Beauty: 'A great big forest grew around, grew around, grew around.' Alas, that then made me think of the later line about how the prince took his sword and cut it down, and I didn't really want to think about Bardo's sword), but just as in she obviously really liked painting things green. And painting the furniture. I did like the painted furniture, and started thinking about how I could paint that old sideboard that had been Simon's grandmother's and maybe one day people would visit my house and ooh and ah over my artistic skills and say that clearly painting the walls a lurid shade of bright green was a sign of my genius and not colour-blind derangement. I also liked the layout, which meant you had to go back outside to get into her bedroom, which I thought was a most satisfactory arrangement preventing irritating children from coming in and jumping on your head in the morning to demand Coco Pops and *SpongeBob SquarePants*. Not, of course, that Virginia had children, but I wondered if perhaps Vanessa Bell made a habit of dropping off rambunctious nephews and nieces for the weekend and Virginia needed to escape?

I did enjoy the blissful experience of wandering round a National Trust property without finding myself halfway to a nervous breakdown as I shrieked 'Don't touch! Leave it! No running! I SAID DON'T TOUCH!' (Why do the National Trust even *sell* family memberships? It's a trick, because you can't really take small children to National Trust properties because they're full of precious and fragile things and there's nothing small children like better than smashing precious and fragile things – things like my SANITY. I no longer took the children to such places, there had been too many … incidents.) I couldn't help but think, though, that it must be much easier to create genre-defying works of deathless prose if you had a quirkily green room full of nice furniture and with no one strewing bastarding fucking loom bands or Moshi dickhead Monsters everywhere underfoot while asking for yet another snack and screaming that their life is now meaningless until you come and find the small, lurid piece of plastic tat they have lost that is apparently the only thing that makes their existence worthwhile.

Walking through the rooms with James, making admiring noises while surreptitiously googling 'Virginia Woolf books synopsis' on my phone, I saw a glimpse of a different, calmer, life. A life with a partner who was not permanently tired and grumpy and didn't wear nasty fleeces and who read intelligent books instead of watching *Wheeler Fucking Dealers* every night. An actual partner, someone who was in tune with me and attuned to me, and my emotions and needs, who would support me instead of playing yet another round of competitive bloody tiredness (for which Simon seemed to be going for Olympic Gold).

We went into the garden and right on cue I stumbled, and James turned and caught me before I went arse over tit into Leonard Woolf's fishpond. I had somehow managed to go flying on an apparently flat and unimpeded piece of ground, and James had had to use both arms to steady me. Arms that were now around me, as he looked down at me.

'Ellen,' he said. 'Ellen, I –'

'We're closing early today, I'm afraid,' chirped the National Trust lady who had stealthily appeared behind us in her sensible shoes. 'Just to let you know you've got another half an hour if you want to quickly look round the gardens and pop into the writing hut. I'm sure you'd like to see it, before we close,' she said firmly, making it clear that we were to go and look at the hut, and there would indeed be no funny business here.

'Of course,' said James, letting me go in embarrassment as I scurried down the garden squawking, 'The shed! The shed, we must see the shed!' as the National Trust lady followed us to inform us that it was in fact a *writing hut*, not a shed, and also clearly to make sure there were no shenanigans in the hallowed shed either.

I wittered all the way back in the car. I don't know what I said, I just had to fill the silence that if left might be filled with other things, things that once said, couldn't be unsaid, and if they *were* to be said, I wanted them said in a more romantic setting than in a Volvo doing 57 mph on the A26. I know I did fall back on my favourite conversational gambit in Awkward Situations of talking about otters and their opposable thumbs, because I then ran into trouble when I started talking about how otters also have pockets to keep their favourite stone in and was halfway through saying 'and that's where the phrase "wetter than an otter's pocket" comes from', when I remembered that while the phrase might have started out innocently enough to describe getting caught in the rain, it had also acquired another, less innocent meaning.

I hastily embarked on my final otter fact, about how they sleep holding hands so they don't drift away from each other, and realised that was also not helpful under the circumstances. I had never dreamed that my fail-safe otter anecdotes would turn out to be so bloody sex-related! Luckily, we were pulling into the hotel car park, and I was out of the car and sprinting across the gravel before James had the handbrake on, waving furiously and shouting, 'Bye! Thanks! Lovely afternoon, see you later!'

Of course, I'd forgotten that I had to get my room key from reception, as did James, which led to a tense lift ride together. We were on the same floor, and he stopped outside the lift and said, 'I had a really nice time this afternoon.'

'So did I,' I muttered, which was true. It had been lovely.

'About earlier –'

'Earlier? What about earlier?'

'In the garden, I –'

'Ha ha ha!' I laughed my best 'nothing to see here' laugh, as though the National Trust lady were still chaperoning us to point out interesting features of the hut, like apparently Virginia Woolf was a bit of a dirty mare and in her day her desk was covered in rubbish and fag butts. I was warming to Virginia and thinking I rather liked her style – apart from the madness and suicide bits, obviously.

'I know, what a clumsy tit I am, thank goodness you were there. Lucky I didn't knock you into the fish pond or I think the National Trust lady would have shouted at us. She wouldn't have let you in the special hut all covered in pond weed, anyway!'

Well done, Ellen, I congratulated myself. Pond weed diffuses any situation. Whatever he was going to say, whether it was something awkward and romantic (oh, how I wished it was, but at the same time how terrified I was of what would happen if one of us finally said something) or something to make it clear I'd actually got completely the wrong end of the stick and we in fact had nothing but a purely platonic friendship based on cigarettes and our mutual love of novels about penguins, and the soulful look as he had gazed into my eyes was just trapped wind, then the pond weed had dealt with it.

'Yes,' said James. 'Yes, I can see her taking umbrage about pond weed. Might've got a lifetime ban from the National Trust for that!'

'You'd have to hand back your membership of the middle classes,' I laughed. 'They probably would tell Waitrose and you'd be banned from there too. The horror! Imagine! Oh look, Room 38! This is me. Um, I'll see you later then.'

'Yeah. Yeah, later. Ellen?'

I turned back, halfway through the door (though not before I had a glimpsed a four-poster bed, no less, and clocked that the hotel biscuits on the tray were KitKats, NICE!). 'Yes?'

'Later – come down and have a drink with me? Early? Before the corporate hell bin fire starts and Sally Thompson makes us stick Post-its to our head and guess who we're supposed to be, and Nigel Kempson starts trying to get us to play Never Have I Ever?'

'Oh, you've heard about our Christmas parties then!' I said. 'Last year Nigel told us about how he had a threeway with his brother and his wife. His *brother*. I don't mean to judge, but there's something weird about having a threesome with your brother, isn't there?'

'Um, yeah. But will you? Have a drink with me?'

'Yes, yes, why not?'

I floated into my room on a cloud of happiness. I hadn't been wrong about how he'd looked at me. He didn't have wind. He wanted to have a drink with me. Just me. Just me and him. Just me and James. I regretted the babbling about otters on the way home, and the pond weed and bringing up Nigel's incestuous threesome. I realised I did want him to say … well, I didn't really know what.

But something had to be said. And more than I wanted something said, I wanted very very badly for him to kiss me under the mistletoe and say my name again like he had in the garden, but without an officious fucking woman with a clipboard appearing to spoil my Moment.

Too late it dawned on me that we had not actually set a time to meet. What time did 'Before' mean? The corporate hell party was supposed to start with a 'drinks reception' at 6 p.m. It was 3.30 p.m. now. Five o'clock? Half past? Four thirty? I didn't want to be there too early, meaning I'd look too keen and also probably would accidently get disastrously pissed through nerves. At the same time I didn't want poor James sitting like Billy No Mates thinking I wasn't coming, but obviously I couldn't *ask* him because *reasons*, so instead I went for the proper middle-class solution and ignored the scandalous price of the mini bar and the stern memo we'd all had about how Cunningham United Nautical Trust was only paying for the room, and all *sundries* would have to paid for by ourselves, and took a large vodka and tonic into the bath.

I took my time over getting ready. I hadn't *had* any time to get ready in a long time, and James or no James, I wanted to make the most of it. I also wanted to look ravishingly beautiful and irresistible for him when I finally went downstairs. Despite the diet my new sexy dress definitely still required Spanx, so I was reassured that I couldn't get too carried away with romance and passion, or at least not beyond a point where I'd have to reveal the swathes of straining Spandex and stout gusseting preserving my modesty, which I was not prepared to do. Not yet, anyway.

I did start to feel a bit guilty about everything, though, as I gazed in the mirror. When had I last made this much effort for

Simon? The guilt was rather eased by a call from Simon at five o'clock though, as I was applying my third coat of mascara. I knew it was the children's dinner time and he'd only be calling with some inane question about how much tomato sauce they were allowed or some other query that was on my very detailed list of instructions, and that I'd just end up annoyed and stressed and worried about the children instead of a serene vision of vodka and Radox and Clinique. If it was important, I reasoned, he'd leave a message. He didn't, but despite my best efforts, I could not abandon him to his fish-fingered fate (homemade because of the Guilt), and I rang him back.

'What?' I snapped rather ungraciously.

'Jane says you don't make them eat vegetables at the weekend?'

'If they didn't have to eat vegetables, would I have gone to all the trouble of preparing vegetables for them?'

'Um, I suppose not. Jane says you let them have Coke at the weekend too?'

'Simon. When have you seen me let them have Coke?'

'I dunno? Is that a no then?'

'Yes.'

'Oh, and Peter says his bum is sore.'

'Did it look red when you helped him wipe?'

'I didn't help him wipe?

'He's only three, he still needs help wiping his arse. It was ON THE LIST.'

'Was it? Well, what should I do?'

'After dinner give him a good clean-up with some baby wipes, then put him in the bath and put some Sudocrem on his bum afterwards.'

'Right. And where are the baby wipes and Sudocrem?'

'IN THE BATHROOM,' I snarled, then hung up and went down to the bar, chuntering to myself that it was hard to feel like an irresistible sex goddess, let alone turn yourself into one, for a man you had conversations about bum cream and arse wiping with.

Unfortunately, neither James nor I had taken into account the fact that everyone who worked at Cunningham United eventually had their soul so crushed by the place that they turned to strong drink, and therefore most of our colleagues would also have had the bright idea of getting a few under their belt before the official 'drinks reception'. The bar was heaving by the time I walked in, and I couldn't even see James. Nigel appeared, though, leering appreciatively at my cleavage and boomed, 'Ellen! Looking very –' He paused, stared hard at my tits, swallowed several times and then finished feebly with a half-hearted 'nice' (I suspected finishing feebly was Nige's signature move). He cleared his throat and dragged his gaze briefly upwards in a last-ditch attempt to make eye contact. 'I say, Ellen,' he murmured in a conspiratorial whisper, 'have I ever mentioned my brother to you?'

'I have to go,' I said hastily, and turned and bumped into Sally, who beamed and said, 'Ellen! What a … brave … dress! Hope we don't lose any Post-its down there later! Don't worry if you do, though, I've got plenty! We're going to have *loads* of fun tonight,' and she opened her enormous sack-like handbag to reveal most of the stock of Ryman's lurking inside, ready for Sally's 'party fun' later. Briefly I wondered which would be the worst fate: Nigel's idea of 'fun' or Sally's?

I attempted to muster an enthusiastic look for Sally's party games, but I was evidently too successful because Sally was struck by a splendid idea.

'Oh!' she said in excitement. 'Ellen, why don't you help me organise the games? That will be super-fun!'

James appeared at my elbow to rescue me in the nick of time before I could find a diplomatic way of telling Sally that I'd rather shit in my hands and clap than organise the Cunningham United Nautical Trust's Christmas party games.

'Ellen!' he said heartily. 'Fancy seeing you here, ha ha ha.'

'Ha ha ha,' I responded in relief.

'You haven't got a drink, let me get you one. Sally, can I get you anything? No? You're happy with your orange squash. Sure? Ellen, what do you want?'

'Err, I'll come to the bar with you,' I said brightly. 'See you in a bit, Sally.'

'You look incredible in that dress,' James breathed in my ear as we fought our way to the bar. 'You literally took my breath away when you walked in. You are easily the most beautiful woman in this room.'

'That's not very hard,' I pointed out pragmatically, though inside I was glowing with joy, and definitely recalling the alternative meaning to the expression about an otter's pocket. He'd noticed I scrubbed up all right. He thought I was beautiful. He liked my dress! This was all particularly gratifying, as when I had showed Simon my dress, he'd looked up briefly from *AutoTrader*, peered at it for a moment and then simply said, 'Won't your tits fall out?', which hadn't been entirely the response I'd been hoping for, as I indignantly explained to him about the wonders of tit tape and considered taping his testicles to his thigh as he slept to show him its holding power as he attempted to peel his crown jewels free without giving himself an accidental bollockectomy (I didn't. Good tit tape is expensive, and I wasn't wasting it on teaching Simon a lesson).

'You'd be the most beautiful woman in any room,' James insisted. It was corny as fuck, and I did cringe a little, but still, I reasoned, a compliment was a compliment after all, and at least it wasn't Nige who'd told me that – Nige saying something similar would definitely make me more than just cringe and want to douse myself in Dettol as my vagina slammed shut, possibly forever, turning into a haunted cavern filled with dusty cobwebs.

I was rapidly downing a large V&T and attempting to make intelligent and enthusiastic conversation with James and his boss Terry, when the summons came to go through to the 'function suite' for the 'drinks reception' (i.e. we were to shuffle into the soulless annexe tacked on at the back of the Georgian house by a bastard 1960s architect, to consume several glasses of tepid sparkling battery acid to get us in a 'festive' mood). Regardless of the quality of the drink to be recepted, it was provided on the company dollar, so the rules were you had to drink as much as possible before it ran out in order to get your money's worth. Even though it wasn't your money paying for it. On the other hand, it was probably your blood, sweat, tears and possibly sanity that had contributed to the company profits that *were* paying for it, and there was no Christmas bonus this year, so all the more important to chase that elusive festive dream of getting alcohol poisoning at the Cunningham United Nautical Trust's expense.

As the throng stampeded out the bar, James put his hand on my back to steer me through the crowd. My bare back, as my dress was extremely low-cut back and front (though it was a decorous length; my mother had instilled in me early that it was tits *or* legs, never both – not that she said 'tits', obviously, going for the more discreet 'decolletage' – and it was a habit I remained unable to break). It felt all fizzy where he was touching me, and the otters were, quite frankly, making for the lifeboats, every otter for himself.

'Are you all right, Ellen?' asked Sally, adding, 'You've gone a funny colour. Dress too tight? Or is it the Change, dear?'

'Change?' I squeaked, acutely aware of James's hand, mere inches from my actual bottom.

'You know, your Time of Life? Are you having a hot flush?'

Sally's squashing comments had at least brought me sufficiently down to earth to stop me turning round to James and shrieking, 'Ride me sideways, NOW!' and I mumbled something about it just being very hot in here.

'I'm surprised you can feel it, in a dress like that,' said Sally, tipping her head to one side in concern. 'It *is* December, you need to be careful you don't get a chill on your kidneys. I've got a nice shrug in my bag I can lend you if you get chilly?'

My phone rang again. It was, unsurprisingly, Simon. 'Two secs,' I said brightly to Sally and James, and 'Yes?' to Simon, who announced that Peter's bum was still sore, and did I think he could have worms? I turned away and hissed, 'Give him some pink Calpol. In the unlikely event he does have worms there's nothing I can do about it now, is there?' and hung up again.

'Everything all right?' asked Sally, now tipping her head to the other side to indicate maternal concern. 'Problems with the kiddies? I never wanted them myself. Just as well, with my plumbing issues! Did I tell you about my fibroids?'

'Ooh, look, Sally,' I said, and hastily pointed out the bored teenage waitresses proffering trays of battery acid to us. Sally seized two and made for a corner. I didn't mean to be unsympathetic to a fellow woman, but I'd heard about Sally's 'plumbing issues' before. At length.

'Thank God,' James breathed in my ear. 'I thought we were going to be stuck with her all night.'

'No, she's gone to top her glasses up from the bottle of vodka in her bag,' I explained. 'She does it every year. You don't think she was really just drinking orange squash in the bar? She's just too tight to buy a proper drink, makes a great song and dance about "hotel prices" and how she's "beating the system". Last year after the Post-its game, she took her bra off, swung it round her head and threw it over the chandelier, then she snogged Nige, and Tony found her asleep in the lift in just her pants at 2 a.m.'

'Gosh,' said James. 'These parties are quite wild then?'

'Depends on your definition of wild,' I said airily, trying to give the impression that I myself was accustomed to much more rock 'n' roll levels of debauchery than the Christmas party could offer.

The next two hours were hideous. I'd not had the wit to sneak in and tamper with the seating plan, and so I was at one table between Nigel and Chris from HR, and James was on the very furthest away table between Sally, and Tara from reception. I was initially paranoid that someone had sensed something between James and me, and had designed the seating plan accordingly, till Chris confided it had actually been drawn up with the intent of keeping Sally and Nigel as far apart as possible.

'Though how we'll manage that when she starts with those bastarding Post-its, I don't know,' he sighed wearily.

Simon also rang another four times, to enquire if Jane could watch *Coraline* before bed, even though it wasn't in the pile of approved bedtime DVDs ('No, it gives her nightmares'), to ask if I knew where the reel for his fishing rod was ('I didn't even know you had a fishing rod'), to check what times their bedtimes were, because Jane said they definitely could stay up late at the weekend

('It's on the SODDING SHEET, and when have you EVER seen them stay up till midnight at the weekend?') and to inform me that they had both watched *Coraline* before bed and were now sobbing hysterically that they couldn't go to sleep lest the Other Mother got them ('Give them half a teaspoon of pink Calpol and tell them it will help them sleep and keep the Other Mother away').

Finally, when dinner was over and we'd sat through the self-congratulatory speech from Sir Jason, the CEO, in which he basically said, 'Thanks for all the hard work. Myself and the shareholders are very much enjoying the profits you have generated for us,' James appeared behind my seat.

'Ellen,' he said, feigning casualness. 'I'm nipping out for a smoke, want to join me?'

'Sure,' I said, equally casually. I suddenly felt sick and all hot and cold. Was this it? Was it finally going to happen? My heart was beating very oddly as I stared at James. I wasn't sure how I felt about this now it was becoming reality. Daydreaming, fantasies, lustful thoughts when surrounded by other people were one thing. But what if he actually kissed me? Exchanges of bodily fluids placed everything on another level altogether, and I wasn't really sure I wanted that. In truth, all my daydreams had stopped round about the moment the lady had interrupted us beside Leonard Woolf's fish pond, only with fewer disapproving National Trust employees in blue Crocs hanging about. The *idea* of being kissed, I suddenly realised, was a much nicer thing than actually being kissed. James's tongue. In my mouth. Tongue. Tongue.

'Ellen?' said James again. 'Are you OK?'

'Yes! Fine!' I said brightly.

'Only you looked all blank and seemed to be mumbling "tongue" to yourself?'

'No, no, erm, time. I was saying time, time for a ciggy!'

'Ooooh,' said Sally, appearing out of nowhere. 'Can I nick a fag?'

'Of course! I didn't know you smoked,' I said in sudden relief.

'I don't really, only after a few drinks. And it *is* Christmas.'

James managed a valiant 'Great! More the merrier' and we all traipsed outside, while I gave serious thought to kissing Sally, instead of James, so grateful was I for her chaperonage, putting off what was going to be a dreadfully awkward encounter either way, whether James kissed me and suggested going to bed, or whether I renounced him forever. A very British part of me considered just shagging him to be polite, on the basis that extra-marital sex would be less awful than an embarrassing conversation.

Sally, swathed in her polyester sequined shrug to keep the chill off her kidneys, was a dreadfully slow smoker, and she was in a chatty mood after her turbo Proseccos.

'Anyone see *EastEnders* last night?' she asked brightly. 'What do you think's going to happen to Phil Mitchell in the Christmas special?'

'Oh, it's so exciting,' I started to say, but James interrupted with a crushing, 'I don't actually watch TV, Sally.'

We both stared at him, stunned. What sort of person doesn't watch TV? I mean, I still haven't managed to convince Simon of the joys of *EastEnders*, but he does watch TV. It's not *normal*, not watching TV. If BuzzFeed Quizzes had existed back then, they'd probably have confirmed 'not watching TV' as one of the top 10 signs that someone is a serial killer (in fairness, they do make their own entertainment, I suppose).

Sally managed to swallow her shock and croaked, 'But what do you *do*? Instead of watching TV?'

James looked smug. 'Read. Listen to music. Discuss current affairs.'

Suddenly I noticed he had a rather weak chin. How had I not noticed that chin before?

Sally shuddered. 'I just don't understand. You don't watch *any* TV?'

'Well,' James conceded. 'I do occasionally treat myself to watching the golf.'

Golf! What the actual fuck? He was a bloody *golfer*? Like *Geoffrey*? Did he bore on with tedious anecdotes about the terribly funny thing Norman said the other day too?

'Golf's, like, the most boring thing ever?' said Sally in disbelief.

Small eyes, James had too. Really very small. And quite close together. Granny Green said never to trust a man with eyes too close together. Oh God, he *was* talking about golf now, mansplaining it to poor Sally, who suddenly sucked down the rest of her cigarette and made excuses about it being time to start organising the party games.

I started to follow her, but James caught my arm.

'Let's have another cigarette,' he said loudly for Sally's benefit, and made a great show of fumbling with the packet until she was safely out of sight and earshot.

'God,' he said. 'I never thought she'd go. I mean, how sad. Who actually watches *EastEnders*? Imagine Sally with her cats of a night, sitting in her winceyette nighty, getting all hot and bothered at the thought of the *EastEnders* Christmas special. Ugh, on second thoughts, don't, what an image!'

'Stop it,' I said. 'Sally's OK. She's just a bit lonely. She's a kind soul, really. Don't make fun of her.'

worried I just want some sordid Christmas one-night stand or office fling, I *don't*. This is real. I want something *real* with you.'

'But you don't *KNOW* me,' I cried again in frustration. 'You *don't* know anything about me. I don't like those stupid books I pretended to like. I like Jilly Cooper, and jazz just sounds like a gang of two-year-olds let loose with a xylophone and some saucepan lids. I've heard better music at Mothers and Toddlers than on that awful CD you lent me and I pretended to rave about, and I don't like those wretched films you kept telling me were "senimal shinema", I mean "seminal cinema". That's quite hard to say when you're a bit pissed, you know! I like *EastEnders*, just like Sally. I'm not who you think I am at all, and I don't think I know you at all either. You don't watch TV and you're a *golfer*!' I had finished my cigarette and lit another in anguish at how I'd been duped.

'OK.' James took a step back and ran his hand through his (rather thinning, and quite mousy) hair. 'OK. But these are details. I can give up golf. We can compromise. I could learn to like *EastEnders*, you could maybe learn to like jazz? But I want to be with you, and I thought you wanted to be with me?'

'No! Don't you see? It's all just been an illusion. Neither of us are what we thought. And if we have to change that much about who we fundamentally are, how can it ever work? What are we going to do? Wreck our families, put our children through all that upheaval, to look at each other in a few months or a year and think, "Who the fuck ARE you?" when we discover that dirty pants left on the floor and lost car keys are still fucking annoying no matter who's doing it, and this is real life. Real life is boring and drudgery and there's no getting away from it, and you just need to find someone who makes you laugh enough to make it bearable, and I'm sorry if that's not your wife for you, but I know it's not going to be me either, and you're definitely not going to be that person for me, and I need to go now, I really do.' I flung my cigarette end away dramatically and turned back into the hotel. My phone started ringing as I did.

'Simon,' I said in relief. 'No, I'm just on my way up to bed. Sally's starting the party games, yeah, the Post-its, so I'm going to turn in with the new Jilly Cooper. Shit, you got me that for Christmas? Sorry, darling, I didn't realise, that was nice of you. Look, just return it and get the new Penny Vincenzi instead, I'm dying to read that too. I don't know, I'll worm Peter tomorrow when I get home.'

Present day

The dream about James on top of the brutal hangover had left me discombobulated, to say the least. I tried my best not to think about him, and certainly not in the context of anything like the dream. It was a guilty and shameful time of my life, but in some ways I was strangely grateful to James. The unfortunate interlude with him had reminded me that I did really love Simon and that I didn't want anyone else. Without that wake-up call for me, I'm not sure we'd have made it through those years with small children.

The James thing had made me realise that I was as responsible for the distance between us as Simon was, that I needed to stop nit picking and shouting at Simon *all* the time, and let him make his own mistakes with the children. It hadn't always gone to plan, of course; he'd continued to miss swimming lessons with abandon and my attempt to take a step back from that had been to shout at him that I hoped his conscience wouldn't keep him awake at night when Jane drowned IN A RAGING TORRENT, and also did he know that you could drown in TWO INCHES OF WATER, but it had certainly made me more tolerant towards him for a while anyway, until we were over the worst of the early years.

But I'd been pushing him away again recently, shutting him out, being so focused on my 'what about meeeee' empty-nest pity party, that I'd rather forgotten that Simon was probably also missing the kids and worrying about what we did now, after all these years of parenting.

It was all quiet when I got home (I'd let everyone else go home at 3 p.m., but thought I'd probably better at least pretend to do some work before I buggered off). I found Simon asleep in the sitting room, all three dogs, including Barry the giant horse dog, snoring on top of him.

'I finished early,' he said blearily as he woke up. 'Ellen, we need to do something about poor Flora.' He gestured at the ancient and frail little Border terrier. 'She had another accident today.'

I opened my mouth to protest that was no reason to 'do' anything about poor Flora, who was happy and comfortable, if a bit leaky, but before I could, Simon went on, 'I'm going to talk to them on Monday about working from home so I can be here with her. With all of them, really. None of them are getting any younger – even Judgy's showing his age these days.' Judgy, my other Border terrier, shot him a malevolent look for being so rude.

'You're going to work from home to be here for the dogs?'

'Yeah. I know you can't, but apart from meetings, I don't need to be in the office all the time. It makes sense.'

'You're rearranging your working life because the dogs are old and incontinent and need company? The dogs you always insisted were *my* dogs?'

'Is that a bad thing? And who am I kidding? They've always been our dogs.'

'No. No, it's a good thing. Thank you. For everything. Simon, I'm sorry.'

'What for? What did you do last night? You haven't been sacked for doing your 'Patricia the Stripper' routine at the Christmas party, have you?'

'No. I don't *think* I did Patricia anyway. No one mentioned it if I did. I'm sorry I've been so busy feeling sorry for myself about the children leaving home that I forgot I still had you.'

'You do indeed. Stuck with me, you are. Shall we get a takeaway for dinner?'

'Actually, that sounds good, yeah.'

Sometimes I thought, looking at Simon sharing his sweet and sour chicken with Flora, while I chastised him over the salt content being bad for her yet surreptitiously giving Judgy and Barry bits of my beef in black bean sauce, it took the most unexpected things to make you realise that you'd made the right choices after all. James would probably have turned out to be a cat person too on top of everything else.

Sunday 10 December

I was just clearing away dinner tonight and having a little glass of wine – it's OK to have wine every night in December because it's *festive*, and it's even more OK to have Baileys, which was what I was contemplating having as a nightcap on finishing the wine – when there was a furious hammering at the front door. I dashed to open it, fearing some emergency, and cursing Simon, who was asleep with the dogs on the sofa again, for not fixing the doorbell, like I'd been asking him to do since August, and found my neighbour Julia standing on the doorstep, looking mildly distraught.

'Julia!' I said. 'What's happened? Are you OK? Come in.'

Julia fell through the door babbling wildly of shoeboxes, she needed shoeboxes STAT and also pound coins, and soap and toothpaste, did I have any such things as shoeboxes and pound coins and soap and toothpaste, because it was an *emergency*. Simon wandered into the hall yawning, followed by the dogs, who'd finally noticed someone was there and decided to bark. Thank goodness Julia was not a serial killer, for all the help my darling husband and loyal wolf pack would be to me.

'Emergency shoe boxes?' said Simon in confusion. 'Who needs emergency shoe boxes? And emergency toothpaste?'

'The school's sodding shoebox appeal, I expect,' I explained, as Julia nodded tearfully and said, yes, yes, the shoebox appeal, and she was so sorry to bother us, but oh thank God I understood.

'Oh yes,' I said. 'I was in thrall to the shoebox appeal for many years. Come and have a glass of wine, Julia, and I'm sure we can find you something. Don't worry, I was a master of the shoebox appeal – they were a staple part of Christmas for many years. I confess it never quite seems like Christmas till I've ransacked the house for a box to fill with cheap toiletries.'

Julia calmed down somewhat for a hefty belt of pinot noir, as she shook her head and told me of the interminable barrages of the school emails, the class WhatsApps, the endless bake sales and Christmas jumper days and furious rows over what to get for the teacher's present, and should the teaching assistant get something too, and should it be of the same value, and what about the office staff, and the janitor and the dinner ladies and had no one thought of the lollipop man, and what about the supply teachers, and that woman who came once to give a talk on guinea pigs, should she get a Christmas present, and on and on and on.

'I thought it would be easier when the boys started school,' whimpered Julia, who had my admiration as she was the mother of twin boys who had just started in Reception. 'I thought all the desperate juggling of childcare, and finances to pay for the child-care, would all magically vanish and I could drop them at breakfast club and pick them up from afterschool club and it would all be fine, and I could go to work and not worry about them all day and actually be a productive member of my team and not get fired for always being late, but it's *worse*.'

'It does get easier, eventually,' I assured her.

'When? When does it get easier?' Julia demanded.

'Well, secondary school? Except then you're worrying about drugs and teenage pregnancies and what the fuck they're posting on TikTok and are they drinking and you have to pick them up from parties in the middle of the night and hope they don't puke in your car because of course they've been drinking, and are you a responsible parent for letting them take some ciders to parties, or are you an utterly irresponsible parent who is setting them up for a lifetime of substance abuse by encouraging social drinking, and are they sending dick pics, or getting sent them, and whatever you do, someone will be there to tell you why you're doing it wrong and to judge you, but it's not quite such a relentless daily grind as primary school. More just a constant ticker tape running through your mind of "Please don't let anything awful happen to them," but then you have that as soon as they are born anyway, don't you?'

'Noooo!' wailed Julia. 'Don't tell me that. That doesn't sound easier. Do they at least stop doing assemblies, though? They've done *two* assemblies this term already, and we're expected to go along and watch. When did this happen? I don't recall my parents ever coming to assemblies, even when I had a starring role as the Little Red Hen!'

'Oh, I loved the assemblies!' I said misty-eyed, sloshing more wine into Julia's glass. 'Jane once played an injured dog called Banjo, waiting for the Mountain Rescue. Or was it Peter?' I frowned. 'Anyway, it was very moving.'

'Was it?' said Julia, looking at me strangely.

'Oh yes,' I insisted blithely. 'Even though she, or maybe he, just lay there, not doing anything.'

'And what about the Open Afternoons? They have an Open Afternoon every month! *Every month!* So we can come and see what they've been working on. They're in sodding Reception, for

Christ's sake. Mostly they are "working" on not eating crayons and learning not to lick the table!'

'Oh, the Open Afternoons were such fun,' I sighed wistfully. 'The children were always so proud to show off their work to their parents, it was very touching. Well, most of the children were. There was one unfortunate incident when Peter was in Reception and he decided he didn't want to show me his pictures of the rainforest, and instead he got hold of the PVA when no one was looking and glued himself to the table. I mean, the gluing himself to the table was bad enough, but for some reason, he decided not to glue his hand to the table, but his penis. It caused quite a stir. We had a very embarrassing interview with the Head, and Peter, who could give no other reason than he thought it would be funny, because "willies are funny". I mean, he's not wrong, but we had to have quite a long chat about how there's a time and a place for things. God, somehow I'd forgotten about that. But apart from that, the open afternoons are magical. Oh, and the one where Jane deviated from the *Titanic* tableau script to give a rabble-rousing speech about socialism and how wrong it was that the first-class passengers escaped while the third-class passengers were left to drown. I think maybe I shouldn't have let her watch the *Titanic* film. But all the others. They were wonderful.'

Julia made a non-committal noise and took another slug of wine. 'God, that is so much better, though no doubt I'll regret it in the morning when Suzie fucking Harper tells me I look "tired", and have I considered that I might be perimenopausal? Yes, Suzie, I probably fucking am, but also I'm tired because I do more than just go to Pilates and send passive–aggressive WhatsApp messages about should we buy an Oxfam goat for the class, and what a shame it was that so few parents bothered to come to the lunchtime Bring and Buy Sale to raise money and awareness for three-legged Mongolian alpacas.'

'I didn't think you got alpacas in Mongolia.'

'You don't. Except for a "charity" Suzie's friend runs, that has four alpacas she has "rescued". So Suzie organised a Bring and Fucking Buy Sale at the school, which cleared me out of pound coins last week, as well as trying to find something respectable for them to Bring, only to discover that they had then Bought the biggest load of tat you ever saw!'

'If she really wants to raise money for the alpacas she should tie some branches to their heads and rent them out as reindeer,' I suggested. 'You should text Suzie and tell her that,' I added helpfully.

'I don't think I'd dare,' groaned Julia. 'Apart from anything else, she might decide we do need reindeer and expect me to organise it and I can barely remember everything I need to remember for December anyway, like the Christmas jumper day, and the Christmas concert AND the carol service, which are not the same thing apparently.'

'No, but they're both lovely in their own way. There's something very heart-rending about the carol service when the tinies sing "Away in a Manger", and the Nativity is always so sweet. I remember when Peter was Joseph. He was marvellous. Sort of. He spent the whole time picking his nose and eating it, which was quite embarrassing. And then there was the year when Mary pushed Joseph off the stage shouting she had told him to book the fucking Hilton, and the Nativity had to be stopped in case Joseph was concussed and Mary's Mummy had quite a lot of explaining to do. Jane had the triangle solo in "O Little Town of Bethlehem" one year. That was nice.'

'I didn't know you got triangle solos,' said Julia in surprise.

'Oh yes,' I assured her. 'They tend to give it to the most unmusical child so everyone feels special, and I think the idea is that no one can really fuck that up. But then Jane fucked it up by just banging the triangle as loudly as she could at random points through the song. So that was quite embarrassing as well. Anyway. The Christmas concert is so nice too in a …' I ran out of festive steam here to find positives in the Christmas concert, which involved a lot of tuneless renditions of 'Jingle Bells'. 'Well, the children are always very *enthusiastic*,' I finished lamely, recalling the smell in the school hall of all the farting children.

'Enthusiastic,' Julia groaned. 'And what about the Christmas party? They have to come home at lunchtime to get ready for the party and we have to provide party food, but under no circumstances can that be grapes or sausages because of choking hazards, and actually Suzie thinks we shouldn't send any fruit that isn't seasonal because of sustainability and climate change, but it's *fucking December*, Suzie. There is no seasonal fruit, and you've already vetoed carrot sticks as little Portia is allergic to them apparently, and *also* announced that there is to be no refined sugar, fizzy drinks or processed foods provided, and also no cling film or Tupperware because microplastics, so what are they meant to do, Suzie, bring some houmous in a fucking shoe and lick it off each other?'

'Oh Julia,' I said. 'You should try to enjoy it! They're not little long!' and I clapped my hands over my mouth in horror at uttering the words I swore I'd never ever say to anyone.

'I'm so sorry. I don't know what came over me! I promise I'll never say that again, I didn't mean it. I'll open another bottle,' I said hastily. As I pulled out the cork, there was another wail from Julia, who had made the mistake of opening her phone.

'Look,' she whimpered. 'Just look. The utter *fuckers*!'

Suzie H: Hope everyone has remembered their boxes for the shoebox appeal tomorrow!

Natalie J: We had a last-minute panic as I have a dedicated shoe storage area in my walk-in closet, so I don't keep shoeboxes, but Chris came to the rescue and gave me some Prada boots as an early Chrimbo pressie, so I used that. Of course, it's much larger than a shoebox, so I've put in lots of extra goodies!

Rosie K: It didn't specify any brands for the soap and the shower gel, or what the hats and gloves were to be made of, so I just got it all from the White Company, hope that's OK?

Suzie H: Natalie, you're not allowed boot boxes, the email was quite specific, you can't have read it properly. It's called a SHOEBOX appeal for a reason, if they wanted BOOTBOXES, they'd have called it the BOOTBOX appeal, wouldn't they? You won't be able to use the bootbox. If you bring your things I will give you one of my spare boxes in the playground, and you'll have to repack it all. I hope you stuck to the list of what was allowed in the box?

Natalie J: I really don't see what the problem is with a bootbox. Did I mention it was Prada? Does that make a difference?

Rosie K: So is White Company OK?

Susie H: I suppose White Company is fine, Rosie, if that's what you've already got. Personally, I think it's nice to send the poor people something a little better than they are accustomed to, so I get my shower gels and handwash from Penhaligon's, and the hats and gloves from John Lewis, but I went cashmere, it's so warm, isn't it?

Natalie J: I went with Jo Malone, actually, but I put in a Diptyque candle.

Susie H: You can't have candles, Natalie. They weren't on the list. And think of the fire risk. Do you WANT these people to lose their few tattered possessions in an easily preventable fire? They live in hovels, Natalie, probably made of cardboard, the whole place would go up in an instant. THIS is why bootboxes aren't allowed, so people can't just put in any old junk.

Susie H: Anyway, don't worry if anyone's forgotten their shoeboxes, I've done ten, because it would be so sad if any of the kiddos missed out on learning the true meaning of Christmas, wrapping the boxes for the less fortunate, so if anyone needs one, come and find me in the playground and I'll make sure to give you one. Of course, it will say 'A Gift from The Harper Family' on it, but it's the thought that counts, isn't it? Natalie, you WILL need to get a shoebox from me too, I'm afraid.

Natalie J is typing

Natalie J deleted a message

'I went to fucking Poundland,' said Julia gloomily. 'There's a whole other WhatsApp thread about the Christmas jumper day with Suzie urging us to make sure they're ethical and sustainable, and obviously I bought the Christmas jumpers in Primark like the monster I am, because clearly I don't care about The Less Fortunate or The Polar Bears. As far as Susie is concerned, I might as well just beat a penguin to death with an impoverished urchin and have done with it!'

'Oh Julia,' I said. 'I always went to Poundland too. If you're that worried about needing fancy soap for Suzie, my knicker drawer is full of nice bars of soap I can't resist buying from museum gift shops and never get round to using so I stick them in the drawer so my pants smell nice. I'll get you some for the Unfortunates' Shoeboxes.'

'*Less* Fortunate,' Julia corrected me. 'Suzie says we mustn't call them "unfortunate".'

'Anyway, Mad Bitch Suzie will never know about the knicker soap. And you can point out that bars of soap are actually much more sustainable and last longer than even the fanciest shower gel, so FUCK YOU, Suzie, *and* you've saved a polar bear! Also, if you really want to one-up Suzie, get the boys to write a note to the Less Fortunate Children, wishing them a Merry Christmas.'

'They can't write, they're in Reception. Ollie ate a felt tip last week.'

'Well, you write it with your left hand then. It gets major smug points, and if Suzie hasn't thought of it she'll be furious, and even if she has she'll still be outraged that her gesture is now not a unique one. Fiona Montague did it for the shoeboxes one year, and it got *right* on Perfect Lucy Atkinson's Mummy's tits. More to the point, Julia, remember that this too shall pass. In the meantime, I need to give you one very important piece of advice. Listen to me. Never, whatever you do, whatever emotional blackmail is laid upon you, however guilty you're made to feel, NEVER join the PTA. That way lies madness, especially with people like Suzie. She's the sort of person who won't ever actually join the PTA, but thinks all the events should be run according to her say-so, and then won't even show up to them, because she's "busy". Help at coffee mornings, donate tombola prizes, but DON'T join.

'It was nearly the end of me. Peter was in danger of a full-blown gambling addiction at the age of eight, due to the hours he'd spend playing the tombola while I was making tea and finding napkins and trying to stop well-meaning volunteers putting the pistachio cupcakes on the allergy-free table, and Jane had to go through MAOM withdrawal after every school fête. You'll be OK. You can do this. Here, let's finish the bottle, and by the time you go home, Steve should've put the boys to bed!'

Julia tottered off into the night, clutching two shoeboxes, which had sadly left my treasured pairs of (sales bargains, but still) LK Bennetts homeless. I hadn't felt I could let her face Natalie and the famous Prada boot box with only an Office box to show. I felt most wise and elder stateswoman-like, though, after being in a position to proffer advice for once. I collapsed on the sofa next to Simon.

'All sorted?' he asked tentatively.

'Yes, thank God. Do you know, I think Julia was an Omen?'

'An Omen? An Omen you should get pissed on a Sunday night?'

'No, an Omen that I should count my blessings.'

'All right, Pollyanna.'

'No, seriously. I'd forgotten, until I was talking to Julia, how miserably *busy* December used to be – all the carol services and Christmas concerts and nativities and Christmas jumper days and school parties and everything. I'd convinced myself how magical it all was.'

'Really? You did nothing but moan about it at the time?'

'I know. But I'd somehow turned it into this fairytale time, of apple-cheeked moppets and carol singing.'

'You only took them carol singing once. Someone threatened to call the police because Jane went off piste and banged on an old lady's door and menacingly bellowed "Once in Royal David's City" through the letterbox before shouting she was to give her some money now. She omitted to mention the bit about how she was with the Brownies and they were collecting for Oxfam.'

'Enough. That's what I'm trying to say. Part of me *is* a bit sad it's all over, because I realised there was never any time to enjoy any of the school Christmas stuff with the children. It just felt like an endless round of demands from people for things. I'd forgotten how hideous the class WhatsApp turns at Christmas too, though fuck knows it was bad most of the year. So I'm *also* feeling very very relieved that I'm freed of the tyranny of Christmas jumpers and bastard shoeboxes and listening to thirty out-of-tune nine-year-olds sing "When Santa Got Stuck up the Chimney" and not sniggering at the line "There's soot on my sack", or keeping a straight face in the nice school church carol service when the angel tells Mary that she'll get knocked up because the Holy Ghost will come upon her …'

'I mean that's not even anatomically possible,' mused Simon. '*Upon* her wouldn't do much, would it? As an archangel, Gabriel didn't really understand human biology.'

'Well, I suppose if he tried to wipe it off and got some on his hand and then … you know, she could get pregnant?' I offered. '*Just Seventeen* was always warning us of the perils of that. As far as they were concerned, so much as a drop of jizz splashed within a ninety-metre radius of us, and we could be gymslip mothers before you could say "Immaculate Conception". And I don't think anyone else would manage to be as convincing as Mary about the whole Virgin Birth thing – that's a one-time-only excuse.'

'So what you're saying is, Mary basically explained away being pregnant by telling Joseph she only got fingered by the Holy Ghost, and everyone knows fingering doesn't really count and so that's what happened, and then God said he had to marry her because she was up the duff?'

I started laughing. 'Only you would put it quite like that,' I said affectionately. 'I mean, that's not quite what I said. I only said *Just Seventeen* said it was still possible to get pregnant even if you didn't actually *do it* do it. I don't think you've missed your calling as a theologian. Anyway, I'm going to have a bath, and relax and enjoy my phone not blowing up with eleventy fucking billion WhatsApps about Prada bootboxes and three-legged alpacas.'

'What?'

'Never mind, darling.'

In the bath, I decided to see if I could have a tiny Instagram stalk of my children, as Jane was still refusing to reply to my texts and Peter's only response was an occasional thumbs-up emoji. They had both blocked me long ago, and Jane declared Instagram to now just be for old people and it was all about TikTok. Peter was oddly fond of the old-fashioned technology of the 'Gram though, and occasionally unblocked me to have a little stalk of his own, and if I happened by luck to chance on one of those brief windows, I could have a rare glimpse into his life. I lived in hope of Jane doing the same, but she never did. Somewhat to my chagrin, she'd once informed me that she hadn't bothered to block me on TikTok, because she knew I couldn't use it.

Embarrassingly, she was right. Despite my best efforts to master the app, I ended up defeated every time. Once in a while one of them would send me a TikTok video they thought was 'funny' and I'd finally manage to open it and get the sound on, only to be entirely baffled by what the 'joke' was supposed to be. I had to check myself from taking the last step into Aging Ludditedom and referring to it as 'The TikTok', mainly because every time I nearly called it 'The TikTok' I could already hear my precious moppets' derisive laughter ringing in my ears.

Oh, HAPPY day. Peter had me unblocked. I scrolled hastily, as these opportunities did not last long before he hit the block button again. What was he doing? He was on a beach. That girl's bikini was very skimpy and she'd better hope there were no jellyfish in the sea, as she could be stung somewhere very unpleasant with so little fabric covering her. And, oh, another photo with Miss Jellyfish. What … what was she doing to my darling? Oh, sinful Jezebel! Not, it had to be said, that my darling appeared to be objecting, and possibly, I squinted, may have instigated it.

Who was in this one? My darling Peter and Hannah's Lucas, a child who was practically my own as well, clinking shot glasses. He wasn't a child though, I reminded myself. He was young, and that is what you do when you are young. You kiss unsuitable people wearing insufficient clothing and drink ridiculous things like Aftershock and, what was Peter holding in this photo of Lucas and Toby and him? A roll-up cigarette, I was sure. Terrible that he was smoking, but definitely just a roll-up ciggy. It must be, as didn't they behead people for drugs in Thailand? Or was that the Middle East? Either way, I was sure the authorities would take a very dim view of it. *Was* it a roll-up, though? I screenshot it, and sent it to Hannah and Sam to be sure.

Hannah: Oh God, what are they doing? They're smoking drugs, aren't they? When was this taken? I haven't heard from Lucas in two weeks and I was starting to think he was dead. Maybe he is? Maybe he's in a Thai jail? My baby!

Sam: I'm pretty sure that's just a roll-up.

Ellen: Please tell me it is.

Sam: Yeah, it's definitely a roll-up, chill out, girls.

Hannah: They're in jail, aren't they? That's why we've not heard from them, because they're rotting in a Thai jail. Should we fly out and rescue them?

Sam: If they were in jail, someone would have told us.

Hannah: Do they get a phone call? Like here? Maybe they were too scared to call us, in case we were angry.

Sam: They're British citizens, if they were in jail, the embassy or consulate or something would've been informed, and they would have told us. They're fucking idiots, but they're not in jail.

Ellen: Yet. They're not in jail YET! They could be arrested at any time. What are they thinking, doing DRUGS?

Sam: It's a roll-up. And even if it's not, it's only a spliff. Not a very good one though, hardly worth the trouble of rolling that, if it's not just tobacco. Anyway, cannabis is legal in Thailand, I checked before they went.

Ellen: Is it? But it's a GATEWAY DRUG! I read a Telegraph article about it. They could be opium fiends by now!

Hannah: What IS an opium fiend? How is it better than just being an addict?

Ellen: I don't know.

Sam: I think you're both overreacting, calm down.

Ellen: Our children could be drug fiends and you're telling us to calm down.

Sam: The boys aren't stupid. The photos are all pretty tame, they know better than to put photos of them with drugs or anything else on their socials, give them some credit.

Ellen: True. But they're SMOKING, Sam.

Hannah: Our babies.

Sam: For Christ's sake, we all smoke. You more than any of us Ellen.

Hannah: I don't smoke.

Sam: You always nick a fag off me after the fourth glass of wine.

Hannah: It doesn't count if you're drinking.

Sam: Well, they're drinking.

Ellen: Are you SURE it's only tobacco and not a special cigarette?

Sam: No. How the fuck can I be sure if I'm not there? But it's unlikely. And worst case scenario – youths smoke a joint at a beach party. Didn't either of you try it when you were that age?

...

...

...

...

Ellen: I didn't inhale.

Hannah: It was the NINETIES. It didn't count in the nineties.

Sam: I rest my case. Just try and let them be young, without pushing them away by being neurotic and overprotective, OK?

Hannah: I know, but it's so hard, especially now Lucas has said he's not coming home for Christmas either.

Ellen: Has he definitely decided?

Hannah: Yes, he's going to 'hang' at this party with Peter. And their opium fiend friends no doubt.

Sam: Well, try and look on the positive side my little Mary Whitehouses – at least if your boys are in Thailand, they'll be puking and causing carnage on a beach somewhere, and not over Ellen's sitting room, like last year when Peter persuaded her to have the after-party for the school prom at her house. Because that was fun, wasn't it, Ellen?

Ellen: Ugh. Don't remind me. Do you know, I spent half of tonight reassuring Julia next door that it gets easier as they get older, and now I'm worrying about Peter and drugs and thinking about that night of the party!

Sam: You're welcome. Seriously though, the boys aren't daft, they'll be fine.

Hannah: Oh God, I hope you're right.

Sam: Call it father's intuition.

Hannah: I can't believe I'm going to have go through all this again in fifteen years with Edward.

Sam: Poor you.

Ellen: Maybe he'll be different. Maybe he'll be an angel child, who never wishes to leave his dear mama's side.

Hannah: Ha. What is the emoji for a hollow laugh?

Ellen: I better go. I'm in the bath and the water's gone cold and I've turned into a prune, and I was wrinkled enough to start with.

Sam: What a lovely image.

I got out of the bath and dripped through to the bedroom. Simon was already in bed with Flora.

'She was cold,' he insisted when I raised my eyebrows.

'Do you remember Peter's party, last Christmas?' I asked.

Simon shuddered. 'I try not to. I still sometimes think I can smell gazpacho and Malibu puke in the sitting room on a warm summer's day.'

One year ago

It all started just before Peter's Sixth Form Christmas Prom. For weeks all I'd heard was who was going with who, who was having pre's where, the significance of that in the school social pecking order, and scandalised tales of brutal break-ups only days before the Prom, meaning that the whole pre's system had had to be rejigged to accommodate broken teenage hearts. I still insisted it was the height of laziness that the Youth referred to the gatherings before the dance as 'pre's' and not 'pre-dance drinks', and had also railed hard against the deplorable American tradition of renaming the school Christmas dance the 'Prom', as if we were all in a John Hughes film (though secretly I'd have quite liked to live in a John Hughes film where all teenage angst was solved by a nice frock and a snog with Andrew McCarthy), but my complaints fell on deaf ears, and the pre's and the Prom they remained.

Everything finally seemed to be settling down. Lucy Walker and Dan Letterby had both been suspended over Snapchatting their naked photos of each other to the rest of the year, after Lucy dumped Dan to go to the Prom with Findlay Atherton, and I had mostly been feeling very glad that I was no longer a teenager with the immensely intense and complicated love life that entailed, when two days before the dance (they can call them Proms all they like but they CAN'T MAKE ME, HA), Peter slouched into the sitting room and opened the conversation with a long drawn out 'Muuuuuuuuuum?' There were at least six syllables in that 'Mum' and I instantly tensed, as every mother knows that the more syllables there are when your child says 'Mum', the more outlandish the request to follow will be.

'Yes?' I said warily.

'Well, like, the thing is, Mum, like, you see, like.'

'Peter, spit it out, for Christ's sake. Whatever you're wanting, I'm not going to be more likely to say yes to it the longer I've got to listen to you prevaricate. Also, *please*, must every second word be "like"?'

'It's, like, not, like every *second* word, though, like, is it? You, like, *totally* exaggerate!'

'You've just said "like" *four times*. In five seconds! I'll make a deal with you – if you can put your entire request to me, without using the word "like" one single time, you can have whatever it is that you want.'

Oh, how I'd come to regret that rash offer. It turned out Peter *was* capable of constructing a sentence without using that fucking word, and what he wished to ask his dear and darling aged Mama was whether she'd extend her generous hospitality to hosting the after-party that was supposed to have been at Jake Anderson's, except his parents had peremptorily cancelled it after coming home unexpectedly early from a Christmas night out to find Jake bonking his girlfriend in their bed.

'Which was *totally* unfair, because Jake doesn't even have a double bed, and they were being *safe*, but they're really pissed off and said since Jake does not seem to respect their boundaries, he definitely can't have a gaff, so I thought they could all come here, Mum?'

'What the devil is a "gaff"?' I demanded in confusion. 'I thought you wanted a party? Is it some sort of rave?'

'Oh my God, Mother! A gaff is a party! Like everybody knows that, how sad are you that you don't know that? And like, no one says "rave" anymore?'

'I'm not sad, I can't help it that the Youth wilfully misuse the English language, can I?'

'Like, whatever, but can I, Mum? Please? Can I have a gaff after the Prom?'

I desperately stalled for time, saying, 'I'll have to talk to your father,' and Peter grumbled, 'But you *said*, if I could tell you what I wanted without saying "like" I could have it,' and I countered that I'd thought we were talking about a lift into town, or a ludicrously expensive shirt from Flannels, not to have the whole year back for a massive gaff. (I felt most hip and youthful as I proclaimed the word 'gaff', and also secretly pleased that at least they were mangling *British* English and not using yet another Americanism.)

'It won't be massive,' he pleaded. 'Not everyone goes on to the after-party. Hardly anyone. Come on, Mum, pleeeeease! Everyone's really upset there's no after-party now, and no one else's mum and dad are letting them do it at short notice –'

'Yes, there's probably a reason for that.'

'So it would be super-cool if I was the one who saved the night. Please?'

'I *said*, I'll need to talk to your father.'

The more I thought about it, though, the more I liked the idea. They would be all dressed up from their dance, so the house would be full of glitteringly beautiful girls in evening dresses and handsome boys in dinner jackets, trooping through the door, cheeks pink from dancing so merrily, arriving to sip on … eggnog? Would eggnog be appropriately festive? Perhaps I could organise party games? A jovial round of Blind Man's Bluff or something. I could hear the jolly laughter echoing already.

The delightful children who attended would talk of it for years. 'Of course, this a good Christmas party, but do you remember the party Peter Russell had? That was the best Christmas party ever. His mother Ellen is truly the spirit of Christmas. Even when I'm old and grey, I will remember how joyfully we sang carols round the piano, our clear voices sounding out across the snowy fields, guiding weary travellers home to rest.' Oh yes. I was going to show these callow youths the TRUE meaning of Christmas. Maybe not eggnog. Might be a bit rich, late at night? Perhaps some sort of champagne cocktail? Not too strong, and not champagne either but cheap Prosecco, but the sentiment would be there. Could I persuade Simon into his ancient and possibly slightly mouldy DJ for the occasion? I'd do a supper, of course. A cold buffet, but maybe some kedgeree? I'd need a playlist, obviously, and a new dress, possibly involving taffeta. I do adore taffeta and mourn its loss from modern fashion – the girls of today don't know what they're missing, never having gone out in a frock with a taffeta bow on their bum! Oh yes! It would be glorious, My Vision, of some sort of *fin-de-siècle* Christmas extravaganza crossed with a Roaring Twenties party vibe. By the time I discussed it with Simon it was a done deal, and his objections fell upon deaf ears.

Needless to say, Peter vetoed the carols, the eggnog, the cocktails, the Blind Man's Bluff, the playlist, the true meaning of Christmas and especially the supper, the kedgeree in particular. I tried arguing for the HAPPY MEMORIES these things would create and the joyous tales that would be told by many a fireside in years to come, but he was having absolutely none of it. Meanwhile, Simon vetoed the taffeta dress, crushingly informing me that the nineties would never be *that* back.

I did find it hard to part with at least the cocktail part of my plan, but Peter said it was a Bit Much and also Quite Wanky, and could I not just get a load of Kopparberg and Corona in, like any normal person.

'What about the girls?' I objected.

'Can't they drink the Kopparberg and the beers?'

'I don't know. Jane drinks Kopparberg, but maybe these girls have more sophisticated tastes. Shall I get some gin? They might fancy a G&T.'

'We don't drink gin and tonics, that's for well old people. Just some beers and ciders will be fine. And maybe some vodka. Everyone likes vodka. Oooh, tequila might be good?'

'I'm not getting you vodka – that encourages irresponsible drinking. And definitely not tequila. You're not doing shots.'

'You are, like, sooooo hypocritical. Two minutes ago you were offering gin. Vodka's no stronger than gin. And last week you went out and did shots with Hannah and Sam, and I found you in the kitchen trying to butter a piece of kitchen roll while you wiped down the counter with your toast!'

'That is different.' I attempted a dignified stand. 'I'm an adult.'

'So are we, technically.'

'Yes, but I'm a grown-up. I know what I'm doing and when to stop when it comes to shots.'

'Usually when you fall over,' Peter muttered.

'Anyway, you won't all be eighteen,' I pointed out. 'So I definitely shouldn't be encouraging drinking spirits.'

'Oh chill, *Mother*, it'll be fine. Anyway,' he cunningly tried to change the subject, 'it'll be nice for you and Dad to have, like, a night away, won't it? Where are you going?'

'What? We're not going anywhere, Peter. If you have this party, we're going to be here.'

'But you can't. That's like mega-embarrassing, Mum. No one has their parents at a gaff. That's, like, the whole *point* of a gaff. No parents.'

'I think you'll find it's the other way round, darling. No parents, no gaff! Sorry, but this is non-negotiable.'

Despite Peter's best Kevin the Teenager impression about the ruination of his life, I stood firm. The party was the next day now, so short of cancelling it – and thus being a *total* loser – he had little option but to go along with it.

Simon duly dropped Peter off at Millie Evans house for the pre's and came home to help me prepare for the Gaff. I was enjoying quite a nice glass of red when he returned.

'Do you think that's a good idea?' he said doubtfully. 'I mean, should we be drinking, if we're going to be in charge of other people's children?'

'Well, they keep insisting they're *not* children, so why not? It's only a tiny glass of Rioja, darling. Here, have one, it's jolly nice. I did get some Prosecco for the girls, I thought they might like it. And I'm going to make a fruit cup.'

'Punch?'

'No, a fruit cup.'

'Alcoholic?'

'Only a tiny bit.'

'A tiny bit. A tiny bit alcoholic "fruit cup" is a punch, Ellen. I remember the last time you made punch. In your flat in Edinburgh, not long after we'd started going out. Well, actually I *don't* remember, that's the problem. No one does, everyone was shitfaced in the first ten minutes of getting to the party. Amy Benson was drunk for three days. Andy Stevens snogged a postbox on the way home at 6 a.m., thinking he'd pulled, and then tried to fight a postman he accused of "looking at his bird". We only even know that because Annoying Shelley was out for an early run and saw him and told everyone. Andy had no recollection at all. So I really don't think your "fruit cup" is a good idea.'

'Nonsense,' I told him airily. 'I found a recipe on the internet. It won't be like last time when we just emptied every variety of booze we could find into the washing-up bowl and topped it up with Um Bongo and Capri-Suns.'

'I think Um Bongo's banned now, I'm not sure whether because of the name or the E numbers.'

'Well, it doesn't matter, does it? Because look, I'm using fresh orange juice, pomegranate juice, Malibu and just a hint of vodka, with lovely strawberries and blueberries in it. Oooh, I've got some Cointreau, look, will I put a splash of that in? Nope … it still needs something else … maybe a dash more Malibu? Oh yes, that's *damn* fine, if I do say so myself. And doesn't it look lovely in my punch bowl?'

'Where did that come from?' asked Simon dubiously.

'Home Bargains,' I told him proudly. 'So many bargains for your home that you didn't know you needed!'

'I thought we talked about this? If you didn't *know* you needed something, then you didn't need it, however much of a bargain it was.'

'Oh tish. Anyway, I *did* need a punch bowl, didn't I? Because of the punch. I mean fruit cup. So there!' I responded cheerily. The fruit cup was very cheering, I reflected. And so fruity and healthy. The moppets would be delighted by my cleverness, I decided.

'Oh God, are you getting belligerent already? How much of that have you had?'

'Not belligerent, actually,' I said crossly. 'Just ver' happy with my luffly punchy cup. You should have some. Make you happy too!'

'Oh fuck it, why not?'

After that we had to go for a little nighty bed before the revellers returned at midnight. We woke up on the sofa with very dry mouths as they all came trooping in. I leapt up like a good hostess and began dispensing fruit cup, with a little glass for myself, just on account of the dry mouth. The boys were more interested in beer, but the girls were most thrilled.

'See, darling!' I said to Peter. 'I knew this was a good idea. Gosh, there's a lot of you, aren't there? Is that more people arriving? How many do you think are coming?'

'About, like, a hundred?' said Peter breezily.

'Well, I'd better make some more fruit cup then.'

Alas, I'd forgotten the *exact* recipe for the fruit cup, but I improvised and it was also delicious. I'd run out of strawberries, but I cleverly chopped up a carrot and popped that in. So cunning. No one would notice. Was *practically* a strawberry. Maybe some tomatoes? Tomatoes were a fruit? No, Ellen, I chided myself, that would be *silly*.

The boys had now taken notice of the fact that the pretty pink girly fruit cup was considerably stronger than their beers and had also started knocking it back, so I hastily made a third batch. I had no more fruit juice, but I found some cartons of gazpacho soup at the back of the cupboard. 'Tomato *is* a fruit,' I reminded myself, as I emptied them into the bowl, along with a bottle of vodka, some brandy, a doubtful bottle of port that I also found at the back of the cupboard, and grated some nutmeg on the top, to be 'festive'. There!

I served it up with panache and tottered outside for a lil' cigarette. Half the party was now outside too, and I surveyed them with concern. The girls were all so pretty, lovely things with masses of swishy hair but their dresses were so very small! They would surely all catch a chill on their kidneys, for none of them wore tights. You didn't have that worry with taffeta. Nice an' warm you were with taffeta. Kidneys *quite* safe. I collapsed on the bench outside the back door and lit up. There was a youth there, vaping away. I tutted at him.

'S'very bad for you,' I chided. 'Why you vaping? Smoking s'much better!'

'Are you Peter's mum?'

'Yesh.'

'Can I have a fag then, if you think smoking's better for me than vaping?'

'Fine.'

'Wow. You're really cool, Peter's mum.'

'Why thank you!'

The Youth drained the rest of his fruit cup and squinted at me. 'An' you're hot too. Hey! Pedro!' he bellowed at Peter, who was just coming out the back door with a blonde girl who seemed to have forgotten most of her skirt. I sighed for her kidneys. 'Pedro, you never told us your mum was such a MILF.'

Peter looked distinctly unimpressed with this statement.

'What are you doing, Mother?' he hissed. 'Dad's gone to bed, don't you think you should go too?'

'No, no,' I said sternly, remembering my responsibilities. 'Need to supervise, yeah? Can't go bed!'

'Yeah, Pete, leave your mum,' said my new Youth Friend. 'She's a fucking legend.'

I beamed smugly at Peter. A fucking legend MILF, that was me. Although I should really have been offended by such a sexist objectification, there's something shamefully delightful as a middle-aged woman to realise that perhaps you *do* still have some sort of sex appeal and are more than a dried husk who does the laundry and makes dinner, that you can still cause a stir in a young man's loins. Even if, I thought guiltily, that young man was quite literally young enough to be your son.

'Would you care for another cigarette?' I asked the Youth generously.

'Mum, smoking's bad for you,' grumbled Peter.

'Not as bad as vaping,' I insisted. 'Peter, darling, are you going to introduce your friend to Mummy?'

'This is Poppy,' said Peter miserably.

'Hi, Mrs Russell,' said Poppy.

What a nice polite young lady, I thought, she'd make an excellent future daughter-in-law.

'Are you having a nice time?' I enquired.

'Yeah, *great* party,' enthused Polite Poppy.

'Get you anything? More fruit cup? Perhaps, some shots?' I suggested, ever the good hostess.

'Oooh, *shots*!' Polite Poppy's eyes lit up.

'And you?' I turned to my new bestie, who was happily puffing away on one of my Camel Blues. 'I don't think I caught your name.'

'Aidan,' he grinned, 'but they call me Donkey because –'

'Because he's an ASS!' interrupted a beetroot Peter. 'That's why, no other reason.'

Donkey winked at me. I suspected the other reason, but was too much of a lady to say.

'So, Aidan. Or do you prefer Donkey? Shots?'

'Fuck yeah!'

'Come on then. I hid the tequila in the shed. And the sambuca. Shots are such fun!'

After three shots each in the shed with my new besties Polite Poppy and Donkey, we were back in the house.

Peter had abandoned Poppy at some point and had been last seen heading outside with a brunette with an even skimpier dress on than Poppy. I decided it was probably best if I didn't look for him too hard, lest my delicate maternal sensibilities be offended – just as long as he didn't do anything stupid and cause me to have grandmaternal sensibilities. I'd given him a packet of condoms before the dance, much to his chagrin and embarrassment, as I exhorted to him to remember to be careful, as the alternatives were kids or the clap, and he didn't want either yet. Well, ever, in the case of the clap. It *was* December, though, I reflected and probably therefore too cold outside for there to be any call for such things.

Donkey had taken charge of the music, turned off Peter's carefully chosen cool playlist, and at my behest was playing Blondie at full volume.

'Come and dance, Peter's Mum,' he yelled.

There were many youths dancing now, to my astonishment, as I'd have thought they would have decreed Blondie to be sad old-people's music, but they all seemed to be having a marvellous time.

I'd forgotten how much I loved dancing. We used to dance all the time – Hannah and me, Simon and me, the children and me, when they were little, though their choice in tunage had been dubious but even so, on days when I had to admit it was too wet for the park and I couldn't stand another episode of *Bala-bastarding-mory*, we'd stick the music on and just dance round the sitting room. Once they started school, though, dancing with their mother was not cool anymore. Doing anything with their mother was not cool anymore. So I was astonished and delighted when Peter appeared, minus the brunette, and joined the dancing, with his arm round Polite Poppy.

'Let's have more shots!' shouted Donkey.

'We can't,' I protested. 'We drank it all.'

'I got some,' Donkey revealed proudly, and lurched out the room to return with, of all things, a bottle of Buckfast Tonic Wine.

I looked at it very dubiously.

'No,' I said firmly.

'It's fine, Mum,' said Peter, who appeared to have given up being embarrassed by me and was going for a 'if you can't beat them, join them' approach.

'We do shots of it all the time, it's really nice,' beamed Donkey.

'S'ok, Mrs Russell, it's well lush,' Poppy assured me.

'There you go, Peter's Mum,' said Donkey (I did wish he'd stop calling me 'Peter's Mum', it didn't really fit with my image of being A Fucking Legend MILF to be constantly reminded that I was in fact old enough to be everyone here's mother). 'Get it down you.'

I sniffed it doubtfully. It actually didn't smell as terrible as I'd expected. Sort of aromatic and herbally. After all, I said to myself, it was made by monks. Holy Men of God. Surely it would go against their vows to make something horrible that would kill people? I took a deep breath and knocked it back. It was really very palatable. Donkey insisted we all had to have another one, and Peter grabbed the bottle and thrust it at me.

'Here, Mum, need a photo of you with it!'

Unfortunately, to take the photo, he had to let go of Poppy, who had been clinging to him rather precariously, and now she developed a distinct list to starboard.

'Are you all right, Poppy?' I asked anxiously.

'S'fine,' she mumbled. 'I jus' feel lil bit –' She retched alarmingly.

'DON'T PANIC!' I yelled, panicking about my carpets. 'I'm on it!' I grabbed the punchbowl and flung the contents out the window. This would have been an excellent plan, if only the windows had been open. Still, I reasoned, better gazpacho up the walls *before* it had seen the inside of Poppy's stomach than *after*.

'Hold her hair,' I ordered Donkey, as I proffered the punch bowl in the nick of time and Poppy heaved mightily into it. Peter regarded the scene with some dismay.

'Thanks, Mum,' he said furiously. 'I was in there.'

'Well, I hope you don't think you are now, she's in no fit state for anything.'

'Obviously not!'

'Peter's Mum?' piped up a pea-green Donkey. 'Peter's Mum, I don' feel ver' well either.'

'Oh Christ!' I couldn't move as I was still holding the punch bowl under Poppy, who continued to do an excellent re-enactment of the eruption of Mount Vesuvius in the medium of Malibu and strawberries. 'Peter, get him outside! Outside now!'

Peter grabbed Donkey and flung him out the French windows into the garden. Unlike his mother, he had the foresight to open them first.

'Sorry,' whimpered Poppy. 'I's been bit sick. I go ni'night now.'

'Nooooo!' I howled as Poppy curled up on the floor. 'You can't go to sleep here, darling. Up. Up! Come on, hey YOU!' I grabbed a large passing youth. 'Help me with Poppy, she can go to bed in my daughter's room. PETER! Come and help too, Donkey will be fine in the lavender.'

'Where does she live?' I demanded of Peter, who didn't look too clever himself but insisted it was just all the sicky sick making him feel sick.

'Her mum and dad are away, and she was meant to be staying at Maisie's, with Olivia and Ruby.'

'Well, find Maisie and tell her Poppy's staying here now, and make it clear that she's staying in *Jane's* room, OK?'

I put Poppy to bed, propped on her side in the recovery position with many pillows and realised she was absolutely comatose. I had possibly been irresponsible enough for one evening, I decided, and I'd have to stay with Poppy and make sure she was OK.

She was firmly wedged in for now, though, so I dashed downstairs where the last stragglers were leaving, reassured Maisie that Poppy was fine and that I'd stay with her, received abject apologies from Donkey's father, who was attempting to load his son into the car as Donkey kept shouting, 'Peter's Mum's a fucking legend, Dad, a fucking legend MILF,' and he hissed, 'Just get in and shut up, Aidan, for Christ's sake.'

'I FUCKIN' LOVE YOU, PETER'S MUM,' bellowed Donkey, as his father slammed the door in relief and scuttled round to the driver's side, saying, 'I am *so* sorry, Mrs Russell, I don't know how he got himself in such a state or thought it was appropriate to use language like that!'

I went back inside with a dejected Peter, to find various other teenagers sprawled asleep over the furniture.

'Their taxi cancelled,' Peter explained. 'So I said they could stay.'

'Right,' I said, removing a still-full can of lager from the hand of one sweetly slumbering oaf and a vape from between the lips of another. 'Well, I don't think we could wake them up, even if we wanted to.'

'Is Poppy OK?'

'Yes, she'll be fine. Hungover, probably, but she'll be fine. Though you weren't that concerned about Poppy when I saw you going outside with that other girl?'

'Oh that was nothing. That's just Lola. She fancies Donkey, and I fancy Poppy, and we were just trying to make them both jealous since they were more interested in doing shots with you.'

'Cockblocked by your own mother,' I said.

'What?'

'Nothing, darling. I'm glad to hear you weren't doing anything with Lola. That is very bad form, two girls in one night.'

'Well, so's giving the girl I was trying to get off with shots and ruining my chances with her!'

'I didn't do it on purpose. Anyway, I need to go and check on her.'

After a fairly sleepless night on Jane's floor, waking with a jolt every twenty minutes or so to check Poppy hadn't moved and was still breathing, I tottered downstairs at 9 a.m. when I heard Simon get up, having reassured myself that Poppy was now just sleeping and not paralytically comatose.

I found him in the sitting room, looking at the recumbent bodies and gazpacho-splattered walls in dismay.

'What the hell happened, Ellen? Was there some sort of *massacre*? Is that blood? Are they *dead*?' he whispered in horror.

'No, gazpacho and no.'

'Gazpacho? Why is there gazpacho all over the walls and windows and curtains?'

'I ran out of fruit juice,' I explained.

'And this?' Simon picked up an empty tequila bottle. 'I thought you said there were to be no shots.'

I looked at it. 'That's not even mine,' I said indignantly. 'I couldn't be everywhere at once, and you'd gone to bed and abandoned me.'

'I took the dogs; they were getting overexcited. Also, after two glasses of that punch, I was buggered, and it was bed or pass out on the sofa surrounded by the Youth!'

'It's not that bad,' I said doubtfully, looking round. 'I mean, a good Hoover will sort it.'

'Burning the house down would sort it!' said Simon grimly. 'I told you this was a bad idea. And I told you the punch was a really *really* bad idea.'

Peter staggered into the sitting room at this moment and looked around. 'Shit. It's a bit of a mess, isn't it? But thank you. It was a really great party, and everyone had an amazing time. You're both legends, 'specially you, Mum.'

I smirked at Simon. 'See? How is bringing festive joy to our son and the younger generation a bad idea?'

'Someone's been sick under the Christmas tree,' Simon announced.

'Fuck. Right, well, let's start clearing up. These oafs can wake up and help, for a start,' I said, gesturing at the happily sleeping teens draped over every available surface. 'COME ON! WAKE UP! There'll be bacon sandwiches for everyone who helps!'

The Youth turned out to be quite amenable to assisting once they were conscious, and the tidying up was going nicely, though it was unfortunate that someone had also been sick in the boots that Simon had left in the hall – he took that quite badly. About an hour into Operation Clear-Up, a sheepish Donkey knocked on the front door, clutching some drooping petrol station flowers.

'My dad said I was a bit much last night, Peter's Mum, so I've come to apologise and help with the mess. These are for you!' he said, thrusting the dying chrysanthemums at me.

'Thank you, Aidan,' I said graciously (I couldn't call him Donkey in the cold light of day). 'You can call me Ellen, you know. You don't have to refer to me as Peter's Mum.'

Donkey's face lit up. 'Can I? Thanks, Ellen. What can I do?'

'Who is that callow youth following you round with a stupid expression on his face?' Simon demanded shortly afterwards.

'Oh, that's just Donkey,' I whispered. 'I think he's got a tiny crush on me.'

'What? That's not appropriate. Are you going to go all Mrs Robinson on me?'

'Of course not. It's just a crush, kids get them all the time. Anyway, I've made him clean the downstairs loo, which was in an awful state, so I don't think the crush will last. Oh God, who is that at the door now?'

It turned out to be a furious Jane, who'd got a lift home from university a day early instead of getting the train the next day as we'd arranged, and had left her house keys in Edinburgh. This was supposed to have been a lovely surprise for us, but Jane was highly unamused to find that we had let Peter have a massive party, which of course was Not Fair as *she* had never had a party like that, and worse, that Poppy was still sleeping happily in her bed.

'Honestly Mother, I've only gone to university and you're letting my room out to strangers,' she shouted. 'And not only did *he* get to have a party, but he gets to have girls stay over? You never let me have boys to stay when I was at school. He might have done it in *my* bed. Oh God, I feel sick. You'll have to burn the bed.'

I attempted to soothe Jane by pointing out that Poppy spending one night in her room was hardly 'letting it out to strangers', and also that Peter had most certainly had no shenanigans going on with Poppy due to the state of her as well as me having to sleep in there with her, while Peter shouted that what boy would want to shag Jane anyway and she yelled her favourite insult that he was to 'die in a hole'. Donkey came out of the downstairs loo to see what all the fuss was about and gazed in open-mouthed awe at the bellowing Jane.

'Pedro, mate!' he said. 'Who the fuck is this?'

'My stupid sister.'

'She's PROPER fit. Like even fitter than your mum. I'm Donkey.'

'Fuck off, Donkey,' said Jane in disgust.

'I'm definitely in there,' beamed Donkey, trailing after Jane, the devoted love light in his eyes that so recently had shone for me being shamelessly transferred with the fickleness of youth.

'Happy now?' I said to Simon. 'There'll be no chance of Mrs Robinsoning!'

'Do you think we'll ever get the smell out the house?' he asked anxiously.

'Which one? The sick, the Malibu, the gazpacho, the Lynx Africa, the aftershave, the perfume, or the stench of rampant and frustrated pheromones?'

'All of them. The curtains are definitely ruined.'

'So's my Home Bargains punchbowl. I can never use it again after Poppy puked in it.'

'Oh well, at least Jane's home, which is nice, and Peter's happy,' Simon sighed, as we heard Jane from the kitchen shrieking, 'Peter, tell your weird fucking sex-pest mate to FUCK OFF, all right,' and Peter screamed back that he wished Jane had never come home and a sleepy Poppy stumbled down the stairs looking mortified.

'They're all in the kitchen.' I pointed her through, wishing I still had the cast-iron constitution of eighteen-year-olds, which enables them to still look gorgeous even when they've puked their guts up and are wearing last night's dress with mascara halfway down their cheeks. Further anarchy broke out with Poppy's arrival in the kitchen, because as far as we could work out from the screaming, Jane had taken it upon herself to strike a blow against the patriarchy by warning Poppy that her loser brother was a twat and to steer well clear.

Donkey meanwhile turned up love struck on the doorstep every day that Jane was home, apart from Christmas Day. Jane ignored him resolutely, but it turned out Donkey was a far more obliging soul than either of my children or their other friends, so I made shameless use of him to take the bins out, feed the chickens, help me take the tree down, and do other jobs my own children deemed beneath them unless I nagged and shouted. I rather missed him when Jane went back to Edinburgh. Possibly more than I missed Jane. And with neither of the children home this year, I'd definitely have no Dogsbody Donkey, either.

Present day

'God,' I said to Simon as I got ready for bed. 'We were really quite lucky with Peter's party.'

'How?' said Simon, looking at me in horror.

'Well, Dad always said the mark of a good party is a divorce, a fight and an unplanned pregnancy. There were no fights, I did think for a minute you might divorce me over the gazpacho, but luckily you saw the funny side, and how we avoided an unplanned pregnancy with all those drunk, randy teenagers around, I don't know!'

'Can you imagine?' groaned Simon. 'Especially if Peter was involved. I'm *not* ready to be a grandfather, so no unplanned pregnancies here, please!'

I'd just started brushing my teeth and I froze.

'What?' said Simon in alarm. 'Ellen, what's wrong?'

I spat in the sink and dashed back to the bedroom to dig out my phone and count back the weeks. Six weeks. More than six weeks since my last period finished.

'Ellen?' said Simon again, following me through.

'Count,' I said desperately. 'Tell me how many weeks it is between now and October 24th.'

'Nearly seven,' said Simon. 'Why?'

'That's when my last period was,' I wailed.

'But didn't you notice you'd missed one?' said Simon in horror. 'I thought you had one of those period tracker apps?'

'I did, but I deleted it because I read about how it sends all your data to tampon companies and stuff so they can bombard you with adverts at the right time of the month, and I've been so busy, I didn't even notice I'd missed one, and now I'm late *again*. And now I come to think of it, my boobs are sore. And I feel a bit sick.'

'Are you sure you're not talking yourself into the other symptoms?' said Simon anxiously. 'You never mentioned anything about sore tits, and you had a lot of wine and a lot of dinner for someone who feels sick.'

'I don't know.' I shook my head. 'I don't know. But what if I *am*, Simon? What if I'm pregnant?'

'Surely not? At your age? You're on HRT. You've got a bloody coil!'

'An unbloody coil,' I said grimly. 'It happens. You can still get pregnant with a coil. You can still get pregnant on HRT, though it's not terribly recommended, and a few women still get pregnant well into their fifties!'

'Really?'

We stared at each other for a long moment.

'Maybe it wouldn't be so bad,' I said hopefully. 'We'd know what we were doing this time. Oh just think, this time next year we could be having Christmas with a tiny new baby. Baby's First Christmas. Again.'

Simon was ashen. 'No. No, we've done Baby's First Christmas. Twice. This is our time. We're past all that, we're too old. You'd be like that woman you thought was the granny at Baby Music who turned out to the mother. If thirty is classed as a geriatric mother, what would they call you?'

'Experienced? Mature? I don't know. We could make this work.'

'How? This is a disaster; how will we make it work? We'll be dead by the time it's eighteen.'

'No, we won't.'

'We will, we'll be dead with stress and exhaustion,' Simon insisted. 'We barely coped the first time round.'

'Yes,' I breathed. 'But this will be different. We've more time, more money. Like I said, we'd know what we were doing.'

Inside, as the initial shock wore off, I thought, 'It's another chance. A chance to put right all the mistakes.' A chance to be a relaxed, chilled-out mummy, who bakes and laughs and doesn't shout because they've broken the eggs all over the floor instead of in the bowl. I could learn to like Play-Doh. We'd do crafts, and I'd proudly stick up their potato-print pictures over the kitchen instead of putting them in the bin and claiming I'd filed them in a special drawer to keep forever. I could buy teeny tiny outfits and marvel at little shoes, and if it was a girl, maybe we could wear matching, impractical, white cheesecloth dresses to stand barefoot together in golden Instagrammable fields, which was something Jane had been very resistant to, but I could get this baby Instagram-ready from birth!

I'd always regretted missing out on the phase on Facebook where every bloody smug mummy seemed to be photographing her darlings dressed in floaty white clothes, ethereally backlit in some kind of delightful meadow. Naturally, mine refused to comply, and my attempts at meadow-frolicking resulted in Jane breaking out into a hideous rash from some kind of pesticide and Peter falling face first smack into a cow pat. Why were there no cow pats and no DDT in everyone else's meadows? Of course, even before that, they'd been arguing and screaming at each other and refusing to hold hands for my perfect picture to post with the obligatory #HappyMemories. But this time it would be different. Already, I could feel a sticky little hand slipping into mine, a tired head heavy on my shoulder, as we wafted home from the cornfield. This time I damn well *would* enjoy it, and #TreasureEveryMoment.

'Simon?' I looked at him, pleading.

'Ellen, I'm not discussing anything until we know for sure. This could be something and nothing. Don't you have any tests left?'

'I don't know. I've not had a scare in so long. I'll look in the bathroom.'

I found an ancient packet at the back of the cupboard, and to my astonishment, they were still in date – well, as good as, dated November this year.

I went back through to the bedroom.

'I found some.' I held them out to Simon.

'Well, they're not much use to me,' he pointed out. 'Don't you think you should do one?'

'Will you come with me?'

'Of course.'

Simon whistled and looked the other way while I peed on the stick, and then we sat down to wait. There are no minutes so long as those spent waiting to see how many lines show up on a little piss-covered stick. Oh, but just imagine, a little stocking hanging over the mantelpiece next year, and yes, either a tiny velvet dress, or a little bow tie and pretend suit to dress Baba in. I wouldn't eat all the pies when pregnant this time, and next Christmas I'd have my figure back and be radiant, as I tossed my hair, still thick and shiny with pregnancy hormones because I'd take ALL the supplements so it didn't go dry and frizzy and fall out, yes, I'd toss my shiny shiny hair, while bouncing the baby on my hip and laughing merrily about oh yes, how *easy* it is third time round, you really know what you're doing and the baby just slots into your life.

I could get one of those backpack thingamajigs, and Simon could carry the baby as we crunched across frosty fields etc, etc, while the bells rang out and then I might get a sheepskin rug for the baby to lie on in front of the fire on Christmas Eve for those all-important Instagram photos. Judgy had pissed on the last sheepskin rug I'd tried putting in front of the fire, but surely even he wouldn't piss on a baby? He had peed on Peter, several times, but Peter had retaliated by trying to pee on him right back, so that was just about even stevens. I'd appeal to Judgy's better nature. Maybe he'd lie on the rug with the baby, and the photos would be so adorable they'd go viral and I'd become an Instagram influencer for later-in-life mothers. What could I call myself? 'MatureMama'? Balls, that was taken. What about 'MatureMumma', much though I loathed the word 'Mumma'? Oh God, that was a sex account! Nooo! Well, I could give the name more than three minutes' thought later on anyway.

Simon meanwhile paced up and down anxiously, while I scrolled through Instagram for the perfect name for my new career. He stopped mid-pace and gave me an anxious look.

'It'll be OK,' he said, only hyperventilating slightly. 'Whatever it says, it'll be OK. We'll make it work.'

Finally, my phone pinged with the timer and I looked at the test. One line.

'Shit,' said Simon.

'For Christ's sake,' I said. 'How many of these have we done over the years? You never remember that's only the line that says the test has worked. It's saying I'm *not* pregnant.' I felt an unexpected wave of sadness wash over me, but I wasn't sure if it was for my lost youth now my womb was barren and dry, or the Instagrammable baby.

'WOOOOHOOOOOO!' yelled Simon punching the air. 'THANK THE FUCKING LORD. OH JOY OF JOYS, we have a dodged a fucking BULLET, sweetheart! But hang on.' He paused suddenly. 'What if it's wrong? Is there another one in the box? Quick, do it too, make sure!'

'I don't know if I have enough wee left,' I protested.

'Oh come on, Ellen, you always need a wee. There hasn't been one single moment since I met you when you didn't need a wee – you can squeeze something out.'

'OK. I'll try.' I sat down again and concentrated very hard. Maybe the test *was* wrong. There was still hope. 'There. Done.'

The test was not wrong. I wasn't pregnant. When Simon finally stopped dancing round the bathroom and singing 'The Hallelujah Chorus', he saw my face.

'What's the matter?' he said. 'Aren't you pleased? You didn't really want to be pregnant, did you? You hated being pregnant, and you were very firm after Peter was born that you didn't want any more children because you wouldn't cope. Christ, every time you had a false alarm after that because you forgot to take your Pill or whatever you were more horrified than I was!'

'I know,' I said. 'I *know*. But that was then. I didn't have the time or energy for another child, I couldn't have coped. But now they're grown up and they don't need me, and I don't know what I'm going to do with myself, it just felt like another chance. To make everything right. To make it *perfect*.' And Instagrammable, I added under my breath.

'To make what right?'

'All the things I got wrong. All the times I was snappy, all the times I was tired and impatient, all the times I lied about what time it was to make them go to bed, all the times I was a mad, overbearing witch, which is why Jane isn't speaking to me and probably never will again. It was a chance to change all that. And now my chance has gone, and all I have in its place is my withering womb.'

'Oh Ellen. You're hardly withering. And another baby wouldn't have changed any of that. You can't change the past. This is our time now, Ellen, our chance to do all the things we've always wanted to.'

'Like what?'

'Um, travel!'

'That's what everyone says. But you hate people and you hate travelling. You're worse than me when it comes to being like Uncle Matthew in *The Pursuit of Love*, when he says, "Abroad is utterly bloody and all foreigners are fiends."'

'He has a point.'

'So what will we do?'

'I don't know. We'll find something. We'll take up gardening, or feng shui.'

'Feng shui?'

'Yes, you know, that exercise thingy where they all stand about under trees deep breathing and waving their arms about,' Simon explained helpfully.

'That's tai chi.'

'Oh. What's feng shui then?'

'Furniture arranging. Well, it's a bit more complicated than that.'

'Maybe not that then. But you're right, we've spent so long as parents we've forgotten who *we* are, and now we get a chance to find out.'

'What if we don't like who are? What if we never find out who we are again and we just drift through the rest of our lives in some sort of anonymous limbo, like … like ectoplasm or something?'

'Ectoplasm? What do you mean?'

'Just like sort of formless and meh. What if we have no personalities left beyond being parents? Or we do, but we're awful people? Or worse, what if only *one* of us is awful? At least if we were both awful, we'd be awful together and so maybe we wouldn't notice. And worst of worst, what if the awful one of us is SO awful they actually think they are the good one, and the good one is awful? WHAT ARE WE GOING TO DO, SIMON? WHAT? WHAT WILL BECOME OF US?'

Simon bent down, pulled me up off the bathroom floor and wiped my face. 'Stop worrying. For starters, come to bed. If you're not pregnant, we can start finding out who we are right now. And don't worry, if you turn out to be awful, I'll tell you. Obviously, *I* am not going to be the awful one. But we've spent twenty years waiting to have time for ourselves, we need to make the most of it, instead of dwelling on what might have been and looking back with rose-tinted glasses.'

Wednesday 13 December

I feel the need to start panicking. But with only Simon and me for Christmas, what is there to panic about? The children want money, and I've got their stocking stuff, such as it is – mostly sweets and socks, since I've wasted so much money on 'fun' stocking fillers over the years, the larger share of which I found stuffed unused under their beds when I gutted their rooms after they left home, or in cupboards still ungifted as I'd put them away 'safely' and forgotten about them. I've bought and wrapped Simon's present, as our tradition seems to be that I just get him a new fleece every year, which I say is a soulless present and he says is an excellent tradition. Ditto scarves for my mother and Sylvia, and port for Michael and Geoffrey, and we agreed to stop buying presents for our siblings and their offspring years ago, a decision Louisa was rather reluctant to agree to – despite her insistence that material possessions mean nothing to her – since her six children meant her side of the family did rather well out of presents.

Nonetheless, it seems most unnatural to have Christmas approaching and not be panicking about presents. Panicking about getting the perfect Christmas presents for people is what I *do*. It is my favourite December hobby, along with drinking

Baileys, of course. I have spent years wasting time studying gift guides in weekend papers and glossy magazines, trying to make sure I give everyone a suitably on-trend gifting experience each year. What is it with those guides? Every year it's the same thing. 'For her' – it's cream or pink cashmere socks/scarves/hats, posh bubble bath, probably with glitter in it, obscenely expensive face cream, pink travel mugs saying something feminist or something about gin, handbags, some kind of birthstone jewellery, posh gin, probably also with glitter in it, and 'amusing' signs/books about gin.

'For him' – now he gets more Manly colours for his cashmere socks/scarves and hats, and beard oil instead of bubble bath, a wide variety of random objects such as iPad chargers and travel mugs, but inexplicably made of leather, so they are Manly and Luxurious, something knife-based, possibly in a leather holder, so Manly, whisky and/or anything 'whisky flavoured' and amusing books/signs about golf.

Your precious moppets – what's for them? Ah yes. While adults get cashmere socks, children get vile tufty nylon affairs in lurid colours with terrifying faces on them that somehow also cost the same as the bastarding cashmere socks, quite quite horrid fleeces made of the same flammable tufty nylon, any shit with unicorns on for girls and stuff about science for boys, because duh, girls like unicorns and boys like science but it's not *sexist* because remember the girls can grow up to be given a glittery pink travel mug with 'Slay the Patriarchy' on it to drink their fluffy hot chocolate ladies' drinks from, while the men drink Manly Coffee from their Manly Leather Travel Mug, before oiling their beards and licking whisky off their knives, while their silly wives neck pink glittery gin in a pink bubble bath and think pretty fucking glittery pink thoughts about FUCKING KITTENS! Oh, and somewhere on the list of presents 'For Children' some bright spark will also have suggested a 'must-have' stylus or something for the newest iPad, costing approximately the GDP of Luxembourg, JUST FOR THE STYLUS, BUT IT IS BLUETOOTH, AND MADE OUT OF POLAR BEARS' TOENAIL CLIPPINGS SO ECO AND SUSTAINABLE AND 0.5% OF PROFITS GO TO REPLANTING THE RAINFORESTS SO TOTALLY WORTH IT, UNLESS YOU WANT THE POLAR BEARS AND THE SLOTHS TO DIE. Do you? Do you want them to die? Because they will, unless you buy this for your child. It's a ludicrous price? Fine, just order them a cheap generic one from Amazon then, YOU SLOTH-KILLING BASTARD.

I think what enrages me most about the annual gift guides is the fact that I fell for them for so many years. Every shiny magazine would proclaim they had 'The Perfect Gifts for Her'. '50 Manly Gifts for Under £50' another would promise, which merely meant that everything cost £49.99. And then there's 'Stocking Fillers They Will Love' – when I was a child, 'stocking fillers' meant a Terry's Chocolate Orange and crap like yoyos and maybe scented felt-tip pens. Now, 'stocking fillers' encompass things like Dior bloody lipsticks and solid-silver handbag mirrors. And even advent calendars, once a shitty piece of cardboard with tiny impossible-to-open doors hiding a bad drawing of a depressed robin, later upgraded to contain a small piece of greasy cheap chocolate, have gone mad and now come from Liberty and Space NK and Diptyque and cost ludicrous sums of money, and I'm definitely not just bitter about this because I really want a Liberty one and yet cannot justify £250 for an ADVENT CALENDAR!

The whole thing is spiralling out of control, and every year I vow that, actually, I'm not buying *any* presents, and instead I'm going to *make* gifts for people – thoughtful, loving gifts, that will show them how much I care, and instead of contributing to evil capitalism and consumerism, and feeling guilty and broke, everyone will feel a warm glow of joy, including the bloody polar bears. Well, maybe not a warm glow for the polar bears, that would defeat the purpose. But anyway, it will be good for the polar bears, and good for our souls and spirits. And then, I remember the year I tried this, and how it turned out.

Fourteen years ago

It was the year after the James Incident, Jane was six going on sixteen, and Peter was four and thought farting was the funniest thing in the world (he still does). It's probably fair to say that it was also the year I was looking for distractions and ways to be a better wife and mother, instead of a Shameless Jezebel, to somehow make it up to Simon and the children for considering abandoning them, even briefly, for a roll in the hay with a weak-chinned golfer. I thought perhaps if I was never going to manage to be a highbrow literary cultured person, I could be a domestic goddess, Nigella-style, instead.

Being a domestic goddess turned out to be quite hard work, though, especially making marmalade, which I thought would be a delightful activity involving the children wrapped in big aprons standing at the stove laughing and stirring, but turned out to mainly be about a vat of sullenly boiling orange goo that tasted of bitter disappointment and burnt sugar. I was not daunted, however, remembering that the 'true success is to labour', and so I was delighted when I stumbled across an old copy of Fanny and

Johnnie Cradock's *Coping with Christmas* in a charity shop, and I pounced on it with glee! It was originally published in the 1960s, but still, I thought – an entire book devoted to *coping* with Christmas, the very title accepting that it was a stressful time and something to be *coped* with, despite every other publication ever attempting to sell you that magical myth that I'd so bought into lock, stock and barrel. Oh ho! I thought. You can bugger off, Nigella, you fibber, and *Good Housekeeping* and *Country Living* and Jamie and even dear St Delia, with your LIES about making Christmas effortless. If Christmas were effortless, the period between Christmas and New Year would not be the busiest time of year for divorce lawyers. No, lovely Fanny was where it was at – Christmas is to be *coped* with, not breezed through without breaking a sweat or turning a hair, and this book – this would show me how to do that coping so I didn't have a breakdown on Christmas Eve and run to the garage to rock and cry with a bottle of Baileys, for I'd be BLOODY COPING!

Fanny gave a detailed rundown month by month of the year's activities in order to Cope. I quickly realised I'd fallen at the first hurdle, for I had not spent January making my Christmas puddings or Christmas cakes (both were plural, though no explanation offered as to why multiple puddings and cakes were required, or why they must be made a year in advance, right when everyone was sick of the sight of Christmas cake and pudding). Nor had I hoarded old nylon stockings to make 'swags' and crucially, oh laggard delinquent that I am, to use Fanny's expression, I had failed to plant my potatoes in February to be ready for Christmas dinner. But all was not lost! There were many preparations to be made in June! I could not make the muscat jelly, whatever that happened to be, using my gooseberry thinnings (again, so delinquent), but behold! Fanny had a delightful recipe to *make your own Christmas pot pourri*. Could anything be more fucking festive than homemade Christmas pot pourri, instead of buying it from Home Bargains and having Simon complaining over the entire festive period that there was a 'funny smell, like something died'?

The first line of instructions should have given me pause for thought. The rose petals had to be collected in the morning sun, but *after* the dew had dried. I wondered if the phase of the moon mattered, or only morning sun and dried dew? Then all manner of complex procedures had to be done to the rose petals involving things I'd never heard of, but this, after all, is why the internet was invented, so I duly sent off for powdered orris root, storax (I had no idea what it was, and only after lengthy arguings with Google about how I wanted to make pot pourri and not buy shelving units did it turn out to be some sort of resin) and oil of bergamot. In fact, between the orris root, the storax, the many different essentials oils and the other plants I had to buy in order to also pick their bastarding petals by the full moon when Mercury was rising to add to the pot pourri, it was starting to make the £330 pot pourri I had goggled at on the Petersham Nurseries website look rather economical. But, I reasoned, labouring I bloody well was, and you could not put a price on the time, love and effort that had gone into the pot pourri, and that – that was what I'd truly be giving people. Fanny turned out to be rather obsessed with the pot pourri, continuing the instructions through the year, insisting each month that you must 'keep the pot pourri mixture going'. But how? Motivational pep talks? Some kind of pot pourri Couch to 5K equivalent? How *do* you 'keep it going'? I put it in the cupboard and decided it probably just needed to mature a bit and would be a fragrant joy come the merry Yuletide.

I had no walnuts to gather to save from the squirrels nor the inclination to cure hams as soon as the weather was cool enough, and, delightful though the book was, I was starting to feel dubious about how freezing runner beans and making chocolate swans and royal icing penguins was really going to help me *cope* with Christmas. I did, however, take their advice to 'gather fir cones for home-made decorations', and felt most smug about this forward planning, even if I did put them in the garage and promptly forget about them.

And then, in early October, Louisa derailed all my smug plans for the Perfect Christmas, before I'd even had a chance to make the bastarding chocolate swans, by issuing the Great Invitation. She decreed that to celebrate the birth of her latest moon child, whose name she was not revealing yet, we were all to come to the Holistic Retreat in Scotland that Bardo had started and that they both insisted was a viable business model despite all evidence to the contrary, and we were to spend Christmas with them. I was doubtful as to the wisdom of this plan, but Sylvia and Michael were also bidden and had already agreed to go, and as Simon pointed out, it *was* his parents turn to see the children this Christmas, and my father and his latest wife had spent the previous Christmas with us, and so we really should go.

'But I had it all planned,' I wailed to Simon. 'I was going to make a centrepiece in the shape of a pineapple out of chrysanthemums.'

'Why?' he asked in confusion.

'Because FANNY SAID SO! I've made prunes in port wine.'

'That sounds disgusting.'

'They're festive. I've been planning for months, and now Louisa is spoiling it all!'

'Come on, Ellen, you might enjoy it – I'm sure the prunes will keep till next year, and if you're that set on a pineapple made of chrysanthemums, I'm sure you can make one for Louisa's table, and you won't have to cook or anything. In fact, you can have a year off. You and Mum can both have a year off, won't that be nice? You'll be able to spend lots of time together, which I think would be really good for you both.'

'Nice,' I agreed faintly. The idea of leaving Fanny's disapproval over my uncured hams and blatant lack of coping, not to mention the fact I hadn't even attempted Home Made Worcestershire Sauce like the LAGGARD DELINQUENT I so clearly was, was rather appealing, though. I'd become morbidly obsessed by the book and more convinced with each passing day that if I'd only gained permission to glean wild chestnuts to make my own *marrons glacés*, not to mention making my own candied fruits, maraschino cherries and ham frills from tissue paper to decorate the non-existent hams that I hadn't cured, then finally, I'd have the perfect Christmas and I'd *cope*! But if we went away to Louisa's, then I could stop lying awake at night resolving that the very next day, however shattered I was after work, however obstreperous the children were, however tiresome Simon was, I'd *definitely* overhaul all Christmas emergency stores (WHAT Christmas emergency stores? What? Tins of peaches and extra batteries and bottled water, like the doomsday preppers who anticipate the end of the world? Or emergency presents for those neighbours you hardly know who annoyingly decide to give you a gift after the shops have closed on Christmas Eve? Or emergency marzipan fruits, JUST IN CASE?), and make lists of the Main Perishable and non-Perishable Goods. Not to mention finishing buying stamps before post office queues develop, even though I had long since stopped sending Christmas cards on the basis that life was too short (Fanny was very firm about the need for stamps, and the dire situations that an inadequate stamp supply may cause to arise). And yet, despite the long lists of things dear Fanny still decreed I must do, I'd never been so ready for Christmas, nor, I feared, would I ever be again, and now Louisa was spoiling all this for me, and the emergency Christmas stores would *never* be overhauled. But Simon was looking at me very hopefully, and this was clearly important to him, and I was resolved to try to be nicer to him if possible, so perhaps the list of Non-Perishable Goods would have to wait.

'OK,' I said, mustering enthusiasm from somewhere dark and obscure. 'Let's do it!'

'Really?'

'Yeah. What's the worst that can happen?'

For fuck's sake. Will I ever learn to stop making stupid statements like that?

We drove for what felt like endless hours to Louisa and Bardo's Holistic Retreat, with a six-year-old Jane and four-year-old Peter in the back of Simon's Audi asking incessantly if we were there yet, and announcing that actually yes, they really *did* need another wee, as Simon hissed that I should stop giving them drinks and then he wouldn't have to keep stopping, and I hissed back that I wasn't fucking dehydrating my children just for his convenience, and I lobbed bag after bag of crisps and sweets into the back seat, while lamenting to myself that perhaps now I should never get the opportunity to make forcemeat baby ducks to decorate my Christmas dinner, and denied that anyone felt sick, telling them firmly it was all in their mind, and attempted to strip down and wash a screaming Jane in Tebay services after Peter puked over her following his enthusiastic consumption of jelly babies in my desperate attempt to shut them up for just *five* minutes. There were endless games of I Spy, games where I seriously started to doubt my children's intellect and whether Peter would ever learn to read or even just master the alphabet, or actually, I'd settle just for them grasping the *concept* of I Spy, which is that you have to be able to *see* the object you spy with your little bastarding eye, after we'd spent forty-five minutes guessing something beginning with 'J', only for Peter to finally blithely inform us that it was in fact 'Scorpion'. When I shouted that you had to be able to see it so we stood a chance of guessing it, he claimed he could 'see it in my head'. So, then we tried The Minister's Cat, which ended abruptly on round two with Jane – I had started nicely with 'The Minister's Cat is an aggravating cat', only for Jane to counter with 'The Minister's Cat is a bastarding aggravating cat'. I thought it best to stop before we got to Peter and the letter C, lest he suddenly reveal he did in fact know the alphabet, and some interesting words beginning with 'C'.

Simon was outraged by Jane's language and demanded to know where she had learnt such words, to which I hastily countered it must be from 'rough children at school' before Jane could sweetly inform her father that Mummy had called the man who cut her up on a roundabout a bastarding son of a whore the previous day, and Simon chuntered she had better not sully Sylvia's sainted ears with such profanity, and I suggested a silence competition, prizes to be announced.

Oh, hallelujah. It worked. There was silence. Golden, blissful silence. Why hadn't I tried this somewhere around Birmingham? Finally, I was *nailing* parenting.

'Mummy,' piped Peter five minutes later.

'I win!' screeched Jane. 'You talked first, I win!'

'That's not fair! Not fair. Why does she win? I was quiet.' Peter burst into tears, sobbing hopelessly about the inequities of his life.

'Because you TALKED FIRST, so I win. Because you're so stupid, you're a stupid baby poo head who can't even do a *silence* competition!' Jane taunted him, completely unmoved by her little brother's distress.

'I AM NOT A STUPID BABY POOHEAD!' roared Peter, and whacked Jane in the face with the large digger he had insisted he couldn't travel without. Jane started screaming too – 'HE HIT ME! HE HIIIIIIT MEEEEEE! MY FAAAAACE! HEEEEE HIIIIIIIIT MEEEEEEE! MUMMMMMMMEEEEEEE!'

'Not a POOHEAD! Not a BAAAAAYBEEEEE!' howled Peter.

'I can't seeeeeeee,' wailed Jane. There was a bruise forming under her eye already.

'For CHRIST'S SAKE,' yelled Simon, veering onto the hard shoulder and stopping the car. The children continued to howl and scream furiously as I got out the car and attempted to calm them down, and ascertain if Jane was blinded, concussed or merely maimed, by the medium of holding up the remnants of the jelly babies and asking how many there were and getting her to follow them with her eyes as I moved them about, while she wept loudly and furiously, and Peter also wept and demanded jelly babies and I told him he was not getting anything for being a bad boy and hitting his sister, and I searched in vain for something use as an icepack on Jane and settled for a baby wipe, hoping against hope that the magic clean-all/cure-all effect of baby wipes would come through for me. I was pleading with Jane to just hold the baby wipe on her face, and telling Peter in no uncertain terms to shut up, while pointing out to Simon that he could also intervene and help referee, and that if we were at home I'd in fact right now be making a rosemary kissing bough, not attempting to heal my maimed children with baby wipes because he'd insisted on packing my first aid kit right at the bottom of the boot, and Simon snapped that he was doing the *driving* and needed to concentrate, and I pointed out that he wasn't actually fucking driving right now, though, was he, so maybe he could help, when the police car pulled up behind us.

'Oh Christ,' I said in despair, surveying my battered, sticky, sobbing children.

'Fuck my life,' said Simon. 'Fucking fuck my actual fucking life.'

'Afternoon,' said one of the officers. 'Why have we stopped? Emergency? Breakdown?'

'Um … emergency?' Simon offered weakly, over the shrieking banshees in the back.

'And what would be the nature of the emergency,' enquired the police officer. 'Given that stopping on the hard shoulder can be liable to up to a £5,000 fine and nine points on your licence?'

'Medical emergency?' attempted Simon. 'My daughter said she was going blind.'

'And *was* she?'

'I don't think so.'

'So *not* a medical emergency then?'

'Well, no, but I didn't know that when she said she was going blind, did I?' Simon rationalised.

'Hmmm,' said the police officer, in doubtful tones. 'I think I'd better have a look at the children. Make sure they're OK. If you could stand aside, madam.'

He peered into the car, a sobbing Jane with a baby wipe pressed to her cheek and a still-wailing Peter, repeating his mantra of unfairness.

'What's this then, young lady?' he asked gesturing at the baby wipe, and looking horrified when Jane removed it to reveal a quite impressive shiner.

'He hiiiiiiit me,' quavered Jane. 'I didn't even do anything and he hiiiiiiit meeeeeee, because he is horrible.'

'I see,' said the officer grimly.

'I AM NOT HORRIBLE! AND I AM NOT A POO POO HEAD LIKE YOU SAID AND I AM NOT A BABY,' bellowed Peter. 'An' I'm GLAD I hit you because it's NOT FAIR that you got a jelly baby and MY DIDN'T.'

Jane's response to this was to lunge across the car and wrest the digger from Peter and wallop him soundly over the head with it. Peter redoubled his roars and Jane continued screeching.

'Jesus,' said the police officer. 'Are they always like this?'

'Yes,' I said. 'Always.'

'Right. Well. Technically, you know, this isn't an emergency. And you shouldn't have stopped. It's extremely dangerous to stop on the hard shoulder.'

'I know, I know,' said Simon earnestly.

'However, this time, I think we won't take it any further. It's Christmas after all, and you seem to have your hands full. Don't stop again, unless it's a genuine emergency, please. You're putting everyone in a lot of danger.'

'I won't, thank you, Merry Christmas, officer, no more hard shoulders for me, say bye bye to the nice policeman, children,' gabbled Simon in relief as I got back in the car.

Once Simon had pulled back into the traffic amid much swearing and I'd dispensed the last of the jelly babies to shut the children up and attempted to inspect the large egg now forming on Peter's head, assuring myself the lump was a good sign that any swelling was going outwards and not in towards his brain, and reflecting that Peter was never going to master I-Spy if Jane didn't give up her habit of inflicting blows to his skull, Simon sighed and shook his head.

'Pity,' he said. 'That's why he let us off. Pity, because our children are so feral.'

'They aren't feral,' I objected. 'They're just expressing some big feelings because they too wanted to see the chrysanthemum pineapple. And he let us off because it's Christmas. Spirit of the season and all that. And it was probably nearly time to get back for his tea break or something, and he couldn't be bothered with the paperwork.'

'No. It was pity. That is what the children have reduced us to. Strangers pity us, because they are so awful.'

'They're not awful. They're just ... spirited. Anyway, I bet they're a sight more civilised than Louisa's children. Shortly, ours shall be delightful paragons of virtue compared with her wolf pack!'

'How many does she have now?'

'I think this is the fourth. Maybe the fifth? I can't keep up.'

'Four or five,' Simon shuddered. 'Imagine *them* – doubled. Why?'

'I assume she enjoys pregnancy and childbirth more than me. Maybe she doesn't puke her guts up quite so much. And maybe she also enjoys the actual child-rearing bit more than we do. It seems to be more of an endurance competition at the moment, rather than bringing much active joy, despite everyone telling me to treasure every moment, and that they're not little long and I'll miss these days when they're gone.'

'Will we? Will we really miss being pitied by police officers, and every long journey being accompanied by a faint whiff of jelly baby vomit?'

'Unlikely,' I sighed.

Predictably, having valiantly fought sleep and each other for the whole journey, both children fell asleep twenty minutes from Louisa and Bardo's. Despite Louisa's twitterings about their 'ain wee heilan' hame' in a worse Scottish accent than Christopher Lambert in *Highlander*, they actually only lived about half an hour north of Glasgow. I was grumbling about this as we pulled up.

'I'm just *saying*, Simon, I'm sure I saw somewhere that Stirling is the Gateway to the Highlands, and they're not even as far north as that, so how *can* it be the Highlands?'

'Don't be pedantic, Ellen.'

'I'm *not* being pedantic. I'm just *saying*, it's not the Highlands. She just *says* that to make it sound more remote and romantic, when really, she's perfectly close to civilisation and just chooses to live in squalor in the woods, when she could have a normal life. But that wouldn't get enough attention, would it?'

'Please, Ellen. Let's just *try* to have a nice family Christmas, OK? Without arguing over geography.'

'She bangs on about foraging and getting back to nature, but she's got a mini M&S ten minutes down the road. And I'm *not* arguing, I'm JUST SAYING!'

Simon sighed. 'It occurs to me sometimes, darling, that I can see where our beloved cherubs get their argumentative streaks from.'

'I'm NOT arguing. I'm simply stating facts. How is that arguing? Oh God, is this it? Are we here? What the fuck is that? Is it … is it a Wicker Man? Surely not? Who are they going to burn?

Oh fuck, do you think they're going to burn me, for telling Louisa she should really give gas and air a go? Ooooh, maybe they're going to burn your mother?' I brightened up somewhat at this thought.

'Don't be ridiculous, Ellen. They're vegans now, remember. I doubt human sacrifice is permitted for vegans!'

'Oh, I suppose so,' I said in disappointment.

Sylvia and Michael came rushing out as we pulled up, Sylvia draped in an even more extravagant number of scarves than usual, for reasons I was quickly to learn were more practical than aesthetic. Michael too, always stoutly betweeded, appeared to be wearing TWO tweed jackets and a waistcoat.

'Keep your coat on, and whatever you do, don't touch the parsnip wine,' he murmured as he hugged me hello.

'Louisa can't come out, she's breastfeeding,' shuddered Sylvia.

'And Bardo is off in his man yurt, apparently consulting his spirit guide about the festivities,' Michael said, his tone making it clear what he thought of Bardo's spirit guide.

'He did ask me to join him,' Michael added. 'But sadly I had to plead a prior engagement. He said you're welcome to join in too, Simon. Just you, Bardo and an ancient Native American chief who comes to speak to him in his dreams. Funny, isn't it, how these spirits of ancient Native American chiefs have nothing better to do than come to speak to over-privileged, middle-class white men. Every hippy fucker has his ancient chief – always a chief too, never some poor bugger who had to pick up the buffalo poo or something, is it? Same as all these people who discover who they were in a past life – always Catherine the Great or Julius Caesar. I met a woman who claimed she'd been Catherine the Great at a party last week, and I said marvellous, maybe she could finally definitively answer the question about whether or not she had shagged a horse. She was a bit shirty with me.'

'Michael,' implored Sylvia. 'Not in front of the children.'

'They're asleep,' I said. 'We're going to have to wake them up, sorry, it's probably going to be hideous.'

Sylvia shuddered again. 'I doubt it can be any worse than their cousins. We'd better go in, before we get any colder standing out here.'

'Er, Sylvia? Before we go in, what exactly *is* that?' I gestured to the Wicker Man standing guard over the cluster of yurts.

'Don't,' Sylvia whimpered. 'Just don't. You'll need to ask Louisa.'

The children took being woken up in a strange, cold, dark place remarkably well, and seemed to have forgotten their earlier enmity. Sylvia peered at them in horror.

'What's happened to them?' she gasped. 'They look like something out of an NSPCC advert.'

'It was a long journey,' I said defensively, though Sylvia had a point. Between Jane's black eye and the egg on Peter's forehead, and the fact that both children were now distinctly sticky and a layer of grime seemed to have then coated the stickiness, there was a definite hint of urchin about them both. I wondered if the police officer would have been so understanding had Simon not been driving such a middle-class car.

'Well, let's get them inside,' Sylvia said. 'To be honest, they'll fit right in here.'

I wasn't sure what she meant, until she ushered us into the largest yurt. There seemed to be small, fat, grubby children everywhere, though on closer inspection they weren't fat, just bundled into many layers. This was understandable, as the yurt was freezing, and dimly lit, with a wood-burning stove sulking at one end, which didn't seem to be doing much except encouraging the pot sat atop it to belch forth a rancid smell. At least, I hoped the smell was coming from the pot. One could never quite be sure with Louisa and Bardo. On the other hand, maybe it was better if the smell *wasn't* the pot, as it was the only thing that suggested there might be some dinner materialising. In the centre of the yurt there appeared to be a large heap of hairy-looking blankets. As we stood there, our eyes adjusting to the gloom (and the smell), the blankets began to heave.

'Christ, is it a rat? Keep the kids away, I'll find something to hit it with,' yelled Simon, grabbing a ukulele, of all things, that was lying in the middle of the floor and brandishing it as menacingly as it is possible to brandish a ukulele.

'What are you doing with Cedric's lute, Simon?' shrieked the blankets, as Louisa's head appeared over the top of them.

'God almighty, Louisa, it's *you* under there,' said Simon furiously. 'I thought it was a rat.'

'It's too cold for rats,' said Sylvia dolefully. 'Even they have probably abandoned us.'

'Are you *still* going on about how cold it, Mother?' demanded Louisa. 'I've told you, overheating is bad for you. You just need to wrap up warm and embrace the cold; it's a much healthier way to live.'

Sylvia shivered again and I attempted to change the subject by asking Louisa what the Wicker Man was for.

'That's for our Naming Ceremony for the baby and the Christmas Eve surprise,' said Louisa conspiratorially. A hairy, bearded figure appeared in the doorway. 'Oh Bardo! There you are, how did your session go?'

'Great,' said Bardo. 'Chief Hawkeye brought me many messages from beyond.' Bardo's pupils looked decidedly peculiar, so I suspected he'd had a little chemical assistance to commune with his chief.

Before Bardo could elaborate further, I thought I'd better try to get us unpacked and settle in.

'Er, Lou ... Amaris? Where are we sleeping?'

'Oh, we've put you all in the best guest yurt. You'll love it!' said Louisa enthusiastically.

'The best yurt. Gosh,' said Simon. 'What about Mum and Dad?'

'We're not staying *here*,' Sylvia said in surprise. 'We're booked into the B&B down the road.'

The best guest yurt was a freezing goaty-smelling tent affair. There was no electricity in it, as the solar panels only provided enough for the main yurt (and I suspected, the 'organic hemp farm' Bardo kept casually mentioning), where, it turned out, Louisa and Bardo and all the children slept, ate and lived.

'All part of our commitment to being 100 per cent off grid and self-sufficient,' said Bardo cheerfully, handing us a box of Waitrose candles and a plastic lighter.

'Right,' Simon said. 'Er, Bardo, I can't help but notice there's only one bed. Where are the kids to sleep?'

'Don't they just sleep in with you?' said Bardo in confusion. 'That's what our kids do. Lovely and cosy, everyone cuddled up together. Anyway, I'll leave you guys to get settled, then dinner shouldn't be long, so come back over to the main yurt and have a glass of wine once you're ready.'

I began to hyperventilate. Bugger the chrysanthemum pineapple, there was no evidence of Christmas here at all.

Jane started crying. 'I don't like it here, Mummy. It's cold and dark and smelly. I want to go home, and it's not Christmassy, not like at home.'

'Wanna go home,' Peter sobbed in solidarity. I was tempted to join them.

I turned to the children and tried to smile brightly. 'Nonsense, darlings, this is an adventure,' I said. 'Think of it like camping!'

'I hate camping,' wailed Jane. In fairness to her, I also loathe camping.

'Not camping then. Definitely an adventure, poppet. Like the Famous Five!'

'Are there going to be smugglers?' whimpered Jane.

'No! Of course not. All right, not the Famous Five. Um. Like *The Railway Children*. Remember when they move to the country and it's all cold and dark and there's no supper and they don't know where anything is? And then they make the best of it, and end up having a lovely time and lots of fun.'

'*The Railway Children* is a rubbish book,' said Jane dolefully.

'Rubbish,' Peter echoed. 'Rubbish, rubbish, rubbish.'

'I haven't even read you *The Railway Children*, Peter, so how do you know it's rubbish?' I snapped.

'Jane says,' Peter insisted obstinately, now apparently regarding his sister as the oracle of everything.

'Well, tough. It's actually a very good book, so that shows what the pair of you know, and what we're going to do now is MAKE THE BEST OF THINGS, aren't we, Simon?' I appealed as he came in from the car with our bags.

'Well, we can try,' he said doubtfully.

'We will. We're not going to be beaten by a bloody yurt. Where's our *esprit de corps*, our Blitz spirit? Come on, it's an adventure, and we're jolly well going to have FUN!'

We'd have more fun, I thought, once I'd taken stock of our supplies. I rifled through the bags and noted with relief I had of course brought the full first aid kit, and had perspicaciously added two extra bottles of TCP and a multipack of baby wipes. There was also a bag of 'sundries' I'd insisted to Simon he fitted in 'just in case', and I had, at the last moment, flung Fanny in my bag, lest more coping was required than I could manage on my own.

Bardo was at least dispensing glasses of cheer as we dutifully returned to the main yurt for dinner. I took a large and much needed gulp, before I remembered Michael's warning about the parsnip wine. Oh God. It was vile.

'Nice, eh, Ellen,' grinned Bardo. 'We make it ourselves, obviously. Out of the water we boil the parsnips in. Nothing is wasted here. And we culture our own yeast for it.'

I could well believe they were culturing all sorts of things in the yurt, looking at the state of Bardo's fingernails.

'Come on, Ellen, drink up!' said Bardo, nudging my elbow and forcing me to take another mouthful of the dishwater parsnip hell brew. 'That's better. Let me top you up before dinner,' and before I could stop him he had refilled my glass from a filthy demijohn that appeared to be stoppered with a rag. 'Don't be shy, we've plenty of it. Michael, Sylvia, are you *sure* I can't tempt you?'

Michael and Sylvia, who had somehow managed to be drinking a nice-looking red from a normal bottle, shook their heads firmly and murmured concerns about not wanting Bardo to run short.

Simon meanwhile had declined the wine and said something about he had brought some beer. Bardo, though, was having none of that, and relieved Simon of his carefully chosen beers, tucked them away in a cupboard and handed him a glass of foaming sludge instead. 'Mushroom mead,' he said proudly. 'All foraged ourselves.'

Simon was sipping at it tentatively, but had cheered up considerably after a couple of mouthfuls.

'Right,' said Bardo. 'Dinner!'

He filled up his glass from the demijohn again, tottered over to the stove and lifted the lid of the pot of noxious doom.

'Mmmmm,' he said. 'Doesn't that smell good? Parsnip and cabbage stew, lovely.'

Louisa apparently would be eating in bed, but Bardo directed the rest of us to sit at the table, which was in fact a collection of planks roughly nailed together and balanced on some cable reels.

'I made it,' said Bardo proudly, gesturing to his 'table'. The chairs were more cable reels.

'I found them,' he said with equal pride.

Bardo sat down and filled his glass from the demijohn again. 'Why is no one eating?' he demanded. 'Everything in this meal was grown right here at the retreat. It has literally zero food miles.'

It could have been the most gourmet meal in the world, but I still wouldn't have been able to take a bite, because the parsnip wine was doing something unspeakable to my insides. I dared not add any cabbage or more parsnips to the mix. Was I the only one affected?

Right on cue, Bardo let out an enormous fart.

'The wine,' he beamed. 'One of its benefits. Flatulence is such a wonderful detoxifying mechanism.'

Simon meanwhile had finished his entire glass of mead and was now staring into his bowl in wonderment.

'The colours,' he breathed. 'They're astonishing.'

I looked into the bowl of murk. There were no discernible colours in it. What was he talking about?

'And the lights. It's amazing. It's all amazing. Look at my hand. My hand, I've never really looked at my hand before. Look at it. It's so … handy.' He held his hand up before his face and waved it around. 'Oh!' he gasped, wiggling his fingers. 'Oh, incredible.'

'Simon?' I said uncertainly. 'Simon, are you OK?'

'I have the most amazing hands,' he announced, standing up and waving them over his head as he continued to gaze at them. 'Why have I never seen how astounding my hands are?' He started to dance, humming gently to himself.

'Bardo, what was in that mead?' Michael demanded.

'Just some mushrooms we foraged and then we brewed up, man.'

'*Just* some mushrooms? What *sort* of mushrooms?'

'All sorts. That's the point of foraging – you use what you find, yeah? So the mead's slightly different each time, and this is a new batch, so I suppose it's *possible* I might have accidentally added some special mushrooms,' Bardo speculated.

'Right. Marvellous,' said Michael. 'You've got my only son completely off his tits on magic mushrooms!'

Simon continued to dance happily around the room. Jane started whining about how hungry she was and how horrible the stew was. Peter followed her lead. I took another slug of parsnip wine and thought I could always blame Bardo for the farting. I decided the lecture that would doubtless follow would be less painful than enduring my children's wails and handed them the emergency Frubes from my ever-present snack bag.

One of the other children, I thought it might be Coventina, stared enviously at the sight of my children sucking down that sugary dairy chemical goodness out of its toxic plastic wrapping, and I feared she was poised to spring. Louisa was delivering the inevitable spiel about how I was poisoning my children when Cedric fortunately provided a distraction by announcing he'd play his lute for us, and picked up the ukulele.

'No,' snarled Coventina. 'Your lute is stupid. You are stupid. Your face is stupid.'

Cedric broke the ukulele over her head and she launched herself at him.

'Never mind,' said Bardo. 'I can easily make another one.'

Neither Louisa nor Bardo seemed to have noticed that one of the other smaller children had collected the empty Frubes wrappers and scuttled into a corner where they were frantically licking them. Michael was sitting with his head in his hands and Sylvia appeared to having a quiet attack of the vapours. Simon was still dancing happily round the room, and Jane and Peter, satiated with processed yoghurt, were investigating a spinning top, having clearly decided to get on as there was safety in numbers while Coventina and Cedric were about.

I stared around the bleak yurt in despair. I'd planned for holly bell pulls and fir cone garlands and perhaps a delicious spread of hors d'oeuvres, but instead I was shivering in some kind of medieval hovel, with a spaced-out husband and traumatised children and not a hint of festive cheer to be seen beyond the foully bubbling demijohn of parsnip wine. I took another gulp anyway.

Bardo suddenly sprang to his feet. He'd topped up his parsnip wine intake with a couple of mugs of the mushroom mead, having seen its effect on Simon, who was now sitting cross legged in the corner, whispering earnestly to a discarded apple core he'd found on the floor.

'I've just had a revelation from Chief Hawkeye,' Bardo declared, swaying alarmingly. He steadied himself against the table and farted again. 'We should take Simon out to the lodge for a regression right now. Hawkeye says he has messages for Simon and he feels Simon is very receptive to hearing him just now.'

'I bet,' I muttered. I could just guess the messages 'Hawkeye' would be relaying to a 'receptive' (i.e. 'susceptible') Simon, messages no doubt relating to how Simon should invest our meagre savings in Bardo's 'organic hemp farm', which I assumed to be a socially acceptable way of saying his cannabis side-line.

'Come on, man.' Bardo attempted to haul Simon to his feet.

Simon shook his head. 'Not goin' anywhere without my friend,' he said, pointing to the apple core.

'Sure man, bring it with you.' Bardo picked up the core and put it in his pocket, and Simon got obediently to his feet.

'Right,' Michael stepped in, 'I think the only place Simon needs to be going is bed.'

'The wheels on the bus go round and round, round and round, round and round,' sang Simon, before collapsing on the floor again in a heap and giggling uncontrollably, then curling up in a ball and falling instantly asleep.

All attempts to rouse him were in vain. The closest to a response we got was a murmur that the driver on the bus goes toot toot toot, and in the end we flung a blanket over him and left him there. Michael and Sylvia announced that they were returning to the B&B, and faced with the prospect of spending the evening with Bardo, who was completely off his tits and still wittering about Hawkeye, and Louisa, who was offering to give me a blow-by-blow account of her latest 'birth journey' ('it was my biggest mucus plug yet, even bigger than the one I had with Nissien. We filmed it, do you want to see!') and the feral children, who were still roaming with no sign of going to bed, I decided that cold, dark and dank though the 'best guest yurt' might be, it was still the better option.

I collected my children with hissed promises of the iPad in the yurt, and we all huddled into the one bed together, snuggled up for warmth, still fully dressed and in hats and extra socks. Jane still smelled quite strongly of sick and Peter was stickier than ever, but it was actually quite nice, with a candle burning by the bed, and telling them stories because alas, my iPad promises had turned out to be false and it was out of charge. I did wonder how Simon was going to fit in the bed too for the next two nights, and concluded I might just have to get him out of his face on mushroom mead and leave him in the main yurt again. It was only 8 p.m. I closed my eyes and thought of my bag of Sundries.

Since we'd gone to bed so early, we were awake super-early the next morning too, though my sleep had been fitful with children kicking me on both sides.

There appeared to be activity in the main yurt, and we went in to find an ashen-faced Simon slumped in a chair by the wood burner with a mug of something green and swamp like. Various children were wandering around gnawing grey slabs that might be bread, and Louisa, obviously, was in bed.

'Morning, Ellen,' she called brightly. 'Do you want tea? Bardo gave Simon some before he went out.'

'What sort of tea?' I asked suspiciously. 'Is it safe?'

'Dandelion tea, apparently,' Simon mumbled. 'What happened last night? I don't remember anything.'

'Bardo accidently put magic mushrooms in his mead and you got completely out of your head, danced around for a while, talked to an apple core, sang "The Wheels on the Bus" and fell asleep.'

'Oh. That would entirely account for why it feels like a badger shat in my mouth,' Simon sighed.

'What's the plan for today, Lou?' he called over to the bed.

'Amaris,' she corrected him huffily. 'Well, Mum and Dad are apparently going last-minute Christmas shopping in Glasgow, and Bardo is preparing for the Surprise tonight.'

'And what about you?' poor Simon enquired innocently.

'What about me? Simon, I'm *breastfeeding*,' Louisa roared indignantly. 'Isn't that enough? I am nurturing life, what more do you want me to do?'

'I dunno, maybe some washing-up?' muttered Simon. 'Nothing, nothing, I didn't say anything.'

'Why don't you and Ellen take the children for a walk in the woods?' Louisa suggested.

That did indeed sound quite a nice and wholesome festive activity, even if it would be more a case of squelching through mud than frolicking through frosty fields. I duly bundled up Peter and Jane, and started cajoling them out the door, when Louisa shrieked, 'Where are you going? You've forgotten the children.'

'No, they're right here,' I said, gesturing to Peter and Jane.

'Not them, the others. I meant take ALL the children.' Louisa extended a grubby arm from her blankets to gesture to the Wolf Pack, lurking feral and sullen around the yurt.

'What, *all* of them?' asked Simon feebly.

'Yes,' Louisa insisted. 'It will be a wonderful chance for you all to get to know each other.'

* * *

We set off, and at the edge of the woods I was struck by a splendid idea.

'Hang on, Simon,' I shouted. 'I just need to get something. You, Coventina, is it? Does Mummy have any big baskets? Go and get one.'

I dashed back to rummage in my bag of sundries, as Coventina appeared with a large wicker basket I was fairly sure had last been seen as part of an autumn rustic tableau in Sylvia's conservatory, and I declared us ready for the adventure.

We returned two hours later, muddy, rosy-cheeked and with Sylvia's rustic basket filled to the brim. I returned all the children to the yurt, quite proud I'd come back with the same number I'd set out with and only three of them had fallen in a stream (including Peter, obviously, but as the washing facilities at the retreat were quite primitive, I consoled myself that at least he'd now be marginally less sticky).

'Louisa, I mean Amaris,' I said bravely, approaching the bed, proffering the basket. 'Would you mind if I just decorated the yurt a bit? Made it a bit more Christmassy? For the children,' I added hastily. *Obviously* it was for the children, and definitely not for me.

'With what?' Louisa demanded.

'These!' I said, hauling out holly boughs and ivy and many many fir cones, and right at the bottom, next to the secateurs I'd packed in the bag of Sundries, 'just in case', was Fanny, with firm instructions for those holly bell pulls and fir cone garlands.

'All right,' said Louisa grudgingly. 'I suppose the Goddess will enjoy you decorating with her bounty to honour her. But no plastic!'

'Of course not,' I said soothingly. The large roll of 'stout wire' Fanny had decreed essential for making decorations most certainly wasn't plastic. Well, maybe just a very little bit plastic-covered, but it was green plastic, so Louisa would never know.

Aided by Fanny, the wire roll and a large packet of Poundland cable ties, which again I reasoned Louisa would never notice, I set the children and Simon to work. There was still no sign of Bardo, who was apparently 'preparing' for the Surprise later, but Louisa gestured to some more of the greyish bread and some jam if anyone wanted lunch. It was quite gritty jam, but practically Cordon Bleu by the standard of catering at the retreat.

We had just finished when a taxi deposited Sylvia and Michael outside, who had obviously combined their Christmas shopping with a very good lunch. They tottered in, and Sylvia stopped in the doorway and clapped her hands in wonder.

'Good Lord,' she said in astonishment. 'It's like in *A Little Princess* when Sara wakes up and her bleak attic room has been transformed in the night. What happened?'

I beamed with pride. Surely there was no greater compliment from Sylvia, as the only thing I felt we had in common was our longing to inspire a love of classic children's literature in Peter and Jane.

'It was nothing,' I murmured, looking round the yurt in satisfaction. I had perhaps not quite achieved the twinkling magic of Ty'r Ywen, but the grimy walls were covered in holly, bright with berries, ivy garlands and fir boughs. The children had made fir cone wreaths that hung from the branches I had cable tied to the yurt supports, and I'd even mastered Fanny's 'holly bell pulls', which were sort of long hanging holly garland-type things. Simon had become restless after about twenty minutes of this wholesome festive activity, so I'd dispatched him to the nearest Sainsbury's with instructions to buy all the candles he could find and just bloody well tell Louisa they were beeswax if she asked, with the result that instead of the single bare bulb that had dangled, bleakly casting a cold, feeble light over the yurt, candles glowed on every surface, wedged into various chunks of wood I had gouged holes in and wreathed in more greenery. I couldn't suppress the notion that Fanny, and Granny Green, would have been proud of me.

'It's all the Goddess's doing,' announced Louisa from her bed. 'She gives her bounty and creates beauty wherever we worship her. This all represents fertility, you know.'

Bollocks was it fuck all to do with Louisa's sodding Goddess, or fertility. It was bloody hard work by me, six small children and £43 worth of candles from Sainsbury's, which Simon was still complaining about – 'I never imagined when you told me to buy all the candles that candles cost so much. I nearly had a heart attack when I got to the check-out.' However, in the spirit of *Christmas* – and *magic*, which was clearly what all this really represented – I was prepared to let it go.

'All we need is a tree,' sighed Sylvia.

'We're not having a tree,' insisted Louisa. 'We're having a much more ancient celebration of the dying year and the return of the light. Oh, here you are, Bardo. Are you ready?'

'Wooh!' said Bardo, staggering into the yurt, eyes wide and pupils dilated. 'Am I like majorly tripping? What happened here?'

'Oh, just a little festive cheer,' I said modestly.

'Cool. Cool. Yeah, Amaris, we're all set. Guys, you ready?'

I wasn't sure what we were supposed to be ready for, but we all nodded assent.

'Come on then, out we go,' cried Bardo.

'Hang on till I get ready!' grumbled Louisa, and she heaved

herself and the baby from her bed and draped herself in some sort of long white robe.

'What is that?' I asked in horror.

'My High Priestess robe, obviously. What did you think it was?'

'Nothing,' I said hastily, banishing images of burning crosses from my mind.

'Come on,' said Bardo. 'We'll explain it all to you outside.'

'I'll just put the candles out,' I said. 'Safety first.'

Outside it was cold and damp and dark, and I saw that Bardo had also donned a long white robe like Louisa's. Bardo announced they would hold the Naming Ceremony first, and then the Surprise would come after. We all gathered in a circle and Louisa stood in the middle, holding the baby up like Simba at the start of *The Lion King*. The rest of us shuffled awkwardly, unsure what we were supposed to do. Suddenly Bardo let out a roar.

'WE SUMMON THE GODDESS TO NAME THIS CHILD!' he bellowed. 'Come to us, come and gift us the name for this child!'

Louisa swayed and made moaning noises with her eyes shut. There was a strong chance the baby would be dropped in the mud before the poor mite even got a name. Louisa snapped her eyes open and gave out a screech.

'THE GODDESS HAS COME TO ME! SHE HAS GIVEN ME THE NAME! The child is to be called … OILELL! Meaning a mythical queen. She shall be strong and independent, and the Goddess has given the gift of music with the name. Bardo, the sacred smoke!'

Bardo sparked up a massive joint (with another plastic lighter, naturally) and ambled into the centre of the circle to blow smoke over the baby while intoning 'Oilell' as Louisa had several large puffs of the 'sacred smoke' too.

'Join in, all of you. Let the Goddess know we have seen her gift!' called Louisa to the rest of us.

'Oilell,' we muttered dutifully.

'And now we will begin the Solstice Ritual!' Louisa shrieked. 'Here, Ellen, you can hold Oilell while I take part in the ritual,' and she thrust the squawking bundle at me. To my surprise, when I saw Oilell close up, she was not a newborn as I'd assumed from Louisa's insistence on staying in bed 'for the breastfeeding' but in fact a fairly hefty beast of around four months. Had Louisa *really* spent the last *four months* lying in bed claiming she couldn't do anything because she was feeding Oilell? It was hardly surprising Bardo was talking to Hawkeye and the children appeared to be auditioning for a junior version of the Hunger Games. I was torn between criticism of her laziness and admiration for her getting away with it. No wonder she was constantly having babies if she got to sit on her arse and do nothing for months on end!

Bardo now led us over to the Wicker Man under the trees and held up his arms.

'This is the Sacred Ceremony of Sacrifice to the Goddess,' he intoned. 'The eternal mother. The divine womb that brings light into the darkest nights. We ask the Goddess to accept our offerings and bring forth the spring again.'

'You're vegans, how can you sacrifice things? Doesn't that go against your beliefs?' demanded Michael. 'What are you sacrificing anyway? A goat? A chicken? Oh no, not one of the *children*. I'm warning you, I'll call the police.'

'Of course I'm not sacrificing one of the children,' snapped Bardo. 'What do you take me for? And not all sacrifices are blood sacrifices, you know? We are sacrificing nuts and berries we gathered in the autumn, by burning them in the holy structure I built, which represents the sacrifice of my labour to the Goddess.'

'We're also sacrificing my placenta,' Louisa reminded him. 'We put it in here after it detached from Oilell, a week after she was born. So it is a *bit* of a blood sacrifice, and it will please the Goddess to have the sacred essence of woman dedicated to her!'

Sylvia opened her mouth and closed it again. Louisa's rotting placenta from Oilell's not-so-recent birth explained the strange smell round the Wicker Man, which I'd unfairly blamed Oilell's nappy for.

Louisa and Bardo stood each side of the Wicker Man, and raised their arms and began to chant.

'Please tell me someone else is seeing what I see,' Michael muttered. Louisa glared at him. The chanting increased in intensity until they both pulled out more plastic lighters from under their robes ('I thought plastic was evil and forbidden?' Simon whispered to me), lit some bundles of dried grass that been placed beside the Wicker Man and hurled them into the structure, before carrying on chanting loudly. The grass burned merrily for a minute and then went out.

Louisa and Bardo stopped chanting and regarded the slightly smoky Wicker Man in exasperation.

'I *told* you we should've put paraffin on it,' said Louisa.

'We don't need paraffin,' insisted Bardo. 'I've carefully constructed the sacrifices in the optimal way to light. We'll try again. Maybe we didn't chant enough?'

'I'm going to get the paraffin.' Louisa marched off towards another shed in the clearing and Bardo continued his chanting, but louder this time, before flinging another bundle of grass into the Wicker Man, just as Louisa reappeared with a plastic jerry can and doused the Wicker Man in several litres of paraffin.

'There,' she said with satisfaction. 'Now *that's* a fire for the Goddess to be proud of!'

'Form a circle,' ordered Bardo. 'Everyone join hands.'

We looked at each other in horror, but Louisa and Bardo were insistent. We shuffled into a circle around the Wicker Man and reluctantly clasped hands. Bardo was holding one of my hands and caressing it disconcertingly with his thumb. He leered at me in the firelight as he announced, 'Now we ask the Goddess for her blessings for the coming year, and tell her what we want her to provide for us.'

'You could ask for a potent man, Ellen,' he breathed hotly in my ear, his damp beard tickling my cheek in a most unpleasant way. I inadvertently glanced down and noticed a definite tent effect to his robe. I handed him Oilell, but he continued to stand too close to me.

'Now we dance,' Louisa shrieked, beginning to galumph around the Wicker Man, Simon clutched in one hand, Cedric in the other. I took the opportunity provided by the dancing to stamp on Bardo's foot quite hard.

'So sorry,' I said sweetly. I was satisfied to see the tent subside a little.

Louisa suddenly stopped dancing and gave a tortured ululating cry.

'O Goddess, hear our prayers,' Louisa shouted. 'Bless our harvests, bless our wombs, bless our seeds, come on everyone, join in! Bless our harvest, bless our wombs, bless our seeds.'

Louisa and Bardo kept chanting this, as the rest of us mumbled something incoherent and stared at the ground until with a final shriek Louisa cried, 'Bless our harvests, bless our wombs, bless our seeds, even the barren wombs of Ellen and my mother, bless them and make them fruitful, bless the seeds of my brother and my father and my lover. Make me fruitful again, O Mother Goddess, we pray the parsnips will be fruitful also!'

'Make my seed potent,' cried Bardo. 'O Mother Goddess, bless me and let me fill Amaris's womb with my seed, make it strong and make it virile. Chief Hawkeye, are you there? What do you want to say? Hawkeye says bless the organic hemp farm, let it be fruitful also as it is truly an excellent business plan.'

'Come on,' said Louisa impatiently. 'The rest of you can ask the Goddess for blessings now too. This is a sacred night, ask for your heart's desire!'

A shallow part of me wondered if the Goddess would heed my pleas for a Mulberry Bayswater bag if I asked very nicely indeed.

'Someone!' insisted Louisa. 'The Goddess will feel slighted if we reject her munificence.'

'I'd like a new car,' announced Simon. 'A new BMW, please.'

'Simon!' said Louisa and I in horror together. 'You can't ask for a BMW!'

'The Goddess will not grant a machine that desecrates her world,' Louisa complained.

'BMW drivers are even bigger wankers than Audi drivers,' I objected.

'You told me to ask for anything!' said Simon sulkily.

'Well, while you think of something better, let's dance and chant again,' demanded Louisa.

'I want an iPad,' yelled Coventina.

'Coventina,' snarled Bardo. 'We've talked about this.'

'More MOSHIS!' howled Peter.

'I want a *Swan Lake* Barbie Princess,' shrieked Jane, capering wildly, as the flames rose higher and higher.

'Jesus Christ, the trees are going up!' yelled Michael. 'Simon, call the fire brigade. Louisa, have you got a fire extinguisher?'

'Of course not,' said Louisa indignantly. 'Do you know how many toxic chemicals are in them?'

'Can't be worse than paraffin! For fuck's sake, a hose or some buckets or something then, before this whole place goes up.'

'I can't get a signal,' said Simon, frantically trying to dial 999. 'Come on, Bardo, you must have a hose.'

'There's one in the organic hemp farm,' he said reluctantly. 'But it's watering the plants right now.'

'You're not going to *have* a fucking organic hemp farm shortly if we don't *do* something,' said Michael rushing into the shed that housed the 'hemp farm' and emerging with a ratty old hose that barely dribbled.

Sylvia dissolved into hysterics while I retrieved Oilell from Bardo and shepherded Sylvia and the other six overexcited children, still bellowing demands for capitalist consumer goods, away from the fire, while Michael hurried up towards the main road to try to find somewhere with a mobile signal. Simon was directing the hose onto the flames to little effect and shouting to Bardo to get some bloody buckets of water, and Louisa was screaming that the fire taking hold was a SIGN from the Goddess that she was PLEASED and Simon was not to douse the Flames of the Goddess. Simon, in a noble act of brotherly love worthy of my own children, had just turned the hose from the fire and squirted Louisa in the face with it, which temporarily shut her up, when by some miracle we heard sirens in the distance and two fire engines appeared and quickly put out the Goddess's fire, despite Louisa's soggy entreaties to let the righteous fire of the Goddess burn.

It turned out a nearby farm had seen the flames of the Wicker Man and, rightly deducing that no one in their right minds would be having a bonfire on Christmas Eve, had called the fire brigade. Due to the dampness of December and all the trees being soaking wet, there wasn't too much damage and the fire hadn't spread, even with the amount of paraffin Louisa had flung on the blaze.

There were, however, some very judgemental looks from the fireman about people in long white robes starting fires, despite Louisa and Bardo insisting theirs were Druidic robes and they'd been having a symbolic sacrifice to their Goddess. It was even more awkward when Louisa invited the firemen to dance with her around the blackened remains of the Wicker Man and the charred trees, and ask the Goddess to bless their seed and potency too. They declined in horror and departed at speed, with the sirens on again to help make their escape.

'Well, I think that went very well,' said Louisa in satisfaction. 'That was a splendid fire for the Goddess – I feel she's really delighted by the sacrifices and she'll definitely continue to smile on us after a fire like that.'

'Now can we watch the iPad?' asked Coventina.

Christmas morning dawned grey and damp, which was probably just as well because despite the weather the Wicker Man was still smouldering slightly. We squelched from the guest yurt to the main one, Sylvia and Michael appeared, and there was a polite but unenthusiastic exchange of gifts. It wasn't quite the same without a Christmas tree, despite Louisa still insisting the previous night's conflagration was vastly superior to a mere Christmas tree. In the absence of a chrysanthemum pineapple, I *had* managed to create a delightful pyramid centrepiece for the rickety table, adorned with yet more holly and ivy. Fortunately, mistletoe rarely grows in Scotland, as with five children already, I didn't think Bardo and Louisa needed any encouragement.

To my immense joy, Sylvia and Michael produced vats of proper booze, sparing us all the parsnip wine and its effects, not to mention the mead. Bardo managed to sink the best part of a bottle of Bollinger in half an hour, before finally rousing himself and announcing it was time to start the Christmas dinner. I wondered what festive iteration of parsnips was to be served today, as after the parsnip stew on our arrival, last night we'd had a parsnip bake and I'd spotted a dog-eared book by the stove entitled *101 Ways with Parsnips*. I wondered what number Bardo was up to, and hoped all the ways were purely culinary.

Two minutes later, Bardo burst back into the yurt with a dramatic flourish Granny Green would have commended.

'The rats,' he declared in a trembling voice, 'have got into the parsnip store.'

'No!' cried Louisa. 'Not the parsnip store.'

'We are ruined,' moaned Bardo in despair, sinking down at the table and grabbing another bottle of Bolly, which he quaffed straight out of the bottle.

'How have we angered the Goddess so?' quavered Louisa, who was also several glasses down, insisting champagne was a very pure sort of wine so would not hurt Oilell. 'What shall become of us? Our poor babes shall starve.'

'Oh, for heaven's sake,' said Michael crossly. 'You'll just have to go to the shops tomorrow, like any normal person. I've just given you a cheque for a grand for you all for Christmas, Louisa. I'm sure that will tide you over until Bardo can replenish the parsnips.'

'Amaris,' said Louisa sulkily, who had been rather enjoying her melodramatic wallow in doom and was unimpressed to have so easy a solution thrust upon her.

'More to the point,' said Michael, 'what are we bloody well going to eat today?'

'I brought a few things,' I piped up. 'And I could see what we could rustle up. There must be some food apart from parsnips?' I opened Fanny once more, as I rifled through Louisa's cupboards, and sent Simon to fetch the Sundries bag in.

An hour later, we sat down to what was, if not an entirely traditional Christmas dinner, a blessedly parsnip-free zone. Sylvia had also rallied to the cause, and between us, Fanny, the Sundries bag, some shrivelled root vegetables we found rolling around in a bucket in the yurt and a tub of dried lentils, I felt we'd acquitted ourselves with honour. There was a celeriac and beetroot salad with a French dressing made using some doubtful oil we'd found and a splash of Michael's excellent Burgundy, which Fanny said could be substituted for wine vinegar. There was a lentil salad, ditto tossed in the French dressing. There was spiced red cabbage, courtesy of a mulled wine sachet from the Sundries bag, and thanks to the fancy cheese board I'd also secreted in the Sundries bag there was a cheese and potato pie for the children, which was really just mashed potato mixed with cheese and the top browned, but by calling it a 'pie' it sounded more like you'd provided a proper meal. There was, of course, lots more cheese for afterwards, provided you weren't militant vegans like Bardo and Louisa, and there were also mince pies – Simon had cracked and bought them at Sainsbury's yesterday – and very posh chocolates from Sylvia and Michael.

Even Bardo was impressed with the Christmas lunch we'd cobbled together. He managed to plonk himself down next to me, and with a mouthful of celeriac and beetroot he started to tell me how he thought I had a lot of useful skills I could bring to the retreat.

I demurred, but Bardo was insistent. 'You should join us. It'd be really good for the children as well, going off grid, so they can't be lied to by the system and turned into capitalist cogs in the giant machine of doom, raping the planet for the benefit of Bill Gates.'

'Bill Gates is raping the planet?' I asked in confusion.

Bardo nodded. 'Don't you know? He's having the birds replaced with robot spy birds, to watch us wherever we go. Soon nowhere will be safe, because the robot birds will be everywhere, watching, listening, reporting to their overlords.'

'Bardo, have you been on the mushroom mead again?'

'It's true, Ellen.' He shook his head. 'Bill Gates, man. He's behind everything. The robot birds are only the tip of it.'

'I'm pretty sure robot spy birds isn't right,' I said. 'And isn't Bill Gates a massive philanthropist, giving away billions to provide vaccine programmes and clean water for the developing world?'

'That's what they want you to think.' Bardo was leaning in far too close now, flecks of beetroot in his beard. His breath could strip paint, Louisa's homemade vegan toothpaste was clearly not a patch on Colgate. 'But what's in those vaccines? What's in the water? He's injecting microchips into children and adding mind-altering chemicals to the water supply so he can build his own army of billions of controllable zombies and TAKE OVER THE WORLD, and the ROBOT BIRDS are watching for dissenters who have seen what is happening and are trying to warn people! That's why we can only talk about this after dark, when the birds are asleep.'

'Why would robot birds need to sleep though?' I asked. 'Surely they could just spy 24/7. Isn't that sort of the point of robots?'

'Yes, but if people saw birds flying about at night, they'd realise something was up. They'd see it wasn't right, and they'd be onto him. Gates is a clever *clever* man, Ellen, he isn't going to reveal the plan until he's ready. There's only a few of us that have worked out what's he's up to. That's why we live without technology, so he can't track us.'

'But what about owls?' I couldn't help but ask, though I knew I'd regret it. 'And nightingales. And nightjars … and I dunno, all the other nocturnal birds? Why wouldn't he just make robot hedgehogs to listen? Everyone loves hedgehogs.'

Bardo froze in horror. 'Owls,' he whispered. 'Goddammit. Owls. Of course. Brilliant, Ellen, brilliant. Owls. And hedgehogs. He's infiltrated the hedgehogs. You see now, how hard it is to stay one step ahead of him?'

'Not really …'

'That was smart thinking, remembering about owls. *This*, this is exactly why you should join us, Ellen. We need minds like yours for the resistance, when the time comes. Bring the children, and you and Simon can come and live here at the retreat. Sell your house and your possessions – all the things that are tying you to the capitalist treadmill – invest yourself in the retreat and the organic hemp farm, and come and live freely! We'll all be one big happy commune.' He gave me another of his salacious winks.

'Um, I don't think so.'

'Amaris,' he called across to Louisa, who obviously was draped across the bed with a grubby child dangling off her tit. 'Ellen's one of us. She's just pointed out about owls and nocturnal birds, and also that the hedgehogs may be watching. I've said they must come and join us!'

'Not owls,' said Louisa firmly. 'Owls are the spirit animal of the Mother Goddess. I'd know when I saw an owl if it was not a true part of the Goddess. But nocturnal birds and *hedgehogs*. Of course. Hedgehogs are so obvious, now you come to think of it, all that rustling about in the undergrowth … yes, Ellen, Simon, come join us. Come!'

'What's going on?' said Simon in confusion, who'd been listening to Sylvia regaling him with the story of Margaret Robinson's daughter's messy divorce.

'Ellen's come up with some new ways that *bastard* Bill Gates is stalking us, as part of his master plan for world domination while he raises his genetically modified armies against us,' Bardo informed Simon excitedly.

'No, I haven't. I just pointed out that *if* you were an evil genius billionaire mastermind intent on taking over the world with robot birds, which for the record I *don't* think Bill Gates is, you'd probably come up with a solution to have the robot spies on duty after dark, instead of just shrugging and saying, "Oh well, we'll just have to see what they're saying in the morning!" And owls are the obvious answer.'

'It was staring us in the face all along,' Bardo cried. 'Come, come join us! Simon, you'll love it here. You can live as a real man, as men were meant to be, at one with nature and your spirit. Hawkeye will find you a spirit guide of your own! Your past lives will show you the true path to manhood!'

'NO!' said Simon and I, in perfect unison for once.

Present day

I wish I could say that Christmas at Louisa's turned me into a free-spirited hippy chick, letting it all hang loose and smiling benevolently at my precious moppets as they communed barefoot with nature and frolicked in corn meadows in golden light. But it didn't. What it did convince me of was that with enough effort – and the right mindset – I can make Christmas happen anywhere. Of course, it's better if you have a turkey instead of parsnips, and the contents of a supermarket at your disposal instead of Louisa's rat-infested yurt, and you can never underestimate the importance of not leaving the provision of cheese to chance, and it's astonishing how useful cable ties are.

It did remind me, however, that Christmas isn't always about Things; that you can substitute the Things, and make do, and still make the magic happen, because what can't be substituted are the people who make Christmas important. Wonderful though Christmas at Ty'r Ywen had been, if Dad hadn't sold the house and we'd gone back for Christmas without Granny after she'd died, all the Dior and Givenchy in the world could never have made it as good as that first year. And so, sad though I am that Jane and Peter won't be here, maybe I need to just be glad that at least I still have Simon, because one day he might be gone too, and so, like that dark, damp Christmas at the Holistic Retreat, I need to focus more on what I do have and not what I don't (and I'll also be very grateful for my central heating, hot water and Majestic wine delivery).

Sunday 17 December

I woke up this morning to snow! Big, fat flakes drifting down like feathers, reminding me of the children's story that snow is the Old Sky Woman plucking her geese for Christmas dinner. I shook Simon awake in excitement.

'Wake up!' I shouted happily. 'Wake up, it's snowing!'

'Mmmmph,' he mumbled, burrowing under the duvet.

'Simon! Wake up! It's *snowing*!'

'So?'

'It's SNOWING! SNOWING! SNOOOOOOWING!'

'So? Is that why you've woken me up?'

'Yes! Isn't it exciting?'

'Not really. Snow is just weather. And weather is not that exciting.'

'How can you say that? Snow is not *weather*. Snow is FUCKING MAGICAL! It's a beautiful blanket of white, covering everything ugly and dismal and making it all pristine and virginal.'

'Till someone walks across it and leaves footprints. Or the dogs piss over it and leave yellow patches everywhere. Or it turns to brown slush. Not very pristine and virginal then.'

'You have no soul,' I remonstrated. 'I don't care what you say, every time it snows it's a magical experience.'

'I do have a soul, a very sleepy soul that wants to enjoy a lie-in,' Simon grumbled. 'Why don't you come back to bed and we can have a different sort of magical experience?' he added hopefully.

'I'm not wasting lovely snow time on shagging!' I said briskly. 'I can shag you anytime, snow is a once-a-year thing. You can stay in bed, I have magic to make.'

I flung on my jeans and warm socks and a suitably jaunty woolly jumper, in keeping with my Frolicking in the Snow Vision, and skipped downstairs to wake the dogs and have them share in the Frolicking Magic.

The dogs were no more impressed to be woken by my joyous cries about snow than Simon had been, and were definitely disgruntled at being dragged out into it. Barry, being an obliging sort, attempted a half-hearted Frolic after some exhortations from me, but Judgy and Flora were having none of it. Judgy sneezed indignantly at the very idea that a Proud and Noble Border terrier should frolic in such nasty, cold, wet stuff, and Flora informed me that she was A Poor Old Dog and it would be best if I lit the fire to keep her warm, instead of her catching her death in the snow. They did all consent to pee on my lovely white snow, leaving the yellow patches Simon had referred to, and alas, Barry's frolicking attempts had just rather churned everything up. But never mind, the snow was still falling and soon all would be perfect white again.

The chickens were also entirely unmoved by the snow and scuttled back into the hen house amid much outraged squawkings about such nonsense, and I was left to frolic alone in my winter wonderland.

Frolicking alone is not actually much fun, I quickly discovered. You can't have a snowball fight by yourself, obviously. And building a snowman gets old very quickly when you do it on your own, though I persevered, if only so Simon couldn't say, 'I told you it was just cold and damp, didn't I?' if I came in too soon, and so I had something to point to as the fruits of my frolicking labours when he asked what exactly I'd been doing out there under the guise of 'Frolicking'. I gave it a willy, to amuse the children when I sent them a photo of it. I managed to resist adding a passive–aggressive 'You should be here doing this with me!' to my snowman messages, though, for which I was quite pleased with myself. To my delight I saw that Jane actually read my text this time, though she didn't reply. Encouraged by this, I texted her again, this time with photos of the dogs frolicking in the snow. She still didn't reply, but at least she was now *reading* my texts, which was a slight improvement.

Finally, shivering and unable to feel my toes, I went back in, in search of tea and toast. I proudly showed Simon my priapic snowman and he shook his head at me.

Despite my determination to be less interfering and not worry so much, Peter had not seen the frankly hilarious photo of the snowman with a stiffy, which obviously sent me into yet another panicked barrage of 'Are you dead?' texts, until he finally responded.

Was diving, am fine.

Oh good, I was just worried about you when I didn't hear from you.

Why do u text 'r u dead' anyway if I was dead I couldn't reply

No, but someone might find your phone and alert your poor, anxious, loving mama to your fate.

u r weirdo

As long as you're ok, darling! Love you!

luv u 2

In the grand scheme of things, I decided this counted as a deep, meaningful and heartfelt communication with both my children, so I was taking that as a win.

By lunchtime the snow was still falling and I'd launched into full survival mode. There wasn't a great deal of launching to do thanks to Fanny's coping strategies, which, although I drew the line at homemade everything, had led to me year on year buying various jars and tins every Christmas 'just in case'. I'd never used any of these, but I hung on to them regardless, like some sort of Festive Prepper, but with chutney and clementine curd instead of bottled water and baked beans. Since I'd never quite embraced the level of Coping that meant Overhauling the Christmas Emergency Stores and Making Lists of the Main Perishable and Non-Perishable Goods, I wasn't quite sure what I had, though I was fairly certain there was a jar of homemade pickled onions from my last-ditch attempt five years ago at Fannying about.

But pickled onions didn't go off, did they? Nothing pickled goes off, that was the *whole point* of pickling, and precisely why I still had one of the jars of pickled beetroot Granny Green had sent us home with all those years ago. What I'd done today, though, was turn all the veg lurking in the bottom of the fridge into three pots of soup, and make two different loaves of bread to go with them. I most definitely wasn't keeping busy to stop myself repeatedly texting the children to beg them to come home because what good was a white Christmas without them? Oh no!

I was embarking on an apple and cinnamon cake when Simon came into the kitchen.

'What *are* you doing?' he said, surveying the vats of soup and the cooling loaves and the mixer churning round for the cake.

'I'm getting ready, in case we get snowed in,' I said excitedly. 'So we'll have lots of delicious and nutritious food to eat and won't have to risk going out in the blizzard like Dr Zhivago to get essential supplies, because I am *ready for it*! I've made all this bread and soup, and I've got four pints of milk in the freezer that I keep for emergencies, so we'll be fine and can *enjoy* being snowed in!'

'The four pints of milk you tell me I'm not allowed to ever defrost and use because that is the Emergency Milk?' said Simon. 'Ellen, you've had the same four pints of milk in the freezer for three years. I don't think the milk *is* usable any more, it's been in the freezer too long.'

'Nonsense,' I said crossly. 'We've talked about this, Simon. There's NO SUCH THING as "being in the freezer for too long". That's the point of a freezer – once something's in there, it lasts forever. Everyone knows that.'

'Then why do things come with how long they can be frozen for? Why do freezers have labels showing how long you can keep things in them for?'

'That's just all a marketing ploy by supermarkets and Big Freezer,' I said airily. 'They're all in it together. They just want to trick us into throwing stuff out and buying more, but it's quite unnecessary. I'm telling you, freezers keep things forever! Just like pickling.'

'I beg to differ,' said Simon. 'You can count me out of the freezer milk, thank you, along with that jar of pickled murk you've had for as long as I've known you. I'll take my chances with Dr Zhivago in the blizzard and go to the shop if we need any more milk than the four pints we also have in the fridge.'

'Simon! You're completely missing the point of being snowed in. You *can't* go to the shop. You're snowed in! And that's the special pickled beetroot you're talking about there.'

'I don't even recall a scene in *Dr Zhivago* where he went to the shop in a blizzard to get milk,' said Simon, rifling through the fridge. 'Though in your great and organised preparedness, darling, you've put all the butter in that cake and now we don't have any.'

'There's a pint of cream in there,' I pointed out. 'I saw on Instagram how to make butter from that in the food processor. It will be just like *Little House on the Prairie*.'

'Where they were, of course, famed for their use of the food processor,' muttered Simon.

'Oh Simon, stop being such a grump! Wouldn't it be blissful fun to be snowed in?'

'No, not really.'

I had a lovely Vision of Simon and me snuggled in rugs by the fire (still not a sheepskin rug, thanks to Judgy, but we could improvise), reading, talking, telling each other stories, and it wouldn't matter that the children weren't there, because they couldn't have got through the snow anyway. Maybe there would be a mystery for us to solve, snowed in alone – a stranger arriving through the blizzard, an unexpected murder, like *The Mousetrap*? And then this would be the Christmas I Solved a Murder, which would be much better than the Christmas the Children Abandoned Me. Apart from for the poor murder victim, of course, but it would probably be someone awful who deserved it anyway. Maybe the vicar did it? I always thought he had a shifty look about him.

I tried to explain this Vision to Simon.

'We could curl up on the sofa in front of the fire with a bottle of wine, and watch old films and eat soup and play board games. We could regale each other with old folklore while the wind howled and the snow fell outside, like in *Old Peter's Russian Tales*. And solve a murder.'

'Seriously, what's with your Russian obsession today? It snows in places other than there, you know? And where the hell has this murder to solve come from? It doesn't count as solving it if you kill me, you know.'

'Shut up. It would be like an Agatha Christie for the murder. You know, a very wholesome sort of a murder. But before the murder happens, I could tell you the story about how the snow is the Old Sky Woman plucking her geese for Christmas.'

'No, thank you.'

'See? NO SOUL! It's a lovely story.'

'Go on then,' Simon sighed.

'Well, er, that's it, really. There's an old woman in the sky, and the snow is the feathers from the geese she's plucking.'

'Really? Gosh, you're right, getting snowed in and having you tell me *fascinating* stories like that would be amazing fun! Have you got any more?'

'There's the one about the woman who drowned her husband in a vat of soup because he had no fucking soul and she needed a wholesome murder to solve,' I muttered. 'Oh come on, Simon.

Being snowed in would be brilliant. Nowhere to go, no rushing around, just lovely together time.'

'A couple of weeks ago you said lovely together time would be the worst Christmas ever.'

'It's different when you're snowed in. Everyone knows that.'

'I remain unconvinced,' Simon sniffed. 'Also, you're very bad at being housebound and cooped up. You go stir-crazy very quickly.'

'How do you know? We've never been snowed in.'

'We've been forcibly housebound, that dreadful chickenpox Christmas.'

'Yes, but you and me being snowed in together would be totally different to being stuck in the house with eleventy fucking billion poxy children and both our sisters!'

'Would it? Would it really?'

'Yes. And if you think about it, the Christmas of the Great Poxing wasn't *that* bad. It was even fun in some ways.'

'What ways? In what ways was it fun?'

'Well, maybe "fun" is the wrong word. It was certainly *character building*.'

'If by character building you mean utter hell, then yes, yes it was. Now if you'll excuse me, I'm going to buy some butter.'

'But I can make it! I'm practically Ma Ingalls,' I called out to his departing back.

'I'll show him,' I muttered to myself as I dumped the cream into the food processor and switched it on. 'No need to go into the blizzard to buy butter, I shall provide buttery goodness with the labour of my own two hands. And the Magimix, of course.'

And actually, Simon was wrong about the Christmas of the Great Pox, I decided. Perhaps I wouldn't have agreed at the time, but despite my fine resolutions to make the most of it just being Simon and me, I'd swap the Pox Christmas for this one looming anytime.

Eleven years ago

The Great Pox began the year after Louisa left Bardo. She was living in France near Michael and Sylvia, and she decided that year that she was going to bestow her presence upon us for Christmas, along with the six children. It was time, she declared, for the cousins to all get to know each other better, and what better time than at the sacred mystical turn of the year?

It didn't seem like there was much option to say no, and since my mother was wetting her knickers that she and Geoffrey had been invited for Christmas dinner by the local Lord of the Manor for some reason, and Dad and wife whatever number it was were golfing in Portugal, and Sylvia and Michael had suddenly decided to book a cruise when they heard Louisa was coming to us for Christmas, and Jessica and Neil were taking the children to an ice hotel in Lapland, which frankly, of all Jessica's bonkers ideas sounded the most unpleasant one yet, I didn't really have any good excuse to proffer about why they couldn't come. It was definitely preferable to be at home, with Nigellas and Delias at my disposal as well as the emergency Fanny, rather than risking Louisa guilt-tripping Simon into us going to them for familial bonding. There had been many life lessons from that Christmas at the Holistic Retreat, but I really felt I'd learned quite enough about cobbling together Christmas dinners from random root vegetables and would instead prefer Ocado to be delivering.

We duly agreed that Louisa and the rest of the travelling flea circus would arrive on 22 December. On 21 December, Jessica rang me in a panic.

'Ellen, I have a problem! Neil has to fly out to Dubai tomorrow, some ghastly problem with this merger he's working on, and it doesn't look like he'll get back for Christmas and what am I going to *do*?'

'Do? Well, you're going to that ice hotel place, aren't you?'

'I can't go by myself.'

'Why not?'

'I have *children*! I can't travel alone with children.'

'People do.'

'I don't know how. I've seen them in airports, all frazzled and cross while the children run amok on those hideous Trunki things, breaking people's ankles. It's awful. I can't, I simply can't. People might think I'm a single mother. And I tried to get Marie-Christine, my nanny, to come with me, but she's going back to Geneva and refused to change her plans, quite rudely actually, and I've given the cleaners the week off too, and they also said they weren't changing their plans and coming into work, and even Alejandra the au pair – we went Spanish this year, it's one of the few languages the children haven't been exposed to, because I'm just not a Spain sort of person – well, even she has refused to stay on and help out, so what am I going to do?'

'I still don't understand the problem, Jessica.'

'Isn't it obvious? I'm going to be left alone with my children for at least a week, and I don't know how I'm supposed to cope!'

'But you always cope, Jessica. That's what you do! You're a coper! An organiser. The person who gets things done!'

'No,' wailed Jessica. 'No, I *delegate*. I organise other people, that's how I *cope*. I can't do it myself. How can I keep track of both children in the airport without Neil to help? What if one of them gets kicked in the head by a reindeer in Lapland and has to be airlifted to hospital and there isn't room for the other child in the helicopter and I either have to abandon one child to their fate with vicious marauding reindeer or else leave my wounded baby alone with the Lapland medical service while I stay behind to fight off the rabid reindeer?'

One thing about Louisa and Jessica, I reflected, was that between them they made me feel very normal. Louisa made me feel like you could definitely be too relaxed and chilled out, and Jessica made me realise that I could ratchet my own catastrophising up several notches and still not even be close to her.

'Please, Ellen, you need to help me!' Jessica pleaded.

Ooooh, I thought. Maybe she was going invite me to the swanky Lapland ice hotel thingy. I mean, it sounded bizarre and brutally cold, but it also sounded better than spending a week with Louisa and the six feral fiendlettes she now had in tow. Simon, I was sure, would understand that my sister needed me, and would cope just fine with his own sister and family, and Jane and Peter. I thought gleefully that an ice hotel would probably be a really good place to drink martinis, because they wouldn't get warm. I could pretend I was the Snow Queen (I always thought she was very misunderstood). Though if I was in Lapland being the Snow Queen, I'd miss out on a vital opportunity to swank as the Festive Queen. But also Snow Queen. And a man to make me martinis. I could probably cope.

But no. Jessica had a *much* better idea than that.

'I thought I could come and stay with you,' she whimpered. 'It would be so nice for the cousins to spend some time together and get to know each other properly.'

I knew once Jessica had made up her mind about something, much like Louisa, there was little option but to do what she wanted. Still, I reasoned, it might be fun! The more the merrier! After all, what was the worst that could happen? Really, you'd have thought I'd have learned by then to stop tempting fate like that.

'When were you thinking of coming?' I asked resignedly, casting my mind over Fanny's instructions for guests, including biscuits and books for spare rooms, writing paper and envelopes and stamps for some reason (Fanny was alarmingly obsessed with stamps), and jigsaws to occupy children after meals – I feared I'd be letting Fanny down horribly as I'd be cramming people in as and where I could, on sofas and floors and airbeds and not a scrap of writing paper to be found. As for the jigsaws, last year I tried to get Jane and Peter to do a Christmas jigsaw and Jane rammed a corner of the Nativity stable up Peter's nostril; we only narrowly avoided A&E by my ad hoc expedient of fishing the ice out my gin and hastily slapping it onto his bleeding nose. The electronic babysitter would suffice, the price of stamps was extortionate so they could buy their own, and if Jessica and Louisa wanted jigsaws, they could supervise and minister to the injured ones. But still, I conjured a jolly image of familial bliss, of rosy-cheeked, laughing cousins, of merry games of *Monopoly* and *Scrabble* (actually not *Scrabble*, my children were too good at the rude-word version and Jessica might faint if they taught Persephone and Gulliver any of their extensive vocabulary), and Dickensian feasts and charades.

I realised Jessica was still on the phone, and squawking. 'Ellen? Are you still there? I said I was going to come tomorrow! Neil is leaving first thing for his flight, then I'll drop Marie-Christine and Alejandra at the airport once the children are up and dressed and packed and ready to go, and we'll come straight on to you after that. We should be with you by mid-afternoon.'

'Right,' I said, still trying to work out where everyone would sleep. 'See you then!'

'Don't worry!' said Jessica brightly. 'I'll bring the pickled beetroot and my Fortnum's Christmas pudding.'

'Why do you even have a Christmas pudding if you were going to Lapland for Christmas?'

'I was going to take it with me. And the beetroot. For tradition,' Jessica said, as if it was the most obvious thing in the world to go all the way to Lapland with a jar of pickled beetroot and a Fortnum & Mason Christmas pudding in your hand luggage.

'Right,' I said again. 'Of course. Well, see you tomorrow!'

I looked around the house, wondering where on earth we were going to put everyone. Still, I reasoned, it was only for a few nights. We'd manage. Somehow. Jessica might have to sleep on the sofa, which she'd be unimpressed by, but she'd just have to make the best of it. I was putting Louisa and the three smallest urchins in the spare room on the basis that I could burn the sheets on their departure, but I couldn't really burn the sofa. At least Jessica was hygienic. The other children would all have to bunk down in Peter and Jane's rooms as best they could on a selection of airbeds and camping mattresses and old duvets.

It would be *fine*, I told myself. It would be better than fine! Imagine all those happy, glowing little faces opening their stockings beside my (really very tasteful and quite fucking magical) Christmas tree! What could be better than two children opening their stockings? Why, *ten* children opening stockings! Ten? Were there really going to be *ten* children? Oh bollocks. *Ten* children? Fine, I reminded myself. It'll be fine. Ten children, four adults, still only fourteen people, still fewer than there had been at Ty'r Ywen, and that had been fine, even though all those people had been adults and none of them had been Louisa. But it would be fine!

Simon was less convinced.

'Seriously? Jessica can't cope with her children on her own for a few days?'

'Apparently not.'

'So why does she need to come here? Why can't she go to your mother's? She's the Golden Child, after all.'

'They're going to Lady Rosalind's.'

'Who?'

'I dunno, but Mum practically orgasms every time she mentions her name.'

'What a hideous mental image.'

'Don't be mean, it's probably the only ones she's ever had since she met Geoffrey,' I said, honour bound to defend Mum.

'But why can't Jessica go on this doubtless very expensive trip they'd planned?' Simon wanted to know.

'People might think she's a single mother.'

'Oh, the humanity.'

'Well, there's only three of them. There's seven from your side, with all Louisa's children, so your family is still adding double the number of people,' I pointed out.

'Yes, but now we have both extremes of the batshittery spectrum descending on us. Halle-fucking-lujah!' Simon threw himself off the sofa and picked up his car keys.

'Where are you going?'

'Majestic. We're going to need a LOT more wine!'

Louisa and fiends arrived first, their arrival heralded by the traditional cloud of black smoke and bangs from the backfiring exhaust of her latest clapped-out camper van, which I was not convinced was legal, MOTed, taxed or insured, since apparently Louisa had bought this one from a man in a pub for cash as it was 'untraceable' and thus the robot birds wouldn't know how to track it.

They piled out of the van and trailed up the path. Louisa froze halfway and eyed a pigeon in horror.

'That's one,' she hissed under her voice. 'Quick, children, look away, don't make eye contact, they scan your retinas.'

The children were rapidly hustled into the house and the door slammed against the innocent and surprised pigeon, who'd been happily chewing down the remnants of a Ginsters cheese and onion pasty someone had abandoned in the gutter.

'You've got to be on your guard *constantly*,' Louisa told me. 'It's been an exhausting journey. Have you noticed the hawks hovering over the motorways?'

Baby Boreas, the last blessing of Louisa's womb before Bardo's betrayal of it with Carol the rich American divorcee, was now in a sling on Louisa's hip, although he looked to be around two. The other children milled around mutinously, gazing in awe at the light fittings, the radiators and the TV.

'It's hot in here,' announced one of them, discarding several layers of grubby rags.

'I know, darlings,' said Louisa, 'it's really not healthy. Ellen, can we get some windows open or something?'

'But then the pigeons will be able to hear you,' I pointed out, glad of such an easy excuse to keep my lovely central-heated air in my nice cosy house. 'Louisa, did you all leave your shoes in the van?'

Louisa looked down at fourteen filthy bare feet. 'Oh no. We don't wear shoes now. We live the barefoot life. It's so much better for you, so grounding, and it really makes it easy to feel the ley lines running below you. You simply can't pick up that sort of energy with your shoes on. I'm standing on one now, actually, it's really rather erotic.'

'But it's December,' I said in astonishment. 'Surely you don't go out and around the place with no shoes on?'

'Oh yes,' said Louisa. 'Cedric, don't eat that,' she put in to her eldest who was excavating something out his ear with a black fingernail. 'Doesn't matter the time of year. Actually, it's better in winter. More primeval, y'know. Try it!'

'I'm OK, thanks. Anyway, do come through.'

'Don't look at the TV, kids,' Louisa urged her offspring as they trudged past the living room and into the kitchen. 'That's another way they scan your retinas.'

'Look,' I said smugly, 'I've got organic, gluten-free vegan mince pies for you all, as a lovely festive treat to celebrate your arrival.'

'Oh dear, no, processed sugar. It's poison, Ellen, pure poison. Coventina, stop! Spit it out. Oh no, you've swallowed it. I'll have to cleanse your aura later. Ellen, I'm concerned about the microwave.'

'What about it?'

'It emits death rays. Can't you get rid of it?'

'No. If you don't like it, you can go back to France for Christmas.'

'I can't,' said Louisa sulkily. 'Mummy called in the exterminators to my house when she heard I was coming here for Christmas. I told her the mice and the black beetles have a right to life, but she wouldn't listen. I insisted they're not to use chemicals and only humane traps and lemon juice, but they still said I can't be in the house for seven days.'

The doorbell rang, and I left Louisa anxiously scanning the kitchen for anything else that might be trying to kill her or spy on her – might the Magimix be in the pay of Big Food Processor?

Jessica stood on the doorstep looking stressed, with Persephone and Gulliver, a mountain of luggage and a small, white puffball.

'I finally made it!' she cried triumphantly, implying her journey had been something akin to Hannibal crossing the Alps rather than a couple of hours down the motorway in a Mercedes 4×4.

'What's that?' I asked, nodding at the puffball.

'That's my dog. BooBoo.'

'BooBoo?'

'The children named her.'

'When did you get a dog?'

'About three weeks ago.'

'She doesn't look like a puppy.'

'No, she's about eighteen months old. I got her from Carl at work; he was moving to the Cayman Islands for tax purposes and couldn't take her, so we were incredibly lucky to get her. They're very rare.'

'What is it?'

'She. She's a cavacockajackasprackapoo.'

'A fucking what?'

'A cavacockajackasprackapoo. Haven't you heard of them, Ellen? I thought you knew about dogs. They're a special hypoallergenic breed.'

'They're bloody mutts!' I said.

'They are not mutts. She cost me four grand.'

'Mutt! Why didn't you tell me you were bringing a dog? What about Judgy?'

'But dogs love playing with other dogs.'

'He's not "other dogs". He's a Border terrier,' I reminded her. 'Well, it's too late now. We'll just have to hope they get on. You'd better come in. Louisa's already here,' I said, looking doubtfully at the huge heap of bags. 'Um, do you really need all that stuff, Jess? Can't some of it stay in the car?'

'No, I need it all,' she insisted, filling my small hallway with her goods and chattels, half of which appeared to belong to BooBoo, but this was a battle for another day and at least Louisa seemed to be travelling quite light (if you didn't count the six children and the emotional baggage).

To my relief, Judgy seemed quite taken with BooBoo, though she was so hairy I wasn't sure which end he was sniffing. BooBoo seemed less enamoured with Judgy, but the main thing was he hadn't turned her into a snackapoo.

I decided, after everyone had been fed according to their varying dietary requirements (hurrah for Fanny's coping strategies) and Jessica had also rejected the mince pies on the same toxic sugar grounds as Louisa (how much simpler my life had become once I'd given up such notions and realised the fine bribery potential of such toxins), that board games would be a good, wholesome way to while away the rest of the afternoon until Simon got home from work and I commenced #OperationFeedTheFiveThousand Round 2. Jessica lobbied hard for *Scrabble* for educational purposes, but fearing just how educational it might be, I told her that Peter had eaten all the vowels. This was a lie, of course, as he had only eaten an 'X' and an 'R', but

Jessica believed me. I put on my *Now That's What I Call Christmas!* CD and exhorted the children to have festive fun, while I opened us a bottle of festive cheer.

Despite Louisa's handwringing over the plastic peril, she found a ley line that told her she could detox the children back in France, and a delightful game of *Twister* was embarked on. The children played several rounds of this, getting hot and sweaty and up in each other's faces, and generally laughing and tumbling and having fun. I was starting to think this might not be the worst way to spend Christmas, when I noticed Persephone scratching her stomach.

'What's that rash on her tummy?' I asked Jessica.

'Oh, it's probably just stress with saying goodbye to Marie-Christine and Alejandra. Oh, and Neil,' said Jessica.

Jane, ever the keen hypochondriac, was on the case, though, and examining her cousin's stomach.

'Chickenpox,' she announced with satisfaction.

'What?' I said in alarm. No, no, no. Pox was not in my Grand Festive Plans. At no point had I considered this. Fanny gave no coping instructions for pox ridden children. Perhaps I could stick a stamp on them and post them elsewhere?

'Definitely chickenpox!' said Jane.

'How do you know?'

'I googled it last week when I had a rash. I hoped it might be chickenpox and I could stay off school.'

'Why didn't you tell me you had a rash?'

'Because I googled it, and it wasn't chickenpox. But *this* is chickenpox, I know what it looks like. So now we'll all probably get chickenpox too, because Persephone has breathed over all of us and she's still infectious.'

Jessica was on her phone, also googling feverishly. 'It *is* chickenpox,' she wailed. 'Oh, my precious baby. Gulliver, come here, let me have a look at you.'

Gulliver, it transpired, was also poxy.

'How didn't you notice?' I demanded.

'Marie-Christine and Alejandra got them dressed this morning. And *you* didn't notice when Jane had a rash last week. Oh God. Do you think I should take them to A&E?'

'For chickenpox? When they're totally fine, apart from a few spots? I don't think so,' I said in my most reassuring tones.

'What about an out-of-hours GP, then? I've got BUPA, we can go privately.'

'Again, probably not really necessary?'

'Can I at least phone 111 to check what I should do?' begged Jessica.

'I think what you should do is take them home,' I suggested. 'If they haven't infected the others by now, they definitely will if you stay and there's really not room to keep them all separated to stop it spreading.'

Jessica clutched my arm in panic. 'No,' she said in horror. 'No, Ellen, you can't send me home. You know you can't. It's *Christmas*. There's no magic in a Christmas alone with chickenpoxy children! I *need* the magic, Ellen.'

'I'm not sure there's going to be much magic here, with said poxy children, Jessica! And it's not just my kids, is it? I mean, if it was just them, I'd say fine, they're bound to get it at some point and it might as well be now. But what about Louisa's kids? If they're not already infected, she might not want them to be exposed.'

'Send *them* home. I'll do anything, I'll pay for a minibus and driver to take them back, or I'll put them up in a hotel or something, just don't make *me* go, please. Louisa doesn't really care about Christmas anyway, she only minds about her pagan stuff.' Jessica was wild-eyed by now.

'OK. We'll ask Louisa. Where is she, anyway?'

She was, it transpired, in the garden, still barefoot, listening to the ley lines away from the 'toxic babble' of my electronics. I explained the situation, and Jessica's various offers, and Louisa, after a moment's contemplation, was quite sanguine about it all.

'We'll stay, Ellen. The Goddess just spoke to me and told me to keep faith with my beliefs. My children won't fall sick – this is a modern Western plague and I've taken too much care of their immune systems for it to affect them.'

'Well, what about you? Have you had chickenpox?'

'I've no idea,' said Louisa vaguely. 'It doesn't matter, though. In a past life I was Madame du Barry, mistress to Louis XV, and he died of smallpox and I didn't get it, so I clearly have a natural immunity. The children probably do too.'

'I'm fairly sure that's not how immunity works,' I said.

'No, no, think about it, Ellen. If I can mentally recall all the experiences and memories of a past life, why shouldn't I carry the physical memories in my DNA as well? It makes perfect sense. It's also why I've never liked tapas, because when I was Blanche of Bourbon I was imprisoned in Spain and poisoned by my cruel husband, King Pedro of Castile.'

'Well, there you go. And I always thought you didn't like tapas because you don't like sharing,' I muttered.

'What?'

'Nothing. They're certainly interesting theories, but I don't think there's much scientific evidence for them.'

'Science is overrated,' Louisa said airily. 'What is science, after all, but theories and ideas.'

'Well, research and evidence? Medicine? Technology? All quite evidence-based.'

'Evidence,' Louisa scoffed. 'What's evidence? I prefer to rely on the tried-and-tested methods of the ancestors.'

'But if they're tried-and-tested and proved to work, isn't that *evidence*?' Louisa's thought processes were starting to give me a headache.

'Semantics, that's all,' Louisa declared. 'Anyway, I may be able to help Persephone and Gulliver. If only it was summer, I could gather feverfew by the light of the moon for them, but as it is I have homemade rosehip syrup and fire cider with me. The Goddess's generosity extends to all, and I will dose them immediately.'

'We were thinking maybe just some Calpol? Not really sure you can go around dosing kids with cider, however organic it is?'

'Oh Ellen! Fire cider isn't *alcoholic*. Come on. The Goddess gave me healing skills among her many gifts.'

Jessica was initially resistant to Louisa's bottles of matter, but was won over by Louisa's repeated assertion that it was *organic*. One of the few things Jessica and Louisa have in common is an unshakeable belief that organic equals good for you and sugar equals certain death.

I convinced Jessica a Christmas film would be a good idea to keep Persephone and Gulliver occupied and 'resting,' and whacked *The Snowman* on. The children were all unimpressed, and under instructions from Jane lobbied hard for *Bad Santa*, which apparently Olly Martin at school had told Jane was 'the best Christmas film.'

Jessica continued to pace and wring her hands and take Persephone and Gulliver's temperature every half an hour. When Gulliver's temperature went up by half a degree, she had to sit down and breathe into a paper bag. Louisa attempted to massage valerian tincture into her temples to calm her, but at this stage I don't think anything could have calmed Jessica down except a shot of ketamine.

'Why did it have to happen at Christmas?' she sobbed. 'Why not Easter? No one cares about stupid Easter.'

Simon, returning from his last day of work before Christmas and filled with festive bonhomie, was alarmed to find Jessica hyperventilating in the corner, Louisa burning the contents of my spice rack to 'purify the air and cleanse the evil humours' and ten children running amok, two of them now covered in what looked to be suppurating sores. I, meanwhile, was self-medicating with Chardonnay, though it was not taking away the lingering burn of the fire cider Louisa had insisted everyone be dosed with, sick or well.

'What the fuck?' was his response to the scenes that awaited him.

'We have the pox,' I informed him gloomily.

'Simon! Here, here, fire cider and rosehip syrup.' Louisa advanced on him threateningly, as Jessica clutched his arm and demanded to know if *he* thought she should call an ambulance.

'And what is that?' he demanded as BooBoo scuttled into the room, closely followed by her faithful swain Judgy, his nose firmly wedged, well, somewhere about her personage.

'BooBoo,' I informed him.

'Oh sweet suffering Jesus fuck.'

* * *

Ten children, four adults and two oversexed dogs in one average-sized house and a small garden for a week is … challenging. The house reeked of calamine lotion by the 23rd and, after Gulliver found a packet of Penguins in the cupboard while Jessica was in the loo, of chocolatey Calpol sick. I determinedly lit cinnamon-scented candles and set the children to studding oranges with cloves to create a festive ambience, which Simon complained reminded him of the pomanders carried in medieval times to ward off the Black Death. I thought valiant thoughts of the Christmas in *What Katy Did*, with poor crippled Katy bravely and stoically creating a wonderful Christmas for her brothers and sisters, and, of course, of the noble March girls in *Little Women* giving away their breakfasts and being so very very good.

The children, however, were *bored*. Jessica and Louisa had both caved in to unlimited screen time, but even that was not keeping them occupied. Inspiration struck on Christmas Eve, for in a moment of madness in October I had resolved to out-Fanny Fanny by making my own hand-stamped wrapping paper with the children, which would be, I was sure, A Most Delightful Christmas Craft. Obviously, once I'd spent a shocking sum on stampers, ink, and polar bear- and rainforest-friendly brown paper, sanity set in, and I put it all in the cupboard and sat down until the notion passed. But now, I thought, this could be charming. All the cousins could gather sweetly round the kitchen table and print lovely wrapping paper to give each other as gifts. In my head they were all somehow going to turn out the sort of masterpieces that you wouldn't even use as wrapping paper, but instead would frame and keep as a memento of that delightful family Christmas Eve. Perhaps, I thought, it could even become a Christmas tradition, and we'd each of us have a gallery wall somewhere of all the beautifully stamped creations from every year.

It started well. Louisa and Jessica both approved of this wholesome pastime, once I lied to them and claimed the ink was organic, made only from natural dyes. The children looked adorable ranged round the table in a variety of old shirts of Simon's that were too wrecked to wear but too good to throw out. I put *Carols from King's* on in the background and explained what they were to do. Perhaps, I thought wildly, I could peel the potatoes while the children stamped, and carve them additional stamps from the odd potatoes, whimsical and magical shapes that would be talked of nostalgically in years to come – 'Do you remember the stamps Aunty Ellen used to carve? She was so creative. I really feel she made me into the artist I am today!'

The children all settled down and began to stamp beautifully. For at least forty-five seconds, it was all magical. Then Cedric allegedly 'breathed' on Jane's paper, and Coventina wanted the stamp that Gulliver was using and Persephone started crying because she'd stamped a reindeer slightly out of kilter with the other reindeer because Peter had nudged her. By the end everyone was crying, including me; the glitter I'd been foolish enough to provide as a 'special treat' if they 'stamped really nicely' had been spilled everywhere and was coating the entire kitchen; and Cedric had had a holly leaf indelibly stamped on his forehead by an enraged Jane. In fact, they were all covered in ink. The table was covered in ink. I was covered in ink. The potatoes were covered in ink. Everything was covered in ink except the sodding paper. Jessica, who'd been watching the news because she's a proper grown-up, and Louisa, who'd been meditating to check in with Madame du Barry on the pox score, came through to see what the noise was.

'Oh dear,' said Jessica. 'Are you sure this was a good idea?'

'Maybe the ink wasn't natural and organic after all, and the toxins have caused this,' suggested Louisa unhelpfully.

Simon came in from his shed, took one look at the kitchen and fetched the Hoover, several flannels, a packet of kitchen roll – and a very stiff gin for me.

Christmas Eve night, though, went rather better than the day. The children were still inky, despite all being thoroughly scrubbed in the bath, which made the poxy ones look even more alarming, but we got them into their pyjamas and I lit the fire in the sitting room, which might only have been gas but still gave a nice effect, and Simon most nobly, if unwittingly, distracted Louisa by apparently having something terribly wrong with his aura, which she demanded to cleanse immediately, and he agreed that she could, if she did it without talking while he watched the Christmas *Wheeler Dealers* on the TV in the kitchen and had a large whisky.

It was time for the children's stockings, and in lieu of a proper fire and chimney to send their wishes up à la *What Katy Did*, we got them to close their eyes and make a wish as they hung up the stockings. Peter and Cedric managed to bang their heads together, but we convinced them that was extra lucky. I suggested a merry sing-song of some carols in the manner of *Little Women*, but it was a hard no, and my Vision of them all clustered round my feet, gazing up in rapt wonder as I read aloud 'The Night Before Christmas', was also thwarted, being declared 'sad', so we compromised by putting on the *Polar Express* DVD and tucking them in, pox and all, in Jane's room, with a further stack of Christmas DVDs (I had hidden *Bad Santa*).

One by one they fell asleep, until we could only hear Jane, Persephone and Coventina whispering. I did rather fear what they might be talking about, Jane having just started 'Living and Growing' (aka Sex Ed) at school and finding the word 'vagina' a most amusing one to throw into conversation, and Coventina, Louisa informed us, had witnessed the birth of Baby Boreas, along with the rest of the children, so I was slightly concerned Persephone might be found in the morning with her hair turned white having gone stark raving mad, but I insisted to myself they were probably just talking about Christmas wishes and imagining they heard sleigh bells.

Louisa had been stuck in to the Prosecco since about 3 p.m., so by the time we got the children settled for the night she'd declared Simon's aura clean enough and passed out on the sofa. We filled the stockings (I'd made an executive decision that I refused to discuss but merely informed Jessica and Louisa of, that with ten children in the house, to avoid fights, they were all getting the same in their bloody stockings, and yes it would be cheap tat and probably even plastic, and fuck the polar bears), then we turfed Simon out of the kitchen and put on *It's a Wonderful Life*, and Jessica and I settled down to peeling the potatoes for the following day, which were about the only thing that everybody would eat.

'We haven't done this together at Christmas since Ty'r Ywen,' said Jessica mistily, taking another belt of Baileys.

'I know. Isn't it nice? It's practically –'

'Arrrghhhh! I've cut myself. I'm bleeding in the potatoes. Oh God, I think I might faint. Is it deep? Why is there so much blood?'

By the time I'd Steri-Stripped Jessica's finger back together and assured her she wasn't going to get tetanus from my knife, no, nor from the potatoes, and she really didn't need to go to A&E, and I'd got Simon to get Louisa off the sofa and lug her up to bed so Jessica could swoon, and I'd finished peeling the potatoes and drunk all the Baileys, it was 3 a.m. and I was exhausted, the house was silent and everyone was asleep. I felt oddly happy and was sure that I could hear the distant ringing of sleigh bells, though that was probably just the Baileys.

Christmas Day started relatively incident free. The children were all far more delighted with the cheap plastic tat in their stockings than with their 'real' presents from their parents, and my strategy of everyone getting the same worked and minimised the fighting.

I pulled out all the stops for Christmas dinner and the turkey was only very slightly glittery after yesterday's craft extravaganza. My children refused vegetables and demanded to eat only pigs in blankets and roast potatoes, which led to mutiny among the cousins who were expected to eat Louisa's lentil bake, and Jessica's moppets who were not permitted to miss their five-a-day even on Christmas Day, so everyone claimed Unfairness and Persephone sobbed about the poor turkeys and decided to have lentil bake too, until she tried it and then got over her reservations about the turkey. Jessica ate only vegetables because I'd followed Nigella's instructions to brine the turkey, which meant Jessica said it would not do for her low-sodium diet. Simon ate everything, largely out of fear. I toyed with a slice of the turkey and wondered why I fucking bothered, so everything was pretty much par for the course so far.

Jessica's Christmas pudding (well, Fortnum's pudding, really) did look lovely, set alight with the brandy, and Louisa announced that the Goddess would be pleased with our fire ritual. Disaster struck, though, when we came to put out the Christmas tea, which Jessica and I were conditioned from childhood to serve, regardless of the fact that everyone was still full from lunch, as

Jessica's precious jar of pickled beetroot was found to be missing. The Christmas Pickled Beetroot was not just any pickled beetroot, but one of the jars Granny Green had given us as we left Ty'r Ywen. We had two jars each that were only brought out on special occasions, to be admired. I had even taken a jar to Louisa's retreat, the year we spent Christmas there, but I'd not put it out, as I did not trust the likes of Louisa and Bardo with my Precious. No one had ever opened the beetroot, much less eaten it, yet it formed an integral part of the Christmas tea. To Jessica and me, the pickled beetroot represented much more than an underrated condiment. It was symbolic to us of tradition, of happier times, of stability when all around us was in flux. It was our last link to Granny and Ty'r Ywen, and it was a Christmas essential. It didn't matter that by this point it was almost certainly inedible. It simply had to be there.

Jessica became distraught again. This was worse than her poxified children. No pickled beetroot meant Christmas was ruined! RUINED! Where was the beetroot? I rifled the cupboard of Fanny Supplies, but her beetroot was not there. I attempted to placate her with one of my jars of beetroot, but Jessica wanted, nay NEEDED, *her own* jar of PICKLED BEETROOT.

And then Jessica spotted Louisa sidling out the door with something concealed under her lumpenly home-knitted jumper.

'What's that, Louisa?' snapped Jessica, her beetroot detector clanging.

'Nothing ...' murmured Louisa, making a bolt for the garden.

Jessica dived after her and grabbed the jar of beetroot just as Louisa was reverently placing it in a puddle by the trampoline.

'That is my Solstice offering to the Goddess. This is a very powerful ley line we're standing on and that is the Goddess's beetroot now,' Louisa shrieked. 'You cannot steal from the Goddess and profane her offerings!'

'FUCK OFF, LOUISA, YOU DEMENTED FUCKING HIPPY TWAT! GIVE ME MY BEETROOT,' roared Jessica.

'I have to give her an offering on this special day, and everything else is contaminated with PLASTIC,' countered Louisa, snatching possession of the beetroot again. 'The Goddess is the one watching over us and keeping us healthy. You spurn the Goddess, and it's YOUR children who have brought the sickness, not mine. I LOOK AFTER my children's health.'

'HOW FUCKING DARE YOU,' bellowed Jessica, now holding the beetroot, which seemed to be becoming some sort of conch shell by which the holder could sling insults at the other. 'I look after my children's health too, and a damn sight better than yours. They get proper medicine and vitamins and healthcare, not bottles of shit and woo woo.'

'MY FIRE CIDER IS NOT WOO WOO,' howled Louisa, beetroot in hand. 'It WORKS! We're not sick, are we? No, not us. It's YOU. Killing your children with modern medicine, and begrudging the GODDESS, who could HEAL your children if you asked, ONE JAR OF LOUSY BEETROOT!'

'FUCK OFF, YOU MAD BINT,' snarled Jessica, thrusting the beetroot down the neck of her cashmere jumper, away from Louisa's grasping, grubby hands. 'How DARE you call this a jar of lousy beetroot, THIS IS ALL THAT'S LEFT OF ANY HAPPINESS FROM MY CHILDHOOD AND YOU CAN'T HAVE IT!' and she sprinted into the house before Louisa could lunge for the beetroot again, and slammed the door, leaving Louisa standing in the garden shouting, 'The Goddess will SMITE YOU FOR THIS, Jessica, just see if she doesn't!'

I gave Louisa a hard stare and went into the house after Jessica, as Simon came out to see what all the commotion was about. She wasn't in the kitchen, or the sitting room, where ten children were sitting glassy-eyed in front of *The Sound of Music*. I called up the stairs but there was no reply. I had a pretty good idea where she was, though. I picked up Simon's good bottle of whisky and went out to the garage.

Jessica was sitting in a sagging deckchair, sobbing. 'Sorry,' she sniffed. 'I'm sorry. All your trouble and then I make a scene about the beetroot that no one eats anyway.'

'It's not just beetroot, though, is it?' I said, getting down another deckchair. 'I understand why it matters. I didn't want her to have our beetroot either. It doesn't mean anything to her, it's just a jar of beetroot.'

'Here,' I said, handing her the bottle. 'I think we've passed the stage of Baileys cutting it. I forgot glasses, sorry.'

'What about germs?'

'It's whisky, it's self-sterilising.'

'Why does that sound like the sort of thing Dad would say?' Jessica hiccupped.

'I might have heard him say that, now I come to think of it.'

Jessica took a slug of whisky and shuddered. 'God, that's strong. Nice though. Why do we always end up in the garage at Christmas?'

I shrugged. 'It's where all the cool kids hang out. Shall I put some Christmas music on my phone?'

'Oh yes, please!'

I took a large gulp of whisky myself and listened to Mariah for a moment before I said, 'Jessica? Do you think we take Christmas too seriously?'

'No!' Jessica yelped indignantly. 'Of course not! The problem is, other people don't take it seriously *enough*! Give me that whisky.'

'Are you sure it's other people who are the problem, and not us?' I said.

'I don't know. Maybe. My therapist says we can only control what *we* do. Not how other people react to it. All we can do is try our best, and hope someone appreciates what we do. Even so,' Jessica went on, 'maybe we *can't* control how people react. But we can keep hoping they'll react properly one day.'

'Did your therapist tell you that too? Isn't that the definition of insanity, doing the same thing over and over and hoping for a different result? I think you need a new therapist.' The whisky was really quite strong.

Jessica was having none of it, though. 'Ellen, think about it. You've tried. You know you've tried. And one day the kids will appreciate how hard you've tried. And I do. And Simon does. Even if it didn't turn out how you wanted. You put a lot of love into it, and that's what really matters.'

'Do you really think so?'

'Yes. Yes, I do. Maybe I have to think like that because I try so hard.'

'Maybe we *should* be more like Louisa, giving no fucks about anyone but ourselves.'

'NO!' snarled Jessica. 'No one needs to be more like her. And someone has to give the fucks. Might as well be us. At least we know how to do it *properly*!'

'We do,' I agreed. 'God, Jessica, do you think we'll ever manage it? The magic, I mean. Do you think we'll ever manage to make Christmas feel like it did at Ty'r Ywen?'

Jessica considered carefully, while taking another gulp. 'I dunno,' she finally pronounced wisely. 'S'ppose part of the magic was jus' that we weren't in charge.'

'But when we're not in charge now, we still don't seem able to stop *wanting* to be in charge,' I pointed out.

Jessica sipped from the bottle again, and then squinted at me. 'Maybe s'cos we's *wants* it too much?' she suggested. 'Wha' was the magic, really? Ever'thing went wrong, Granny couldn't cook, ever'body got pissed and we jus' had pickled beetroot.'

'Gimme whisky! I think that *was* the magic,' I said sadly. 'That ever'thing went wrong, an' Granny jus' made ever'body not care and *think* it was magic. But how we *do* that?'

'Dunno. This whisky *broken*, Ellen. Oh no, you put lid on. Why you do that? But Granny tried too, din' she? She worked ver' hard, jus' bloody Aga wen' out. Wouln't been magic if she'd not tried and jus' said fuck it, here's some fucking beetroot, would it?'

'No. Fuckin' hell, Jess'ca, you's drunk all Shimon's whishky! So. We gotta do the trying, AN' we not gotta givva fuck when it all goes wrong. S'easy, innit? Then's it all be maghical. Fuckin' maghical.'

Present day

The hangover suffered by Jessica and me on Boxing Day certainly was not magical, nor was Simon's 'disappointment' that we'd drunk all his whisky, nor Louisa's martyrdom over our spurning of her Goddess. And despite my best efforts to not give any fucks when things went wrong, somehow I just couldn't make that happen. It was one thing sailing to the rescue and being the hero of the hour by providing a beetroot Christmas dinner at Louisa's yurt, but I don't think I could have borne the shame had my own inadequacies been the cause of a beetroot dinner, the way Granny had simply decanted it all into the best china and carried on as if it were a Michelin-starred meal.

Yet where had all this got me? Nowhere. Because no one had ever warned me that perhaps you can try too hard, that in the quest for perfection you just become an annoying tit and irritate everybody, and in your striving for everything to be right you end up going very very wrong, pushing away the very people who are the ones who really make Christmas magical. And now there was not even anyone to try for, except Simon, I thought, stirring my last vat of cock-a-leekie.

Maybe Jessica was right, and we just wanted the magic *too* much, and since I'd been too pissed back then to really pay attention to her when she told me that, this year it was finally time to start properly trying to stop giving a fuck. After all, Simon wouldn't mind that much if it all went wrong anyway. And there was always soup, and I wouldn't have to resort to beetroot again. I wondered if there was any value in texting Jane to tell her that I'd attempt to stop trying so hard, if she'd only talk to me again. I suspected not. If I hadn't lured her into communication with dog photos, I wasn't sure what would. Even Barry with antlers tied on to look like Max out of *The Grinch* hadn't done the trick, and Barry was her favourite dog and *The Grinch* her favourite Christmas story. Also, there was something a bit try hard about a text promising to be less try hard.

I was putting all my many soups in the freezer when Sylvia rang. I immediately panicked that something must have happened to Michael, but no, Sylvia was just calling, she informed me, 'for a little chat'.

Simon had told Sylvia that the children were not coming home for Christmas, and Sylvia apparently wanted to talk to me about this. She understood how hard it was, she told me, the first time they don't come back for Christmas, that that's when you realise you have to start letting go and appreciate that they've grown up and are making their own way in the world. I was too dumbfounded by Sylvia's unexpected sympathy and understanding to say anything in response.

'I know you thought I was a clingy old bat, Ellen dear,' Sylvia continued.

'No, no I didn't.' I hastily got myself together enough to lie.

'I was. I couldn't bear it. The children had been my life, especially Simon. Louisa and I always had a more difficult relationship but I was very close to Simon, and then suddenly there he was with his own family – and I thought I'd been left out in the cold. That wasn't the case, of course, yet it felt like it at the time. And I nearly pushed Simon away completely, trying to muscle in where I wasn't wanted, upsetting you. It's the hardest part of parenting, Ellen, learning to let go.'

'I don't think I've made a very good job of it,' I said miserably. 'Jane's not talking to me right now because I didn't let go enough.'

'Give her time, and some space,' Sylvia soothed. 'She'll come round, just let her come to you. And you'll adapt too, Ellen. This first Christmas without them is the hardest, but it does get easier, I promise you. You find ways to cope, things to do. You still miss them, but you learn to have fun and make your own traditions, just you and Simon. And you can do lovely decadent things for a couple of years, like lie in the bath all Christmas morning with a bottle of champagne and a box of chocolates, instead of sweating in the kitchen and wrestling with a giant bloody turkey. You'll be doing that again soon enough when the children return with the grandchildren.'

'*If* they return with grandchildren,' I said gloomily. 'Though decadent baths and champagne do sound nice,' I admitted.

'See? There's one thing you're very good at, Ellen, and that's looking on the bright side. Find your silver lining, and you'll get through it. Like Pollyanna and Sara Crewe.'

'I always forget you're the only other person I know who appreciates those books.'

'I know, dear, though we tried our best with Jane.'

'She told me last year rather snidely that at least if she ever found herself at a pub quiz with a round on "Plucky, Impoverished Heroines of Victorian Children's Literature" that she'd ace it. Though she also said that it would almost certainly never be a pub quiz topic.'

'A *pub* quiz?' said Sylvia. I could almost hear her wrinkling her nose in distaste. 'Oh how ghastly. Anyway, I must go. Michael's calling me to play bridge. We do it on the internet now, isn't that *marvellous*? So no one has to go out, and we can all drink as much as we want without worrying about anyone driving home! So clever! Anyway, goodbye, dear. We'll try and FaceTime on Christmas Day.'

I have to confess that Sylvia was the last person I'd expected to offer comfort at this moment in time, but I did feel better for talking to her. I hoped she was right about Jane, but I wasn't so sure it would be that easy. I decided to take Sylvia's advice in any case, and stop trying to push Jane into forgiving me. Jane was an adult, and I needed to let her make her own decisions, even the ones about me. And if Christmas Day was just me and Simon, well, I'd take Sylvia's advice about that too, and to hell with the turkey and the stuffing and the potatoes. We'd just feast on delightful nibbly things, quaff champagne, make passionate love on the rug in front of the fire (well, obviously not, because of the dogs, but we could have a tender embrace and then retire somewhere where it wouldn't shock them) and do exactly what we wanted. If it wasn't going to be a traditional family Christmas, well, I was just going to Pollyanna the fuck up and create some new traditions. And it would be bastarding magical, even if it killed me.

Saturday 23 December

Bollocks. Big buggering stinky bollocks. I completely forgot to change my Marks and Spencer's order to scale it down for just Simon and me. Unfortunately, due the fact I found doing the Christmas food shopping online quite delightful instead of death wrestling pensioners for the last box of mince pies in Sainsbury's, and so popped all manner of random and delicious things in my trolley with no proper thought of cost or who was going to eat them, because it was just virtual and wasn't real, we now have what's technically known as a 'fuck tonne' of bloody Christmas food.

Simon looked at me in horror as I staggered in the door, laden with bags.

'What have you done?' he wailed, as I sheepishly explained how late-night online shopping in October, combined with wine, for an event that at the time was so very far away as to barely be comprehensible as an actual thing, so fuck it, a whole *brie en croute*, into the trolley it goes, was a very bad idea, but on the plus side, we probably wouldn't need to do a food shop again until February.

'But it will go out of date,' Simon complained, as I insisted it would all freeze and would be perfectly fine.

'I'm not sure I'll want to be eating mini beefburgers in February,' he said doubtfully, rifling through the bags. 'How many different kinds of stuffing did you buy?'

'Err, all of them. I just put all of them in the basket and thought I could narrow it down later, but I forgot.'

'Two different sorts of turkey crowns *and* a three-bird roast?

'Well, I couldn't decide which one to get. I'd always wanted to try the three-bird roast, but I wasn't sure what you'd think, and if we went with turkey I was torn between stuffed and unstuffed, so I just put them all in and thought I'd ask you later what you thought, and take out the ones we didn't want but –'

'Let me guess. You forgot.'

'A little bit.'

'And a ham?'

'Well, ham's nice for Boxing Day. People might look in, so we'll need something to offer them.'

'Ham? You're just going to offer them slices of ham? Wouldn't a mince pie do?'

'I dunno. I had a sort of –'

'Vision? Did you have a Vision?'

'I did, how clever of you,' I enthused. 'A Vision of a lovely Boxing Day buffet with cold cuts and Stilton.'

'You hate Stilton. You say it tastes of feet.'

'Yes, but it's Christmas. And look, it comes in this delightful jar.'

'Oh, you've bought a Stilton too. For the Boxing Day Vision, that who exactly is going to eat?'

'Um, you know. Carol singers, maybe?'

'You don't get carol singers on Boxing Day. Carol singers are for before Christmas. And we've never ever had carol singers come round any other Christmas, so where are your mysterious Boxing Day carol singers going to materialise from?'

'I don't *know*. Anyway, it'll keep,' I insisted. 'It's already mouldy, so it can't go off.'

Judgy sneezed to indicate that if there was a problem with an excess of cheese, or ham, or any other tasty morsels, he, Judgy, would be most willing to oblige and help out with using them up.

'You're not having Stilton, Judgy,' I told him sternly. 'You get bad enough cheesy bum on mousetrap.'

Judgy remonstrated that this was a most unfair accusation, a quite terrible thing to say about a Proud and Noble Border terrier, and it was definitely Barry who was responsible for the cheesy farts. He, Judgy, So Proud and So Noble, would do nothing so vulgar as fart.

Simon went off to his shed, and I got on with unpacking the shopping. Lovely though the peace and quiet and lack of pressure were, I couldn't help but feel a pang of sadness for the busy Christmases of old. All right, yes, I'd frequently shouted that it was all TOO MUCH and also that I hated humanity, but they had been *festive*. It was very nice not to have to defend the food from ravening children, while screaming 'LEAVE IT, LEAVE IT, IT'S FOR CHRISTMAS,' but it just didn't feel right without Jane and Peter. As Sylvia said, however, that was something I was going to have to get used to, with them growing older and having families of their own, and in-laws, and starting their own traditions that suited their own lives.

I'd never expected *quiet* to feel so sad, though. I thought of the days when the children were little and how I'd beg, plead, pray for five minutes' quiet, when I couldn't even go for a wee in peace without someone banging on the door and screaming for something, and how I used to fantasise about repeatedly smacking Simon round the head very hard with the loo brush on account of his infuriating habit of thinking it was acceptable to vanish for half an hour on Saturday and Sunday mornings for his Very Important Shit, which he had to undertake in perfect peace, while I couldn't even go for a single piss without having to deal with incidents ranging from Peter concussing himself while pretending the sofa was a great white shark he was wrestling (no, I've no idea where he came up with that idea) to Jane standing outside the door complaining vociferously because the carrots I'd lovingly cooked for their dinner were apparently cut into 'the wrong shape, and you *know* I don't like carrots cut like that'. Now that I could cut the carrots into whatever shape I liked and wee without fear of carrot-shaped repercussions, I reflected that I didn't really like carrots.

At 9 p.m. I was still playing fridge-and-freezer Jenga (the freezer being somewhat full of soup) and promising myself a delightful little glass of wine at any moment now, just as soon as I was done, when my phone buzzed and Jane's name flashed up on the screen. Jane was calling me! I grabbed my phone in delight, reminding myself that she might have just sat on her phone, and pressed answer, trying to sound cool.

'Hi Jane.'

'Mummy ...' came a miserable wail down the line. 'Mummy, are you busy?'

'No, darling. What's wrong?'

'I'm at the service station at Stafford.' Jane made a sort of unattractive gulping snuffling sound, 'Can you come and get me, Mummy?'

'I'm on my way. Are you OK? Are you hurt?'

'No, I'm fine. I just want to come home.'

After a hell-for-leather drive up the M6, I loaded a tearful Jane and a remarkably small amount of luggage for a week's skiing into the car (though I didn't mention that she couldn't possibly have enough warm clothes in that rucksack), and drove her home. It took all the willpower I could muster not to demand to know what had happened and offer to rain fire and vengeance upon the heads of whoever had upset my baby girl, but I heeded Sylvia's advice to let Jane come to me, and contented myself with a brief 'Do you want to talk about it?'

'No,' hiccupped Jane with another sob, before relating the whole sorry tale.

It seemed that Rich Rafferty's charms had been dwindling for a little while now, ever since she'd met his parents for dinner a couple of weeks ago when they came to see him in Edinburgh. Apparently they were utterly ghastly Brexiteer types, his father repeatedly asking the waitress in the restaurant where she *really* came from until, when she was on the verge of tears, he finally extracted the information that her grandmother was from Trinidad, at which point he'd triumphantly demanded to know if she supported England or the West Indies at cricket. When she said she had no interest in cricket, he took this as evidence that clearly, therefore, she wasn't *really* British, just as he'd suspected all along. Rafferty's father sounded like he'd get on like a house on fire with Geoffrey.

'I should've chucked him there and then,' said Jane tearfully. 'But I thought maybe I'd made too much of it, maybe they weren't as bad as I thought, or even if they were, that it wasn't Raff's fault and he was OK.' Post the parentals, though, Jane had noticed more and more things about Rafferty that reminded her of his parents, but by then she felt it was too close to Christmas to callously dump him.

'And miss your ski holiday,' I added slightly heartlessly.

'That wasn't anything to do with it,' Jane lied unconvincingly.

'Oh, don't worry, darling, I'm not judging you. I'd have probably done the same at your age.'

There was more trouble on the drive from Edinburgh to get their flight from Bristol, as apparently Rafferty's parents had insisted they all travel together tomorrow on Christmas Eve, with Rafferty loudly criticising any women drivers they passed and announcing that really, women shouldn't be allowed to drive on the motorway because they're no good at it.

'I'd never been on a motorway with him before, nor really spent any time in a confined space with him, and I suddenly realised he was *awful*. All the things I thought he said as a joke and to be "ironic", he wasn't actually joking about. He might have pretended he was – and he told me I was being too uptight if I said he was being a prick – but he really meant it, Mum. And then he started saying he hoped I wasn't expecting a ring for Christmas, because isn't that why women go to university, to find a husband, ha ha ha, lighten up, take a *joke*, can't you and all that *shit*, and I thought, "You are such a fucking knob."'

So when Rafferty stopped for petrol at Stafford, Jane got out the car and told him he could get to everlasting fuck and walked off, leaving him behind bleating, 'But what will I tell my parents?' To which Jane responded that he could tell them to get to everlasting fuck as well, and that when they all got there, they could fuck off some more.

'And then I looked back at him standing on the forecourt in his stupid bloody red trousers, with his stupid little Audi, and I thought, "What on earth was I thinking?" My mother brought me up to value myself more than this, so why the fuck haven't I been? Don't answer that, Mum, because I really don't know. I don't. He was just so confident about everything, and had this way of making me feel stupid if I questioned him, and oh, I don't *know*, Mum, but please don't say I told you so.'

Unfortunately, finding herself alone in Stafford services, Jane's independent feminist principles had not offered much in the way of transportation, so she'd called me.

'I'm so glad you did, darling.'

'I wasn't even sure if you'd come. I haven't been very nice to you.'

'It doesn't matter, Jane. I'm your mother – I'll be there for you, and I'll always come and get you, as long as I live.'

'I know. I knew really that you would come. I'm sorry about all the stuff I said.'

'You were right. I do interfere, I do try to control things. Especially at Christmas. And especially at the thought of you not coming home for Christmas, and it just being me and Daddy. But I'm trying not to, I'm really trying not to.'

'I know. I could see you looking at my bag and desperately wanting to say something. I was impressed you didn't. But I was thinking, while I was waiting at the services, I suppose that although it's annoying that you're always there fussing about stuff, that's just it, you're always there.'

'I know you have to grow up, Jane, and I have to stop fussing. It's just not easy. It's not something you can turn off like a switch. I've spent so many years worrying about you both, it's ingrained in my DNA now. I have to make a conscious effort *not* to. Or at least, not to annoy you with it.'

'It's OK,' said Jane. 'It's quite nice, knowing I have you there when things go wrong.'

'I'll always be there. I'd do anything for you, Jane.'

'Would you help me bury a body?'

'Why? What have you done? Oh my God, have you murdered Rafferty?'

'No! Why would you think that?'

'Because you just asked if I'd help you bury a body!'

'I meant *hypothetically*, Mother. I can't believe you could think I'd murder Raff!'

'Well, he sounds like he deserves it. It would depend entirely on the circumstances of who and why you had murdered, whether I'd help you bury the body.'

'Bollocks, you'd *totally* help me bury a body. You wouldn't be able to help yourself, you'd want to make sure it was done right.'

'Well, maybe,' I admitted.

'Mum?' said Jane. 'I got you something at the service station. Look!'

I glanced over. Jane was holding a jar of pickled beetroot.

'I know it's important to you at Christmas. And I thought you might not have bothered for just you and Dad. So I got you some.'

'Oh darling. Thank you.'

'Are you crying?'

'No, I've just got something in my eye.'

'So now you have to help me bury a body.'

'Are you quite sure you haven't murdered Rafferty? I promise I won't be cross, I *have* always wanted to solve a murder.'

'MUM!'

Sunday 24 December

CHRISTMAS EVE

I was shattered when I woke up on Christmas Eve. Jane and I hadn't got home till 3 a.m., and the dogs were so incandescent with joy to see her that they'd all had to go out for extra wees, so by the time everyone was settled and in bed it was 4 a.m. But I was still delighted to wake up with Jane back in the house.

It was strange, though, to wake up on Christmas Eve not feeling utterly stressed and despairing, my first waking thought not being about a vast to-do list with vats of potatoes to be peeled and presents still to be wrapped and mothers or mothers-in-law to be placated and overexcited children to be calmed down and the carefully chosen stocking fillers I bought in the sales last January to be located in whatever 'safe' place I put them, and meals still to be made around the prep going on for The Meal, THE Meal, which inevitably causes far more work and hassle than seems feasible for what Simon insists is just a big roast chicken dinner!

Thanks to the munificence of Marks and Spencer's ('See?' I said to Simon, 'it's just as well I bought all that food, *Jane* is home!' Simon responded that yes, Jane was home, just Jane, not the 5,000 I was apparently attempting to feed), all I had to do today was tidy up the house a bit and then I could spend a lovely Christmas Eve with Jane. I was glad I'd not, after all, arranged a Christmas Eve soirée with Hannah and Charlie, and Sam and Colin, ironically because I'd been too gloomy about my abandonment, and now I was free to Be Festive with Jane.

Jane, however, when she surfaced at lunchtime, announced she had other plans, and was going out with Emily and Sophie, her two best friends and the daughters of Hannah and Sam.

Even though I swallowed my wail of 'But what about meeeeee?', the disappointment must have shown in my face, as Jane suggested I invite Hannah and Sam and their husbands over for an impromptu bijou Christmas Eve soirée after all.

Sam and Colin said they'd be delighted. 'If I can actually get in the bathroom for a shower,' complained Sam. 'Sophie's been in there for an hour.'

'So's Jane,' I said delightedly. 'Isn't it marvellous them being home?' Sophie having returned a week before Jane, Sam said he was finding the novelty to be wearing off.

Hannah, however, had a problem in the form of her darling four-year-old, Little Edward, being abandoned by her babysitter Emily, and her husband Charlie having to work Christmas Eve because he was a very busy and important doctor.

'Just bring Edward,' I said blithely. 'We'll plug him into the iPad. Unlimited *Paw Patrol* can be an early Christmas present.'

'Are you sure?' said Hannah.

'Of course,' I said. 'It'll be nice to have a little one in the house again, and we can do the whole mince pie and a glass of something restorative for Father Christmas and a carrot for the reindeer thing.'

I thought with some excitement that maybe I could get a few Christmas crafts out for Little Edward to do, so I hauled my old box of craft supplies out of the hall cupboard to see what there was left in it. I was sorting through old scraps of tissue paper and dried-up tubes of glue while perusing Pinterest for suitable ideas when Jane came in.

'Ooooh, glitter!' she said, opening a jar of bright pink sparkles and trying to shake some onto her hand. 'I love glitter.'

Jane and I had both forgotten the first rule of glitter, though, which is that there is no such thing as 'some' glitter. There is only ALL the glitter, and we watched in dismay as a pink cloud settled over the kitchen.

'Do you know,' I said, hastily packing up the box again, 'I'm not sure crafts with Edward is such a good idea?' Suddenly, I'd found my nostalgia for creativity with small children vanishing somewhere into the centre of that sparkle bomb that Jane had unleashed.

With the stamina of youth, Jane (still slightly glittery) had vanished mid-afternoon to hit the town with Sophie and Emily, and the house seemed more silent than ever after her brief presence.

And then, just as I was finishing drying my (still slightly glittery) hair and getting ready for my soirée with a little glass of wine, the doorbell rang. I cursed my wretched friends, who must have got the time wrong. I bellowed to Simon to get the door, adding that they'd just have to entertain themselves until I was ready as they were at least an hour early, but just then he appeared at the bedroom door and shepherded in a rather tear-stained Jessica.

'Jessica! What are you doing here?' I exclaimed.

'I'm here because I've left Neil,' she announced dramatically, collapsing on my bed, grabbing my glass and draining it in one.

'You'd better go and get a bottle,' I said to Simon, who was hovering in the doorway, keen to know what was going on.

'You've left Neil,' I repeated, gaping at Jessica in astonishment.

'That's what I said, isn't it?'

'But why?'

'Why do you think?' said Jessica wearily. 'Because like every other fucking predictable middle-aged man having a mid-life crisis, he's having a fucking affair!'

'*Neil*? Having an *affair*?' I gawped at Jessica in astonishment. I felt terribly sorry for her, of course, but mostly I was astonished that my incredibly dull brother-in-law had managed to do something as *interesting* as have an affair. Not to mention that he'd somehow dredged up enough charisma to get someone to have an affair with him. I'd never understood why my clever, beautiful sister had married someone as mind-numbingly boring as Neil, but they'd seemed happy, and that was what mattered. 'How did you find out?'

'It was all too bloody *Love Actually* for words,' said Jessica. 'I was looking for Sellotape in his desk drawer to wrap his present and I found a receipt from Tiffany's dated earlier this month. Diamond earrings. Two grand he'd spent. They were naff too – I looked them up on the website afterwards. I thought it must be my Christmas present, but the parcel under the tree definitely wasn't Tiffany earrings.'

'Maybe he was planning to surprise you with them tomorrow?' I suggested.

'No. I asked him outright and he admitted it. The earrings were for some little tart from work he's been shagging. So I left him.'

'What's happened?' demanded Simon, returning with a bottle and another glass and filling us both up.

'Jessica's left Neil because he's a cheating bastard.'

'Really?' Simon was equally astonished.

'Oh yes,' Jessica sniffed, and took another belt of wine.

'Jessica, what about the children?' I asked.

'The children?'

'Persephone and Gulliver,' I reminded her. 'You haven't just left them with their cheating father on Christmas Eve, have you?'

'No, of course not. Gulliver is off somewhere living up a tree or something, protesting about fracking with Just Stop Oil, and Persephone is going to a Christmas rave in Ibiza, she tells me.'

'But I thought they were home for Christmas? You said you were having a nice family Christmas with just the four of you.'

'Did I?' said Jessica vaguely, taking another swig of wine and picking up my foundation and examining it. 'This looks nice. Is it any good? Oh, all right! I didn't want to admit that my perfect family was fucked and my children wouldn't come home for Christmas,' said Jessica sadly. 'I couldn't tell you it was just going to be me and Neil.'

I was astonished. 'I thought it was just me!' I said, stunned. 'Peter isn't coming home either, and Jane wasn't meant to be until she made a surprise appearance last night because she's split up with her boyfriend. It was going to be just me and Simon, and I was so jealous of you having yours both home and I didn't want to tell you either.'

'Really? God, do you think we're like Mum sometimes, always worrying what people think? Anyway, yours were probably not coming home because you've brought them up to be independent and adventurous, mine aren't coming home because they don't want to see me, because I'm too controlling.' Jessica swallowed hard and wiped away what looked suspiciously like a tear. I tried not to feel too smug that Jessica of all people thought I was #Winning at #Parenting.

'Oh Jess. You did your best. Jane said I was also too controlling, if that makes you feel any better and she's here now, isn't she? Anyway, I'm sure that's not it. I mean, Christmas raves and fracking protests sound pretty bloody independent and adventurous, don't they?'

'Do you think?' Jessica sniffed a bit. 'Gulliver said he couldn't justify the time away from the movement to walk home, and when I offered to come and pick him up I got a long lecture about the evils of fossil fuels. I assumed it was just an excuse.'

'What happened to Cambridge?'

'He jacked it in for the tree house. He said he saw Bardo at the protest, by the way, and Louisa and some of the children.'

'That sounds about right. But you never said about Gulliver leaving Cambridge?'

'How could I, after the fuss I made about him going there?'

'Oh, Jessica. You need to stop worrying about what people think all the time. We both do. Look at how much of our lives we've messed up doing that. You're right, it's exactly what Mum does, and it's not made her happy either.' I felt very wise all of a sudden. 'I've been doing a lot of thinking with Jane and Peter not coming home, and I've realised trying to make everything perfect, even just for Christmas, doesn't work! Come on. Hannah and Sam and Colin are coming round, and I take it you're staying? You'll have to have Peter's room. I'll open the windows and try to get the worst of the smell out for you.'

The Mini Beef Wellingtons had all been eaten and the wine was flowing. Jessica had drunk enough to forget she didn't eat gluten *or* red meat, or partake of anything except herbal tea after six o'clock, and she'd shouted 'bollocks to the intermittent fasting' and gulped down fistfuls of canapés. I decided I'd had quite enough of *Christmas Party Hits*.

'Time for dancing,' I yelled, turning off the Pogues and putting on 'Patricia the Stripper'. 'I'm a grown-up again,' I told Simon, 'not just a parent, and it's FUN! I'm going to get new hobbies! Ooooh, maybe I'll learn to pole dance! That would be fun!'

He looked both excited and terrified at this notion.

'C'mon, Jessica, Hannah, let's dance.' I dragged them to their feet. 'I'm so glad you're my sister and my best friend. Simon, c'mon, DANCE. An' you Colin, I love you too. Where's Sam? We need Sam. All my favourite people, an' now we'll have more time together, now we don't have school runs and all the laundry and all that. Sorry, Hannah. But it's not forever, is it, an' we'll still be here when Edward grows up. Does anyone want some glitter? Bastarding glitter!'

Sam came in from having a cigarette and announced it was snowing heavily.

'Oh hurray,' I said rapturously. 'It's magical!'

Sam shook his head. 'I don't think so. It's a bloody whiteout. I don't think anyone's getting home tonight.'

We all dived for our phones. Unfortunately Sam was right. Charlie was stuck at the hospital, and couldn't pick Hannah and Edward up.

'Where is Edward, anyway?' said Hannah suddenly, realising we hadn't seen him in some time.

It turned out that Little Edward had sneaked off with a bottle of Baileys when no one was looking and was now sleeping blissfully. Hannah looked at him anxiously.

'I'm torn between feeling like the worst parent in the world and wondering if I can't give him a shot of Baileys every night instead of his bedtime milk,' she admitted. 'But how I am going to get him home? I can't get a taxi because a) they won't have a car seat for him and b) how can I get in a taxi with a four-year-old comatose on Baileys. They'll call social services.'

'You can't get a taxi anyway,' said Sam. 'I've tried them all. They're all fully booked and say the drivers are all going home despite the bookings because they can't get through with the weather.'

'Oh God, what am I going to do? What if he gets alcohol poisoning? Or chokes in his sleep?' Hannah wailed. 'An ambulance won't be able to get here!'

'He's not comatose,' I said, trying to be helpful. 'I mean, it's ten o'clock, way past his bedtime, so it's no wonder he's asleep. He didn't have that much Baileys anyway. When I was a baby, apparently, my grandmother dosed me with whisky in my bottle when I had a cold, and the vicar came round to see her while I was passed out on the sofa in a whisky stupor. When he left, Dad said that he thought the vicar might have a drink problem, and Granny had to admit the smell of whisky was actually coming from me. And I was *fine*.'

I wasn't sure I was helping, but I was very glad that those pregnancy tests had been so firmly negative. The golden cornfield Instagrammable baba was one thing, the real-life practicalities of small children quite another. *And* Little Edward had wiped snot on my lovely velvet palazzo pants. I'd forgotten about the snot wiping. And come to think of it, salt-dough decorations and gift tags never came out looking like the ones on Pinterest, and drinking whisky yourself was much more fun than leaving it out for Father Christmas, the greedy fat fuck.

'I think you might be stuck here, Hannah,' said Sam grimly. 'I think we all might be.'

'Never mind,' I said brightly, 'the more the merrier. Shall we do shots?'

Oh what bliss! Shots on Christmas Eve instead of peeling bastarding potatoes. What on earth had I been so worried about? This was the life!

'Do you think I should?' said Hannah anxiously. 'Do you really think Edward's OK?'

'Yes! Look, he's waking up!'

'Oh God, no, don't wake him.'

Edward opened his eyes blearily and asked if Father Christmas had been yet. Hannah told him not yet, and he was going to have a sleepover at Aunty Ellen's house, but Father Christmas would definitely find him, not to fret, and no, he couldn't have any more of Aunty Ellen's special chocolate milk, maybe some water would be a good idea. Astonishingly, Edward accepted all this and – to everyone's great relief – went straight back to sleep on the sofa, as a wide-awake child was most certainly not conducive to the shots I'd set my heart on.

More worrying, as the night wore on, was the fact we could not get hold of any of the girls. At ten o'clock we'd been unconcerned, assuming they were in a noisy pub and couldn't hear their phones. We had another tequila and said we'd try them all again in a bit. By midnight panic had set in, and apart from Jessica, we were sobering up rapidly. The snow was now positively blizzarding outside and you couldn't even see to the end of the garden. Somewhere out there in that were our daughters.

'Toby's at home now, but he's not heard from them, and he didn't see them when he was out,' said Sam.

'Do you think we should call the police?' I whimpered. 'What if they're lost in the blizzard, or dead in a doorway like in *The Little Match Girl*?'

'I don't think you can call the police and ask them to go and check all the doorways in town in case your child's huddled there over a box of matches,' pointed out Simon.

'I'se FaceTiming Persephone with my shots,' slurred Jessica in the background. 'Hi darling, s'Mummy, I been doing shots.'

'Ask her if she's heard from Jane,' I demanded.

'Pershephone shays Jane sent her a WhashApp at 11.15,' Jessica announced.

'Thank God. Wait. Is that 11.15 UK time or Ibiza time?'

'Ibeefa.'

'So 10.15 here. So Jane was still OK at 10.15, and the girls know to stay together. Maybe the police could trace them from the WhatsApp.'

'I'm going to try Sophie again,' said Sam. 'Oh come on! Pick up!'

'Oh look! Look! Jane's calling! Jane! Jane! Are you OK? Are you dead in a doorway like the Little Match Girl? Mummy can't come and rescue you because I've had all the shots and there's too much snow, even though I said I'd always come and get you. Jane, where are you, why haven't you answered?'

'Why do I have like thirty-nine missed calls from you, Mother?' demanded Jane. 'And twenty-seven texts going, "Are you OK, Mummy loves you?" Are you drunk?'

'Only a very little bit, and we were very worried. Are Sophie and Emily there?'

'Yes, we've gone back to Emily's because we couldn't get a taxi for love nor money because of the snow and Christmas Eve, so we just walked back to Emily's house.'

'They're all at yours, Hannah,' I announced joyfully to the anxious assembled faces.

'Seriously, Mum. Chill out,' said Jane crossly. 'I thought you weren't going to do this anymore.'

'I'm your mother. I'll always worry, it's what mothers *do*. Are you all right, though? Are your feet wet? Have you got frostbite? Did you wear your ski socks out? Make sure you warm up, have a hot drink!'

'Mum, we've been back for hours, we're fine.'

'Why didn't any of you answer your BLOODY PHONES THEN?'

'The snow must've knocked out the mobile signals. We literally had no calls until all of a sudden I had a million missed calls. Sophie's in the loo and Emily's in the kitchen making popcorn. I'm sure they'll call in a minute too.'

'I'm just so glad you're OK! I love you!'

'Mum! CHILL!'

'MORE SHOTS,' I cried joyously, as Jane hung up.

'Thish is fun,' I mumbled to Hannah and Jessica later as the three of us squashed into my bed. 'S'like sleepovers when we were young again.' (Little Edward was in Jane's bed, but when Hannah had attempted to join him there he'd kicked out like a mule, so she'd retreated in with Jessica and me. Simon, to his indignation, was relegated to the sofa, and Sam and Colin were in Peter's room.)

'Including the B-52s,' Hannah mumbled back. 'Why'd we drink B-52s? They wash bad idea when we wash fifteen, they'sh worsh idea now.'

'Feel bit sicky,' groaned Jessica. 'Urrrgh.'

'S'OK.' I rubbed her back. 'No be shicky, Jeshica, be fine.'

Jessica suddenly sat bolt upright, and I feared she was about to spew over the whole bed.

'The BEETROOT!' she howled. 'I forgot to bring the BEETROOT becaush Neil is fucking cheating bashtard.'

'S'ok,' I assured her again. 'I'sh got beetroot. Gotta lotta beetroot. S'all fine. Ni'ni', Jeshica. Ni'ni', Hannah.'

Monday 25 December

CHRISTMAS DAY

Christmas Day, needless to say, started badly. I was awoken by the dulcet tones of my only sister hurling her guts up, as she's entirely unaccustomed to shots. I had a vague recollection of her insisting I take a video of her downing a line of Baby Guinnesses to send to Persephone to prove her mother was cool. I feared Jessica was regretting that decision now.

Ten seconds later Little Edward barrelled into the room clutching the stocking we'd cobbled together for him at 3 a.m. from the box I'd found at the back of a cupboard of all the stocking fillers I'd bought over the years and lost before Christmas and rediscovered each January. He seemed unimpressed as he flung himself on the bed, landing squarely on my bladder, shouting loudly about Father Christmas NOT USING HIS LISTENING EARS because none of this was what Edward had asked for. The noise was hideous to my delicate sensibilities, and I left Hannah to it. So much for a civilised Christmas lie-in. Poor Hannah, how did she still do this *every day*?

Downstairs, Simon was still snoring on the sofa. I gathered all the glasses strewn about the place, fearing my soirée had ended with considerably less elegance than it had begun with, and started stacking the dishwasher.

I'd had a delightful champagne breakfast planned for Simon and me, but that was now obviously out the window, so I made a big jug of Buck's Fizz with cheap Prosecco and set about scrambling the two dozen eggs I'd somehow ended up with as part of my random Christmas stockpiling. I may not have biscuits beside the spare-room bed, nor indeed a single stamp in the house, but Fanny, I thought, would approve.

After breakfast (Jessica declined and fled back to bed when I offered her both the Buck's Fizz and the bacon), we went outside. The vast snow drifts and Dr Zhivago-esque conditions of the night before were vanishing, and the road looked passable again.

'Looks like we can go home,' said Hannah. 'And we've still got time to get to Mum's for Christmas dinner. Oh, hang on, my phone's ringing.'

Hannah came back in five minutes later. 'That was Mum,' she said. 'She's only twenty miles away, but apparently the snow is still terrible there and they're cut off. So we can't get over there. And Charlie texted to say he's got three emergency appendectomies and an emergency gall bladder removal to do and he won't be home till God knows when. And I took all the Christmas food to Mum's yesterday morning and there's nothing to eat at home because it's all at Mum's. So we're going to have to have a turkey Ginsters out the garage for Christmas dinner!'

'Stay here,' I offered. 'Simon's not had any Buck's Fizz, because he was going to try to pick up Jane and drop off Sam and Colin, so why doesn't he just pick up all the girls and bring them here. He could get Toby too, Sam, and you and Colin can all stay for Christmas dinner. Stay tonight so no one worries about driving, we can all squash in again! What do you think? Oh please, please say yes – won't it be fabulous?'

'Are you *sure*?' said Colin. 'Do you have enough food? Can you be arsed? What about your lovely relaxed Christmas you kept saying you were looking forward to?'

'I've got years ahead for that,' I said airily. 'Anyway, Christmas is about people, isn't it?' I added, going over to the freezer and taking my emergency milk out, just in case. I briefly looked in the cupboards and wondered if I needed to start showing off by conjuring up marvellous delicacies out of nothing; there was a jar of truffled artichokes for reasons that escaped me. Perhaps I could do something delightfully hors d'oeuvrey with them, but then I saw sense and decided I'd far rather get pissed with my friends and family than fanny around (I chuckled to myself at my cunning pun) with truffled artichokes.

Simon duly delivered Toby and the girls, who were greeted by Little Edward sweetly informing them that Father Christmas was a fucker because he hadn't brought Edward a real gun like he'd asked him for.

By three o'clock we were all squashed round my dining table and mildly pissed again. None of the crockery or glasses matched, and the charming tablescape of candles and flowers I'd arranged on Christmas Eve had been jettisoned in order to fit everyone in. Even Jessica had rallied and managed a couple of glasses of wine, and she was now FaceTiming Persephone again, who'd been very impressed by her mother's shot-downing skills the night before. Jane had told me at least eleventy fucking billion times to 'CHILL', but had said nothing untoward about any of the useful or the whimsical gifts I'd given her for Christmas.

'Listen,' I cried. 'Listen to that! In the distance.'

'Carol singers!' said Hannah in excitement.

'Oh my God,' said Jessica. 'How amazing. I haven't heard carol singers in years.'

'Do you think they're coming here?' said Colin.

'What will we give them?' I said in a panic. 'Is there any ham left? I had ham for carol singers, but I think we might have eaten it all.'

'You can't just give carol singers ham anyway,' Simon insisted. 'Why do you keep wanting to give carol singers ham?'

'Figgy pudding then.'

'It's probably not even carol singers,' said Jessica. 'It's probably just your neighbour with the speakers turned up too loud.'

'They're not very good carol singers, are they?' agreed Sam. 'They don't know half the words. Maybe Julia's doing some sort of Christmas karaoke?'

'I love karaoke,' I said. 'Maybe we could go and join in? No, there's too many of us. I'm sure I've still got an old karaoke microphone in the attic somewhere. Do you remember, Jane, I got you one for Christmas years ago and you never used it? Let's get it down and have a sing-song.'

Jane rolled her eyes. 'Seriously, Mum? Karaoke?'

'Why not?' I said stubbornly. 'I've always had a Vision of us all singing carols round the piano at Christmas. Well, we don't have a piano, so we'll go for the twenty-first-century version and have Christmas karaoke carols. Come on! It'll be fun! Simon, go and find the microphone. It's in a box on the left-hand side of the attic labelled "Jane", I think.'

'No!' everyone shouted. 'Enough Visions, Ellen!'

'But karaoke,' I pleaded. 'It doesn't have to be carols. Don't spoil the Christmas magic. It's not too late for me to go to the garage with the Baileys, you know.'

'I don't think you want to take the Baileys to the garage. Edward was drinking it out of the bottle, and he tends to drool into things like that,' Hannah pointed out. She was attempting to wrestle the Lego gun he'd made off Edward, as he was pointing it at Toby and yelling 'Stick 'em up!'

'Seriously, where does he learn phrases like that?' she despaired. 'It's not from *Hey Duggee*.'

'*Hey Duggee* is rubbish,' Edward informed her. 'I like YouTube. I saw a YouTube with nudey ladies and willies!'

'How has he turned off the parental controls?' whimpered Hannah. 'And what has he been watching? No, Edward, no one wants to see your willie.'

'Simon! The microphone,' I reminded him, as he watched Little Edward in horror. I could see him thinking, 'Thank fuck that's not us,' and despite the whole withering womb thing, I was in full agreement. Simon sighed, put down his fork and went out to the hall.

'Ellen,' he shouted. 'Ellen, I think you'd better come out here! Hannah, you too.'

I dashed into the hall, visions of burst pipes or dog diarrhoea flashing through my head. But instead, standing on the doorstep, stood Peter, Lucas and an unknown blonde girl. As they saw us, Peter and Lucas burst into an incredibly tuneless rendition of 'We Wish You a Merry Christmas'.

'What?' I gasped.

'Why?' said Hannah.

'How did you get here?' said Simon.

It turned out it was mainly down to Ciara, Peter's new girlfriend.

'I was telling her about you, Mum. About how you're such a pain in the arse all the time and think I'm dead when I don't answer a text. Ciara said I was lucky to have a mum like you. And I realised I was. And Ciara said Christmases with you sounded great, and I realised actually you do always make it really enjoyable. Like the year we all made that wrapping paper with the stamps. That was so much fun.'

I was astonished and incredibly touched that Peter's memories were so different to mine. Maybe there *had* been magic and I'd been too stressed to notice? 'But everybody cried,' I said. 'Including me. Your cousin Cedric still had a holly leaf stamped on his forehead when he went home in the New Year.'

'Really? I just remember the fun. And Ciara said' – it seemed I'd better get used to the phrase 'Ciara said', but since she clearly talked a lot of sense and seemed a very sweet girl, I thought I could live with that – 'Ciara said that you obviously put in a lot of work to make Christmas so entertaining, and she wished she'd had Christmases like we did, and then I thought, she's right, and wouldn't it be great to bring Ciara for Christmas. So I said to Lucas, let's go home, because I didn't want to leave him on his own, and I knew you wouldn't mind and Ciara would love it. And I wanted you to meet her, because she's really cool, Mum, really cool, and I'm thinking of popping the question soon.'

I was so busy feeling incredibly proud of being the cool mum that Peter could bring his cool girlfriend home to meet, and realising that all the stress, the crying and the beetroot had not been for nothing, that it took me a second to register the last part of what Peter was saying.

'YOU ARE *WHAT*?'

'Chill, Mum, what's the big deal?'

'You're way too young to get married.'

'Who said anything about getting married?'

'You said you were popping the question!'

'Yeah. I'm gonna ask her to be my girlfriend, like Officially?'

'You've brought her home for Christmas and to meet your family, surely that makes her your girlfriend?'

'Not till I ask her. Officially. I'm going to do it later today.'

I shook my head at the complicated dating rituals of The Youth of Today. But I was still wasn't sure how he'd got back from his trip.

'Oh, we got a mega-cheap flight that got in first thing this morning. Donkey was on it too. He said to say Merry Christmas to my MILF mum, and he's coming over tomorrow to see if you need any help with anything.'

'That's nice of him. And how did you get from the airport?'

'We hitchhiked.'

'You … you hitchhiked?' I took several deep breaths, and decided I could rock and cry in the corner about the hitchhiking later when no one was around.

'Anyway, I'm starving, Mum. Any food?'

The boys and Ciara were all very thin and sickeningly brown, and despite having been travelling for the best part of twenty-four hours, as well as being raveningly hungry, were in fine party spirits.

'Oh God, I hope we have enough booze!' I said anxiously.

'Don't worry! We brought supplies,' said Peter, as they produced a duty-free bag containing a bottle of Sambuca, a bottle of tequila and a bottle of doubtful-looking schnapps.

'So!' said Peter, slinging an arm round my shoulders. When did he get so *tall*? 'Shall we do shots then, Ma?'

* * *

Much much later, I looked round the carnage of my sitting room. There were bodies everywhere. The candles from my tablescape were burning precariously on the bookcase. Lucas, Ciara and Peter were asleep on the sofa. Sam, Toby and Jessica were still doing shots. Colin and Hannah were watching *Titanic* and mopping each other's eyes. The girls were upstairs and there was a lot of shrieking and laughter from Jane's room. Little Edward was ... where was Little Edward? Oh fuck, Little Edward was trying to start a fire under the table. I removed the matches and firelighters from his outraged sticky grasp, and handed him the iPad and a box of Ferrero Rocher instead. He seemed to find this a satisfactory exchange and settled down happily. I decided not to ask him what he was doing on the iPad.

I passed Simon in the kitchen on his way to let the dogs out.

'Hang on a minute, Ellen,' he said.

'What?' I said impatiently.

'Just this,' he grinned, and produced a piece of mistletoe from behind his back and gave me a huge kiss.

'There,' he smirked, then opened the door to let Flora out for yet another wee.

Jessica suddenly lurched into the kitchen and yelled, 'THE BEETROOT!'

'In the cupboard by the cooker,' I said.

She staggered back to the sitting room bearing the precious jar and placed it carefully on the bookcase between the candles, like a little pickle shrine.

'There,' she said in satisfaction. 'Thass better. Ellen, I's had an "pifnee".'

'A what?'

'A PIFNEE. You know epiffiwhatsit.'

'Epiphany?'

'Tha's it. Persephone likes me 'gain. So now I need to make Gulliver like me. So I's going to stop being corporate lawyer, and get 'nother job. Savin' the polar bears or something.'

'Are you sure, Jessica?'

'Well –' Jessica thought for a moment. 'Maybe I'll jus' get an electric car for my next company car. Thass good for the polar bears!'

Suddenly I noticed Jessica's dress.

'You're wearing the Dior,' I said.

Jessica nodded. 'Couldn't bear to leave it behind. Put it on 'bout ten minutes ago. D'you still have the Givenchy?'

'Yes, but I can't get into it. I should give it to Jane.'

'What a good idea. I'll give the Dior to Persephone and they can wear 'em together! 'Nother shot, please, Sam. You have one too, Ellen.' She raised her glass to me. 'S'practically water, darling.'

'Practically water, darling.' I clinked my glass against hers.

'Look at this,' said Jessica, gesturing around her. 'Jus' look. S'not what you planned, is it?'

'No,' I said. 'But you know what it is, right?'

'Oh yes,' said Jessica.

'MAGICAL!' we said together.

Acknowledgements

Once again, there are such a huge number of people to thank, but no one more than my marvellous editor Katya Shipster. I truly couldn't do this without you. Jenny Hutton's editorial skills and insights are also amazing – thank you so much! All the team at HarperCollins – thank you! I love working with you all so much, and you make it such incredible fun! Particular thanks, though, to Tom Dunstan and his brilliant sales team, Hetty Touquet, my fantastic publicist, and Sarah Hammond, the organisational genius who keeps us all on track. Mark Bolland, my copy editor, has once again done a great job of wading through a sea of exclamation marks and dubious punctuation, turning the manuscript into something readable, so thank you(!).

A huge part of these books are the stunning cover designs with the glorious drawings by Tom Gauld, so my undying gratitude and eternal thanks to Tom, and to Claire Ward for once again blowing me away with another perfect and brilliant cover.

Paul Baker, my lovely agent – we've survived another book, so thank you! They've discontinued Patrón XO Cafe, so we'll need to find another way to celebrate. I have faith we'll manage.

To all my fabulous friends, thank you for putting up with me. Jo Middleton, thank you for your eternal joie de vivre, even when crying in the back of a car. You bring so much fun to my life. And as always, Alison, Eileen, Lynn, Mairi, thank you for being you and always being there for me. Helen and Sarah, thank you for the martinis and Marbella, even if they did delay the book a bit. And an enormous thank you to the eternally divine Jilly Cooper for her wonderful friendship and generous permission to name a dog character after Rupert Campbell-Black.

And as ever, last but not least, my husband and children. Thank you for everything! And of course, the Proud and Noble Border terriers Billy and Buddy. I'm not sure what exactly I'm thanking you for, because you're pig dogs, but you'll sulk if you don't get a mention.